YEAR'S BEST FANTASY

Edited by David G. Hartwell

Year's Best SF
Year's Best SF 2
Year's Best SF 3
Year's Best SF 4
Year's Best SF 5
Year's Best SF 6

YEAR'S BEST FANTASY

EDITED BY DAVID G. HARTWELL
AND KATHRYN CRAMER

EOS

An Imprint of HarperCollins*Publishers*

This is a collection of fiction. Names, characters, places, and incidents are products of the authors' imaginations or are used fictitiously and are not to be construed as real. Any resemblance to actual events, locales, organizations, or persons, living or dead, is entirely coincidental.

EOS
An Imprint of HarperCollins*Publishers*
10 East 53rd Street
New York, New York 10022-5299

ISBN: 0-7394-1939-0

Printed in the U.S.A.

This book is dedicated to Arthur D. Saha, who edited a fine *Year's Best Fantasy* and as well co-edited the Donald A. Wollheim *World's Best SF* for two decades or more. Rest in peace, Art, you are remembered with fondness and respect. And to Caitlin Blasdell, for enthusiasm and editorial support over a number of difficult years.

Contents

Acknowledgments

We would like to acknowledge the continuing value of Mark Kelly's short fiction reviews in *Locus*, and of the various short fiction reviewers of the *Tangent* Website. And to thank Jennifer Marcus and Kathy Morrow for last minute help. And again to acknowledge Diana Gill for catching the balls in the air under difficult circumstances. Next year it'll be easier. We hope.

Introduction

Welcome to the first volume of our new paperback series, the *Year's Best Fantasy*. We hope that this book will give you a convenient reference to what's going on now, to who is writing some of the best fantasy fiction published, and will provide a collection of excellent stories for your reading pleasure. In this book, and this anthology series, we will use the broadest definition of fantasy (to include wonder stories, adventure fantasy, supernatural fantasy, satirical and humorous fantasy). We believe that the best-written fantasy can stand up in the long run and by any useful literary standard in comparison to fiction published out of category or genre. And furthermore, that out of respect for the genre at its best we ought to stand by genre fantasy and promote it in this book. We have been editing fantasy anthologies together since the 1980s, and each of us separately has won a World Fantasy Award for best anthology. So we feel up to the challenge of doing a *Year's Best Fantasy*.

What we hope for in a fantasy story is a well-told tale with a memorable image—a flurry of bloodthirsty leaves, a sleeping beauty on exhibit in the British Museum. We believe that writers publishing their work specifically as fantasy are up to this task, so we set out to find these stories, and we looked for them in the genre anthologies, magazines, and small press pamphlets. Some fine fantasy writers will still be missing. A fair number of the best fantasy writers these days write only novels; or, if they do write short fiction, do so only every few years, and sometimes it is not their best work. We will find the good examples and reprint them when we can.

We found that the good fantasy short fiction this year is notably international. Although all but one of the writers in this book write in English, many of them live and work outside the United States, in Canada, Australia, the British Isles, Yugoslavia. Australia is still full of energy a year or two after the 1999 Melbourne World Science Fiction Convention. *Eidolon* and *Aurealis* are the leading magazines, and Australian fantasy novelists are continuing to break out worldwide, at least in the English language. Canadian SF is still thriving, and Canada is still introducing new world-class fantasy writers to the world stage each year. *Interzone* has grown into one of the three or four leading SF magazines. *Realms of Fantasy* and *F & SF* are its peers. And the best new semi-professional fiction magazine of the year, publishing both fantasy and SF, is *Spectrum SF*, from Scotland. The World Fantasy Convention is to be held in Montreal, Quebec, in 2001.

There were a number of good original anthologies, including especially *Dark Matter*, edited by Sheree R. Jeffers (the first SF and fantasy anthology specifically devoted to Black writers); *Black Heart, Ivory Bones*, edited by Ellen Datlow and Terri Windling, the sixth and final in their distinguished series of fairy tales retold anew for our times; and *Graven Images*, edited by Nancy Kirkpatrick and Thomas Roche, an original anthology of fantasy tales of gods and goddesses. There are also the magazines, from *Interzone* and *Realms of Fantasy* and *F & SF*, which publish substantial amounts of fantasy, to *Century* and *Eidolon* and *On Spec* and *Weird Tales* and *Marion Zimmer Bradley's Fantasy Magazine* (now suspended), and several others. The small press has been since the 1980s a force of growing strength and importance in the field, in part due to the availability of computers within reach of the average fannish budget and in part due to the new economies of instant print, now prevalent in the USA and soon to reach everywhere. And the books from the more established small publishers, from Golden Gryphon, Ministry of Whimsy, Borderlands, and others, continue to impress. The field lost two fine magazines this year, *Marion Zimmer Bradley*'s and *Amazing* (which published both fantasy and SF), but a perceptible increase in the number and quality of small press publications helped to cushion the loss, as did the announcement of several high-paying online short fiction markets.

It would be comforting to be able to say that this was an especially good year for fantasy, but it was not. Still, there were more than enough excellent stories to consider to let us fill this book and have some left over. And there are a lot of promising signs, and talented new writers in unexpected places. Now that we have finished our first annual volume, we are confident of the quality of future books.

—David G. Hartwell & Kathryn E. Cramer
Pleasantville, NY

Everything Changes

John Sullivan

John Sullivan lives in Gaithersberg, Maryland, with Max, "the one-eyed pirate cat," and works as a journalist covering the wireless telecommunications industry. He holds a Bachelor's degree in Geography and, in 1999, attended the Clarion writing workshop. He's on the Web at www.sff.net/people/johnsullivan. "Everything Changes," his first publication in the genre, appeared in the magazine Adventures of Sword & Sorcery, *one of the better small press fantasy magazines—it has been published for a number of years and often contains stories of high quality. He also published a story in a mystery anthology called* Crafty Cat Crimes *(apparently a thriving subgenre) that Stefan Dziemianowicz put together for Barnes and Noble at about the same time.*

In "Everything Changes," humans have come to regard the dragon as a powerful weapon to be used or destroyed, or as a figurehead to be manipulated. Sullivan says that this story "is an argument in favor of the wisdom that comes with experience. That experience can be a powerful tool, even when the world around you has become very different from the one you knew. I love dribbling bits of technology—gunpowder, electricity, what have you—into fantasy settings to see what happens." This examination bears interesting fruit: The dragon, who is older and wiser, resists lobbying, political pressure, threats, and objectification to lead the people better than can the human kings.

I am sunning myself on the west terrace when Gilyan comes. Still languid, I fold one wing back against my body to clear his path.

He stands before me and makes the ancient gesture of fealty. "Great Lord, emissaries of Caladin enter the pass from the east," he says.

The late summer sun and the warm stone beneath my scales make me slow. "Let them through," I rumble. "If your people have needs, you may tax them a bit."

"They're not merchants, Great Lord. The King himself comes, with officials and soldiers. He seeks audience with you."

I stretch my limbs and scratch one long, thin claw across the marble as my blood speeds up again. "The King himself? Something to do with this war you mention?"

"It must be," says Gilyan. "He must want protection. Travelers say war will come before winter, and Caladin isn't ready."

If soldiers attack through my pass, I am involved in their petty affairs, whether I wish it or not. I breathe slowly, rasping, and tense my claws.

"I will receive him," I say at last. "But not here, and not in the pass. On the high table. And him alone."

Gilyan bows and backs toward the doors.

"Gilyan?"

"Yes, Great Lord?"

"This King. What is his name now?"

"Mindaran the ninth, Great Lord. The people call him 'the Kind.' "

The ninth already. They come and go so quickly, and I can't tell one from the next.

A minute's flight brings me to the windswept rocks at the highest summit, but the King takes hours to climb to me. When he comes he is flushed and panting. An old man, not used to climbing my mountains alone. There is fear in his eyes as he leans against one of the ancient statues to catch his breath.

"Mindaran the Kind," I roar over the wind. "What do you seek from me?"

He trembles at the sound, but steps forward and looks up at me. "Mighty Teliax, my people are in danger. Tadroth's armies will invade my nation soon, before the snows. Their soldiers will march through your pass, supported by cannon and horse. We will not be able to stop them. As those who loved justice did in days long past, I come to beg for your help."

"You cannot defend yourselves?"

"For three years the rains have been weak, the harvests bad. I've had to deplete my treasury to feed the people. There's been no money for powder and guns, but when the children starve, what good is an army to protect the dead land? What else could I do? Mighty Teliax, the pass is yours. You can prevent this. Hear my cries and save my people."

He tries to use the ancient forms of address, but he does not understand them. He simply hopes they will flatter me into doing what he wants.

"I have heard you. Leave me now."

* * *

The winds carry me over the northern plains, so high that my shadow is only a faint cross sliding across the ground far below. But my eyes are hunter's eyes. Movement draws them, even from this high. Once, when the people below sensed my shadow sweeping over them, they felt an ancient fear. Something buried deep inside them recognized a hunter's shadow.

They were illiterate savages then, huddling around their fires at night, praying I would suffer them to live. I was old even then, and at last I gained wisdom and left them in peace.

They built a great empire, uniting the plains on both sides of my mountains. They taught the children that their God had sent me to embody his vigilance and his anger, but in time they forgot why they had built the public buildings and the great temples. They tore them down to make walls around their villages from the stone. Then, when they could no longer remember why they had needed walls, they used the stone to build houses. Again in time, the houses were abandoned, and the stone made roads to cities long forgotten now.

Always I have been above them, guarding the pass through the mountains. I am eternal, as they are ever-changing.

Now comes a new change. Below me Tadroth's army practices its maneuvers with different weapons than the old sword and bow. The tang of powder smoke rises on the wind now, and the faint crack of muskets. The soldiers are too busy to notice my passage as they form their shifting patterns of infantry, cavalry and artillery. If they looked up, would they still feel the old fear, or have their weapons made them fearless?

When Tadroth's ambassador arrives, he leads a regiment of soldiers and a great train of gifts. Gold and jewels, bolts of silk, and dozens of marble statues. The wagons creak and the oxen strain to climb the pass.

So they think of me as another petty princeling now,

with power to be measured against their armies. Will they try to buy my strength with their trinkets?

I fly down to meet them halfway up the pass. Let them feel the wind my wings can raise, and smell my sulfur breath. Let them feel a touch of the old fright again. Gilyan advises against this. They are powerful, he says. They are dangerous.

I swoop down out of the dying autumn sun and land before them, kicking up gravel and frightening their horses. While they calm the animals, I approach the ambassador.

"Are these merchants," I growl, "carrying trade goods through my pass?"

He struggles to maintain his composure. "Mighty Teliax," he says, "I bring you greetings and gifts of friendship from my Lord, King Serian of Tadroth." He makes a sweeping gesture to the wagons.

"You should speak quickly," I rumble, "for your lives are fleeting. You wish to attack your neighbors across my pass, do you not?"

"Mighty Teliax," the ambassador sputters, "you among all creatures know that Tadroth and Caladin were one from the earliest days. Our cause is just. It is time to reunify the land under one King again. We offer you tribute and friendship if you will join your power to ours. Together we will rebuild the glories of the past."

His men unload the chests of gold and the gleaming statues. Behind them the soldiers grow restless. They finger their muskets and watch me as I prowl back and forth across the pass.

"So you would have me join your armies then." My claws scratch furrows in the ground and I let smoke surge from my nostrils. "You would have me burn your enemies for the glory of your kingdom, little fleck? In a thousand years Tadroth will be only a legend. In two thousand, even the legend will be forgotten. When you and all you make are dust in a grave, only I will remain. Why should I care how many kings rule this land for a season? Why should I care if your Serian lives or dies?"

The ambassador is indignant, huffing and red-faced. My

brain conjures an image of my claws pressing his screaming body against the ground as my jaws pull his head from his shoulders and swallow it. Perhaps I will still do that.

"You have overstepped your place," I snarl. "Do not think yourselves so important that I will raise my fire to serve your territorial ambitions. Do not think your baubles will seize my eye and bind me to you. Go from here and trouble me no more. Your war is of no interest to me."

The horses rear and cry again as I rise into the air on my powerful wings. I fly up, spiraling tightly around them. A few of the wagon drivers turn and run back down the pass. From a few hundred feet up, I swoop down on their column and seize one of the oxen pulling the lead wagon. I rip it from the harness and carry it, shrieking, away.

One of the soldiers panics, shoulders his musket and fires. There is a brief pinprick of pain in my side. I wheel and bellow flame into the air. The hot stream of it lances over their heads and splatters against the nearby rocks. They break then, turning and galloping back down the road to Tadroth. The remaining oxen trample their tack and flee as well. Only the shattered wagons remain, and the cluster of fine statues, gleaming white in the setting sun.

Gilyan is unhappy, but knows he must remain silent. He serves me faithfully, as did his father, and his father before him, back so many generations I cannot count them. His people were my priests long ago. Now they maintain my castle, and herd my sheep in the high mountain pastures so that I may hunt. They tax the merchant caravans in the pass for their needs and to increase my useless store of wealth. They remember more of the old ways than anyone else, but even they do not understand me. How can they, when ten thousand years have been stuffed one after the next into the deep well of my memory? What can I share with these flickering things? They cannot see beyond the horizon of their brief lives. Every little thing is so important to them.

As the sun sets, I call Gilyan to the terrace, and he

comes, looking at me expectantly, with love and concern.

"You think I was wrong to rebuff the embassy from Tadroth."

"No, Great Lord, I don't." He pauses, thinking. "But if they can't call you their friend, they will call you their enemy. That's how they are. And they make powerful enemies."

"So you fear for me in the storm of their wrath. But in your heart you do not want me to help them, do you?"

I gesture to the east with one wing. "You want me to protect the others. Caladin."

He stammers for a moment. "They're weak, Great Lord, and Tadroth will use them cruelly."

"You see the strong oppress the weak and think this is wrong. You love me, and you want me to uphold the right so that you can be proud of me."

I have embarrassed him now. "Great Lord . . ."

"Fifty generations ago it was Caladin that slaughtered the children of Tadroth, though neither used that name then. Did you know that?"

"No, Great Lord."

"And what does it matter now? The winners and losers are equally gone. Only I am left to remember them. No, Gilyan, their wars are beneath us. Let their fires burn themselves out. I will not help them, but neither will I stop them. Let all your kind do as you will."

Gilyan frowns. "As you wish, Great Lord."

"You may go now." He turns to leave. "You do not understand, Gilyan," I say to his retreating back. "But in the end that does not matter either."

With the dawn, there are trumpets in the pass and the sound of many horses and men. Gilyan and a number of the shepherds come to me with frightened chattering.

"Tadrothi troops, Great Lord," Gilyan says, still breathing hard. "Nearly a hundred horsemen and cannons. They're forming a line in the northern approaches!"

The old instincts rise up in me. Defend the nest, destroy the enemies. I struggle to push them down.

"Are they bound for Caladin? Or can they mean to attack us?" The idea is incredible.

"They're not in cannon range of the castle, Great Lord. But this can't be the invasion. There aren't enough of them. I think they're testing you, to see if you'll let them pass."

I soar from the northern tower into the chill morning sky. The soldiers are arrayed below me, in uniforms of bright blue and white. Pennants flutter in the wind. Their cannon are lined up in the center of the road, the horsemen massed to either side.

When they see that I have come, they fire off a volley of cannon shot. A terrible roar, as great as my own, echoes off the mountains, amid fire and smoke. As the smoke clears, it leaves behind a bed of white marble rubble where the statues stood.

An officer steps forward and unrolls a gilt scroll. His shouting voice booms from the rock walls of the pass as he reads.

"Mighty Teliax, for longer than any man remembers, you have dwelt in our mountains, and been a friend to man. It saddens us that you now break this ancient faith. But we cannot suffer an enemy so close to our borders. Removing you will delay the reunification of our land. Yet, when this is done, no man will dare stand against those who have overcome such a power from the dawn of time. In this way, your death can still serve the cause of justice which you have forsworn in life. King Serian III. Dragonslayer."

I scarcely know what to think as they head back down the pass. I take flight out over the familiar plains, once more turning brown with the approach of winter. I was the fang and the burning flame of God to them once. But they forget everything in time. Each generation struggles to reclaim the wisdom gained by the last and then lost in their passing.

Perhaps they need a display of the strength they once feared. Yet they are stronger now as well. Have their weapons made us equal at last? Have I been reduced to just another worldly power among many?

Back in the castle, Gilyan awaits, with a number of the others behind him.

"They weren't expecting you to refuse them," he says, "and now it's almost winter. They won't be able to mount an attack on the pass itself until spring." He nods grimly. "You've given Caladin that much time at least."

He wants to say more, but fears to. I reach out to him with one long talon. "Speak freely, Gilyan. Do you fear them?"

"As you should, Great Lord," he says suddenly, spilling out the words before he loses the courage. "I've read the old tales of times when nothing could threaten you. Those times are gone.

"They can kill you. You're stronger than they know, and they'd pay a terrible price, but in the end bullets and cannon shot are a match for your scales and your claws, and even your fire."

"So what would you have me do, Gilyan?"

"Leave here. The world is large. You'll find other mountains. You must go where you'll be safe, Great Lord."

"And you? What will you and the others who serve me do?"

"Stay here, since we can't follow you. We'll defend the pass as long as we can. In the end, Caladin will die, but perhaps something can be saved. There's nothing else to do."

The others agree with him, I see. They are looking at the end of all they know.

"You wanted me to protect Caladin, but you want to protect me even more?"

"Everything changes in time, Great Lord, but I can't imagine a world without you in it. You must survive, for the thousands who came before that live only in your memory now. There's no other way, Great Lord."

The world is changing again. Perhaps I must at last change with it. I wasn't wrong to give these creatures peace, but perhaps I have forgotten how little they remember. I know I had forgotten how brave forgetting makes them.

"No, Gilyan. I won't abandon you or your ancestors. Prepare messengers, and bring me the accounting of my wealth. There is much to do before spring."

The Tadrothi army advances into the pass with a spring wind at its back. They are many more now, a brightly colored column stretching back into the plains. An advance guard of cavalry leads them, followed by Serian himself with his officers and guards at the center of the artillery. The rolling of their drums echoes like thunder off the rocks.

I await them crouched in the roadway at the top of the pass, wings spread, talons ready. The Tadrothi see me and Serian orders the charge. The advance guard rushes up the pass, eager to test their bullets and cannon against my scales.

I let them come until they reach two hundred yards, then I let out a great bellow. My followers, the shepherds and carpenters, farmers and stewards, rise from their positions above them on both sides of the pass. Their black uniforms are not easily spotted against the rocks, and the Tadrothi see only the enemy ahead. My forces bring their guns to bear and fire a volley down into the road. The second rank rises and fires as the first reloads, and then the third rank follows. In seconds the pass is choked with smoke and the screams of dying men rise over the fading echoes of our volleys.

The shattered advance guard lies in blood and dust below. My men have already reloaded and stand ready to open fire on the next section of the column. Farther down the pass, my remaining troops rise and click back the locks of their muskets.

The stunned Tadrothi realize I have outmaneuvered them. Serian himself looks up the pass to where I still wait motionless on the road. His hand clenches the ornate butt of a pistol as he waits to die for his misjudgment.

"King Serian, Dragonslayer," I call to him. "You will not earn that name here today, I think. You found weapons that could pierce my scales and thought that made you my equal. You are mistaken. They are only one of my weapons. I have lived ten thousand years. I have learned much, I have amassed great resources. I have earned the loyalty of brave men. Overcome these if you can. Then you may face my scales, and my fire."

"Spare my men, great Teliax," he calls. "Let them return safely to their homes and we will have peace!"

"I have been too apart from you too long and you have forgotten too much about me. Now I have reminded you, but you are short-lived and forget too easily. I will not make that mistake again. Your men will return home. You will come to me and we will set the terms of peace in this land."

The orders are given. My troops raise a cheer and brandish their muskets as the column turns and retreats back to the plains. Their King rides forward to meet a fate he is still uncertain of. Behind me Gilyan leads the emissaries from Caladin up the trail to my castle. There will be peace in the land, and Gilyan practically gleams with his pride in me. He will fade and die in little more than a moment. At best he will tell his children of this day, but it will be just a story to them. And yet, as I fly back to my castle in the peaks, I find that his pride is important to me, and I will keep it long after all else has been forgotten.

A Troll Story

Lessons in What Matters, No. I

Nicola Griffith

Nicola Griffith emerged as a strong feminist voice in science fiction in the 1980s and early 1990s. Born in Leeds in the UK, she lives in Seattle, Washington, with her partner, Kelly Eskridge. She has won the James Tiptree, Jr. Award, and the Lambda Award, and is the author of the science fiction novels Ammonite *and* Slow River, *and the detective novel* The Blue Place, *featuring the sexy lesbian private detective Aud Torvington. Her female central characters are capable and engaging without falling into perkiness and spunkiness. Griffith's new novel in 2001 is* Red Raw. *Her Web site is at www.sff.net/people/nicola.*

"A Troll Story" appeared in Realms of Fantasy, *edited by Shawna McCarthy, a magazine that had a strong year and published a lot of the better fantasy stories of 2000. Told to a child who has broken a boy's nose, this is a gory and exciting Norse tale of heroism, guilt, and the emergence of conscience. Being a conventional hero, it seems, involves learning to "forget that sucking sound a sword makes when you pull it from a woman's stomach." Interestingly, the gender of the child to whom the tale is told is not specified.*

No, don't turn on the lamp; who I am is not important. The lamp wouldn't work, anyway. If you shout for your parents, they won't hear you. Are you afraid? There's no need, I'm here only to tell you a story. If you wish you may pretend I'm a figment of your imagination, product of a fever dream. Oh, yes, I know about your fever. Your mother thinks you're coming down with something, but it's not that, is it? It's guilt. You feel bad and there's no one to tell. Such a small thing, too, to punch a boy on the nose and make it bleed, and in a noble cause, for what else can a person do but step in when a bully is hurting the weak? Unexpected though, the sound of breaking bone, eh? That noise, that meaty creak, makes it all real. Tomorrow you'll pluck up the courage to tell your mother, and she will wipe away your tears and snot and tell you it doesn't matter, to forget it, that you did the right thing. Which is why I'm here. It does matter, you see, and nine is not too young to learn these things. Everything you do is a step toward who you will become. We are born in blank ignorance, a kind of darkness, if you will, and every act, every thought is a little piece of knowledge that illuminates the world and leads us farther from the nothing of our beginning. We don't always like what we see but it is important that we look, otherwise the steps mean nothing, and we become lost.

I see your hand by the lamp switch once more. Very well, try it if you must. You see? I told you the truth. Everything I will tell you is true, at least in the ways that matter. There's no need to scrunch up in a heap like that, no reason to fear me. Perhaps the light bulb simply needs replacing.

But light can be such a comfort, can't it? There are some times and places, some circumstances which only make it more so. I am here to tell you about one such time and place. Listen carefully; it matters.

In Norway a thousand years ago, all dreaded *morketiden,* the murky time of winter when the Sun hides below the horizon for weeks on end and the very rock sometimes stirs to walk the steep *fjell* in troll form. Families lived in lonely seters, and in winter, trapped by snow and darkness, the only comfort was to lift a burning twig from the hearth and touch it to the twisted wool wick floating in a bowl of greasy tallow, to watch light flare yellow and uncertain, and to hope the wind that howled down the *fjell* would not blow it out, leaving nothing but long twisting shadow from the fire, whose coals were already dying to deepest black tinged with red.

In the Oppland lived one such family, a hard-working man called Tors and his strong-minded wife, Hjorda, and their sandy-haired daughters Kari and Lisbet, better off than most. They had a fat flock of sheep and fine cows for milk, their seter was large and well covered with living sod and surrounded by sturdy outbuildings, and in addition to their bond servants, they could afford a shepherd in winter, two hired men to tend the fields and mend the walls, and a dairymaid. At this time it was the end of summer and the livestock were fat, the grass green, and the storehouse full, but Tors and Hjorda were worried. Oh, it was not their daughters, who ran about the fields like little plump geese, not a care in the world. Nor was it the hired men or the dairymaid they both mooned after. No, it was that even as the nights began to draw in, Torsgaard did not have a winter shepherd.

Hjorda decided that Tors must go to the All-Meet, the Thing, that year. "For while it is not always true, more heads may on occasion lead to greater wisdom."

So Tors went to the Thing, and he and his neighbors from Gjendebu and Leine and other places as far away as Dragsvik talked of fields and sheep and the price of oats. On the last night they drank vast quantities of mead. "Last winter trolls came to walk the *fjell*," Tors said. "Our shepherd disappeared and no local man will be persuaded to watch the sheep this year." This was very bad, and no one had any advice to offer. Eventually, many horns of mead later, Grettir, a farmer from the richer lowlands of Leine, stroked his beard and said, "There is a man, a strange, rough man, Glam by name, who might watch your sheep. But I would not want him watching my sheep if I had daughters." Despite the mead, Tors was not a stupid man, and he agreed that it is better to lose one's sheep than one's daughters. Especially if you have a woman like Hjorda to deal with at home.

The next day, he woke up feeling as though his head were seven times too big for his hat and his legs three times too weak for his body and, to top it all, his horse was gone. None of his neighbors could spare him even a nag; he would have to walk the long, long path home. Mid-morning found him tramping the springy turf of a narrow valley between two hills. Autumn berries grew bright around him but the air was chill, and he worried about what Hjorda might say when he returned to Torsgaard not only without a shepherd, but without his horse. And then, crossing his path, was a man, a huge bundle of faggots on his back. If the bundle was huge, the man was more so.

"What is your name?" asked Tors in amazement, looking up at the massive brow, ox-like shoulders, and the muscles of his bare arms which were plump as newborn piglets, but white.

"They call me Glam." His voice was harsh, like the grinding together of granite millstones, and he tossed the bundle to the ground as though it weighed less than his hat—a greasy leather thing. His hair, too, was greasy, black and coarse as an old wolf's. The face under it was pale and slippery looking, like whey, and his eyes were a queer, wet, dark gray-green, like kelp.

"Well, Glam, I need your help." Tors had been about to ask for directions to a farm or settlement where he might buy a horse, but his head ached, and he felt out of sorts, and thought perhaps if he didn't tell Hjorda about Grettir's warning, all might be well. "Grettir tells me you might be persuaded to work for me at Torsgaard as my winter shepherd."

"I might, but I work to please myself and no one else, and I do not like to be crossed."

His harsh voice made Tors' head ache more. "Name your terms."

"Where is your last winter shepherd?"

"We are haunted by trolls. He was afraid." No need to mention the fact that he had disappeared on the *fjell*, where the trolls walked.

"A troll will provide me with amusement during the long winter nights."

They bargained, and Glam agreed to start work on *haustblot*, the celebration that marks the first day of *morketiden*. As soon as they spat on their hands and shook, Glam slung his bundle up onto his back without even a grunt, and though his walk was shambling and crablike, it was fast, and he was gone behind a stand of aspens before Tors could think to ask about a nag. But scarcely was Glam out of sight when from behind the very same stand of aspens came trotting Tors' very own horse. Its eyes were white-ringed and it was sweating, but it seemed pleased to see Tors, and it was only later that he began to scratch his beard and wonder at the odd coincidence. So he went home a hero, with his horse and his promise of a winter shepherd, and waited for *morketiden*.

The people of Torsgaard and the surrounding farms went to the hov to celebrate *haustblot*: to welcome the winter season and implore Thor to protect them against disease, sorcery, and other dangers, and Frigg to ensure warmth and comfort and plenty in the home during the time of dark and bitter cold. With all the fine white beeswax candles lit, the strong light showed men in their best sealskin caps and women with dried flowers woven into their hair. All made merry, for soon the dark would come. Amid the singing and laughter and drinking came Glam.

He wore the same greasy hat and despite the cold his arms were still bare. All his possessions were bundled in a jerkin and slung over his back. He walked through the suddenly quiet people toward Tors, and Tors' two hired men stepped in front of the dairymaid, and Tors himself looked about for Hjorda and his girls, and people moved from Glam's path, from his queer gaze and hoarse, ill breath. Hjorda appeared from the crowd and stood at Tors' elbow. "Husband," she whispered, "tell me this is not our shepherd."

Glam stopped some distance from them and folded his arms. He shouted, so all could hear. "It is *morketiden* and I am come to look after Tors' sheep." A murmur went up in the hov, and Hjorda said privately, "Husband, look how the very candles sway from his presence. Send him away." But Tors did not want to be gainsaid before his neighbors, so he turned to Hjorda with a ghastly smile and said, "Hard times need hard remedies." Raising his voice he called to Glam, "Welcome to Torsgaard. Now our sheep will be safe." And it was done.

The rest of *haustblot* passed uneasily, with Glam tearing into a great ham and draining horn after horn of feast mead, and Tors telling people Glam would no doubt be on the *fjell* every day with the sheep, and manners after all were not everything.

And, indeed, the next morning Glam left with the sheep before Tors woke and did not come back until the evening fire was dying. And as the days passed, even Hjorda had to admit that Glam was a master of sheep herding: They seemed terrified of him, and all he had to do was call out in that terrible hoarse voice and they huddled at his direction. Days turned to weeks, and he lost never a single sheep. But not a man or woman or child would go near him, except as they must when he called for meat and drink, and even the dogs slunk away when they heard his tread.

Many weeks passed in this fashion and the days drew in upon themselves and the nights spread until even noon became just a thin, pale dream of daytime and nothing seemed real but the cold, the howling wind, and the red flickers of firelight. And still Glam called for his sheep in the dark of every morning and led them up into the hills to find grass, and every night he came back in the dark, face white as clabbered milk despite the cold.

Midvintersblot was a day sacred to Frey, when all the people of Torsgaard gathered to beg Frey to ensure fruitfulness for people and animals and crops during the coming year. It is a day of fasting until the evening feast, when holiday mead is brought out and the plumpest hog roasted, and the people feast by torchlight all night and don't sleep until dawn. That *midvintersblot*, Glam rose as usual in the dark and called for bread and meat. The noise woke Kari, the eldest daughter. His shouting grew louder—no one seemed to be attending him—followed by a great thump as if he had sent a man flying with a casual blow with the back of his hand.

Kari rose from her bed. "Today is *midvintersblot*. We fast until the evening to honor the gods."

Glam sneered. "I have never seen a god and I have never seen a troll. And who are you to say whether I should eat or drink? Now go get my food!" And he stepped aside so Kari could see the bondservant lying senseless by the cold hearth. Kari, frightened, brought his food. When he stepped out into the dark, shouting in that horrible voice for his sheep, she went to her mother and spoke of what had happened.

Hjorda saw to the bondservant, then sought Tors and told him of events. "Glam must be paid off and turned out, husband."

"But what of the sheep, wife? Besides, the man was probably just hungry."

"The servant's cheek is broken, and he is only now recovering his wits. He would have done the same to Kari, had she not obeyed."

"Nonsense. No doubt the girl misunderstood, frightened by his loud voice." He turned back to the warmth of his wolfskin coverlet and slept. He didn't hear the rising note of the north wind, the first flurries of driving snow. He didn't hear Glam roaring above the wind for his sheep, the shouts getting fainter and fainter and farther off. By the time he rose, Glam could not be heard and the snow was settling in fat white folds on sills and stoops. The hours slipped by, with all the servants and the women of the house working over spits and ovens and Tors working over his tally sticks. The flurries became a blizzard and the dairymaid, when she went to milk the cows, could not see her hand before her face.

The scents from the kitchen grew more delicious, the wind climbed to a high-pitched howl. The trenchers were laid on the board, and still Glam did not return. The hired men and several male servants came to Hjorda. "It's cruel outside, but if you asked we would venture into the cold and dark and wind, as some misfortune might have befallen Glam."

"No, no," said Hjorda, thinking quickly. "Glam is strong and wily. No doubt he can look after himself, and the sheep have fine wool coats. See that you don't bother Tors with this."

"Certainly not, mistress," they said, knowing full well that Tors might take them up on their offer—and the bondservant with the addled wits and broken cheek being a friend of theirs.

And so the feast was laid out and eaten without Glam, and not a soul missed him until it was long past midnight and Tors asked, "But where is our winter shepherd?" By this time, the snow lay hip deep and the wind was cold enough to freeze people's breath in their throats, turn their eyeballs to ice, and crack open their very bones. Tors declared no man could step forth and live, so they turned their backs to the door and drank barrel after barrel of ale, cask after cask of mead, and sang loudly enough to drown out the terrible noises and deep vibrations that rolled down the *fjell*—though Lisbet, the youngest daughter, who had fallen asleep on a bearskin after her third horn of mead, had strange and awful dreams of dark shapes battling on snow. Not long before dawn, sodden with celebration, they slept.

They woke after noon. Headaches and guilt are fine partners, so Tors did not have to urge the men to put on their boots and fur capes and caps and set off up the mountain. The pale winter Sun shone brilliant on the new-fallen snow and the air lay still. Snow crunched and one of the hired men could be heard groaning softly to himself every time his boots thumped down. They walked and walked, and eventually they heard the faint bleat of a sheep, and suddenly sheep were all around them; some nothing more than frozen woolly mounds in the snow, some bleating pitifully, some standing lost on crags or caught in bushes. Past the sheep they found a place where great boulders and trees had been torn from the ground and the snow beaten down in some mortal struggle. They walked faster now, and found a bloody, leveled place where Glam lay on his back, his strange seaweed eyes open to the sky and covered in snow, which did not melt. His skin was mottled and bloated, as though he had been dead a long, long time. Huge tracks, the size of barrel hoops, filled with frozen blood, led off to a deep and narrow gully. Something had fallen and splashed blood—hogsheads of the stuff—all about, but there were no more tracks so the men could not follow. The hired man stopped groaning long enough to peer into the gully, look at the blood, and say, "Nothing, not even a troll, could have survived that." There was general agreement, and the hired men and bondservants returned to Glam's body.

The bolder among them tried to move him, but it was as if his bones had turned to stone and he would not shift. Nor could they close his eyes. They herded up the sheep and returned to Torsgaard. "Glam is dead," they said to Tors. "He killed the troll and most of the sheep are living. We tried to bring him down but his body is strangely heavy."

"Well, take a yoke of oxen up the mountain and drag

him down if necessary," said Tors. "We must bring him back to the hov for a proper send off."

"No," said Hjorda, "take faggots and tallow to the gully and burn him there, like carrion."

"Yes," said Kari.

"Yes," piped up Lisbet, whose dreams still hung about her.

"No," said Tors, and the men tried not to sigh. They took the oxen up the mountain, and some rope, but even with the oxen Glam's body, black as Hel now and bloated as a bladder, would not move even along level ground. After hours of this, with his men surly and tired and his own fingers and toes going white with cold, Tors unyoked the oxen. "He seems to want to stay here, so let him. We will cover him with stones."

So it was done, and they walked back to the women and a warm hearth.

Three days later, Lisbet woke in the middle of the night and ran to her mother. "Glam walks in my dreams!" Hjorda cuddled her close and they both fell back to sleep. They were awakened in the morning by a shriek from the dairymaid, who had opened the door and tripped over a dog—or what was left of a dog—on the stoop. Later that morning, the haunch of mutton on the spit was found to be green and black on one side, and the servant who tended the ovens was clean out of her wits: "Glam came down the chimney, Glam came down the chimney, Glam came down the chimney," was all she could say, over and over.

Glam did not lie easy in his grave. He came again, and again, and again, driving more people mad, sending one hired man—who had taken the sheep out—headlong down the *fjell*, falling and breaking his neck, and the dairymaid running away to another farm, snow or no snow.

Hjorda found Tors. "You must burn him, husband."

But upon toiling up the mountain with faggots and tallow, and heaving aside the stones, they found nothing. When he returned, Tors told this to his wife, who nodded. "The troll lives in his bones and walks abroad wearing his skin, even under the Sun."

While Glam could appear during the day, it was at night that he spread true terror. He ran on the rooftops until the beams buckled, he rolled great boulders down the *fjell*, destroying some outbuildings entirely, and he laughed. His deep horrible laughter ground over Torsgaard and the farms of Oppland, crushing the spirit of men, driving cattle mad, and women to weeping in their terror that Glam was coming for *them*. The dairymaid who had escaped to another farm was found beside a barn, used and torn and tossed aside, like a broken doll. The still-living hired man ran mad and took an axe up the mountain, foaming at the mouth, vowing to chop Glam to pieces. The man's head, and pieces of his torso, rained down on Torsgaard all that night. The whole countryside felt disaster looming. Hjorda bade her daughters to sleep in her alcove, and they carried eating knives in their belts that were a little too long and a little too sharp for manners.

But as the days grew longer and the Sun stood higher in the sky, the hauntings lessened.

"Summer Sun is not kind to trolls," Hjorda observed. "But when winter comes he will be back, and no one in Oppland will be safe."

Tors did not want to hear it. He hired more men and a new dairymaid and worked to rebuild the broken outbuildings. His wife insisted that he strengthen the doors and roof beams of Torsgaard. And when this was done she sent him to the Thing, only this time she sent Kari with him. "Find a good strong man," she told her daughter, "one who can do more than tend the sheep during winter. Spend your portion to hire him if you must—for what good is a dowry to a dead maid?"

Now it happened that at this time a ship came into the *fjord* and Agnar the Strong, who was tired of adventuring in foreign lands, came to the Thing and heard that Tors of Torsgaard needed a winter shepherd but that no man would take up his offer. He sought out Tors and asked of him, "Why will no one take up this offer of yours?"

"The last shepherd, Glam, died on the *fjell* and there is some superstition attached to his name," said Tors evasively. "Have some of this mead." Now Tors was generally an honest man, and his shame at speaking false would have been apparent even to a lesser man of the world than Agnar. Agnar declined the mead and watched thoughtfully as Tors walked away, ashamed.

"Sir, allow me to offer you the mead again," came a woman's voice from behind him. He turned to face the maid with bright blue eyes. "I am Kari Torsdottir. Drink the mead and I will tell you of Glam." He did, and she did, leaving nothing out, and finishing, "—and so if you would look after our winter sheep and keep them safe, you could have my marriage portion and welcome."

"Money is no good to a dead man."

"My mother says that if you are but a strong man, good and true, and willing to listen to her, you will prevail, for trolls, even trolls who wear a man's skin, are stupid, being made mostly of rock."

And so Agnar the Strong agreed to come to Torsgaard and be the winter shepherd, but instead of waiting for *morketiden*, he returned directly with Tors and Kari, for he was curiously unwilling to let Tors' daughter out of his sight.

His open face, clear blue eyes, and ox-wide shoulders were welcomed by all. He noted the great gashes in the doors and the rents and holes in walls and gates but kept his own counsel. All through the summer, Agnar helped at the farm. He repaired stone walls and cut huge trees to reinforce roof beams, he helped herd cattle, and walked with Kari and Lisbet when they went berry-picking. As the evenings drew in, he held their yarn while they spinned and Hjorda did not fail to notice that he was always willing to fetch a cape for Kari, or pump the bellows to coax the fire hotter when she sat by it. A good man.

On the eve of the first day of *morketiden*, Hjorda drew him aside. "Glam will return, perhaps as soon as tomorrow."

"Glam doesn't frighten me!"

"Then you are more of a fool than I thought. He is more stone troll than man, and more heartless. Alive he was twice as powerful as a brace of bulls. Now even bulls would flee. And he wants to destroy this farm and all the people in it, only this time he is stronger and will be after choicer fare than the dairymaid." Hjorda noted Agnar's quick glance at Kari, combing her hair before the hearth. "Yes. Glam will come for the eldest daughter of the house. If you wish to save her, you will listen to me." But Agnar knew in his heart he needed nothing but his own strong back, and he laughed, and walked away.

That night the ground shook as Glam stalked the farm, his bones so heavy his feet sank ten inches into the turf. His awful, grinding laugh filled the dark as he tore off chunks of wall and gate. A rending crash and a high-pitched scream split the dark, followed by the terrible sound of a large animal being torn limb from limb, and the splash and spatter of blood on the iron-hard ground of the barn enclosure. Then with a roar of satisfaction he ran up the mountain and was gone. When the people crept from the hearth hall the next day, they found Tors' poor horse ripped into quarters and its guts arranged in a rune of challenge.

The next night, Agnar the Strong, who had been a-viking as far as Novgorod and the shores of Ireland, who had burned priests and fought the hordes of Rus, who was famed for his strength and bravery from Oppland to Hordaland to Rogaland and beyond, sought out Hjorda, the woman of Torsgaard. "If you speak on this subject, I will listen, and do as you say."

And so as the Sun went down that evening, Tors found himself strangely sleepy, and while the great fire still roared in the hearth, he fell sound asleep and snored on his wallbed by the inglenook. Hjorda directed Agnar to pick up her drugged husband and bundle him into the bed at the far end of the hall, away from the passage that led to the door. Then she dressed Lisbet in her warmest clothes, and the two of them stole out to hide in the barn, cosy in the straw with the cattle. Then there was only Kari and Agnar. They stood opposite each other by the hearth.

Agnar, forgetting himself in his fear for her, took her by the hand. "It's not too late to hide with your mother and sister."

"You will need me," she said. "We must bring Glam inside."

When the embers began to die, Kari, still wearing her clothes, left the curtain between the passage and the hall open, and lay down on the wallbed by the inglenook; Agnar, similarly dressed, wrapped himself like a sausage in an old, heavy fur cloak so that one end was tucked tightly under his feet and the other securely under his chin, leaving his head free so he could look about. Then he settled himself on the wall bench opposite Kari's bed. In front of the bench lay a bench beam, a huge ancient thing set into the floor when the farm was built. He set his feet against it and straightened his legs so he was firmly braced between the beam and the wall. And then he waited.

The embers glowed then dulled then sighed into ash. Kari's breath grew soft and slow and regular. Once, there was a rattle as a gust of wind shook the only gate still standing. Far, far away he heard the lonely howl of a wolf. But Agnar's heart did not beat soft or easy, it hammered like a smith beating hot iron into an axe-head, and he touched the sword at his belt constantly. The hilt was cold as only iron can be, and he could no longer quite feel his feet.

Sudden as an avalanche, something leaped onto the roof and thundered about, driving down with its heels, until the new beam buckled and splintered and the roof almost fell in. Glam. The walls shook and Glam jumped down, and the earth trembled as he strode to the door. A sharp creak as he laid his huge horny hand on the door and suddenly it was ripped away, lintel and all, and moonlight briefly lit the hearthroom. But then Glam blocked out all light as he thrust his huge head through. The whites of his strange eyes gleamed like sickly oysters, and Agnar's heart failed him. Glam's head brushed the roof of the passage as he came into the hall.

"Glam," said a soft voice, and Kari stood there slim and

brave by the door, her hair silver in the moonlight. "I will come with you, but it is cold outside and I must have a bearskin to lie on. Bring that old cloak on the bench by the fire. I'll wait for you outside." And Agnar's heart filled with admiration for her and there was no room left for fear.

Glam strode to the sausage-shaped bundle of fur, and tried to pick it up with one hand. Agnar was braced and ready. He made no sound and the fur did not move. Glam pulled harder, but Agnar braced his feet all the more firmly. He was sweating now. Glam grunted, and laid two hands on the bundle, and now a titanic struggle began, Glam hauling up, Agnar fighting to push against the bench beam with all the strength of his muscle and sinew yet make no noise. But then Glam put his back into it and the old cloak tore in two. He stood there, the fur in his hands and his horrible eyes staring, and Agnar flung himself at the troll, gripped him around the waist and set his feet. With a massive grunt, he squeezed tight and started to bend the monster backward. It would not be the first time he had snapped a man's spine in a wrestling match.

But Glam was now more, much more than a man, his bones were made of the rock of the mountain, and with a single heave he had Agnar off his feet and was flinging him about. But Agnar had been in many wrestling matches and he did all he could to brace his legs against roof beam or hearth edge, bench or wall. In the passageway he strained until the veins stood out in his neck and sweat sprang out on his forehead, and always he avoided the ruined doorway. It was bad enough in the enclosed spaces of the hall; outdoors, it would be seven times worse. Closer he was drawn to the door, and closer still. Sweat poured from him. With a furious wriggle, he eeled around in Glam's grip until his back was to the awful face and bull-like chest. He dug his heels against the threshold stone and with a strength that was equal parts fear, determination, and desperation, he leaned in toward the last breath of warm, indoor air. As Glam hauled backward with all his might, so too did Agnar thrust *backward*, and his last strength and the inhuman force of Glam's heave hurled them both outside. Glam, with Agnar still clutched to his breast, landed spine down across a rock. The spine parted with a loud *crack*, a sound that would live in Agnar's mind for the rest of his days.

Agnar could not rise; all he could do was lie like a gasping fish in the dying troll's grasp, drained not just by the effort of fighting a monster, but by the awful touch of its skin against his own. His strength ebbed and ebbed, until his muscles were made of lead and his bones felt like lace and he could not even touch the hilt of his sword with his fingertips. And then Glam spoke, hoarse and horrible in his ear.

"You will live, Agnar the Strong, but you will never be the same. You will always look into the dark and see my face, hear my voice, and know yourself." And the troll laughed, dark and full of wickedness. At the laugh, Agnar felt the strength flow back. He sprang to his feet, pulled free his sword, and swung. Once, twice, three times, and the muscle and sinew and bone of Glam's neck parted, and the head, like some vile rock, rolled free, and Agnar did not laugh, but wept.

The Moon tugged clear of its cloud, and Kari ran to his side, and Hjorda and Lisbet emerged from the barn. Even Tors stumbled up from his drugged sleep and stood blinking and beaming with happiness on the soiled turf. "Agnar the Strong! You can have anything of mine you name!" And Kari took his hand and kissed it, and laid it against her cheek. Agnar held her close but could not meet her gaze.

He stood, numb and tired, while Kari wrapped him in the wolfskin and the servants brought him mead warmed by the hurriedly stirred fire, and while Hjorda ordered in a great voice that the hired men bring faggots and tallow and waste not a minute.

They burned Glam right there, outside the hall. And then they burned the ashes. And when the ashes were cold they were gathered in the torn cloak and wrapped tight, and Hjorda saw to it that it was thrown into a chasm, and huge boulders hurled down on top of it.

Torsgaard celebrated all day and into the evening, with men and women arriving from all over Oppland to share the good news. In all that time, Kari remained at Agnar's side, and she noted how he shook with fatigue. Eventually the fire dwindled and the torches were doused. Everyone slept. In the middle of the night, Kari was awakened up by a strange noise, like a child crying. It was Agnar, trying to light the torch, and rocking back and forth. "He will come for me. He will come for me."

"He is dead, beloved."

"I am all alone and he will come for me!"

"You will never be alone again." But he would not hear her, he just rocked and rocked, back and forth.

And the story goes that though Kari stayed by his side every living minute, much to the disapproval of the very traditional Opplanders, and married him not long after, his fear grew worse and he began to rock back and forth and light torches even in the daytime. In the end, they say he ran out, barking mad, and Kari was left without a husband and the hall at the Oppland farm gradually declined. No flowers ever grew on the chasm where they had thrown Glam's ashes.

And that's the end of the story. Agnar was a hero. He saved a household from Glam, the man who became a troll. But before that he was called a hero for slaughtering women and children, roasting priests on the spit, and burning down churches while he drank the altar wine and laughed. "Never mind," his father would have said after that first trip a-viking, "forget that sucking sound your sword makes when you pull it from a woman's stomach."

And so you punched a bully on the nose and broke it, and some will call you a hero, and some will think you a beast, and you feel so confused you have worked yourself into a fever, and it's not something your mother can kiss away in the morning. Nor should she, for if you pretend it never happened you will never bring it into the light to examine and it will fester there in the dark and grow strong, as a troll does, and one day when you are grown and you punch a man on the nose, the weight of all the things you have done and tried to forget will rise up and eat you up from inside.

There, now, you're sweating; perhaps the fever is breaking. In a little while you will sleep, and your mother will wake and come sit by your bedside, and in the morning she will be the first thing you see. You may pretend that this never happened, that I was never here, that this was all a dream. If you like. It's your choice, weigh it carefully before we meet again.

The Face of Sekt

Storm Constantine

*Storm Constantine became an icon of Goth literary culture in the 1980s with the publication of the Wraeththu trilogy (*The Enchantments of Flesh and Spirit, *1987;* The Bewitchments of Love and Hate, *1988;* The Fulfillments of Fate and Desire, *1989), featuring the hermaphroditic race of the Wraeththu. She has since published eleven more novels, three short story collections, and numerous short stories, including many set in ancient civilizations. Constantine lives with her husband, Jim Hibbert, and nine cats in a Bohemian household of varying size in Stafford in the UK. The Official Storm Constantine Web Site is at http://members.aol.com/Malaktawus.*

"The Face of Sekt" appeared in Graven Images, *a substantial fantasy anthology of original stories about myth and magic edited by Nancy Kilpatrick and Thomas Roche. In this tale of temple intrigue, the avatar of the goddess Sekt is lured from her den. Kathryn says, "This story recaptures for me some of the wonder at ancient Egypt I felt upon reading Bram Stoker's* The Jewel of Seven Stars *when I was a twelve-year-old." It is unusual these days for a fantasy story to capture as well as this one does the uncanniness of the ancient deities.*

I am the lioness. I speak with her voice. I look out through her eyes. I am she. I doze in the hot bars of sunlight that come down through the temple roof. I breathe in the scent of flowers. Priests come to me and ask questions so I will talk. It doesn't matter what I say, because all the words of the goddess have meaning. They prostrate themselves and then Meni, the high priest, will raise himself before the others. "Oh mighty Sekt, beloved of Aan, queen of fire, lady of the red flower, hear our petitions."

Aan, I might mention, is my husband, whom I have never met. He lives in another temple somewhere. They say his face is beautiful, but the chances are I will never find this out for myself.

"Speak," I say, yawning.

The questions are too tedious to relate. I have to let my mind go blank so the answers will come. Say this prayer, do that ritual task, cast scent, rake the sand, spill blood. It's all they want from me.

The crown of the goddess covers my head, my face, and rests upon my shoulders. It is fashioned from beaten leaves of gold, shaped and painted. Wearing it, I resemble the black basalt statues of the goddess that line the courtyards and populate the darkest niches of the temple: lioness-headed women. The mask was put upon me in my fifteenth year, a decade ago, and comes off rarely. No one may see the true face of the goddess. My handmaidens withdraw from my chamber before I remove it to sleep.

There are no mirrors in my chamber. If I looked upon myself I might die, for the body that carries this goddess is still that of a woman. It is frail. I dare not even touch my face for fear of what my fingers might explore. When the mask was put upon me, Sekt entered my flesh. I wash myself in a sacred fountain, so that only the water may touch my face and hair.

At one time, our land was a province of the sacred kingdom of Mewt, and although those empire days are but distant memories, our culture is still saturated, if subtly, with Mewtish things. Originally, Sekt was a goddess of war, whose fierce countenance gazed down from the banners of Harakhte the conqueror. The temple he built here is a labyrinth of immense chambers, full of shadows, and tiny shrines where a priestess might mutter in the dark. It is called the Sektaeon.

As a representation of Sekt on earth, I am privileged above all other women. I have no secret yearning to escape the temple, or even this mask. I can bask in the sun all day if I want to. Long ago, my people embraced Sekt as a national goddess. At first this may have been due to fear, but later it was because they saw her power to work for them. She listened to their prayers, and very soon afterward Harakhte was killed in battle by the king of Cos, and Jessapur regained her independence. She has never lost it since. I like this irony. I believe Sekt loves us.

But every day, priests and priestesses in fire red robes walk the temple from end to end, renewing the magical seals over every entrance, however small. This is to keep the ancient spirits at bay, the djinn of the arid wilderness beyond the city and its fertile girdle of land. The djinn are born of fire and are therefore attracted to a goddess of that element. They desire also to wear flesh, and who better to steal a body from than a priest or priestess of fire? Sometimes, I think the djinn are long dead, and the precautions are only tired old ritual, but at other times, when the wind blows hot through the long reaches of the night, I hear a voice from the wilderness, in my heart rather than my ears, and it unnerves me.

Meni, my high priest, came to me this morning, in my solarium, which is actually a shady, green place. He glided between the lush trees and plants, dappled by the sunlight that found its way through the waving fronds of the vines. I was reclining upon some cushions, surrounded by lionesses, who lay licking their paws at my feet. We were being serenaded by the water garden. The rivulets conjured different notes as they ran through the various mechanisms hidden among the ferns. I was not in the best of moods as, during the night, the wind had blown with exceptional passion from the wilderness, carrying with it a scent of burning meat. I had turned restlessly, woken up from a dream of smoke. The darkness in my chamber had seemed watchful, almost sly. A flavor of the haunted night remained with me. I wondered whether it was a portent, and perhaps it was, for the high priest clearly hid a certain agitation beneath his serene and flawless countenance.

Meni stood before me and bowed. "Your reverence, there is a matter for your attention."

I have nothing to do most of the time, so it really perplexes me why every possibility of action seems only an irritant. "Oh, what, Meni? Can't you see to it?"

He bowed again. "Your reverence, it is a matter of importance. King Jaiver himself has requested that you turn your divine face toward it."

"What matter is it?"

"It concerns the Prince Reevan. He has a malady."

One of Sekt's aspects is a goddess of plagues, but she is equally adept at averting human illness. "I shall burn a pouch of incense for the boy and direct Sekt's healing force in the direction of the palace."

Meni paused. "It is rather more than that," he said. "The king has requested your presence."

That made me sit up. "Indeed?" I did not have to go. I was a goddess, who obeyed no one, yet I was intrigued as to why the king desired my physical presence. Was the prince so desperately ill? But that did not make sense. The most ailing of royals were generally carried to the temple, where they could be nursed by the priestesses, close to the presence of Sekt. "What is the nature of this malady, Meni?"

He shrugged. "I have not been told, your reverence. All I know is that Jaiver humbly requests your presence and has already made a sizable donation to the temple treasury."

"Then prepare my litter."

Meni bowed and departed, and presently a retinue of servants came padding to my garden, where they attended to my needs. They washed my hands and feet, and rubbed the palms and soles with red ochre. They applied cinnamon perfume to my wrists and throat, and veiled me in scarlet voile from head to foot. Beyond the temple, I would be concealed behind the curtains of my litter, but sometimes in the labyrinth of the city, strange winds can arise, which might blow the curtains apart. We have to take precautions so that common people never behold the face of the goddess.

The tasseled litter was carried by four eunuch priests. Before it marched a dozen priestesses in the red and gold robes of Sekt. They scattered petals of scarlet poppies before my path. At the head of the procession, Meni rode upon a beautiful nut-colored horse. Behind my litter strode three priests who also acted as my bodyguards. And behind them was a company of neophyte priests and priestesses, on hand to collect any spontaneous donations onlookers might wish to make.

Thus we processed through the faded grandeur of old Madramarta. I love my city, although I rarely get to see it. It is like a ghost of what it used to be, yet still beautiful. The ancient palaces are now tenement buildings full of low-caste workers, or else they have been turned into bazaars. The temples of forgotten gods stand rotting amid jungled gardens. In the dusty streets, forlorn peacocks trail their tails in the dirt, crying plaintively for the ordered landscapes of their ancestors. Everywhere there is evidence of a past opulence, now lost. As a province of Mewt, we prospered, for the Mewts loved the idea of sacred blood—such as the ichor that runs in the veins of our aristocratic families—and honored our country. They were not harsh governors and shared with us their knowledge of arts both occult and scientific. Now, in a time of independence, internal politics ravage the heart of Jessapur. The lowborn have turned our palaces into warrens. They spit on the idea of divine providence and seek power for themselves. The king still reigns, but just. His palace is a citadel.

We passed through the first series of gates and towers, into open parkland, where pale deer run. In the distance, we could see the ghost of the white palace shimmering in the heat. It is called Jurada, which means home of the high god. Only as you draw close to it can you tell it is not a mirage. Trefoil lakes surround it, and mock temples, and ornate gardens. Even though so many of the ancient houses have fallen into disrepair, Jurada still gleams as if new. It is said the entire remaining wealth of the country is divided between the upkeep of the temple of Sekt and that of the royal palace.

My party had to walk for nearly an hour along a shady avenue to reach Jurada. We came to a halt by a pool full of exotic fish in front of the main entrance. A scrum of servants ran out from the cool depths of the hall and laid down a carpet of ferns for me to step upon. I was offered saffron water and a piece of sugared coconut, which I accepted with grace. Meni went ahead of me into the palace and the rest of my retinue surrounded me protectively. The priestesses sang in rapturous high voices while the priests hummed an accompanying undertone. I put my sacred feet upon the ferns and walked the short distance to the hall. I left scarlet footprints.

The king was waiting for us in his throne room, which seemed a little inappropriate to me. I felt we should have been conducted directly to the royal family's private apartments, where the prince must lie in his sickbed. Was this a subtle affront? I was alert for strangenesses. A memory of my dream of smoke came back to me. Queen Satifa was present, magnificent in cloth of gold with a diadem of emeralds upon her regal brow. She sat on a golden throne beside the king, who was surrounded by courtiers in dark robes, the magi who counseled him. The chamberlain, chief conjuror over this clutch of demons, stood imperiously to the left of the king's throne. There was no sign of the crown prince, nor indeed of any of the other royal children or wives. The king's expression was grave.

He inclined his head to me, as I did to him, my hands raised, palms together, before my breast. "Oh mightiness, you have called for me. How may I aid you?"

The king made a nervous, abrupt gesture with one hand. "I am grateful for your presence, revered lady. My concern is Prince Reevan. He is sorely afflicted."

"Take me to him. I will assuage his hurts."

"It is not that simple."

I narrowed my eyes slightly, although no one would be able to tell because of the mask. All they'd see was the snarling face of the goddess, dimly through my veil. "Please explain the difficulty, your mightiness." I glanced at the queen. Her head was lowered. She would not look at me.

"A demon has possessed him," said the king.

I paused. "A demon, mightiness?" This would explain, then, the reluctance to bring the prince to the temple.

He looked slightly uncomfortable. "Yes. That is the diagnosis."

"By whom, may I ask?" I turned my head toward the vizier so he'd be sure I was looking at him.

"A wise man has come to us," said the king.

"A wise man?" I said haughtily. Who was it making diagnoses of royal ailments—indeed possessions—before I? "Are you sure his appraisal of the situation is sound? There are old legends concerning possession by demons, but now our more enlightened understanding is that in most cases when people were said to be hag-ridden, they were in fact afflicted by a malady of the mind. You must tell me, your mightiness, of your son's symptoms."

"This I will do," said the king. "Then you may see him

and reach your own conclusion. But first, I must inform you of the events that led to it."

Eight days before, I was told, news had come to the court of a master magician who was creating something of a stir in the tearooms of the more affluent corners of the city. His illusions, it seemed, were so convincing they could inspire terror, obsessional devotion and dark hatred. He claimed he could drive people mad with his magic, mad for love or envy, mad for despair. The illusions themselves were so astounding, so beautiful, that many were moved to tears. One man said he was transported back into the most golden day of his childhood, when he had become aware in his heart of the spirit of the sky—a moment he had never before recaptured. Another man spoke of how his long-broken heart was healed of hurt as the woman who'd sundered it came to him and asked for his forgiveness. There were many stories such as these. It was all illusion, of course, but it touched people, and word of it came to the king. "Send for this man," he'd said. "Let him show the court his expert trickery." And so the magician was sent for.

As I was told this story, I could picture the man's charlatan's garb, all flouncing colorful robes and extreme hand gestures. I listened patiently while the king described the wonders this paragon of tricksters performed for the court. "It was all the usual fare and more," he said. "Not only could he make serpents dance to the music of a flute, but they would come out of their baskets and choose dancing partners from among the ladies. Then they would turn somersaults, before tying themselves into a complicated knot and flinging themselves back in their baskets."

I nodded. "Mmm."

"Then, he filled the air with flowers that turned to bubbles when you touched them. He made a servant boy climb up a rope he flung into the air, and which stayed there taut. The boy came down again and told us all of a magical land he'd found at the top, where the sky was red and the trees were bright yellow. The magician then took the hand of my old mother and turned her back into the girl she'd once been. The effect lasted for over an hour, and my mother has not stopped weeping since." The king raised his arms. "I have never beheld such wondrous magic. He is a powerful man indeed."

"Indeed. Does he have a name, this man?"

"He calls himself Arcaran."

"I see. How is his arrival connected with your son's illness?"

The king tapped his lips with restless fingers. "Ah, well, the two events go together, but not in any way you'd imagine. On the morning I sent for the magician, Reevan seemed out of sorts on awaking. He felt tired, listless. He could barely move. When my physician examined him, Reevan spoke of bad dreams, a night during which he had been hunted by demons through a strange and terrifying landscape. The experience had exhausted him. The physician proclaimed that Reevan had a slight fever which had caused hallucinations in the night. The prince was given a posset to soothe him.

"But the illness only became worse. It was as if his life was draining away, and it happened so quickly. In the space of a day. I decided Reevan must be sent to the temple, but Arcaran intervened at this point. He came into the sickroom, unbidden, and there made a terrible hissing noise, all the while drawing symbols in the air around him. I was naturally aghast and affronted and about to order him out, but he said to me, 'Great king, you are familiar with the stinging salamander?'

"I can't remember how I answered this bizarre and inappropriate question, but Arcaran raised his hands against my bluster and said, 'There is a stinging salamander on your son's back. It is feeding upon him.'

"I could see no such thing and said as much, although I remember my flesh went cold.

" 'Oh, it is there,' said the magician. 'It is an elemental being, the cause of the prince's torpor. It must be removed, and quickly, for it is already laying eggs.'

"When I heard these words, I went utterly cold. It was as

if I could smell something foul in the room, something evil."

The king shook his head, and would have continued, but I decided it was time to interrupt this preposterous narrative. "Eggs? Salamanders? Perhaps it is time I saw the phenomenon for myself." I paused. "I trust no action has yet been taken to remove this alleged elemental?"

The king shook his head. "Indeed not. Arcaran was most insistent that your aid should be sought first."

"How polite of him," I said. Quietly, I wondered why the charlatan showed such consideration.

Accompanied only by his vizier, King Jaiver led Meni and me to the prince's bedchamber. Here, dark drapes were drawn against the heat of the day, so that the light was brownish. I saw the boy lying on golden pillows, covered by a thin tasseled blanket. His body gleamed with sweat, but I sensed that should I touch him, his flesh would be cold. I could tell at once that this was more than a fever, but I could not credit the idea of unseen parasites.

I walked around the bed for a few moments, sniffing the air. The strange thing was that I could not smell sickness. The air was dry and faintly redolent of smoke. They had been burning an acrid incense in there. I forcibly repressed a shudder. "I really think he should be moved to the temple," I said. "He needs light and air."

"But the demon creature," said the king. "You should not carry one across the threshold of the Sektaeon. Surely that would be dangerous?"

I made my voice cold and harsh to indicate that my patience was fraying. "I and my priesthood are quite capable of dealing with any eventuality."

The king bowed. "Great lady, we have no choice but to obey your word, but I have to say that your decision distresses me greatly. In the temple of fire, the elemental could acquire great strength and take what is left of my son's life."

"You must trust me," I said.

Then, a faint hiss and a dry rattle emanated from one of the dark corners of the room and a man emerged from the shadows. He had, of course, been present the entire time, but for whatever reason had concealed his presence until now.

He bowed slightly and extended his arms in an expansive gesture. Such theatre! "Great lady, you must not take the boy into your temple."

I put as much sneer into my voice as I could muster. "Ah, you must be the *physician* who diagnosed the case. Your presence is no longer required. I am here now."

The magician stole forward. He was not garbed in the flamboyant robes I'd expected, but in dark, close-fitting garments, such as those worn by nomad warriors of the wilderness. "You are skeptical," he said mildly, "and that I understand, but perhaps if you and I could be alone with the prince for a short time, I could show you the nature of the affliction."

"Now is not the time for illusions," I said briskly. "We can all see the prince is gravely ill. Now, if you will step aside, my priest will carry his highness to my litter."

"No," said the magician, and for a brief moment his strange dark eyes burned with an amber spark. He held my eye for a while, almost as if he could see through my mask, and during that time it was as if he and I were the only people in the room. I had never encountered such an intensity of gaze. Within it, I saw passion, fire and knowledge, but also a fierce kind of tragedy. It shocked me.

"I am an illusionist, yes," said the magician softly, "but not just that. There are times for illusions and there are not. I am aware of the distinction, lady."

I hesitated for a moment, then said, "Leave us. Everyone."

There were murmured assents from the king and his vizier, but forthright protests from my high priest. "Your reverence," Meni said in a strained voice. "Is this wise?"

I turned my head to him. "There is nothing to fear. Please, leave. I will call you shortly."

Alone, Arcaran and I faced each other across the bed, where the prince moved feebly, uttering sighs.

"I appreciate this," said the magician. "You will—"

I interrupted him coldly. "Do you know who I am?"

He frowned briefly, then bowed again, smiling. "You are the avatar of Sekt, the goddess on earth."

"Yet you speak to me with little respect. It's clear to me that the king dances to your tune. Who and what are you? Why are you here? What is your aim in this?"

He continued to smile, apparently unflappable. "I appreciate your curiosity and concern. Here are the answers you seek. I am what you perceive me to be. I am here because I was summoned. My aim in this is to heal the prince."

It was clear he sought to charm me, yet there was something—*something*—utterly compelling about this man. Merely being in his presence seemed to inform me he had seen many wonders of the world, that he possessed great knowledge. Perhaps he, too, wore a mask. However, I would not let him win me over that easily. "You prey upon the rich," I said. "You dupe them of their riches with your illusions."

He grimaced, head tilted to one side. "That is a sour depiction of my profession, but not without some basis of truth. Still, I am a creature of many facets. Not all of them are based upon deception."

I made myself totally still. "Show me this parasite, then. No tricks. The truth."

Without further words, he leaned over the prince and gently turned him onto his stomach. He drew down the blanket. Reevan's flesh appeared sallow in the dim light, the sharp ladder of his spine too close to the surface of his skin. The magician lifted the prince's hair from his neck. "Look closely," he said. "To see it, focus beyond the prince's skin. Try to look inside him."

"I am not easily suggestible."

"This is no illusion. Do as I say. You are Ṣekt. You must be able to see this creature."

For some moments, I concentrated as he suggested, blurring my sight until my eyes watered. Then, it came. I saw nothing with my physical sight, yet, in my mind, I sensed pulsing movement, many legs and a presence of malevolence. If it had a form at all, it was a filthy smoky suggestion of a shape. I drew back, uttering an instinctive gasp.

Even then, I was aware of the power of suggestion. This did not have to be real simply because I'd perceived it, yet there was no doubt an evil odor of malice oozed upward from the bed. It was like being in the presence of a crowd of people, all of whom hated me utterly. I made no comment, confused in my own thoughts.

"You see?" said the magician.

"I *see* nothing," I replied carefully. "But I sense something. This may, of course, be an illusion emanating from you."

"It is not," said the magician softly. "Come now, great lady. You are Sekt, a goddess. The goddess perceives all, does she not?"

It came to me swiftly then how wrapped up I was in the trivia of mundane life. I lived fully in the corporeal senses, lolling around in the sun, uttering the first words that came into my head. And yet I was supposed to be divine, to see and sense all. Perhaps I had been too much the lazy lioness. "There are ancient rituals in the temple library," I said slowly, "which are designed to deal with possession by bodiless entities. It would perhaps do no harm to perform them." I stood up straight. "I must summon my priest."

"No," said the magician.

"It is not your decision."

"I have another suggestion. Will you hear it?"

"Very well."

"I have traveled in many lands and have seen many strange things. My knowledge has been gathered from every corner of the world. I have seen cases such as this before, and once a fire witch taught me how to treat the condition. The prince is afflicted by a spirit of the wilderness, a creature of fire. The people of this city have mostly abandoned the old ways, and while, in some respects, this ignorance has weakened the ancient spirits, in other ways it has made the people vulnerable to them. They have forgotten how to protect themselves, how to fight back."

I remembered the dreams I had had, the smell of burned meat around the temple. "I have always believed that new gods drive out the old. Sekt is mistress here now."

"Yes, a goddess of fire. She is not that different. Like calls to like. What reason would she have to drive out her own denizens, only because they are known by a different name? This is why *you* can remove this parasite. In a way, it is your servant."

I stared down at the prince. If this was true, I felt no kinship to the thing on the boy's back. I could barely sense it. I realized then that the priesthood of Sekt had lost a lot of their magic. We were fat and domesticated lions, dozing by pools, licking our paws. Where was the lioness of the wilderness, breathing fire? Did she still exist within me? I had no doubt the magician had also thought these things. Perhaps he despised me for what I was: a mask with nothing behind it. "What was the suggestion you had to make?" I said.

"That you and I take the prince out into the wilderness, where I will teach you what the fire witch taught me."

"Why to the wilderness? Why not here?"

"We need the elements around us. We need to tap their power. Too long have you hidden behind stone, my lady. I am offering you a great gift. If you are wise, you will take it."

"You are importunate!" I snapped. "I am Sekt."

"Are you? Then banish this creature of fire now. Take it by the tail and toss it from the window." He stood back with folded arms, appraising me.

I was breathing hard. My veil fluttered before my face. Meni would never allow me to venture out into the wilderness alone with this man. He would not let me be so foolish and, if necessary, would physically restrain me. Yet I felt a wild desire to take what the magician offered me. I sensed he spoke the truth. I wanted to be alone with him, buffeted by hot winds beneath an ardent canopy of stars. I wanted to conjure fire spirits, be the lioness of the desert. "It would be regarded as unseemly for me to venture out with you alone," I said.

"Do they watch you so stringently?"

"Are you suggesting deception? How will you spirit the prince from his bed without detection?"

He smiled and I realized he was beautiful, like the sky is

beautiful, or the raging of a storm. I had met no one like him before. "Remember what I am," he said.

"When? How?" I asked, breathless.

"Tonight," he said simply. "Why delay? Will you be able to get away?"

I thought about the sleeping temple, the dozing guards, the great air of torpor that hung over its colonnaded halls from dusk until dawn. I could slip like a wraith from shadow to shadow, leap the wall like a lioness, land without making a sound.

"I know what you are," he said. "You are a goddess, yes, but are you not also a woman? Are you not also a lioness? You crave adventure, even the hunt. You crave the ecstasy that freedom brings. Indulge yourself, my lady. Who will ever know?"

He was a friend to me. I had known him many lifetimes. In the night, in the wilderness, he would be a black lion, gliding at my side.

Once the king and Meni returned to the prince's bedroom, I told them that I would perform the ancient rituals the following evening, that I would need a day to prepare. Meni seemed a little bemused by my decision, and I knew that later he would quiz me about it, but he was loyal and did not voice his concern in public.

Outside the palace, back in my litter, I felt dizzy, almost sick. What was I doing? How had I become so infected with these alien feelings? The magician had conjured illusions for me, but I knew they could be real, because they did not involve magical ropes, phantom flowers or even bittersweet memories. They were possibilities, a revelation of what could be. I had never craved freedom, yet now it seemed the most heady thing on earth. I had never felt the stirrings of desire for a man, nor even curiosity, yet here it was, hot and burning in my belly.

I should have known then, sent word to the king, had the magician drowned or beheaded. Yet, instead, I lay back among my cushions, swooning like a lovesick girl.

I could not wait to dismiss my servants from my presence that evening. The air was full of a tension only I could feel. Candle flames bent into a wind that was not there. Incense smoke curled to the side. Even now, I entertained a dangerous hope. I thought of Aan, the husband I had never met, he whose face is beautiful. Had he found some way to escape his temple? Had he come to me wearing the face of a man? How could I think such things? And yet, I did not find myself thinking about the fate of Prince Reevan, or even about what the magician would show me tonight. I thought only of his face, of being near him, of the vast expanse of wilderness around us, the infinite sky above. I ran my fingers over the mask that shrouded me. The gold felt hot like fevered skin. I felt it might crack like the skin of a serpent and then I would slither out of it, reborn. If he did not wither before me, he would be the one, but dared I take that chance?

At each hour, boy priests sang litanies to the goddess and her heavenly entourage. At the hour after midnight, when only the young priests were awake, I slipped from my bed, took up the mask and placed it over my head. I dressed with speed and covered myself with a dark hooded cloak that I wear to walk through the gardens in the rainy season. As an afterthought, I clasped around my neck a golden chain, from which hung a lion's-eye stone, striped dark crimson and gold. Perhaps instinctively, I sought to provide myself with some kind of protection.

The temple was quiet, and yet I thought I heard in the distance a rumble of thunder. For a moment, I wondered whether I would ever return, and such was my excitement that at the time I did not care.

It was as if I were invisible. I hurried past the open doors, beyond which lay sleeping servants. I undulated like smoke past guards who lounged at their posts, their eyes wet slivers that looked only upon dreams. The gardens were held in a humid caul of air. Lionesses sprawled beneath the trees, some upon their backs with their paws curled over their chests. I ran among them and none stirred. Lightning scratched across the night, but there would be no rain. The sky was a robe of stars.

Then the garden wall was before me. I yearned to leap it,

but it would not be necessary. Flights of steps run up to the top of the wall at regular intervals, so that guards can patrol it or else temple staff might sit there and watch the life of the city. I chose one of these flights at random and ran up, then stood for a while on the wall, looking down. The city was spread out ahead of me, a mass of dim glows and hulking shadows. Now I had to jump, for there were no steps on the other side of the wall. It looked so far, yet I knew it was not. I glanced behind, fearful for a second that someone was watching me, but the temple and the gardens were still and silent, as if enchanted. I drew in my breath and leapt.

I landed on all fours on the short wiry grass and, for some moments, felt I should continue my journey in this manner, that I had discarded the body of a woman altogether. Then I stood up and saw that, yes, I still had arms and legs and that running on all fours would be both ungainly and slow. Quickly, I ran to a grove of tamarinds near the road, which was a glaring pale ribbon in the darkness. The wilderness was very near. I had only to follow the road for a short time, then take a narrower track to the east. The wilderness is always there around us. If people should abandon the city, it would soon revert to a strange and tangled waste, dry and tough and desert-colored.

I had arranged to meet Arcaran at the edge of the waste, by a forest of broken towers, which were all that remained of a city older than ours. Their shattered fingers cast eerie shadows on the ground and I was sure that ghosts lingered there. For a while I could not find the magician and ran about in circles among the looming ruins. Then he stepped out of the shadow of a tower in front of me. He was a creature of night, yet I could see his face clearly: its sculpted planes, the faintest breath of dark beard about the jaw.

"I am here," I said. "Where is the prince?"

"I have hidden him in the ruins. I thought you were not coming."

"Take me to him."

"We must venture farther from the city. We are too close here."

Prince Reevan lay with his head resting on a broken column. He looked young and vulnerable, his eyes staring blankly at the stars. I thought for a moment that he was dead, then he made a small sound and a thread of drool fell from his lips. I was alarmed by his condition and knelt at once to place my hands upon him, but Arcaran cried, "No, don't touch him."

"Why?"

"The parasite could transfer itself to you. We are not yet prepared."

I stood up. "Then we should proceed quickly."

Arcaran lifted the prince in his arms and began to walk away through the ruins. I followed, looking about myself. I did not feel afraid, or if I did, the sensation felt pleasurable. It did not cross my mind that I was essentially, despite my title and status, a young woman alone with a strange man far from my sanctuary. I had always believed I was a goddess, but in truth did I really possess a goddess's powers? I did not know how to smite a man if he should attack me. I did not even know how to defend myself with human strength. Yet there I was, following him. It seems senseless now.

Beyond the ruins was a rocky valley, surrounded by high spiky cliffs. We went down into it and there I saw that a fire had been built and already lit, flames leaping hungrily at the sky, shedding showers of sparks.

The magician laid the prince down on the ground and I awaited the preparations for what I was convinced would be some arcane ritual. As he arranged the prince's limbs, the magician said, "I have spent a lot of time in Mewt, my lady. I have visited the great temples there of Sekt and of her sister, Purryah, the cat goddess. The priests revealed to me some of their knowledge. It is a wisdom that never came here. For a century, your people have had an incomplete belief system."

"The original priestess of Sekt in Madramarta was trained by Senu, High Priestess of Akahana," I said. "How do you know what we have or have not learned?"

"I know because you are unaware of what to do now. A true avatar of Sekt would know."

"And so, presumably, do you."

He nodded, squatting before me, his long, expressive hands dangling between his knees. "I do, and I will tell you, but it may alarm you."

I stood stiffly before him, wondering what would be said and whether it would be true.

"You must expel the breath of Sekt into the boy," said the magician. "You must conjure it. Do you know how?"

I wanted to answer that I did. I wanted him to think I was something more than just a mask, but I couldn't answer, because I didn't know.

He ignored my silence and said, "First you must remove your mask."

"No! It is forbidden. I may only do so when I'm alone. You should know that." But, in my heart, that leap of hope.

He looked at me steadily. "The mask should be removed for certain types of work. This is one of them. Don't you know why you are masked?"

"Because I am the goddess and her presence in me has changed me. I am too terrifying to look upon. I would wither you."

He laughed softly. "It would take more than that to wither me. Do you think you are hideous beneath it, a gorgon to turn me to stone?"

Again, I could not answer. "It is the law," I said.

He stood up and came toward me. He drew back the cloak of my hood and put his fingers against the hard skin of the mask. Beneath it, I burned. It was I who was turned to stone. "I can see your eyes," he said. "I can see your mouth. You wear this mask to contain your power. The High Priestess in Akahana wears hers only for state occasions, but you are bridled here, held back."

I felt I would die from suffocation. I could not breathe. The mask constricted me. I was more aware of its presence than I'd ever been.

"Take it off," he said. "I am not afraid. Nor should you be. Claim what is yours, what you've never truly had."

My hands moved automatically. I had no choice. He took a step back and watched me as I lifted the mask from my head and shoulders. Immediately, the wind felt too hot on my skin. My hair was lifted by it. His expression did not change. I felt exposed, impotent. Was all of my courage contained within the mask? I had no strength now. He came toward me, put his hands upon my face. I expelled a cry, for his touch burned me. "I know you," he said. "I have always known you."

Some instinct made me pull away. I glanced down at Prince Reevan and saw that his entire body was covered in a crawling black smoke. It was as if he was being devoured by a swarm of insects. The magician's face looked black too, yet his eyes burned wildly. They were blue now, yet surely only a moment ago, they'd been dark?

"Don't be afraid," he said. "Accept. You can see now, *truly* see."

I gulped the searing air. My eyes were weeping tears of flame. "The prince," I managed to burble.

The magician laughed and with a flick of his hand made a gesture. "The brat doesn't matter. He is only a decoy. Watch." At once, the enveloping darkness rose from the prince's body into the air. He cried out; his limbs jerked. "It is done," said the magician. "Simple. The salamander was my creature. I put it there. It was you I wanted. It was always you."

I backed away from him, incapable of thought, of reason.

He stalked me. "You people are pathetic," he said. "You were given a power you could have developed. You did nothing but lie complacently in the temple until the power fell asleep from ennui. I can wake it, lady. It is already mine. I have come for you. Do you understand? For all it has atrophied, something was created here in Jessapur. I smelled it. It drew me. You are more than Senu ever could have been, yet you do not know it." He drew himself up to his full height and it seemed to me as if his flesh was smoking. I could smell charred meat again. His eyes were smoldering blue flames. "Do you know what I am?"

I knew. Part of me, a part of me that should have been greater, had always known. "Djinn!" I said. Hungry, envious of flesh, full of guile.

"They let me in," he said. "You let me in. Look at you. A gargoyle. The *mask* has more life in it."

I put my hands to my face and all I could feel was a frozen snarl, made of ivory. I had the wedge-shaped muzzle of a cat, a cat's sharp teeth. If ever I had been a normal woman, now I truly was a semblance of Sekt, lioness-headed, a statue made flesh. Hideous. Monstrous. This was the secret the mask had hidden. Now, the lioness had been released, but she had no strength. She had been domesticated.

"You have the potential power of the red fire, the white fire," said the magician, "that which is stronger than the orange fires of hearth or altar. You are most powerful free of your mask, lady, but also, paradoxically, most vulnerable."

Arcaran made a sudden movement and grabbed hold of my arms. It was strange, because there was no substance to him. He was smoke, yet I could not escape him. From the waist down he had transformed into a boiling column of darkness. He dragged me toward the fire and I could hear the song of sparks. The flames leapt higher as if in anticipation. "We shall be one," he said. "I shall have Sekt's essence. You do not deserve it."

He was never flesh, I can see that now. Even his body was an illusion. He wanted mine, and the gift of fire that lay slumbering within it. To him, I was naive and stupid, a posturing child with no true understanding of the goddess's power. Perhaps he saw himself as a denizen of Sekt and sought to reclaim her, release her. But most of all, he wanted my body. I knew that when I returned to the temple, I would no longer be me, and that a prince of djinn would hold sway in the hallowed precincts. No one would ever guess.

The flames licked at my clothes. Soon, it would be over. I could not help but fight, even though I felt my predicament was helpless.

Then she moved within me. I felt a flexing in my muscles

and bones, a great sense of outrage. A voice roared from my throat. "I am Sekt!"

I breathed in the flames, and expelled them in a gust of bloodred sparks. Arcaran uttered an inhuman scream and fell backward into the fire. The leaping hot tongues enwrapped him and he lay there staring up at me in fury. I snarled at him and he snarled back, but he was no longer the one in control. "Do not presume," I growled. "Don't *ever* presume."

Then I turned my back on him and put my hands against my face. I was no longer snarling. I felt pliant flesh, slightly furred. The golden mask stared up at me from the ground. It was a lifeless thing. I sensed him move behind me and turned round. He looked like a man again, a beautiful man, although his long hair was smoking.

"You cannot have this flesh," I said. "It is mine. I have provenance over this land."

"Sekt," he said, "you misunderstand. I sought only to wake you."

I snarled at him again. "Fool! I know what you sought—a way into my temple, and thus to create your own reign of fire over the land and its people."

"It has already begun," he said. "You cannot stop it, but should join with me. Look at this land. It is dying. The divine kings are shorn of grace and power. My influence smokes through the streets of Madramarta, inspires its slaves to revolt."

I shook my head. "You are deluded. You were banished once, because you could not, or would not, help the people of Jessapur against their conquerors. You have no true might, merely a sneaking creeping insolence that finds a home only in the hearts of the ignorant and debased."

"The greatest changes will always be born in the darkest gutter," said the magician. "What happens in a noble court or an enclosed temple affects only the privileged few. That is not change, but indulgence."

"Perhaps there is some truth in your words," I said. "But now the people have me. I will serve them here as I served them in Mewt. I always will."

"Brave words," hissed Arcaran. "It is most likely that all you will do is fall asleep again. You need my influence."

I snarled and stamped my foot, and the ground shook for a great distance around us. "Smite you!" I hissed.

He raised his hands. "I am already smitten, as you pointed out. Is there to be no peace between us?"

"There cannot be. You cannot be trusted."

His face twisted into an evil leer. "Go back to your temple, then. Be alone. But rue this day, Sekt. Remember it. It will haunt you."

I stared at him unblinking for some moments, then turned away. I went to the prince, who lay unconscious near the fire, and lifted him in my arms.

"Sekt," said the magician. "You cannot contain me. You will return. You will call for me. You know you will. Like speaks to like. I woke you."

For some moments I considered his words, then I carefully placed the unconscious prince back on the ground. Arcaran was sitting amid the flames of the fire, the most beauteous sight I could imagine, the most treacherous. I lifted the lion's-eye pendant in one hand and held it up before my face on its chain. "I will never be without you," I purred. "I both love and hate you, and will hold you forever against my heart."

He grinned at me, confident.

I dropped my jaw into a smile and spoke in a voice of command. "I call upon the light at the center of the universe!"

"What are you doing?" said Arcaran. The smile had disappeared from his face.

"Great powers, attend me!" I roared. "Hear now the voice of Sekt! Give me your power of compulsion!"

"No," said Arcaran. The features on his face had begun to twist and flex.

"Yes," I answered softly, then raised my voice once more, arms held high. "By the power of the creative force, I compel thee, prince of djinn. I command thee. Enter into this stone. I am Sekt, queen of fire. You will obey."

A searing wind gusted past me, pressing my robes

against my body, lifting my hair in a great tawny banner. Sparks fountained out of the fire.

Arcaran expelled a series of guttural cries and his body writhed amid the flames. I do not know whether he felt pain or not, but very swiftly, he reverted to a form of smoke. I sucked his essence toward me, then blew it into the lion's-eye pendant. It felt hot for some moments, and glowed with an eerie flame. Then it went cold and dark. I placed it back against my breast once more. He would always be with me, but contained, a genie in a stone.

I lifted the prince once more and glanced down at the golden mask lying nearby. Already ashes from the fire had drifted over it. I would not wear it again. There might be another mask, and sometimes I would wear it, but it would be of my own design and I would don it through choice.

It seemed my altercation with the djinn had taken only minutes, but as I walked back toward the ruins, I saw that already the light around me was gray with dawn. Soon the pink and gold would come, the morning. As I walked, I breathed upon the prince's face. His eyes moved rapidly beneath their closed lids. He would recover swiftly from his brief ordeal. I had breathed the white fire into him. He was mine. I would make a true king of him, for all the people.

Near the temple, I passed a peasant woman with her children taking fish to the market. When I drew near, they fell to the ground before me, their hands over their heads. "I am Sekt," I said to them. "Look upon me."

The woman moaned and uttered prayers, but even so, raised her head.

"You are blessed," I said. "Carry word to the city that Sekt walks amongst you. She is unmasked and awake. Remember her face."

Now, I am home. I can sense Meni awaking in his chamber. I will go to him, show myself to him. I am Sekt.

Chanterelle

Brian Stableford

Brian Stableford is an energetic and prolific writer and critic who continues to produce annually an astonishing variety of excellent fiction, reviews, and essays. He has been doing this since the 1970s, and has built a worldwide reputation as a scholar of literary history as well as a writer of international prominence. A sociologist by training, he was a lecturer in sociology at the University of Reading until he quit to write full time in 1988. He is now teaching an M.A. course in "Writing for Children" at King Alfred's College Winchester. His 2001 publications include The Cassandra Complex *(Tor) and a translation from the French of Paul Fval's* Knightshade *(Sarob Press). He is an expert on the Romantic Fantastic in eighteenth- and nineteenth-century literature, from which the contemporary literature of fantasy has descended.*

He regards "Chanterelle," which appeared in Ellen Datlow and Terri Windling's excellent fairytale anthology Black Heart, Ivory Bones, *as one of his best stories, as do we. It is about a brother and sister in the forest and has the feel of the genuine article from the Romantic era, the power and glory of the Romantic movement, the feeling of incomprehensible menace and genteel decay, that most modern-day fairytales lack. Despite its archaic feel, this story is not a retelling of an old story; rather it takes from a number of sources to make something new.*

There was once a music-loving carpenter named Alastor, who fell in love with Catriona, the daughter of a foundryman who lived in a Highland village near to the town of his birth. Catriona was known in the village as the Nightingale, because she had a beautiful singing voice. Alastor loved to play for her, and it was while she sang to his accompaniment that she fell in love with him.

When Alastor and Catriona were married, they left the Highlands for the Lowlands, taking up residence in the nation's capital city, where Alastor was determined to make a living as a maker of musical instruments. Their first child, a son, was born on the first Monday after New Year's Day, which is known throughout Christendom as Handsel Monday.

A handsel is a gift made to celebrate a new beginning, as a coin might be placed in the pocket of a freshly tailored coat. Alastor knew that his son might be seen as exactly such a gift, bestowed upon his marriage, and he was determined to make the most of him.

"Should we call him Handsel, do you think?" Alastor asked Catriona.

"It is a good name," she said.

Every choice that is made narrows the range of further

choices, and when the couple's second child was due, Alastor said to Catriona: "If our second-born is a girl, we must not call her Gretel. There is a tale in which two children so-named are abandoned in the wild forest by their father, a poor woodcutter, at the behest of their stepmother. The tale ends happily enough for the children, but we should not take chances."

"You are not a woodcutter, my love," Catriona replied, "and we live in the city. We left the wild forest behind us when we left the Highlands, and I am not sure that we should carry its legacy of stories and superstitions with us."

"I think we should," said Alastor. "There is a wealth of wisdom in that legacy. We may be far away from the haunts of the fairy-folk, but we are Highlanders still. There have been those in both our families who have had the second sight, and we have no guarantee that our children will be spared its curse. We should be careful in naming them, and we must take care that they hear all the stories we know, for whatever their guidance might be worth."

"Here in the city," said Catriona, "it is said that children must make their way in the real world, and that stories will only fill their heads with unreasonable expectations."

"They say that," admitted Alastor, "but the city-dwellers have merely devised a new armory of stories, which seem more appropriate to the order and discipline of city life. I would rather our children heard what *we* had to tell—for they are, after all, *our* children."

"What name did you have in mind?" Catriona asked him.

"I hope that our son might choose to follow me in working with his hands," Alastor said. "I would like him to master the grain of the wood, in order that he might make pipes, harps, fiddles, and lutes. I hope that our daughter might complement his achievements with a singing voice the equal of your own. Let us give her a name which would suit a songstress."

"Ever since I was a girl," said Catriona, "I have been nicknamed Nightingale—but if you mean what you say about the wisdom of stories, we should not wish *that* name upon our daughter. No sooner had it been bestowed upon me than I was forced to listen to the tale of the little girl who fell into the care of a wicked man who knew the secret of training nightingales to sing by day. Even today I shudder when I think of it."

"She was imprisoned in a cage by a prince, was she not?" said Alastor. "She was set to sing in the depths of the wild forest, but suffered misfortune enough to break her heart, and she refused to sing again, until she fell into the clutches of her former master, who—"

"Please don't," begged Catriona.

"Well," said Alastor, "we must certainly avoid the name that was given to *that* girl—which was Luscignole, if I remember rightly. I wonder if we might call our daughter—if indeed the child you are carrying should turn out to be a daughter—Chanterelle, after the highest string of a musical instrument?"

"Chanterelle is an excellent choice," said Catriona. "I never heard a story about a girl named Chanterelle. But what if the baby is a boy?"

There is no need to record the rest of the conversation, for the child *was* a girl, and she was named Chanterelle.

When Handsel and Chanterelle were old enough to hear stories, Catriona was careful to tell them the tales that were popular in the city as well as those she remembered from her own childhood in the Highlands, but it was the Highland tales that they liked better. Although there was not the faintest trace of the fairy-folk to be found in the city, it was the fairy-folk of whom the children loved to hear tell.

Handsel, as might be expected, was particularly fond of the tale of Handsel and Gretel. Chanterelle, on the other hand, preferred to hear the tale of the foundryman who was lured away from his family by a fairy, until he was called back by the tolling of a church bell he had made, which had fallen into a lake. Catriona told that story to help her children understand the kind of work her father did, although she assured them that he was not at all the kind of man to be seduced by a fairy, but it was Alastor who told them the story of the little girl whose wicked guardian knew the secret of making nightingales sing by day. Catriona could not tell that story without shuddering, and she did not altogether approve when her husband told the fascinated children that *she* had once been nicknamed Nightingale, even though she had always been able to sing by day.

"In actual fact," Catriona told her children—using a phrase she had picked up in the city—"nightingales are not very good singers at all. It is the mere fact of their singing by night that is remarkable, not the quality of their performance."

"Why can we not hear them?" Handsel asked. "I have never heard *any* bird sing by night."

"There are no nightingales in the city," she told them. "They are rare even in the forests above the village where I was born."

"As rare as the fairy-folk?" asked Chanterelle.

"Even rarer, alas," said Catriona. "Had more of my neighbors heard one, they might have been content with my given name, which comes from *katharos*, or purity."

As Alastor had hoped, Handsel soon showed an aptitude for woodwork, and he eventually joined his father in the workshop. He showed an aptitude for music too, and was soon able to produce a tune of sorts out of any instrument he came across. Chanterelle was no disappointment either; she proved to have a lovely voice. She sang by day and she sang by night, and on Sundays she sang in the choir at the church that Alastor and Catriona now attended.

All was well—until the plague came.

"It is not so terrible a plague as some," Alastor said to Catriona, when Handsel was the first of them to fall ill. "It is not as rapacious as the one in the story of the great black spider—the one which terrified and blighted a Highland village, infecting the inhabitants with fevers that sucked the blood and the life from every last one. This is a disease which the strong and the lucky may resist, if only fortune favors them."

"We must do what we can to help fortune," Catriona said. "We must pray, and we must nurse the child as best we can. He *is* strong."

The instrument-maker and his wife prayed, and they nursed poor Handsel as best they could—but within a week, Chanterelle had caught the fever too.

Alastor and Catriona redoubled their efforts, praying and nursing, fighting with every fiber of flesh and conviction of spirit for the lives of their children. Fortune favored them, at least to the extent of granting their most fervent wishes. Handsel recovered from the fever, and so did Chanterelle—but Catriona fell ill, and so did Alastor.

The roles were now reversed; it was the turn of Handsel and Chanterelle to play nurse. They tended the fire, boiled the water, picked the vegetables, and cooked the meat. They ran hither and yon in search of bread and blankets, candles and cough-mixture, and they prayed with all the fervor of their little hearts and high voices.

Catriona recovered in due course, but Alastor died.

"I was not strong enough," Handsel lamented. "My hands were not clever enough to do what needed to be done."

"My voice was not sweet enough," mourned Chanterelle. "My prayers were not lovely enough for Heaven to hear."

"You must not think that," Catriona said to them. "Neither of you is at fault."

They assured her that they understood—and it seemed that Handsel, perhaps because he was the elder, really did understand. But from that day forward, Chanterelle refused to sing. She would not join in with the choir in church, nor would she sing at home, by day or by night, no matter how hard Handsel tried to seduce her voice with his tunes.

Catriona and Handsel tried to complete the instruments that Alastor had left unfinished. They even tried to begin more—but Handsel's hands were only half grown and his skills less than half trained, and Catriona's full-grown hands had no woodworking skill at all. In the end, Catriona and her children had no alternative but to sell the shop and their home with it. They had no place to go but the Highland village where Catriona's parents lived.

The journey to the Highlands was long and by no means easy, but their arrival in the village brought no relief. The plague had left the highest parts of the Highlands untouched, for no fever likes to visit places that are too high on a hill, but it had insinuated itself into the valleys, descended on the villages with unusual ferocity. When the exhausted Catriona and her children finally presented themselves at the foundry, they found it closed, and the house beside it was dark and deserted.

Neighbors told Catriona that her mother had died, and her mother's sister, and her father's brother, and her father's brother's wife, and both their sons, her only cousins.

The catalogue of catastrophe was so extended that Catriona did not notice, at first, that her father's name was not included in it—but when she did, the flicker of hope that burst forth in her frightened mind was quenched within a minute.

"Your father," the neighbors said, "was driven mad by loss and grief. He fled into the wild forest, determined to live like a bear or a wolf—for only bears and wolves, he said, know the true joy of unselfconsciousness. Before he went he cast the bell that he had made for our church into the tarn, declaring that the spirits of the lake were welcome to roll it back and forth, so that its echoes would toll within his heart like the knell of doom. He had heard a story, it seems, about another founder of bells who went to dwell in the wild forest, among the fairy-folk."

"He told me the story half a hundred times, when I was a child," Catriona admitted. "But that was a tale of vaulting ambition, about a man who sought unprecedented glory in the mountain heights because he was seduced by a fairy. If what you say is true, my father has been stolen rather than seduced, by demons and not by fairies."

"We are good Christians," the neighbors said piously. "We know that there is no difference between demons and fairies, no matter what those with the second sight may say. The house is yours now, by right of inheritance, and the foundry too—you are welcome to make what use of them you will." Perhaps that was honest generosity, or perhaps the villagers thought that the foundry and house were both accursed by virtue of the death and madness to which they had played host. In either case, the donation was useless; if Catriona and Handsel could not run a workshop in the city, they certainly could not run an iron-foundry in a Highland village.

"There is only one thing to be done," Catriona told the children. "I must go into the wild forest to search for my father. If only I can find him, I might make him see sense. At least I can show him that he is not alone. Pray that the idea of meeting his grandchildren for the first time will persuade him that it is better to live as a human than run wild as a bear or a wolf."

"Will he not be a werewolf, if he has been away too long?" Handsel asked. "There is a story, is there not . . . ?"

"You are thinking of the tale in which an abandoned boy became king of the bears," Catriona told him, firmly, although she knew that he was thinking of another bloodcurdling tale of Alastor's. "He called upon their aid to reclaim his inheritance, if you remember, and they obliged. What I must do is help my father to reclaim *his* heritage."

"But what shall we do," Chanterelle asked, in the whisper that was now her voice, "if you are lost, and cannot return? What shall we do if the fairy-folk take you away, or if the werewolves eat you? What will become of us then?"

"I *will* return," said Catriona, even more firmly than before. "Neither fairy nor werewolf shall prevent me." She knew even as she spoke, however, that there were too many stories in which such promises were made and never kept—and so did Chanterelle.

Handsel had sense enough to hold his tongue, and wish his mother well, but Chanterelle was too frightened to do anything but beg her not to go. Handsel had enough of the city in him to know that stories were not always to be taken literally, but Chanterelle—perhaps because she was younger—did not. Catriona could not comfort her, no matter how hard she tried.

Catriona realized that when *she* had been a child she had known the reality of the wild woods as well as the stories that were told about them, while Chanterelle knew only what she had heard in stories. Alastor had overlooked that point of difference when he had insisted that the children must be told the stories that he had known when he was a boy.

"Please don't be afraid, Chanterelle," Catriona said, when she finally set out. "The fairy-folk never harmed me before."

"But they will not remember you," said Chanterelle. "You're a stranger now. Don't go."

"I must," said Catriona. "What earthly use is an iron-foundry without an iron-master?"

The two children found that the charity of their new neighbors lasted a full week. At first they were able to go from door to door, saying: "We are the grandchildren of the village iron-master and our mother has gone to search for him in the wild forest. Could you spare us a loaf of bread and a little cheese, or perhaps an egg or two, until our mother returns?"

As the days went by, however, the women who came to the door when they knocked began to say: "We have fed you once: it is someone else's turn"—and when the children pointed out that everyone in the village who was willing had taken a turn, the women said: "We have no guarantee that your mother will ever return, and even if she does, she has no means to repay us. The parish has its own poor; you are strangers. We have done all that we must, and all that we can."

When ten days had gone by without any sign of their mother, Handsel and Chanterelle went to the village church and said to the priest: "Advise us, please, as to what we should do. We have prayed long and hard, but our prayers have not been answered."

"I am not surprised, alas," said the priest. "Your grandfather was a good man once, but in casting the bell intended for our church into the dark waters of the tarn he committed an act of sacrilege as well as an act of folly. There is a story, you see, about an iron-master who was seduced away from faith and family when a church-bell he had founded was lost in a lake. Your grandfather was knowingly putting himself in that man's place, asking for damnation. It is good of you to pray for his return, but if he does not ask forgiveness for himself, one can hardly expect Heaven to grant it, and even then—"

"Yes," said Handsel, "we understand all that. But what shall we *do*?"

"There is no living for you here, alas," said the priest with a sigh. "You must go into the forest in search of your mother, and pray with all the might of your little hearts that *she* can still be found. It is possible, after all, that she is still alive. The forest is full of food, for those bold enough to risk its hazards. It is the season for hazelnuts, and bramble-berries, and there are always mushrooms. It is time to commit yourself to the charity of Heaven, my little darlings. I know that Heaven will not let you down, if you have virtue enough to match your courage. There is a story about a boy named Handsel, as I recall, and his little sister, which ended happily enough—not that I, a priest, can approve of the pagan taint which such stories invariably have. In the final analysis, there is only one *true* story, and it is the story of the world."

"That isn't so, sir," said Chanterelle. "There are hundreds of true stories—perhaps thousands. I only know a few, but my grandfather must be old enough to know far more."

"You are only a child," the priest said tolerantly. "When you are older, you will know what I mean. If your grandfather can recover his lost wits, he will be wise to forget all the stories he ever knew, except for the one which holds the promise of our salvation. I wish you all the luck in the world, little Gretel, and I am sure that if you deserve it, Heaven will serve you well."

"My name is Chanterelle, not Gretel," Chanterelle corrected him.

"Of course," said the priest serenely, "and you can sing like a nightingale, Chanterelle, as your mother could when she was young and lovely?"

"My mother is lovely still," Chanterelle replied, with unusual dignity in one so young, "and she can still sing—but I have never heard a nightingale, so I don't know which of them is better."

"When we say that a human sings like a nightingale," the priest said, with a slightly impatient smile, "we do not mean it *literally*. That is to say, we do not mean it *exactly*."

"Thank you," said Handsel, taking his sister's hand. "We shall take your excellent advice." Even Chanterelle could tell by the way he said "excellent" that he did not mean it *exactly*—but the advice was taken nevertheless. On the morning of the next day, Handsel and Chanterelle set off into the wild forest to search for their mother. Their new neighbors waved goodbye to them as they went.

The priest had told them the truth, at least about the season. There were indeed hazelnuts on the hazel-trees and ripe bramble-berries on the brambles. The only problems were that hazel-trees were not easy to find among all the other trees, none of which bore any edible nuts, and that brambles were equipped with ferocious thorns that snagged their clothing and left bloody trails on their hands and arms.

There were mushrooms too, but at first the two children were afraid to touch them.

"Some mushrooms are poisonous," Handsel told his sister. "There are death-caps and destroying angels, and I do not know how to tell them apart from the ones which are safe to eat. I heard a story once which said that fairies love to squat on the heads of mushrooms, and that although those which the good fairies use remain perfectly safe to eat, those which are favored by naughty fairies become coated with an invisible poisonous slime."

Even Chanterelle did not suppose that this story was entirely trustworthy, but she agreed with Handsel that they ought to avoid eating mushrooms, at least until the two of them became desperate with hunger. By the end of the first day they were certainly hungry, but by no means desperate, and it was not until they had been searching for a second day that desperation and its cousin despair began to set in. On their first night they had slept long and deep, but even though they were exhausted they found it more difficult to sleep on the second night. When they finally did go to sleep, they slept fitfully, and they woke up as tired as they had been when they settled down.

Unfortunately, the wild forest was not consistent in its nature. Although the lower slopes were host to hazel-trees and brambles, such plants became increasingly scarce as the two children went higher and higher. Their third day of searching brought them into a region where all the trees seemed to be dressed in dark, needlelike leaves and there was nothing at all to eat except for mushrooms. They had not yet found the slightest sign of their mother, their grandfather, or any other human soul, even though Handsel had shouted himself hoarse calling out to them.

"Well," said Handsel as they settled down to spend a third night in the forest, bedded down on a mattress of leaf-litter, "I suppose Heaven must be on our side, else we'd have been eaten by wolves or bears before now. If we're to eat at all tonight we must trust our luck to guide us to the most nourishing mushrooms and keep us safe from the worst."

"I suppose so," said Chanterelle, who had been keeping watch on all the mushrooms they passed, hoping to catch a glimpse of a fairy at rest. She had seen none as yet, but that did not make her any happier while they made their first meal of mushrooms, washed down with water from a spring. They found it difficult to sleep again, and tried to comfort one another by telling stories—but they found the stories comfortless and they slept badly.

They made another meal of white mushrooms, which settled their hunger after a fashion and caused their stomachs no considerable upset. As the day's journey went higher and deeper into the forest, however, they found fewer and fewer of that kind.

Handsel continued to shout occasionally, but his throat was raw and his voice echoed mockingly back at him, as if the trees were taunting him with the uselessness of his attempts to be heard. Chanterelle helped as best she could, but her voice had never been as strong as it was sweet, even when she sang with the choir, and it seemed much feebler now.

When darkness began to fall yet again, and the two of them were badly in need of a meal, Handsel proposed that they try the red mushrooms with white patches, which were much commoner in this region than the white ones they had gathered on the lower slopes. Chanterelle did not like the look of them at all and said that she would rather go hungry.

"Oh well," said Handsel, "I suppose the sensible thing to do would be for *one* of us to try them, so that their safety can be put to the proof."

Again they found it difficult to go to sleep, but they decided to suffer in silence rather than tell discomfiting stories. The forest, of course, refused to respect their silence by falling silent itself; the wind stirred the branches of the trees restlessly—but tonight, for the first time, they heard another sound.

"Is that a nightingale?" Chanterelle asked her brother.

"I suppose so," Handsel replied. "I never heard of any other bird that sings at night—but it's not as sweet a singer as the birds that were kept in cages by people in the city. They had at least a hint of melody about their songs."

"It may not have much melody," said Chanterelle, "but I never heard a song so plaintive."

"If it *is* a nightingale," said Handsel, "I can't begin to understand why the old man in the story thought the secret of making them sing by day so very precious."

"I can," whispered Chanterelle.

When she finally fell asleep, Chanterelle dreamed that an old man was chasing her through the forest, determined to make her sing again, even if he had to do to her what the old man in the story had done—first to the nightingales, and in the end to Luscignole. Usually, such nightmares continued until she woke in alarm, but this one was different. In this one, just as the old man was about to catch her, a she-wolf jumped on his back and knocked him down—and then set about devouring him while Chanterelle looked on, her anxious heart slowing all the while as her terror ebbed away.

When the wolf had finished with the bloody mess that had been the old man, she looked at Chanterelle and said: "You were right about the mushrooms. They'd been spoiled by fairies of the worst kind. You'll have a hard job rescuing your brother, but it *might* be done, if only you have the heart and the voice."

"Mother?" said Chanterelle fearfully. "Have you become a werewolf, then? Is Grandfather a werewolf too?"

"It's not so bad," said the she-wolf, "but Grandfather was wrong to think he'd find the solace of unselfconsciousness in the world of bears and wolves. Remember, Chanterelle—*don't eat the mushrooms.*"

Having said that, the she-wolf ran away into the forest—and Chanterelle awoke.

Handsel was already up and about. He appeared much fitter than he had been the previous day, and he was much more cheerful than before, but he seemed to have lost his voice. When he spoke to Chanterelle, it was in a hoarse and grating whisper.

"You must eat *something*, Chanterelle," he told her. "We must keep our strength up. The red-capped mushrooms are perfectly safe, as you can see. I've suffered no harm."

Had Chanterelle not had the dream, she might have believed him, but the dream made her determined to leave the red-capped mushrooms alone.

"Did you dream last night?" Chanterelle asked her brother.

"Yes I did," he croaked, "and rather frightening dreams they were—but they turned out all right in the end."

"Was there a wolf in your dream?"

"No. There were other monsters, but no wolves."

"I can't eat the mushrooms," Chanterelle told him. "I just can't."

"You will," he said, "when you're hungry enough. You'll need all your strength, I fear, because I can't raise my voice at all. It's up to you now. You have to sing out loud and clear."

"I can't do that either," said Chanterelle, her voice falling to a whisper almost as sepulchral as his. She was afraid that he would become angry, but he didn't. He was still her brother, even if he had eaten mushrooms enslimed by naughty fairies.

"In that case," she said, "we'll have to hunt for mother without calling out."

That was what they did, all morning and all afternoon. The forest was so gloomy now that even the noonday hours hardly seemed daylit at all. The dark-clad branches of the pines and spruces were so dense and so extensive that it was difficult to catch the merest glimpse of blue sky—and where the sun's rays did creep through the canopy they were reduced to slender shafts, more silver than golden. For four days they had wandered without catching sight of any predator more dangerous than a wildcat, although they had seen a number of roe deer and plenty of mice. That afternoon, however, they were confronted by a bear.

It was not a huge bear, and its thinning coat was showing distinct traces of mange, but it was a great deal bigger than they were, and its ill-health only made it more anxious to make a meal of them. No sooner had it caught sight of them than it loped toward them, snuffling and snarling with excitement and showing all of its yellow teeth.

Handsel and Chanterelle ran away as fast as they could—but Chanterelle was smaller than Handsel, and much weaker. Before they had gone a hundred yards she was too tired to run any farther, and her legs simply gave way. She fell, and shut her eyes tight, waiting for the snuffling, snarling bear to put an end to her with its rotten teeth. She felt its fetid breath upon her back as it reached her and paused—but then it yelped, and yelped again, and the force of its breath was abruptly relieved.

When Chanterelle opened her eyes she saw that Handsel had stopped running. He was snatching up cones that had fallen from the trees, and stones that had lodged in the crevices of their spreading roots. He was throwing these missiles as quickly as he could, hurling them into the face of the astonished bear—and the bear was retreating before the assault!

In fact, the bear was running away. It had conceded defeat.

"He wasn't hungry enough," Handsel whispered when the bear had gone. "Are *you* hungry enough yet, Chanterelle?"

"No," said Chanterelle, and tried to get up—but she had twisted her ankle and couldn't walk on it. "It'll be all right soon," she said faintly. "Tomorrow, we can go on."

"If the bear doesn't come back," Handsel said hoarsely. "When it's hungry enough, it might. If we can't search any longer, you really ought to sing. A song might be heard where shouting wouldn't."

"I can't," said Chanterelle.

Handsel said no more. Instead, he went to gather redcapped mushrooms. When he came back, his shirt was bulging under the burden of a full two dozen—but all he had in his hands was a tiny wooden pipe.

"I found this," he murmured. "It couldn't have been hollowed out without a proper tool, and the finger-holes are very neat. Mother had nothing like it, but I suppose it might be Grandfather's. Perhaps Father made it for him long ago, and gave it to him as a parting gift when he took Mother away to the town. If it's not Grandfather's, it's the first real sign we've found of the fairy-folk. I think I have breath enough to play. Perhaps, if you have a tune to follow, you'll be able to sing."

So saying, Handsel sat down beside his sister and began

to play on the little pipe. He had no difficulty at all producing a tune, but it was as faint as his voice if not as scratchy. It was pitched higher than any tune she had ever heard from flute or piccolo.

"It *must* be a fairy flute," said Chanterelle anxiously. "All the stories say that humans must beware of playing elfin music, lest they be captured by the fairy-folk."

Handsel stopped playing and inspected the pipe. "I could have made it myself," he croaked. "Smaller hands than mine might have made it as easily, I suppose."

"Elfin music loosens the bonds of time, in the tales that Mother used to tell," said Chanterelle, "and time untied has weight for no man . . . whatever that's supposed to mean."

"I think it means that while a fairy flute plays a single song, years may pass in villages and towns," said Handsel. "I only wanted to help you sing, Chanterelle—but now the dusk is falling and the darkness is deepening. I couldn't see a bear by night, Chanterelle. I couldn't hurt his nose and eyes with pinecones. If the bear comes back, it will gobble us up. *Are you sure you cannot sing, even if I play a tune?*"

"Even if you play a tune, dear Handsel," Chanterelle told him, "I could not sing a note. Even if you were to do what the old man in the story did—"

"I never understood how that was supposed to work," Handsel said, his voice like wind-stirred grass. "On nightingales, perhaps—but what good would it do to run red hot needles into poor Luscignole's eyes? Will you eat some mushrooms, Chanterelle? I fear for your life if you won't."

"A she-wolf warned me against them," said Chanterelle. "I dare not—unless she comes to me again by night and tells me that I may."

Handsel would not press her. He set about his own meal quietly—but he was careful to show her that he had only eaten half the mushrooms he had gathered, and would save the rest for her.

* * *

When night fell, Chanterelle tried to sleep. She wanted to see her mother again, even if her mother had to come to her in the guise of a wolf. Alas, she could not sleep. Hunger gnawed at her stomach so painfully that she soon became convinced the bear could have done no worse. She tried to fight the pain, but the only way she could do that was to call up a tune within her head, and the only tune she could summon was the tune that Handsel had begun to play on the wooden pipe which had somehow been left for him to find.

It was an old tune, perfectly familiar, but she had never heard it played so high. Chanterelle was afraid that it might be the key in which a tune was played that made it into elfin music, rather than the tune itself. At first, when the tune went round and round and round in her sleepless mind, there was nothing but the sound of the pipe to be "heard," but as it went on and on it was gradually joined by a singing voice: a voice that was *not* her own.

Eventually, Chanterelle realized that although the sound of the pipe was in her head, conjured up by her own imagination, the voice was not. The voice was real, growing in strength because the singer was growing closer—but how could it be, she wondered, that the imaginary pipe and the real voice were keeping such perfect harmony?

Chanterelle sat up and began to shake her sleeping brother, who responded to her urging with manifest reluctance.

"Let me sleep!" he muttered. "For the love of Heaven, let me sleep!"

"Someone is coming," she hissed in his ear. "Either we are saved, at least for a while, or lost forever. Can you not hear her song?"

The singer was indeed a female, and when she came in view—lit by the lantern she bore aloft—Chanterelle was somewhat reassured, for she was taller by far than the fairy-folk were said to be. The newcomer wore a long white dress and a very curious cape made from bloodred fur, flecked with large white sequins. She had two dogs with her, both straining at the leash. They were like no dogs Chanterelle had ever seen: lean and white, like huge spectral greyhounds, each with a stride so vast that it could have out-sprinted any greyhound in the world.

"*Bad* dogs," said the lady, who had stopped singing as soon as her lantern revealed the two children to the inspection of her pale and penetrating eyes. "*This* is not the prey for which you were set to search. These are children, lost in the wilderness. Were you abandoned here, my lovelies?" As she spoke she looked down at Chanterelle. Her eyes seemed strangely piercing; it was as if she could look into the inner chambers of a person's heart. Chanterelle hoped that it was a trick of the lantern-light.

"We came in search of our mother," said Chanterelle. "Have you seen her?"

"I've seen no one, child," the lady replied. "I'm hunting a she-wolf which has plundered my birdhouse once too often. I thought that Verna and Virosa had her scent, but it seems not. What are your names?"

"I'm Chanterelle, and this is my brother Handsel."

"Why are you whispering, child?" the lady asked, although her own voice was low and her singing had been soft, in spite of the notes she had to reach.

"Misfortune and too much shouting have weakened our voices," Handsel explained. "Have you bread, perchance—my sister will not eat the mushrooms which grow hereabouts, because she fears they have been poisoned by the fairies."

"Those old wives' tales are best forgotten," the lady said, "but I have bread at home, and meat too, if you can walk as far as my house."

"I can," whispered Handsel, "but Chanterelle cannot. She twisted her ankle while fleeing from a bear."

"Well," said the lady, without much enthusiasm, "I suppose I can carry her, if you will hold the lantern and my dogs—but you'll have to be strong, for they can pull like the Devil when they're of a mind to do so."

"I can do that," said Handsel.

The lady gave the lantern and the two leashes to Handsel, and bent to take Chanterelle in her arms. For a fleeting instant the warmth of her breath reminded Chanterelle of the bear, but it was sweeter by far—and the lady's slender arms were surprisingly strong.

"Who are you?" Chanterelle asked as she was borne aloft.

"My name is Amanita," the lady said, turning around to follow the dogs, which had already set off for home with Handsel in tow.

"I hope your house is not made of gingerbread," murmured Chanterelle.

"What a thing to say!" the woman exclaimed. "Indeed it is not. Whatever made you think it might be?"

"There is a story about a boy named Handsel, who was lost with his sister in a wild forest," Chanterelle told her. "They found a house of gingerbread and began to eat it—but the witch who owned it caught them and put them in a cage."

"It's exactly as I said," the lady observed. "Old wives' tales are full of nonsense, and mischief too. Do you think I'm a witch?"

"You were singing a song," said Chanterelle uneasily. "I was remembering a tune, and your song fitted the tune. If that's not witchcraft, what is?"

"You poor thing," said the lady, clutching Chanterelle more tightly to her, so that Chanterelle could feel the warmth of the bloodred fur from which her cape was made. "You've been sorely confused, I fear. Don't you see, dear child, that it must have been my song that started the tune in your head? Your ears must have caught it before your mind did, so that when your mind caught up it seemed that the tune had been there before. But you're right, of course; if there's no witchcraft there, there's no witchcraft anywhere—and that's the truth."

Chanterelle knew better than to believe it. She had heard too many stories in her time to think the world devoid of magic. She knew that she would have to beware of the lady Amanita, whatever her house turned out to be made of.

* * *

The sleep that Chanterelle had been unable to find while she lay on the bare ground, fearful of the bear's return, came readily enough now that she was clasped in Amanita's arms. The lady did not carry her quite as tenderly as her mother would have, but the warmth of the red cape seemed to soak into Chanterelle's enfeebled flesh, relaxing her mind. In addition, the lady began to sing again, albeit wordlessly, and the rhythm of her voice was lullaby-gentle and lullaby-sweet.

In such circumstances, Chanterelle might have expected sweeter dreams, but it was not to be. This time, she found herself alone by night in a vast and drafty church—vaster by far than any church in the town where she had lived, let alone the village whose priest had advised them to search for their mother in the forest. Its wooden pews formed a great shadowy maze, and Chanterelle was searching that maze for a likely hiding place—but whenever she found one, she would hear ominous footsteps coming closer and closer, until they came so horribly close that she could not help but slip away, scurrying like a mouse in search of some deeper and darker hidey-hole. She never saw her pursuer, but she knew well enough who he must be and what he must be holding in his gnarled and arthritic hand. She knew, too, that no she-wolf could come to her aid in such a place as this—for werewolves cannot set foot on consecrated ground, no matter how noble their purpose might be, nor how diabolical the schemes they might seek to interrupt.

When Chanterelle awoke, she realized that she was in a bed with linen sheets. When she opened her eyes she saw that the bed had a quilt as red as Amanita's cape, patterned with white diamonds as neatly sewn as any she had ever seen. It was obvious that the lady Amanita was an excellent seamstress—which meant, of course, that she must possess a sharp, sleek, and polished needle.

Bright daylight shone through a single latticed window the shape and size of a wagon-wheel. Handsel was already up and about, as he had been the morning before. As soon as he saw that his sister was astir, he rushed to her bedside.

"Isn't this wonderful?" he said, gesturing with his arm to indicate the room in which they had been placed. As well as the bed on which Chanterelle lay, it had a number of chairs, one of them a rocking-chair; it also had a huge wooden wardrobe, a chest of drawers, a wooden trunk, and a tiny three-legged table. The walls were exceptionally smooth, but their gray surfaces were dappled with black, and the curiously ragged shelves set into them were an offensive shade of orange.

"No gingerbread at all?" Chanterelle whispered.

"None," said Handsel, who had obviously recovered the full use of his voice during the night. "I'll bring you some *real* bread. It's freshly baked."

Handsel left the room—passing through a doorway that was far from being a perfect rectangle, although the door fit snugly enough—before Chanterelle could ask where a woman who lived alone in the remotest regions of the Highland forest could buy flour to bake into bread. When he returned a few minutes later, Amanita was with him, carrying a tray that bore a plate of what looked like neatly sliced bread and a cup of what looked like milk.

Alas, the bread had neither the odor nor the color of wheaten bread, and the milk had neither the color nor the viscosity of cow's milk.

"I can't," said Chanterelle weakly.

"Of course you can," said Handsel.

"It's not poison," said the lady Amanita—but Chanterelle did not believe her.

"You're a bad fairy," said Chanterelle to Amanita.

"You're a silly fool," said Amanita to Chanterelle.

"This is pointless," said Handsel, to no one in particular. "We can't go on like this—and if we don't go on, how will we *ever* find our mother?"

"You won't," said Amanita. "This isn't like one of your stories, you know. This is the real world. Your mother never had the slightest hope of finding your grandfather, and you don't have the slightest hope of finding your mother. They'll both be dead by now—and you ought to count yourselves very lucky that you're not dead yourselves. You will be, Chanterelle, if you won't eat."

"Poor Chanterelle," said Handsel, who seemed even fitter and bolder today than he had when he drove off the bewildered bear, and was in far better voice. "Can't eat, can't walk, can't sing, can't do anything at all. How can we save you, little sister?"

"Find Mother," Chanterelle replied. "Leave me, if you must, but *find Mother*."

"Handsel won't go on without you, Chanterelle," said Amanita. "If you won't get better, he'll stay with you until you die." *And after that*, she didn't add, *he'll stay with me*.

"Find Grandfather," whispered Chanterelle. "Please leave me, Handsel. Find Grandfather, because he can't find himself. The bell in the tarn can't toll, you see. Its chimes can't echo in his heart like the chimes of conscience, drawing him back to his hearth and home. Find Mother, before she loses herself entirely. Find them both, I beg of you. If you love me, go."

"You'll regret it if you do," said Amanita to Handsel.

Handsel seemed to agree with her; he shook his head.

"One more day, Handsel," whispered Chanterelle. "If you'll search for just one more day, I'll eat something. That's a promise. Even if you fail, I'll eat—but *you have to try*."

That argument worked, as Chanterelle had known it would. "If you're sure you'll be all right," Handsel said dubiously, "I'll go." Even as he said it, though, he looked at Amanita. It was as if he were asking her permission.

Amanita shrugged her shoulders, whose narrowness was evident now that she was no longer wearing the speckled cape. "You might as well," she said, "although I'm sure that there's nothing to find. I'll lend you Verna and Virosa if you like. If there's anything out there, they'll track it down—but you'll have to be strong if you're to hold on to them."

"No," said Chanterelle quickly. "Don't take the dogs. Don't take that little pipe either. Your voice will be enough, now that you've got it back. Search *hard*—you have to find them today, if they're to be found at all."

Again Handsel looked at Amanita, as if for permission. Again Amanita shrugged her narrow shoulders.

"Look after my sister," Handsel said to the white-clad lady. "If anything were to happen to her—"

"Nothing will," said Amanita. "She's safe here. Nothing can hurt her, if she doesn't hurt herself—but if she won't eat—"

"She will," said Handsel firmly. "She will, if I keep my part of the bargain." And having said that, he left.

When the door closed behind him, Amanita looked down at Chanterelle for a full half minute before she put the bread that wasn't wheaten bread and the milk that wasn't cow's milk on the three-legged table. Then she sat down in the rocking-chair, tilting it back so that when she released it she moved gently to and fro. She never took her eyes off Chanterelle, and her brown eyes were exactly as piercing now as they had seemed by tricky lantern-light.

"That was very brave of you, my dear," the lady said at last, "if you really believe what you said about my being a bad fairy."

"I do," said Chanterelle, "and I'm *not* a silly fool."

"That," said the lady, "remains to be seen."

Chanterelle tested her injured ankle by stretching the toes and turning it to the left and the right. The pain she felt made it evident that she still wasn't able to walk, and wouldn't be able to for quite some time. The pain nearly brought tears to her eyes—but the anguish wasn't entirely unwelcome, because it distracted her attention from the awful hunger that felt as if it were hollowing out her belly with a fork.

The fake bread and the fake milk were beginning to seem attractive, in spite of the fact that they were not what they seemed to be. Handsel had obviously eaten them, just as he had eaten the red-capped mushrooms, but Chanterelle couldn't be certain that Handsel was still what he seemed to be.

"I wish you would eat, my dear," said Amanita after a

long silence. "If you don't eat, you'll never recover your strength. If you do, you might even recover your voice. You mustn't let stories make you afraid—and in any case, you can see readily enough that my house isn't made of gingerbread."

Chanterelle put out a hand to touch the wall beside the bed. It was softer than she had expected, and warmer. It had a curious texture unlike any wall she'd ever felt before. It wasn't brick or stone, and it wasn't wood or wattle-and-daub.

"It's a mushroom," whispered Chanterelle. "The whole house is a gigantic mushroom. How did it grow so big? It must be magic—*black* magic."

"Magic is neither black nor white, my dear," said Amanita. "Magic either *is* or *isn't*."

"The witch in the house of gingerbread tried to fatten Handsel for the cooking-pot," Chanterelle observed. "She wanted to eat him. Bad fairies and witches are much of a muchness, in all the stories I ever heard."

"Did the witch succeed?" asked Amanita.

"No," said Chanterelle. "Gretel—Handsel's sister, in the story—put an old stick in the witch's hand every time she reached into the cage to see whether Handsel was plump enough to eat yet. The witch was nearsighted, and couldn't tell that it wasn't Handsel's arm. When the witch finally grew impatient and tried to cook Gretel instead, Handsel pushed her into her own oven and cooked *her*. Then the children took the witch's hoard of gold and jewels back to their father, so that they would never be poor again."

"I see," said Amanita. "I fear, dear child, that I am not nearsighted. Were I what you suspect me to be, you'd have no chance at all of escaping me. In any case, it would do you no good if you did bundle me into my own oven. I have no hoard of gold and jewels, and you have no father. Your brother told me *another* story, about a little girl with a marvelous singing voice, who lost the will to sing when her heart was broken—but she was found by the old man who'd kept her when she was a child, who knew the secret of making nightingales sing by day. You know that story, of course."

"I know," whispered Chanterelle fearfully.

"Well," said Amanita, "that's nonsense too. All you need to set *your* voice free is a little bread and milk."

"The bread isn't wheaten bread and the milk isn't cow's milk," said Chanterelle. "The bread is baked from mushrooms and the milk is squeezed from mushroom flesh."

"That's true, as it happens," admitted Amanita. "As you've observed yourself, there's not much food fit for children growing wild in *this* part of the forest. There are insects a-plenty, and animals which eat insects, and animals which eat animals, but children can't hunt. Fortunately, the mushrooms with the red caps *do* make nourishing food. Handsel is as bold and strong as he ever was, don't you think? *He* isn't afraid to eat my bread and drink my milk."

"Handsel will find Mother today," whispered Chanterelle, "and Grandfather too. Then we shall all go home."

"Go home to what?" asked Amanita. She stopped the chair rocking and leaned forward to stare at Chanterelle even more intently than before. "To an empty foundry, which had failed long before the plague came and your grandfather tipped the unfinished church-bell into the tarn? Do you know why no one can hear it tolling in the dark current, least of all its maker? Because it has no tongue! It cannot ring, dear child, any more than you can sing."

"Mother will know what to do," said Chanterelle, so faintly that she could hardly hear herself.

"When Handsel returns," Amanita told her coldly, "you'll understand how foolish you are. Remember your promise, Chanterelle. When Handsel returns, you must eat and drink."

Having said that, Amanita got up and stalked out of the room, her white skirt swirling about her. The rocking-chair was thrown into violent motion by the abruptness of Amanita's abandonment, and it continued rocking back and forth for what must have been at least an hour.

* * *

Chanterelle tried to stay awake, but she was too weak. When she drifted off to sleep, however, the pain in her ankle made it difficult for her to sleep deeply. She remained suspended between consciousness and oblivion, lost in a wilderness of broken dreams.

She dreamed of mournful she-wolves and decrepit bears, of ghostly hunting-dogs which bounded through the forest like malevolent angels, of sweet-smelling loaves of bread which broke to reveal horrid masses of blue-green fungus, of cups of milk infested with tiny worms, of long ranks of club-headed mushrooms which served as cushioned seats for excited fairies, and of wizened old men who knew the secret of making nightingales sing by day.

When she woke again, the room was nearly dark. The patch of blue sky that had been visible through the latticed window had turned to velvet black, but the stars were out and the moon must have been full, for the room was not *entirely* cloaked in shadows.

At first Chanterelle couldn't tell what it was that had awakened her—but then she realized that the door had creaked as it began to open. She watched it move inward, her heart fluttering in dread because she expected to see Amanita.

When she saw that the person coming into the room was Handsel, not Amanita, Chanterelle felt a thrill of relief, which almost turned to joy when she saw the excited expression on his face. For one delicious moment she read that excitement as a sign that he must have found their mother—but when he came closer, she realized that it was something else.

"Oh, Chanterelle!" Handsel whispered as he knelt down beside the bed and put his head on the pillow beside hers. "You've no idea what a day I've had."

"Are you hoarse from shouting," she whispered back, "or are you afraid of waking Amanita?"

"Amanita's not here," Handsel said in a slightly louder voice. "She must have gone out again with those dogs of hers to hunt the she-wolf. I shouted myself hoarse all morning, as I knew I must, but no one answered. Then I stopped to pick and eat more mushrooms. Then I began to shout again, but it was no use at all. I had lost my voice—*but I had gained my sight!*"

"You never lost your sight," said Chanterelle faintly.

"I never *had* my sight, dear sister. I always *thought* that I could see, but now I know that I never saw clearly before today. I had never seen the trees, or the earth, or the air, or the sun.

"Today, for the first time, I saw the life of the trees, the richness of the earth, the color of the air and the might of the sun. Today, for the first time, I saw the world as it truly is. I saw the fairy-folk about their daily business. I saw dryads drawing water from the depths and breathing for the trees. I saw kobolds churning the soil to make it fertile. I saw sylphs sweeping the sky and ondines bubbling the springs.

"Oh Chanterelle, you were right about the mushrooms—and yet so very wrong! The fairy-folk swarm about them, hungry for pleasure, and make them grow tall and red, but there's no *poison* in them. There's only nourishment, for the mind as well as the body. Those who eat of the mushrooms tended by the fairy-folk may learn to see as well as growing strong. You must not be afraid of eating, Chanterelle. You must not starve yourself of light and life."

"I *am* afraid," said Chanterelle, and shut her eyes for a moment. She knew that the sight Handsel had discovered must be the *second* sight of which the stories told, which was sometimes a blessing and sometimes a curse. She had always thought that if either of them turned out to have the second sight, it would be her, and she felt a sharp pang of jealousy. She, after all, was the one who could sing—or *had* been able to sing, before grief took the melody out of her voice.

When she opened her eyes again, Handsel was no longer there—or, if he was, he was no longer Handsel. Kneeling beside her bed was the strangest creature she had ever seen. It was part human, having human legs and human arms, but it was also part insect, having the wings and head of a hawk-moth. Where the human and insect flesh met and fused, in the trunk from neck to hip, there was a soft carapace mottled with white stars. Even in the dim light, Chanterelle could see that the color of the carapace was crimson, exactly like Amanita's cape.

The huge compound eyes looked at Chanterelle with what might have been tenderness. The principal part of the creature's mouth was a pipelike structure coiled like a fernleaf, which gradually uncoiled and stiffened, so that the tip reached out to caress her face.

When the creature spoke to her, its words sounded as if they were notes produced by some kind of flute, and every sentence was a delicate musical phrase.

"The sweetest nectar of all is fairy blood," the monster informed her, "but the fairy-folk offer it willingly. Human blood is bitter, spoiled as anything is spoiled that is kept for far too long. Iron bells are hard and cold, and their voices are the tyrants of time. The bells of forest flowers are soft and beautiful, and their voices can unloose the bonds of the hours and the days. When humans go mad, they usually become bears or wolves, but find neither solace nor liberation. The fairy-folk are forever mad, forever joyous, forever free. Children may still be changelings if they choose. While the true sight has not quite withered away, children may find the one true path. While the true voice is not yet lost, children may soar on wings of song."

If only the monster had chosen its words more carefully, Chanterelle thought, it might have contrived a melody of sorts—but she had heard the songs of the skylarks and thrushes that the city-dwellers kept in cages, and she knew full well that even they had little enough talent for melody. Nightingales, for all their fame, were merely plaintive.

Chanterelle shut her eyes again and counted to ten. When she opened them, the monster was gone and Handsel was himself again.

"What did you say?" asked Chanterelle, in a voice as faint as faint could be.

"I said that we might be safe and happy here," murmured Handsel, in a voice that was not quite lost. "If we can only persuade Amanita to take us in, we might live here forever. She must be lonely, must she not? She has no husband, and no children of her own. She might accept us as her children, if we promise to be good. Wouldn't you like to live in an enchanted forest, sister dear?"

"I would rather find my mother," said Chanterelle.

"We have tried and failed," said Handsel sadly, "and must make the best of things. Would you rather starve than eat? Would you rather go down to the valley, where no charity waits us, than stay in the wild forest and live as the fairy-folk live? You promised, did you not, that you would eat Amanita's bread and drink her milk if I could not find our mother or our grandfather in one more day of searching? I have tried, and failed; I have lost my voice, but I can see. Will you eat, dear sister, and live—or will you break your promise, and die?"

"I will eat and drink in the morning," whispered Chanterelle. "If Mother has not found us by then, I will eat Amanita's mushroom-bread and drink her mushroom-milk."

Handsel stood up and turned toward the door.

"Don't go!" said Chanterelle.

"I have my own room now," said Handsel, "and my own bed."

No sooner was Chanterelle alone than the room grew noticeably darker. A cloud must have drifted across the face of the moon. Chanterelle moved her injured foot from left to right and back again, and then she stretched her toes. The result was agony—but it was the kind of agony that chased sleep away, and delirium too. Her mind had never been sharper.

Because she had no voice, Chanterelle cried out silently for her mother and her grandfather. *If you don't come by morning*, she thought with all the fervor she could muster, *you will come too late. If you don't come by morning, I shall be lost.*

In stories, she knew, such silent cries sometimes brought results. In stories, panic was sometimes as powerful as prayer. She prayed as well, though, in the hope that even if her mother and her grandfather could not help her, Heaven might.

As before, the pain could not keep sleep at bay indefinitely, but the sleep to which Chanterelle was delivered was shallow and turbulent.

She dreamed that she was running through the forest yet again, still pursued by an old man who carried a long needle in each hand. All night long his footsteps grew closer and closer, until at last she sank exhausted to the ground and waited for the inevitable.

The old man had no chance to use the needles; he was knocked flying by the paw of a bear, which then limped away into the forest with its ancient head held low. When the old man attempted to rise again, he was confronted by a she-wolf whose gray coat was flecked with blood. For a moment or two it seemed that he might try to defy the she-wolf, which was limping almost as badly as the bear, but when she showed her bright white teeth, he thought better of it and ran off, taking his needles with him.

"Thank you," Chanterelle whispered to the she-wolf.

"Don't thank me," said the wolf, sinking down beside her. "I can't help you. I can't even help myself." The wolf began licking at her wounds. Both her hind legs had been bitten, and her belly too. It was obvious that the hounds had almost brought her down.

"Who will help me if you cannot?" asked Chanterelle. "Must I trust in Heaven?"

The she-wolf stopped licking long enough to say: "Heaven is a poor ally to those still on Earth, else plague would have no power to consign us to damnation. Had you kept your promises, you'd be beyond help already—and those who are less than honest can hardly look to Heaven for salvation."

"Then what will become of me?" asked Chanterelle.

The wolf was too busy feeding on its own blood to give her an immediate answer, but when her fur was clean again she looked the child full in the face with sorrowful eyes.

"I wish I knew," the wolf said. "I can't even tell you the answer to your other question."

"What other question?" asked Chanterelle.

"Why the girl sang again when she was captured for a

second time by the man who knew the secret of making nightingales sing by day. I don't know the answer. All I know is that there's no more joy in being a wolf than there is in being a bear. I have to go away now. If I stay in this part of the forest, the hounds will have me for sure—and a wolf shouldn't have to live on mice while there are sheep in the valleys."

"Please don't go," begged Chanterelle. "If only you could save me, I think I *might* be able to sing again."

"It's too late," said the wolf as she disappeared into the darkness of the forest.

"It's too late," said Amanita, as Chanterelle woke to morning daylight. "You must eat now, or it will be too late."

Amanita was sitting no more than an arm's reach away from Chanterelle's head, having drawn a chair to the side of the bed—not the rocking-chair, but one of the others. The white-clad woman was holding a bowl full of steaming soup, which had the most delicious scent. The soup was thick and creamy, with solid pieces of a darker hue half submerged beneath the surface.

"Mushroom soup," said Chanterelle very faintly.

"The best mushroom soup in the world," said Amanita. "Not all mushrooms are alike, you know. These are the very best. They're called chanterelles—did you know you had a mushroom's name, my dear? I had to hunt far and wide to find them for you, but I knew that I'd have to find them even if it took all night. Luckily, the moon was full. Only eat this, and you'll be yourself again—or perhaps for the first time ever."

"I don't want it," whispered Chanterelle.

"But you don't have any choice," said Amanita. "You promised Handsel that you'd eat if your mother and grandfather were still lost. You don't understand what's happening here. You don't understand who and what you are. When your father named you Chanterelle, he thought it was a safe name for a nightingale, but he forgot the other meanings of the word. He knew that the highest string of a musical instrument was a chanterelle, but he *should* have known that a chanterelle is the most delicious kind of edible mushroom, and an imitation bird used to draw others into traps. Fate plays these little tricks all the time, you see. You thought you were supposed to be a singer, but you never knew how to find your voice, or how to use it, until you came to me. All children are kin to the fairy-folk, dear Chanterelle, but only a few have the chance to cross over, to see the world as *we* see it, with the *second* sight. You have that chance, but you must seize it. You must welcome it, because the cost of refusal will be more terrible than you imagine."

"Where's Handsel?" asked Chanterelle. "I must see Handsel."

"In the hope that he can seize me and throw me in my own oven, to burn me alive? In the hope that you and he can run away, laden down with gold and gems? Handsel can *see* now, my darling. Handsel will be my lover now, my darling boy, the sweetest of the sweet."

"I must see Handsel," whispered Chanterelle.

Amanita called out to Handsel to come and see his sister—and Handsel came. He stood beside Amanita, with his arm about her shoulder and his cheek next to hers.

"You must eat, Chanterelle," he said. "If you can't eat, you'll never sing."

"Can't you see that she's a wicked fairy?" Chanterelle asked in a voice so faint as hardly to be there at all.

"I *can* see," said Handsel. "I never could before, but now I can. I never want to be blind again. I couldn't stand it."

"The poor girl thinks that she's a nightingale," said Amanita, softly and sadly. "She can't believe what she really is, and she's starving herself to death because of it. But you know—don't you, darling Handsel?—how nightingales can be taught to sing by day. Tell me what the secret is, darling Handsel."

"The old man trained the nightingales to sing by day by running hot needles into their eyes," Handsel said calmly. "Afterward, they thought eternal night had come, and that was their idea of Heaven—so they sang, and sang, and sang in celebration. When Luscignole first saw what the old man did, she ran away, but that was because she didn't understand her true nature and her true destiny. She lost her voice when her heart broke, and the only way she could find it again was to find Heaven where she had never been able to look before: in eternal darkness."

"We don't need to do anything nearly as unkind as that," said Amanita. "Chanterelle will find her voice if she'll only eat the chanterelles. Eat, dear child, and discover what you truly are!"

Chanterelle could not believe that what was being done to her was any kinder than what had been done to Luscignole. She opened her mouth and tried to scream, but no scream came out. Instead, a spoon went in, bearing a full load of the impossibly delicious soup.

Chanterelle would have swallowed the soup if she had not gagged and choked, but the reflex saved her, and sprayed the contents of the spoon all over the bosom of Amanita's white dress, flecking it with gray and brown. So astonished was Amanita that she dropped the bowl and howled with anguish as the hot liquid flooded the thin fabric of her skirt.

Chanterelle, fearful for her very life, threw back the crimson coverlet that had kept her warm for two nights and a day and made her bid for freedom. She flew across the room to the open window, beating her wings with all the force and skill of long-frustrated instinct, and soared into the welcoming sky.

Some months later, on the first Monday after New Year's Day, Handsel and Amanita were walking in the wild forest by the light of the full moon. Their two ghostly hunting-dogs were beside them, neither needing a leash.

Amanita wore her favorite cape of bloodred fur, flecked with silver sequins. Handsel wore a fur cloak cut from the hide of a brown bear, trimmed along the edges with the silkier fur of a gray she-wolf. The body of the fur was a trifle mangy in places but the cape was warm in spite of the spoiled patches.

"How beautiful the sylphs are as they dance on the moonbeams," Handsel said, "freshening the air with their agility."

"Indeed they are, my love," said Amanita.

"I like the dryads even more," said Handsel. "They know the very best of elfin music, and they love to play their pipes when the wind blows. I was a piper myself once, and a plucker too, but I was never very good. One should leave the exercise of such arts to those who know them best."

"Indeed one should, my darling," said Amanita.

"There is another song in the air tonight, is there not?" said Handsel, pausing suddenly and cocking his ear. "There is another voice, even more distant and more plaintive than the dryad pipes. I have heard it before, but never by day and always very faint. What is it?"

"It is the song of a nightingale," said Amanita. "There is a way to make one sing by day, if you remember—but you would have to snare it first, and hold it very still. Would you like me to do that, Handsel? I think I can sing a song which will tempt it from the tree, if you wish. Birds are silly creatures, easily lured by artifice."

Handsel remained where he was for a moment longer, considering this proposition. He frowned as he listened to the plaintive voice, redolent with loss. It seemed, somehow, to be trying to lure him away from Amanita—but he was not the kind of creature who could be tempted by a song.

"What would be the point?" he said. "The poor thing cannot hold a melody at all."

Path of the Dragon

George R.R. Martin

*George R.R. Martin has reinvented himself in recent years as a bestselling fantasy writer with the advent in the mid-1990s of the Song of Ice and Fire series (*A Game of Thrones; A Clash of Kings; A Storm of Swords, *and continuing to total six volumes). In his other personae he has been a Hugo and Nebula Award-winning science fiction writer, a mainstream/horror writer (*Fevre Dream, *1982), a screenwriter, and an anthologist. In the 1980s he created and edited the six-volume Wild Cards series of superhero anthologies. He was the Story Editor for* The Twilight Zone, *and Executive Story Consultant, Producer, and Co-Supervising Producer for* Beauty and the Beast, *both on CBS; and Executive Producer for* Doorways *on CBS. He won his first Hugo in 1975, and over the intervening quarter-century has written an impressive array of stories in the science fiction, fantasy, and horror genres. He can be found on the Web at* www.georgemartin.com.

"Path of the Dragon" appeared in Asimov's, *which occasionally prints fantasy among the science fiction stories, and is an outtake from his new novel* A Storm of Swords. *Although his great fat fantasy series is marketed in the manner of followers of Tolkien, "Path of the Dragon" feels much closer to Samuel R. Delany's innovative* Tales of Neveryon, *set in a fantasy world more like that of Robert*

E. Howard's Conan stories than of Tolkien's, with some of Delany's attention to issues of slavery, economics, race, class, and gender. It is a very different resonance from the Terry Goodkind story in the Tolkien tradition.

A Queen at Sea

Across the still blue water came the slow steady beat of drums, and the soft swish of oars from the galleys. The great cog groaned in their wake, the heavy lines stretched taut between. *Balerion*'s sails hung limp, drooping forlorn from the masts. Yet even so, as she stood upon the forecastle watching her dragons chase each other across a cloudless blue sky, Daenerys Targaryen was as happy as she could ever remember being.

Her Dothraki called the sea *the poison water,* distrusting any liquid that their horses could not drink. On the day the three ships had lifted anchor at Qarth, you would have thought they were sailing to hell instead of Pentos. Her brave young bloodriders had stared off at the dwindling coastline with huge white eyes, each of the three determined to show no fear before the other two, while her handmaids Irri and Jhiqui clutched the rail desperately and retched over the side at every little swell. The rest of Dany's tiny *khalasar* remained below decks, preferring the company of their nervous horses to the terrifying landless world about the ships. When a sudden squall had enveloped them six days into the voyage, she heard them through the hatches; the horses kicking and screaming, the riders praying in thin quavery voices each time *Balerion* heaved or swayed.

No squall could frighten Dany, though. *Daenerys Stormborn*, she was called, for she had come howling into the world on distant Dragonstone as the greatest storm in the memory of Westeros howled outside, a storm so fierce that it ripped gargoyles from the castle walls and smashed her father's fleet to kindling.

The narrow sea was often stormy, and Dany had crossed it half a hundred times as a girl, running from one Free City to the next half a step ahead of the Usurper's hired knives. She loved the sea. She liked the sharp salty smell of sea air, and the vastness of limitless empty horizons bounded only by a vault of azure sky above. It made her feel very small, but free as well. She liked the dolphins that sometimes swam along beside *Balerion*, slicing through the waves like silvery spears, and the flying fish they glimpsed now and again. She even liked the sailors, with all their songs and stories. Once on a voyage to Braavos, as she'd watched the crew wrestle down a great green sail in a rising gale, she had even thought how fine it would be to be a sailor. But when she told her brother, Viserys had twisted her hair until she cried. "You are blood of the dragon," he had screamed at her. "A *dragon*, not some smelly fish."

He was a fool about that, and so much else, Dany thought. *If he had been wiser and more patient, it would be him sailing west to take the throne that was his by rights*. Viserys had been stupid and vicious, she had come to realize, and yet sometimes she missed him all the same. Not the cruel weak man he had become, by the end, but the brother who had once read to her and sometimes let her creep into his bed at night, the boy who used to tell her tales of the Seven Kingdoms, and talk of how much better their lives would be when he became a king.

The captain appeared at her elbow. "Would that this *Balerion* could soar as her namesake did, Your Grace," he said politely, in bastard Valyrian heavily flavored with accent of Pentos. "Then we should not need to row, nor tow, nor pray for wind. Is it not so?"

"It is so, Captain," she answered with a smile, pleased to have won the man over. Captain Groleo was an old Pentoshi like his master, Illyrio Mopatis, and he had been nervous as a maiden about carrying three dragons on his ship. Half a hundred buckets of seawater still hung from the gunwales, in case of fires. At first Groleo had wanted the dragons caged and Dany had consented to put his fears at ease, but their misery was so palpable that she soon changed her mind and insisted they be freed.

Even Captain Groleo was glad of that, now. There had been one small fire, easily extinguished; against that, *Balerion* suddenly seemed to have far fewer rats than she'd had before, when she sailed under the name *Saduleon*. And her crew, once as fearful as they were curious, had begun to take a queer fierce pride in "their" dragons. Every man of them, from captain to cook's boy, loved to watch the three fly . . . though none so much as Dany.

They are my children, she told herself, *and if the maegi spoke truly, they are the only children I am ever like to have.*

Viserion's scales were the color of fresh cream, his horns, wing bones, and spinal crest a dark gold that flashed bright as metal in the sun. Rhaegal was made of the green of summer and the bronze of fall. They soared above the ships in wide circles, higher and higher, each trying to climb above the other.

Dragons always preferred to attack from above, Dany had learned. Should either get between the other and the sun, he would fold his wings and dive screaming, and they would tumble from the sky locked together in a tangled scaly ball, jaws snapping and tails lashing. The first time they had done it, she feared that they meant to kill each other, but it was only sport. No sooner would they splash into the sea than they would break apart and rise again, shrieking and hissing, the salt water steaming off them as their wings clawed at the air. Drogon was aloft as well, though not in sight; he would be miles ahead, or miles behind, hunting.

He was always hungry, her Drogon. *Hungry and grow-*

ing fast. Another year, or perhaps two, and he may be large enough to ride. Then I shall have no need of ships to cross the great salt sea.

But that time was not yet come. Rhaegal and Viserion were the size of small dogs, Drogon only a little larger, and any dog would have outweighed them; they were all wings and neck and tail, lighter than they looked. And so Daenerys Targaryen must rely on wood and wind and canvas to bear her home.

The wood and the canvas had served her well enough so far, but the fickle wind had turned traitor. For six days and six nights they had been becalmed, and now a seventh day had come, and still no breath of air to fill their sails. Fortunately, two of the ships that Magister Illyrio had sent after her were trading galleys, with two hundred oars apiece and crews of strong-armed oarsmen to row them. But the great cog *Balerion* was a song of a different key; a ponderous broad-beamed sow of a ship with immense holds and huge sails, but helpless in a calm. *Vhagar* and *Meraxes* had let out lines to tow her, but it made for painfully slow going. All three ships were crowded, and heavily laden.

"I cannot see Drogon," said Ser Jorah Mormont, as he joined her on the forecastle. "Is he lost again?"

"We are the ones who are lost, ser. Drogon has no taste for this wet creeping, no more than I do." Bolder than the other two, her black dragon had been the first to try his wings above the water, the first to flutter from ship to ship, the first to lose himself in a passing cloud . . . and the first to kill. The flying fish no sooner broke the surface of the water than they were enveloped in a lance of flame, snatched up, and swallowed. "How big will he grow?" Dany asked curiously. "Do you know?"

"In the Seven Kingdoms, there are tales of dragons who grew so huge that they could pluck giant krakens from the sea."

Dany laughed. "That would be a wondrous sight to see."

"It is only a tale, *Khaleesi*," said her exile knight. "They talk of wise old dragons living a thousand years as well."

"Well, how long *does* a dragon live?" She looked up as

Viserion swooped low over the ship, his wings beating slowly and stirring the limp sails.

Ser Jorah shrugged. "A dragon's natural span of days is many times as long as a man's, or so the songs would have us believe . . . but the dragons the Seven Kingdoms knew best were those of House Targaryen. They were bred for war, and in war they died. It is no easy thing to slay a dragon, but it can be done."

The squire Whitebeard, standing by the figurehead with one lean hand curled about his tall hardwood staff, turned toward them and said, "Balerion the Black Dread was two hundred years old when he died during the reign of Jaehaerys the Conciliator. He was so large he could swallow an aurochs whole. A dragon never stops growing, Your Grace, so long as he has food and freedom." His name was Arstan, but Strong Belwas had named him Whitebeard for his pale whiskers, and most everyone called him that now. He was taller than Ser Jorah, though not so muscular; his eyes were a pale blue, his long beard as white as snow and as fine as silk.

"Freedom?" asked Dany, curious. "What do you mean?"

"In King's Landing, your ancestors raised an immense domed castle for their dragons. The Dragonpit, it is called. It still stands atop the Hill of Rhaenys, though all in ruins now. That was where the royal dragons dwelt in days of yore, and a cavernous dwelling it was, with iron doors so wide that thirty knights could ride through them abreast. Yet even so, it was noted that none of the pit dragons ever reached the size of their ancestors. The maesters say it was because of the walls around them, and the great dome above their heads."

"If walls could keep us small, peasants would all be tiny and kings as large as giants," said Ser Jorah. "I've seen huge men born in hovels, and dwarfs who dwelt in castles."

"Men are men," Whitebeard replied. "Dragons are dragons."

Ser Jorah snorted his disdain. "How profound." The exile knight had no love for the old man, he'd made that plain from the first. "What do you know of dragons, anyway?"

"Little enough, that's true. Yet I served for a time in King's Landing in the days when King Aerys sat the Iron Throne, and walked beneath the dragonskulls that looked down from the walls of his throne room."

"Viserys talked of those skulls," said Dany. "The Usurper took them down and hid them away. He could not bear them looking down on him as he sat his stolen throne." She beckoned Whitebeard closer. "Did you ever met my royal father?" King Aerys II had died before his daughter was born.

"I had that great honor, Your Grace."

Dany put a hand on the old man's arm. "Did you find him good and gentle?"

Whitebeard did his best to hide his feelings, but they were there, plain on his face. "His Grace was . . . often pleasant."

"Often?" Dany smiled. "But not always?"

"He could be very harsh to those he thought his enemies."

"A wise man never makes an enemy of a king," said Dany. "Did you know my brother Rhaegar as well?"

"It was said that no man ever knew Prince Rhaegar, truly. I had the privilege of seeing him in tourney, though, and often heard him play his harp with its silver strings."

Ser Jorah snorted. "Along with a thousand others at some harvest feast. Next you'll claim you squired for him."

"I make no such claim, ser. Myles Mooton was Prince Rhaegar's squire, and Richard Lonmouth after him. When they won their spurs, he knighted them himself, and they remained his close companions. Young Lord Connington was dear to the prince as well, though his oldest friend was Arthur Dayne."

"The Sword of the Morning!" said Dany, delighted. "Viserys used to talk about his wondrous white blade. He said Ser Arthur was the only knight in the realm who was our brother's peer."

Whitebeard bowed his head. "It is not my place to question the words of Prince Viserys."

"King," Dany corrected. "He was a king, though he never

reigned. Viserys, the Third of His Name. But what do you mean?" His answer had not been the one she'd expected. "Ser Jorah named Rhaegar the last dragon once. He had to have been a peerless warrior to be called that, surely?"

"Your Grace," said Whitebeard, "the Prince of Dragonstone was a most puissant warrior, but . . ."

"Go on," she urged. "You may speak freely to me."

"As you command." The old man leaned upon his hardwood staff, his brow furrowed. "A warrior without peer . . . those are fine words, Your Grace, but words win no battles."

"Swords win battles," Ser Jorah said bluntly. "And Prince Rhaegar knew how to use one."

"He did, ser. But . . . I have seen a hundred tournaments and more wars than I would wish, and however strong or fast or skilled a knight may be, there are others who can match him. A man will win one tourney, and fall quickly in the next. A slick spot in the grass may mean defeat, or what you ate for supper the night before. A change in the wind may bring the gift of victory." He glanced at Ser Jorah. "Or a lady's favor knotted round an arm."

Mormont's face darkened. "Be careful what you say, old man."

Arstan had seen Ser Jorah fight at Lannisport, Dany knew, in the tourney Mormont had won with a lady's favor knotted round his arm. He had won the lady too; Lynesse of House Hightower, his second wife, highborn and beautiful . . . but she had ruined him, and abandoned him, and the memory of her was bitter to him now. "Be gentle, my knight." She put a hand on Jorah's arm. "Arstan had no wish to give offense, I'm certain."

"As you say, *Khaleesi*." Ser Jorah's voice was grudging.

Dany turned back to the squire. "I know little of Rhaegar. Only the tales Viserys told, and he was a little boy when our brother died. What was he truly like?"

The old man considered a moment. "Able. That above all. Determined, deliberate, dutiful, single-minded. There is a tale told of him . . . but doubtless Ser Jorah knows it as well."

"I would hear it from you."

"As you wish," said Whitebeard. "As a young boy, the Prince of Dragonstone was bookish to a fault. He was reading so early that men said Queen Rhaella must have swallowed some books and a candle whilst he was in her womb. Rhaegar took no interest in the play of other children. The maesters were awed by his wits, but his father's knights would jest sourly that Baelor the Blessed had been born again. Until one day Prince Rhaegar found something in his scrolls that changed him. No one knows what it might have been, only that the boy suddenly appeared early one morning in the yard as the knights were donning their steel. He walked up to Ser Willem Darry, the master-at-arms, and said, 'I will require sword and armor. It seems I must be a warrior.' "

"And he was!" said Dany, delighted.

"He was indeed." Whitebeard bowed. "My pardons, Your Grace. We speak of warriors, and I see that Strong Belwas has arisen. I must attend him."

Dany glanced aft. The eunuch was climbing through the hold amidships, nimble as a monkey for all his size. Belwas was squat but broad, a good fifteen stone of fat and muscle, his great brown gut crisscrossed by faded white scars. He wore baggy pants, a yellow silk bellyband, and an absurdly tiny leather vest dotted with iron studs. "Strong Belwas is hungry!" he roared at everyone and no one in particular. "Strong Belwas will eat now!" Turning, he spied Arstan on the forecastle. "Whitebeard!" he shouted. "You will bring food for Strong Belwas!"

"You may go," Dany told the squire. He bowed again, and moved off to tend the needs of the man he served.

Ser Jorah watched with a frown on his blunt honest face. Mormont was big and burly, strong of jaw and thick of shoulder. Not a handsome man by any means, but as true a friend as Dany had ever known. "You would be wise to take that old man's words well salted," he told her when Whitebeard was out of earshot.

"A queen must listen to all," she reminded him. "The highborn and the low, the strong and the weak, the noble and the venal. One voice may speak you false, but in many there is always truth to be found." She had read that in a book.

"Hear my voice then, Your Grace," the exile said. "This Arstan Whitebeard is playing you false. He is too old to be a squire, and too well-spoken to be serving that oaf of a eunuch."

That does seem queer, Dany had to admit. Strong Belwas was an ex-slave, bred and trained in the fighting pits of Meereen. Magister Illyrio had sent him to guard her, or so Belwas claimed, and it was true that she needed guarding. She had death behind her, and death ahead. The Usurper on his Iron Throne had offered land and lordship to any man who killed her. One attempt had been made already, with a cup of poisoned wine. The closer she came to Westeros, the more likely another attack became. Back in Qarth, the warlock Pyat Pree had sent a Sorrowful Man after her to avenge the Undying she'd burned in their House of Dust. Warlocks never forgot a wrong, it was said, and the Sorrowful Men never failed to kill. Most of the Dothraki would be against her as well. Khal Drogo's *kos* led *khalasars* of their own now, and none of them would hesitate to attack her own little band on sight, to slay and slave her people and drag Dany herself back to Vaes Dothrak to take her proper place among the withered crones of the *dosh khaleen*. She hoped that Xaro Xhoan Daxos was not an enemy, but the Qartheen merchant had coveted her dragons. And there was Quaithe of the Shadow, that strange woman in red lacquer mask with all her cryptic counsel. Was she an enemy too, or only a dangerous friend? Dany could not say.

Ser Jorah saved me from the poisoner, and Arstan Whitebeard from the manticore. Perhaps Strong Belwas will save me from the next. He was huge enough, with arms like small trees and a great curved *arakh* so sharp he might have shaved with it, in the unlikely event of hair sprouting on those smooth brown cheeks. Yet he was childlike as well. *As a protector, he leaves much to be desired. Thankfully, I have Ser Jorah and my bloodriders.*

And my dragons, never forget. In time, the dragons would be her most formidable guardians, just as they had been for Aegon and his sisters three hundred years ago. Just now, though, they brought her more danger than protection. In all the world there were but three living dragons, and those were hers; they were a wonder, and a terror, and beyond price.

She was pondering her next words when she felt a cool breath on the back of her neck, and a loose strand of her silver-gold hair stirred against her brow. Above, the canvas creaked and moved, and suddenly a great cry went up from all over *Balerion*. "Wind!" the sailors shouted. "The wind returns, the *wind!*

Dany looked up to where the great cog's sails rippled and belled, as the lines thrummed and tightened and sang the sweet song they had missed so for six long days. Captain Groleo rushed aft, shouting commands. The Pentoshi were scrambling up the masts, those that were not cheering. Even Strong Belwas let out a great bellow and did a little dance. "The gods are good!" Dany said. "You see, Jorah? We are on our way once more."

"Yes," he said, "but to what, my queen?"

All day the wind blew, steady from the east at first, and then in wild gusts. The sun set in a blaze of red. *I am still half a world from Westeros*, Dany told herself as she charred meat for her dragons that evening, *but every hour brings me closer.* She tried to imagine what it would feel like, when she first caught sight of the land she was born to rule. *It will be as fair a shore as I have ever seen, I know it. How could it be otherwise?*

But later that night, as *Balerion* plunged onward through the dark and Dany sat crosslegged on her bunk in the captain's cabin, feeding her dragons—"Even upon the sea," Groleo had said, so graciously, "queens take precedence over captains"—a sharp knock came upon the door.

Irri had been sleeping at the foot of her bunk (it was too narrow for three, and tonight was Jhiqui's turn to share the soft featherbed with her *khaleesi*), but she roused at the knock and went to the door. Dany pulled up a coverlet and tucked it in under her arms. She slept naked, and had not expected a caller at this hour. "Come," she said when she saw Ser Jorah standing without, beneath a swaying lantern.

The exile knight ducked his head as he entered. "Your Grace. I am sorry to disturb your sleep."

"I was not sleeping, ser. Come and watch." She took a chunk of salt pork out of the bowl in her lap and held it up for her dragons to see. All three of them eyed it hungrily. Rhaegal spread green wings and stirred the air, and Viserion's neck swayed back and forth like a long pale snake's as he followed the movement of her hand. "Drogon," Dany said softly, "*dracarys.*" And she tossed the pork in the air.

Drogon moved quicker than a striking cobra. Flame roared from his mouth, orange and scarlet and black, searing the meat before it began to fall. As his sharp black teeth snapped shut around it, Rhaegal's head darted close, as if to steal the prize from his brother's jaws, but Drogon swallowed and screamed, and the smaller green dragon could only *hiss* in frustration.

"Stop that, Rhaegal," Dany said in annoyance, giving his head a swat. "You had the last one. I'll have no greedy dragons." She smiled at Ser Jorah. "I don't need to char their meat over a brazier any longer."

"So I see. *Dracarys?*"

All three dragons turned their heads at the sound of that word, and Viserion let loose with a blast of pale gold flame that made Ser Jorah take a hasty step backward. Dany giggled. "Be careful with that word, ser, or they're like to singe your beard off. It means *dragonfire* in High Valyrian. I wanted to choose a command that no one was like to utter by chance."

Mormont nodded. "Your Grace," he said, "I wonder if I might have a few private words?"

"Of course. Irri, leave us for a bit." She put a hand on Jhiqui's bare shoulder and shook the other handmaid awake. "You as well, sweetling. Ser Jorah needs to talk to me."

"Yes, *Khaleesi.*" Jhiqui tumbled from the bunk, naked and yawning, her thick black hair tumbled about her head. She dressed quickly and left with Irri, closing the door behind them.

Dany gave the dragons the rest of the salt pork to squabble over, and patted the bed beside her. "Sit, good ser, and tell me what is troubling you."

"Three things." Ser Jorah sat. "Strong Belwas. This Arstan Whitebeard. And Illyrio Mopatis, who sent them."

Again? Dany pulled the coverlet higher and tugged one end over her shoulder. "And why is that?"

"The warlocks in Qarth told you that you would be betrayed three times," the exile knight reminded her, as Viserion and Rhaegal began to snap and claw at each other for the last chunk of seared salt pork.

"Once for blood and once for gold and once for love." Dany was not like to forget. "Mirri Maz Duur was the first."

"Which means two traitors yet remain . . . and now these two appear. I find that troubling, yes. Never forget, Robert offered a lordship to the man who slays you."

Dany leaned forward and yanked Viserion's tail, to pull him off his green brother. Her blanket fell away from her chest as she moved. She grabbed it hastily and covered herself again. "The Usurper is dead," she said.

"But his son rules in his place." Ser Jorah lifted his gaze, and his dark eyes met her own. "A dutiful son pays his father's debts. Even blood debts."

"This boy Joffrey might want me dead . . . if he recalls that I'm alive. What has that to do with Belwas and Arstan Whitebeard? The old man does not even wear a sword. You've seen that."

"Aye. And I have seen how deftly he handles that staff of his. Recall how he killed that manticore in Qarth? It might as easily have been your throat he crushed."

"Might have been, but was not," she pointed out. "It was a stinging manticore meant to slay me. He saved my life."

"*Khaleesi*, has it occurred to you that Whitebeard and

Belwas might have been in league with the assassin? It might all have been a ploy to win your trust."

Her sudden laughter made Drogon *hiss*, and sent Viserion flapping to his perch above the porthole. "The ploy worked well."

The exile knight did not return her smile. "These are Illyrio's ships, Illyrio's captains, Illyrio's sailors . . . and Strong Belwas and Arstan are his men as well, not yours."

"Magister Illyrio has protected me in the past. Strong Belwas says that he wept when he heard my brother was dead."

"Yes," said Mormont, "but did he weep for Viserys, or for the plans he had made with him?"

"His plans need not change. Magister Illyrio is a friend to House Targaryen, and wealthy . . ."

"He was not born wealthy. In the world as I have seen it, no man grows rich by kindness. The warlocks said the second treason would be for *gold*. What does Illyrio Mopatis love more than gold?"

"His skin." Across the cabin Drogon stirred, steam rising from his nostrils. "Mirri Maz Duur betrayed me. I burned her for it."

"Mirri Maz Duur was in your power. In Pentos, you shall be in Illyrio's power. It is not the same. I know the magister as well as you. He is a devious man, and clever—"

"I need clever men about me if I am to win the Iron Throne."

Ser Jorah snorted. "That wineseller who tried to poison you was a clever man as well. Clever men hatch ambitious schemes."

Dany drew her legs up beneath the blanket. "You will protect me. You, and my bloodriders."

"Four men? *Khaleesi*, you believe you know Illyrio Mopatis, very well. Yet you insist on surrounding yourself with men you do *not* know, like this puffed-up eunuch and the world's oldest squire. Take a lesson from Pyat Pree and Xaro Xhoan Daxos."

He means well, Dany reminded herself. *He does all he does for love*. "It seems to me that a queen who trusts no one is as foolish as a queen who trusts everyone. Every man I take into my service is a risk, I understand that, but how am I to win the Seven Kingdoms without such risks? Am I to conquer Westeros with one exile knight and three Dothraki bloodriders?"

His jaw set stubbornly. "Your path is dangerous, I will not deny that. But if you blindly trust in every liar and schemer who crosses it, you will end as your brothers did."

His obstinance made her angry. *He treats me like some child.* "Strong Belwas could not scheme his way to breakfast. And what lies has Arstan Whitebeard told me?"

"He is not what he pretends to be. He speaks to you more boldly than any squire would dare."

"He spoke frankly at my command. He knew my brother."

"A great many men knew your brother. Your Grace, in Westeros the Lord Commander of the Kingsguard sits on the small council, and serves the king with his wits as well as his steel. If I am the first of your Queensguard, I pray you, hear me out. I have a plan to put to you."

"What plan? Tell me."

"Illyrio Mopatis wants you back in Pentos, under his roof. Very well, go to him . . . but in your own time, and not alone. Let us see how loyal and obedient these new subjects of yours truly are. Command Groleo to change course for Slaver's Bay."

Dany was not certain she liked the sound of that at all. Everything she'd ever heard of the flesh marts in the great slave cities of Yunkai, Meereen, and Astapor was dire and frightening. "What is there for me in Slaver's Bay?"

"An army," said Ser Jorah. "If Strong Belwas is so much to your liking you can buy hundreds more like him out of the fighting pits of Meereen . . . but it is Astapor I'd set my sails for. In Astapor you can buy Unsullied."

"The slaves in the spiked bronze hats?" Dany had seen Unsullied guards in the Free Cities, posted at the gates of magisters, archons, and dynasts. "Why should I want Unsullied? They don't even ride horses, and most of them are fat."

"The Unsullied you may have seen in Pentos and Myr

were household guards. That's soft service, and eunuchs tend to plumpness in any case. Food is the only vice allowed them. To judge all Unsullied by a few old household slaves is like judging all squires by Arstan Whitebeard, Your Grace. Most are strong, and skilled, and supremely disciplined. Put ashore in Astapor and continue on to Pentos overland. It will take longer, yes . . . but when you break bread with Magister Illyrio, you will have a thousand swords behind you, not just four."

There is wisdom in this, yes, Dany thought, *but* . . . "How am I to buy a thousand slave soldiers? All I have of value is the crown the Tourmaline Brotherhood gave me."

"Dragons will be as great a wonder in Astapor as they were in Qarth. It may be that the slavers will shower you with gifts, as the Qartheen did. If not . . . these ships carry more than your Dothraki and their horses. They took on trade goods at Qarth, I've been through the holds and seen for myself. Bolts of silk and bales of tiger skin, amber and jade carvings, saffron, myrrh . . . slaves are cheap, Your Grace. Tiger skins are costly."

"Those are *Illyrio's* tiger skins," she objected.

"And Illyrio is a friend to House Targaryen."

"All the more reason not to steal his goods."

"What use are wealthy friends if they will not put their wealth at your disposal, my queen? If Magister Illyrio would deny you, he is only Xaro Xhoan Daxon with four chins. And if he is sincere in his devotion to your cause, he will not begrudge you three shiploads of trade goods. What better use for his tiger skins than to buy you the beginnings of an army?"

That's true. Dany felt a rising excitement. "There will be dangers on such a long march. . . ."

"There are dangers at sea as well. Corsairs and pirates hunt the southern route, and north of Valyria the Smoking Sea is demon haunted. The next storm could sink or scatter us, a kraken could pull us under . . . or we might find ourselves becalmed again, and die of thirst as we wait for the wind to rise. A march will have different dangers, my queen, but none greater."

"What if Captain Groleo refuses to change course, though? And Arstan, Strong Belwas, what will they do?"

Ser Jorah stood. "Perhaps it's time you found that out."

"*Yes!*" she decided. "I'll do it!" Dany threw back the coverlets and hopped from the bunk. "I'll see the captain at once, command him to set course for Astapor." She bent over her chest, threw open the lid, and seized the first garment to hand, a pair of loose sandsilk trousers. "Hand me my medallion belt," she commanded Jorah, as she pulled the sandsilk up over her hips. "And my vest—" she started to say, turning.

Ser Jorah slid his arms around her.

"Oh," was all Dany had time to say, as he pulled her close and pressed his lips down on hers. He smelled of sweat and salt and leather, and the iron studs on his jerkin dug into her naked breasts as he crushed her hard against him. One hand held her by the shoulder while the other slid down her spine to the small of her back, and her mouth opened for his tongue, though she never told it to. *His beard is scratchy*, she thought, *but his mouth is sweet.* The Dothraki wore no beards, only long mustaches, and only Khal Drogo had ever kissed her before. *He should not be doing this. I am his queen, not his woman.*

It was a long kiss, though how long Dany could not have said. When it ended, Ser Jorah let go of her, and she took a quick step backward. "You . . . you should not have . . ."

"I should not have waited so long," he finished for her. "I should have kissed you in Qarth, in Vaes Tolorro. I should have kissed you in the red waste, every night and every day. You were made to be kissed, often and well." His eyes were on her breasts.

Dany covered them with her hands, before her nipples could betray her. "I . . . that was not fitting. I am your queen."

"My queen," he said, "and the bravest, sweetest, and most beautiful woman I have ever seen. Daenerys—"

"*Your Grace!*"

"Your Grace," he conceded, "*the dragon has three heads* . . . remember? You have wondered at that, ever since you heard it from the warlocks in the House of Dust. Well, here's your meaning: Balerion, Meraxes, and Vhagar, ridden by Aegon, Rhaenys, and Visenya. The three-headed dragon of House Targaryen—three dragons, and *three riders*."

"Yes," said Dany, "but my brothers are dead."

"Rhaenys and Visenya were Aegon's wives as well as his sisters. You have no brothers, but you can take husbands. And I tell you truly, Daenerys, there is no man in all the world who will ever be half so true to you as me."

Unsullied in Astapor

In the center of the Plaza of Pride stood a red brick fountain whose waters smelled of brimstone, and in the center of the fountain a monstrous harpy made of hammered bronze. Twenty feet tall she reared. She had a woman's face, with gilded hair, ivory eyes, and pointed ivory teeth. Water gushed yellow from her heavy breasts. But in place of arms she had the wings of a bat or a dragon, her legs were the legs of an eagle, and behind she wore a scorpion's curled and venomous tail.

The harpy of Ghis, Dany thought. Old Ghis had fallen five thousand years ago, if she remembered true; its legions shattered by the might of young Valyria, its mighty brick walls pulled down, its streets and buildings turned to ash and cinder by dragonflame, its very fields sown with salt, sulfur, and skulls. The gods of Ghis were dead, and so too its people; these Astapori were mongrels, Ser Jorah said. Even the Ghiscari tongue was largely forgotten; the slave cities spoke the High Valyrian of their conquerors, or what they had made of it.

Yet the symbol of the Old Empire still endured here, though this bronze monster had a heavy chain dangling from her talons, an open manacle at either end. *The harpy of Ghis had a thunderbolt in her claws. This is the harpy of Astapor.*

"Tell the Westerosi whore to lower her eyes," the slaver Kraznys mo Nakloz complained to the slave girl who spoke for him. "I deal in meat, not metal. The bronze is not for sale. Tell her to look at the soldiers. Even the dim purple eyes of a sunset savage can see how magnificent my creatures are, surely."

Kraznys's High Valyrian was twisted and thickened by the characteristic growl of Ghis, and flavored here and there with words of slaver argot. Dany understood him well enough, but she smiled and looked blankly at the slave girl, as if wondering what he might have said. "The Good Master Kraznys asks, are they not magnificent?" The girl spoke the Common Tongue well, for one who had never been there. No older than ten, she had the round flat face, dusky skin, and golden eyes of Naath. *The Peaceful People*, her folk were called. All agreed that they made the best slaves.

"They might be adequate to my needs," Dany answered. It had been Ser Jorah's suggestion that she speak only Dothraki and the Common Tongue while in Astapor. *My bear is more clever than he looks*, she reflected. "Tell me of their training."

"The Westerosi woman is pleased with them, but speaks no praise, to keep the price down," the translator told her master. "She wishes to know how they were trained."

Kraznys mo Nakloz bobbed his head. He smelled as if he'd bathed in raspberries, this slaver, and his jutting red-black beard glistened with oil. *He has larger breasts than I do*, Dany reflected. She could see them through the thin sea-green silk of the gold-fringed *tokar* he wound about his body and over one shoulder. His left hand held the *tokar* in place as he walked, while his right clasped a short leather whip. "Are all Westerosi pig ignorant?" he complained. "All the world knows that the Unsullied are masters of spear and shield and shortsword." He gave Dany a broad smile. "Tell her what she would know, slave, and be quick about it. The day is hot."

That much at least is no lie. A matched pair of slave girls stood in back of them, holding a stripped silk awning over their heads, but even in the shade Dany felt a little light-headed, and Kraznys was perspiring freely. The Plaza of

Pride had been baking in the sun since dawn. Even through the thickness of her sandals, she could feel the warmth of the red bricks underfoot. Waves of heat rose off them shimmering to make the stepped pyramids of Astapor around the plaza seem half a dream.

If the Unsullied felt the heat, however, they gave no hint of it. *They could be made of brick themselves, the way they stand there.* A thousand had been marched out of their barracks for her inspection; drawn up in ten ranks of one hundred before the fountain and its great bronze harpy, they stood stiffly at attention, their stony eyes fixed straight ahead. They wore naught but white linen clouts knotted about their loins, and conical bronze helms topped with a sharpened spike a foot tall. Kraznys had commanded them to lay down their spears and shields, and doff their swordbelts and quilted tunics, so the Queen of Westeros might better inspect the lean hardness of their bodies.

"They are chosen young, for size and speed and strength," the slave told her. "They begin their training at five. Every day they train from dawn to dusk, until they have mastered the short sword, the shield, and the three spears. The training is most rigorous, Your Grace. Only one boy in three survives it. This is well known. Among the Unsullied it is said that on the day they win their spiked cap, the worst is done with, for no duty that will ever fall to them could be as hard as their training."

Kraznys mo Nakloz supposedly spoke no word of the Common Tongue, but he bobbed his head as he listened, and from time to time gave the slave girl a poke with the end of his lash. "Tell her that these have been standing here for a day and a night, with no food nor water. Tell her that they will stand until they drop if I should command it, and when nine hundred and ninety-nine have collapsed to die upon the bricks, the last will stand there still, and never move until his own death claims him. Such is their courage. Tell her that."

"I call that madness, not courage," said Arstan Whitebeard, when the solemn little scribe was done. He tapped the end of his hardwood staff against the bricks, *tap tap*, as if to tell his displeasure. The old man had not wanted to sail to Astapor; nor did he favor buying this slave army. A queen should hear all sides before reaching a decision. That was why Dany had brought him with her to the Plaza of Pride, not to keep her safe. Her bloodriders would do that well enough. Ser Jorah Mormont she had left aboard *Balerion* to guard her people and her dragons. Much against her inclination, she had locked the dragons below decks. It was too dangerous to let them fly freely over the city; the world was all too full of men who would gladly kill them for no better reason than to name themselves *dragonslayer*.

"What did the smelly old man say?" the slaver demanded of his translator. When she told him, he smiled and said, "Inform the savages that we call this *obedience*. Others may be stronger or quicker or larger than the Unsullied. Some few may even equal their skill with sword and spear and shield. But nowhere between the seas will you ever find any more obedient."

"Sheep are obedient," said Arstan when the words had been translated. He had some Valyrian as well, though not so much as Dany, but like her he was feigning ignorance.

Kraznys mo Nakloz showed his big white teeth when that was rendered back to him. "A word from me and these sheep would spill his stinking old bowels on the bricks," he said, "but do not say that. Tell them that these creatures are more dogs than sheep. Do they eat dogs or horse in these Seven Kingdoms?"

"They prefer pigs and cows, your worship."

"Beef. Pfag. Food for unwashed savages."

Ignoring them all, Dany walked slowly down the line of slave soldiers. The girls followed close behind with the silk awning, to keep her in the shade, but the thousand men before her enjoyed no such protection. More than half had the copper skins and almond eyes of Dothraki and Lhazerene, but she saw men of the Free Cities in the ranks as well, along with pale Qartheen, ebon-faced Summer Islanders, and others whose origins she could not guess. And some had skins of the same amber hue as Kraznys mo Nakloz, and the bristly red-black hair that marked the ancient folk of Ghis, who named themselves the harpy's sons. *They sell even their own kind*. It should not have surprised her. The Dothraki did the same, when *khalasar* met *khalasar* in the sea of grass.

Some of the soldiers were tall and some were short. They ranged in age from fourteen to twenty, she judged. Their cheeks were smooth, and their eyes all the same, be they black or brown or blue or grey or amber. *They are like one man*, Dany thought, until she remembered that they were no men at all. The Unsullied were eunuchs, every one of them. "Why do you cut them?" she asked Kraznys through the slave girl. "Whole men are stronger than eunuchs, I have always heard."

"A eunuch who is cut young will never have the brute strength of one of your Westerosi knights, this is true," said Kraznys mo Nakloz when the question was put to him. "A bull is strong as well, but bulls die every day in the fighting pits. A girl of nine killed one not three days past in Jothiel's Pit. The Unsullied have something better than strength, tell her. They have discipline. We fight in the fashion of the Old Empire, yes. They are the lockstep legions of Old Ghis come again, absolutely obedient, absolutely loyal, and utterly without fear."

Dany listened patiently to the translation.

"Even the bravest men fear death and maiming," Arstan said when the girl was done.

Kraznys smiled again when he heard that. "Tell the old man that he smells of piss, and needs a stick to hold him up."

"Truly, your worship?"

He poked her with his lash. "Not, not truly, are you a girl or a goat, to ask such folly? Say that Unsullied are not men. Say that death means nothing to them, and maiming less than nothing." He stopped before a thickset man who had the look of Lhazar about him and brought his whip up sharply, laying a line of blood across one copper cheek. The eunuch blinked, and stood there, bleeding. "Would you like another?" asked Kraznys.

"If it please your worship."

It was hard to pretend not to understand. Dany laid a

hand on Kraznys's arm before he could raise the whip again. "Tell the Good Master that I see how strong his Unsullied are, and how bravely they suffer pain."

Kraznys chuckled when he heard her words in Valyrian. "Tell this ignorant whore of a westerner that courage has nothing to do with it."

"The Good Master says that was not courage, Your Grace."

"Tell her to open those slut's eyes of hers."

"He begs you attend this carefully, Your Grace."

Kraznys moved to the next eunuch in line, a towering youth with the blue eyes and flaxen hair of Lys. "Your sword," he said. The eunuch knelt, unsheathed the blade, and offered it up hilt first. It was a short sword, made more for stabbing than for slashing, but the edge looked razor sharp. "Stand," Kraznys commanded.

"Your worship." The eunuch stood, and Kraznys mo Nakloz slid the sword slowly up his torso, leaving a thin red line across his belly and between his ribs. Then he jabbed the swordpoint in beneath a wide pink nipple and began to work it back and forth.

"What is he doing?" Dany demanded of the girl, as the blood ran down the man's chest.

"Tell the cow to stop her bleating," said Kraznys, without waiting for the translation. "This will do him no great harm. Men have no need of nipples, eunuchs even less so." The nipple hung by a thread of skin. He slashed, and sent it tumbling to the bricks, leaving behind a round red eye copiously weeping blood. The eunuch did not move, until Kraznys offered him back his sword, hilt first. "Here, I'm done with you."

"This one is pleased to have served you."

Kraznys turned back to Dany. "They feel no pain, you see."

"How can that be?" she demanded through the scribe.

"*The wine of courage,*" was the answer he gave her. "It is no true wine at all, but made from deadly nightshade, bloodfly larva, black lotus root, and many secret things. They drink it with every meal from the day they are cut, and with each passing year feel less and less. It makes them fearless in battle. Nor can they be tortured. Tell the savage her secrets are safe with the Unsullied. She may set them to guard her councils and even her bedchamber, and never a worry as to what they might overhear.

"In Yunkai and Meereen, eunuchs are often made by removing a boy's testicles, but leaving the penis. Such a creature is infertile, yet often still capable of erection. Only trouble can come of this. We remove the penis as well, leaving nothing. The Unsullied are the purest creatures on the earth." He gave Dany and Arstan another of his broad white smiles. "I have heard that in the Sunset Kingdoms men take solemn vows to keep chaste and father no children, but live only for their duty. Is it not so?"

"It is," Arstan said, when the question was put to him. "There are many such orders. The maesters of the Citadel, the septons and septas who serve the Seven, the silent sisters of the dead, the Kingsguard and the Night's Watch . . ."

"Poor things," growled the slaver, after the translation. "Men were not made to live such. Their days are a torment of temptation, any fool must see, and no doubt most succumb to their baser selves. Not so our Unsullied. They are wed to their swords in a way that your Sworn Brothers cannot hope to match. No woman can ever tempt them, nor any man."

His girl conveyed the essence of his speech, more politely. "There are other ways to tempt men, besides the flesh," Arstan Whitebeard objected, when she was done.

"Men, yes, but not Unsullied. Plunder interests them no more than rape. They own nothing but their weapons. We do not even permit them names."

"No names?" Dany frowned at the little scribe. "Can that be what the Good Master said? They have no names?"

"It is so, Your Grace."

Kraznys stopped in front of a Ghiscari who might have been his taller fitter brother, and flicked his lash at a small bronze disc on the swordbelt at his feet. "There is his name. Ask the whore of Westeros whether she can read

Ghiscari glyphs." When Dany admitted that she could not, the slaver turned to the Unsullied. "What is your name?" he demanded.

"This one's name is Red Flea, your worship."

The girl repeated their exchange in the Common Tongue.

"And yesterday, what was it?"

"Black Rat, your worship."

"The day before?"

"Brown Flea, your worship."

"Before that?"

"This one does not recall, your worship. Blue Toad, perhaps. Or Blue Worm."

"Tell her all their names are such," Kraznys commanded the girl. "It reminds them that by themselves they are vermin. The name disks are thrown in an empty cask at duty's end, and each dawn plucked up again at random."

"More madness," said Arstan, when he heard. "How can any man possibly remember a new name every day?"

"Those who cannot are culled in training, along with those who cannot run all day in full pack, scale a mountain in the black of night, walk across a bed of coals, or slay an infant."

Dany's mouth surely twisted at that. *Did he see, or is he blind as well as cruel?* She turned away quickly, trying to keep her face a mask until she heard the translation. Only then did she allow herself to say, "Whose infants do they slay?"

"To win his spiked cap, an Unsullied must go to the slave marts with a silver mark, find some wailing newborn, and kill it before its mother's eyes. In this way, we make certain that there is no weakness left in them."

She was feeling faint. *The heat*, she tried to tell herself. "You take a babe from its mother's arms, kill it as she watches, and pay for her pain with a silver coin?"

When the translation was made for him, Kraznys mo Nakloz laughed aloud. "What a soft mewling fool this one is. Tell the whore of Westeros that the mark is for the child's owner, not the mother. The Unsullied are not permitted to steal." He tapped his whip against his leg. "Tell her that few ever fail that test. The dogs are harder for them, it must be said. We give each boy a puppy on the day that he is cut. At the end of the first year, he is required to strangle it. Any who cannot are killed, and fed to the surviving dogs. It makes for a good strong lesson, we find."

Arstan Whitebeard tapped the end of his staff on the bricks as he listened to that. *Tap tap tap*. Slow and steady. *Tap tap tap*. Dany saw him turn his eyes away, as if he could not bear to look at Kraznys any longer.

"The Good Master has said that these eunuchs cannot be tempted with coin or flesh," Dany told the girl, "but if some enemy of mine should offer them *freedom* for betraying me . . ."

"They would kill him out of hand and bring her his head, tell her that," the slaver answered. "Other slaves may steal and hoard up silver in hopes of buying freedom, but an Unsullied would not take it if the little mare offered it as a gift. They have no life outside their duty. They are *soldiers*, and that is all."

"It is soldiers I need," Dany admitted.

"Tell her it is well she came to Astapor, then. Ask her how large an army she wishes to buy?"

"How many Unsullied do you have to sell?"

"Eight thousand fully trained and available at present. We sell them only by the unit, she should know. By the thousand or the century. Once we sold by the ten, as household guards, but that proved unsound. Ten is too few. They mingle with other slaves, even freemen, and forget who and what they are." Kraznys waited for that to be rendered in the Common Tongue, and then continued. "This beggar queen must understand, such wonders do not come cheaply. In Yunkai and Meereen, slave swordsmen can be had for less than the price of their swords, but Unsullied are the finest foot in all the world, and each represents many years of training. Tell her they are like Valyrian steel, folded over and over and hammered for years on end, until they are stronger and more resilient than any metal on earth."

"I know of Valyrian steel," said Dany. "Ask the Good Master if the Unsullied have their own officers."

"You must set your own officers over them. We train them to obey, not to think. If it is wits she wants, let her buy scribes."

"And their gear?"

"Sword, shield, spear, sandals, and quilted tunic are included," said Kraznys. "And the spiked caps, to be sure. They will wear such armor as you wish, but you must provide it."

Dany could think of no other questions. She looked at Arstan. "You have lived long in the world, Whitebeard. Now that you have seen them, what do you say?"

"I say *no*, Your Grace," the old man answered at once.

"Why?" she asked. "Speak freely." Dany thought she knew what he would say, but she wanted the slave girl to hear, so Kraznys mo Nakloz might hear later.

"My queen," said Arstan, "there have been no slaves in the Seven Kingdoms for thousands of years. The old gods and the new alike hold slavery to be an abomination. Evil. If you should land in Westeros at the head of a slave army, many good men will oppose you for no other reason than that. You will do great harm to your cause, and to the honor of your House."

"Yet I must have some army," Dany said. "The boy Joffrey will not give me the Iron Throne for asking politely."

"When the day comes that you raise your banners, half of Westeros will be with you," Whitebeard promised. "Your brother Rhaegar is still remembered, with great love."

"And my father?" Dany said.

The old man hesitated before saying, "King Aerys is also remembered. He gave the realm many years of peace. Your Grace, you have no need of slaves. Magister Illyrio can keep you safe while your dragons grow, and send secret envoys across the narrow sea on your behalf, to sound out the high lords for your cause."

"Those same high lords who abandoned my father to the Kingslayer and bent the knee to Robert the Usurper?"

"Even those who bent their knees may yearn in their hearts for the return of the dragons."

"May," said Dany. That was such a slippery word, *may*. In any language. She turned back to Kraznys mo Nakloz and his slave girl. "I must consider carefully."

The slaver shrugged. "Tell her to consider quickly. There are many other buyers. Only three days past I showed these same Unsullied to a corsair king who hopes to buy them all."

"The corsair wanted only a hundred, your worship," Dany heard the slave girl say.

He poked her with the end of the whip. "Corsairs are all liars. He'll buy them all. Tell her that, girl."

Dany knew she would take more than a hundred, if she took any at all. "Remind your Good Master of who I am. Remind him that I am Daenerys Stormborn, Mother of Dragons, the Unburnt, trueborn queen of the Seven Kingdoms of Westeros. My blood is the blood of Aegon the Conqueror, and of old Valyria before him."

Yet her words did not move the plump perfumed slaver, even when rendered in his own ugly tongue. "Old Ghis ruled an empire when the Valyrians were still fucking sheep," he growled at the poor little scribe, "and we are the sons of the harpy." He gave a shrug. "My tongue is wasted wagging at women. East or west, it makes no matter, they cannot decide until they have been pampered and flattered and stuffed with sweetmeats. Well, if this is my fate, so be it. Tell the whore that if she requires a guide to our sweet city, Kraznys mo Nakloz will gladly serve her . . . and service her as well, if she is more woman than she looks."

"Good Master Kraznys would be most pleased to show you Astapor while you ponder, Your Grace," the translator said.

"I will feed her jellied dog brains, and a fine rich stew of red octopus and unborn puppy." He wiped his lips.

"Many delicious dishes can be had here, he says."

"Tell her how pretty the pyramids are at night," the slaver growled. "Tell her I will lick honey off her breasts, or allow her to lick honey off mine if she prefers."

"Astapor is most beautiful at dusk, Your Grace," said the slave girl. "The Good Masters light silk lanterns on every terrace, so all the pyramids glow with colored lights. Pleasure barges ply the Worm, playing soft music and calling at the little islands for food and wine and other delights."

"Ask her if she wishes to view our fighting pits," Kraznys added. "Douquor's Pit has a fine folly scheduled for the evening. A bear and three small boys. One boy will be rolled in honey, one in blood, and one in rotting fish, and she may wager on which the bear will eat first."

Tap tap tap, Dany heard. Arstan Whitebeard's face was still, but his staff beat out his rage. *Tap tap tap*. She made herself smile. "I have my own bear on *Balerion*," she told the translator, "and he may well eat me if I do not return to him."

"See," said Kraznys when her words were translated. "It is not the woman who decides, it is this man she runs to. As ever!"

"Thank the Good Master for his patient kindness," Dany said, "and tell him that I will think on all I learned here." She gave her arm to Arstan Whitebeard, to lead her back across the plaza to her litter. Aggo and Jhogo fell in to either side of them, walking with the bowlegged swagger all the horselords affected when forced to dismount and stride the earth like common mortals.

Dany climbed into her litter frowning, and beckoned Arstan to climb in beside her. A man as old as him should not be walking in such heat. She did not close the curtains as they got underway. With the sun beating down so fiercely on this city of red brick, every stray breeze was to be cherished, even if it did come with a swirl of fine red dust. *Besides, I need to see.*

Astapor was a queer city, even to the eyes of one who had walked within the House of Dust and bathed in the Womb of the World beneath the Mother of Mountains. All the streets were made of the same red brick that had paved the plaza. So too were the stepped pyramids, the deep-dug fighting pits with their rings of descending seats, the sulfurous fountains and gloomy wine caves, and the ancient walls that encircled them. *So many bricks*, she thought, *and so old and crumbling*. Their fine red dust was everywhere, dancing down the gutters at each gust of wind. Small wonder so many Astapori women veiled their faces; the brick dust stung the eyes worse than sand.

"Make way!" Jhogo shouted as he rode before her litter. "Make way for the Mother of Dragons!" But when he uncoiled the great silver-handled whip that Dany had given him, and made to crack it in the air, she leaned out and told him nay. "Not in this place, blood of my blood," she told him, in his own tongue. "These bricks have heard too much of the sound of whips."

The streets had been largely deserted when they had set out from the port that morning, and scarcely seemed more crowded now. An elephant lumbered past with a latticework litter on its back. A naked boy with peeling skin sat in a dry brick gutter, picking his nose and staring sullenly at some ants in the street. He lifted his head at the sound of hooves, and gaped as a column of mounted guards trotted by in a cloud of red dust and brittle laughter. The copper discs sewn to their cloaks of yellow silk glittered like so many suns, but their tunics were embroidered linen, and below the waist they wore sandals and pleated linen skirts. Bareheaded, each man had teased and oiled and twisted his stiff red-black hair into fantastic shapes, horns and wings and blades and even grasping hands, so they looked like some troupe of demons escaped from the seventh hell. The naked boy watched them for a bit, along with Dany, but soon enough they were gone, and he went back to his ants, and a knuckle up his nose.

An old city, this, she reflected, *but not so populous as it was in its glory, nor near so crowded as Qarth or Pentos or Lys*.

Her litter came to a sudden halt at the cross street, to allow a coffle of slaves to shuffle across her path, urged along by the crack of an overseer's lash. These were no Unsullied, Dany noted, but a more common sort of men, with pale brown skins and black hair. There were women among them, but no children. All were naked. Two Astapori rode behind them on white asses, a man in a red silk *tokar* and a veiled woman in sheer blue linen decorated with flakes of lapis lazuli. In her red-black hair she wore an ivory comb. The man laughed as he whispered to her, paying no more mind to Dany than to his slaves, nor the overseer with his twisted five-thonged lash, a squat broad Dothraki who had the harpy and chains tattooed proudly across his muscular chest.

"Bricks and blood built Astapor," Whitebeard murmured at her side, "and bricks and blood her people."

"What is that?" Dany asked him, curious.

"An old rhyme a maester taught me, when I was a boy. I never knew how true it was. The bricks of Astapor are red with the blood of the slaves who make them."

"I can well believe that," said Dany.

"Then leave this place before your heart turns to brick as well. Sail this very night, on the evening tide."

Would that I could, thought Dany. "When I leave Astapor it must be with an army, Ser Jorah says."

"Ser Jorah was a slaver himself, Your Grace," the old man reminded her. "Hire sellswords to be your army, I beg of you. A man who fights for coin has no honor, but at least they are no slaves. Buy your army in Pentos, Braavos, or Myr."

"My brother visited near all the Free Cities. The magisters and archons fed him wine and promises, but his soul was starved to death. A man cannot sup from the beggar's bowl all his life and stay a man. I had my taste in Qarth, that was enough. I will not come to Pentos bowl in hand."

"Better to come a beggar than a slaver," Arstan said.

"There speaks one who has been neither." Dany's nostrils flared. "Do you know what it is like to be *sold*, squire? I do. My brother sold me to Khal Drogo for the promise of a golden crown. Well, Drogo crowned him in gold, though not as he had wished, and I . . . my sun-and-stars made a queen of me, but if he had been a different man, it might have been much otherwise. Do you think I have forgotten how it felt to be afraid?"

Whitebeard bowed his head. "Your Grace," he said, "I did not mean to give offense."

"Only lies offend me, never honest counsel." Dany patted Arstan's spotted hand to reassure him. "I have a dragon's temper, that's all. You must not let it frighten you."

"I shall try and remember," Whitebeard said, with a smile.

He has a good face, and great strength to him, Dany thought. She could not understand why Ser Jorah mistrusted the old man so. *Could he be jealous that I have found another man to talk to?* Unbidden, her thoughts went back to the night on *Balerion* when the exile knight had kissed her. *He should never have done that. He is thrice my age, and of too low a birth for me, and I never gave him leave. No true knight would ever kiss a queen without her leave.* She had taken care never to be alone with Ser Jorah after that, keeping her handmaids Irri and Jhiqui with her aboard ship, and sometimes her bloodriders as well. *He wants to kiss me again, I can see it in his eyes.*

What Dany wanted she could not begin to say, but Jorah's kiss had woken something in her, something that been sleeping since Drogo died, who had been her sun-and-stars. Lying abed in her narrow bunk, she found herself wondering how it would be to have a man squeezed in beside her in place of her handmaid, and the thought was more exciting than it should have been. Sometimes she would close her eyes and dream of him, but it was never Jorah Mormont she dreamed of; her lover was always younger and more comely, though his face remained a shifting shadow.

Once, so tormented she could not sleep, Dany slid a hand down between her legs, and gasped when she felt how wet she was. Scarce daring to breathe, she moved her fingers back and forth between her lower lips, slowly so as not to wake Irri beside her, until she found one sweet spot and lingered there, touching herself lightly, timidly at first and then faster, but still the relief she wanted seemed to recede before her. Only then her dragons stirred, and one of them screamed out across the cabin, and Irri woke and saw what she was doing.

Dany knew her face was flushed, but in the darkness Irri surely could not tell. Wordless, the handmaid put a hand on her breast, then bent to take a nipple in her mouth. Her other hand drifted down across the soft curve of belly, through the mound of fine silvery-gold hair, and went to work between Dany's thighs. It was no more than a few moments until her legs twisted and her breasts heaved and her whole body shuddered. She screamed then, or perhaps that was Drogon. Irri never said a thing, only curled back up and went back to sleep the instant the thing was done.

The next day, it all seemed a dream. And what did Ser Jorah have to do with it, if anything? *It is Drogo I want, my sun-and-stars,* Dany reminded herself. *Not Irri, and not Ser Jorah, only Drogo*. Drogo was dead, though. She'd thought these feelings had died with him there in the red waste, but one treacherous kiss had somehow brought them back to life. *He should never have kissed me. He presumed too much, and I permitted it. It must never happen again.* She set her mouth grimly and gave her head a shake, and the bell in her braid chimed softly.

Closer to the bay, the city presented a fairer face. The great brick pyramids lined the shore, the largest four hundred feet high. All manner of trees and vines and flowers grew on their broad terraces, and the winds that swirled around them smelled green and fragrant. Another gigantic harpy stood atop the gate, this one made of baked red clay and crumbling visibly, with no more than a stub of her scorpion's tail remaining. The chain she grasped in her clay claws was old iron, rotten with rust. It was cooler down by the water, though. The lapping of the waves against the rotting pilings made a curiously soothing sound.

Aggo helped Dany down from her litter. Strong Belwas was seated on a massive piling, eating a great haunch of brown roasted meat. "Dog," he said happily when he saw Dany. "Good dog in Astapor, little queen. Eat?" He offered it with a greasy grin.

"That is kind of you, Belwas, but no." Dany had eaten

dog in other places, at other times, but just now all she could think of was the Unsullied and their stupid puppies. She swept past the huge eunuch and up the plank onto the deck of *Balerion*.

Ser Jorah Mormont stood waiting for her. "Your Grace," he said, bowing his head. "The slavers have come and gone. Three of them, with a dozen scribes and as many slaves to lift and fetch. They crawled over every foot of our holds and made note of all we had." He walked her aft. "How many men do they have for sale?"

"None." Was it Mormont she was angry with, or this city with its sullen heat, its stinks and sweats and crumbling bricks? "They sell eunuchs, not men. Eunuchs made of brick, like the rest of Astapor. Shall I buy eight thousand brick eunuchs with dead eyes that never move, who kill suckling babes for the sake of a spiked hat and strangle their own dogs? They don't even have names. So don't call them *men*, ser."

"*Khaleesi*," he said, taken aback by her fury, "the Unsullied are chosen as boys, and trained—"

"I have heard all I care to of their *training*." Dany could feel tears welling in her eyes, sudden and unwanted. Her hand flashed up, and cracked Ser Jorah hard across the face. It was either that, or cry.

Mormont touched the cheek she'd slapped. "If I have displeased my queen—

"You *have*. You've displeased me greatly, ser. If you were my true knight, you would never have brought me to this vile sty." *If you were my true knight, you would never have kissed me, or looked at my breasts the way you did, or . . .*

"As Your Grace commands. I shall tell Captain Groleo to make ready to sail on the evening tide, for some sty less vile."

"No." Groleo watched them from the forecastle, and his crew was watching too. Whitebeard, her bloodriders, Jhiqui, everyone had stopped what they were doing at the sound of the slap. "I want to sail *now*, not on the tide, I want to sail far and fast and never look back. But I can't, can I? There are eight thousand brick eunuchs for sale, and

I must find some way to buy them." And with that she left him, and went below.

Behind the carved wooden door of the captain's cabin, her dragons were restless. Drogon raised his head and screamed, pale smoke venting from his nostrils, and Viserion flapped at her and tried to perch on her shoulder, as he had when he was smaller. "No," Dany said, trying to shrug him off gently. "You're too big for that now, sweetling." But the dragon coiled his white and gold tail around one arm and dug black claws into the fabric of her sleeve, clinging tightly. Helpless, she sank into Groleo's great leather chair, giggling.

"They have been wild while you were gone, *Khaleesi*," Irri told her. "Viserion clawed splinters from the door, do you see? And Drogon made to escape when the slaver men came to see them. When I grabbed his tail to hold him back, he turned and bit me." She showed Dany the marks of his teeth on her hand.

"Did any of them try to burn their way free?" That was the thing that frightened Dany the most.

"No, *Khaleesi*. Drogon breathed his fire, but in the empty air. The slaver men feared to come near him."

She kissed Irri's hand where Drogon had bitten it. "I'm sorry he hurt you. Dragons are not meant to be locked up in a small ship's cabin."

"Dragons are like horses in this," Irri said. "And riders, too. The horses scream below, *Khaleesi*, and kick at the wooden walls. I hear them. And Jhiqui says the old women and the little ones scream too, when you are not here. They do not like this water cart. They do not like the black salt sea."

"I know," Dany said. "I do, I know."

"My *khaleesi* is sad?"

"Yes," Dany admitted. *Sad and lost.*

"Should I pleasure the *khaleesi*?"

Dany stepped away from her. "No. Irri, you do not need to do that. What happened that night, when you woke . . . you're no bed slave, I freed you, remember? You . . ."

"I am handmaid to the Mother of Dragons," the girl said. "It is great honor to please my *khaleesi*."

"I don't want that," she insisted. "I don't." She turned away sharply. "Leave me now. I want to be alone. To think."

Dusk had begun to settle over the waters of Slaver's Bay before Dany returned to deck. She stood by the rail and looked out over Astapor. *From here it looks almost beautiful*, she thought. The stars were coming out above, and the silk lanterns below, just as Kraznys's translator had promised. The brick pyramids were all glimmery with light. *But it is dark below, in the streets and plazas and fighting pits. And it is darkest of all in the barracks, where some little boy is feeding scraps to the puppy they gave him when they took away his manhood.*

There was a soft step behind her. "*Khaleesi.*" His voice. "Might I speak frankly?"

Dany did not turn. She could not bear to look at him just now. If she did, she might well slap him again. Or cry. Or kiss him. And never know which was right and which was wrong and which was madness. "Say what you will, ser."

"When Aegon and Dragon stepped ashore in Westeros, the kings of Vale and Rock and Reach did not rush to hand him their crowns. If you mean to sit his Iron Throne, you must win it as he did, with steel and dragonfire. And that will mean blood on your hands before the thing is done."

Blood and fire, thought Dany. The words of House Targaryen. She had known them all her life. "The blood of my enemies I will shed gladly. The blood of innocents is another matter. Eight thousand Unsullied they would offer me. Eight thousand dead babes. Eight thousand strangled dogs."

"Your Grace," said Jorah Mormont, "I saw King's Landing after the Sack. Babes were butchered that day as well, and old men, and children at play. More women were raped than you can count. There is a savage beast in every man, and when you hand that man a sword or spear and send him forth to war, the beast stirs. The scent of blood is all it takes to wake him. Yet I have never heard of these Unsullied raping, nor putting a city to the sword, nor even plundering, save at the express command of those who lead them. Brick they may be, as you say, but if you buy them henceforth the only dogs they'll kill are those *you* want dead. And you do have some dogs you want dead, as I recall."

The Usurper's dogs. "Yes." Dany gazed off at the soft colored lights and let the cool salt breeze caress her. "You speak of sacking cities. Answer me this, ser—why have the Dothraki never sacked *this* city?" She pointed. "Look at the walls. You can see where they've begun to crumble. There, and there. Do you see any guards on those towers? I don't. Are they hiding, ser? I saw these sons of the harpy today, all their proud highborn warriors. They dressed in linen skirts, and the fiercest thing about them was their hair. Even a modest *khalasar* could crack this Astapor like a nut and spill out the rotted meat inside. So tell me, why is that ugly harpy not sitting beside the godsway in Vaes Dothrak among the other stolen gods?"

"You have a dragon's eye, *Khaleesi*, that's plain to see."

"I wanted an answer, not a compliment."

"There are two reasons. Astapor's brave defenders are so much chaff, it's true. Old names and fat purses who dress up as Ghiscari scourges to pretend they still rule a vast empire. Every one is a high officer. On feastdays they fight mock wars in the pits to demonstrate what brilliant commanders they are, but it's the eunuchs who do the dying. All the same, any enemy wanting to sack Astapor would have to know that they'd be facing Unsullied. The slavers would turn out the whole garrison in the city's defense. The Dothraki have not ridden against Unsullied since they left their braids at the gates of Qohor."

"And the second reason?" Dany asked.

"Who would attack Astapor?" Ser Jorah asked. "Meereen and Yunkai are rivals but not enemies, the Doom destroyed Valyria, the folk of the eastern hinterlands are all Ghiscari, and beyond the hills lies Lhazar. The Lamb Men, as your Dothraki call them, a notably unwarlike people."

"Yes," she agreed, "but *north* of the slave cities is the

Dothraki Sea, and two dozen mighty khals who like nothing more than sacking cities and carrying off their people into slavery."

"Carrying them off *where?* What good are slaves once you've killed the slavers? Valyria is no more, Qarth lies beyond the red waste, and the Nine Free Cities are thousands of leagues to the west. And you may be sure the sons of the harpy give lavishly to every passing khal, just as the magisters do in Pentos and Norvos and Myr. They know that if they feast the horselords and give them gifts, they will soon ride on. It's cheaper than fighting, and a deal more certain."

Cheaper than fighting. If only it could be that easy for her. How pleasant it would be to sail to King's Landing with her dragons, and pay the boy Joffrey a chest of gold to make him go away. *"Khaleesi?"* Ser Jorah prompted, when she had been silent for a long time. He touched her elbow lightly.

Dany shrugged him off. "Viserys would have bought as many Unsullied as he had the coin for. But you once said I was like Rhaegar. . . ."

"I remember, Daenerys."

"Your Grace," she corrected. "Prince Rhaegar led free men into battle, not slaves. Whitebeard said he dubbed his squires himself, and made many other knights as well."

"There was no higher honor than to receive your knighthood from the Prince of Dragonstone."

"Tell me, then—when he touched a man on the shoulder with his sword, what did he say? 'Go forth and kill the weak?' Or go forth and defend them? At the Trident, those brave men Viserys spoke of who died beneath our dragon banners—did they give their lives because they *believed* in Rhaegar's cause, or because they had been bought and paid for?" Dany turned to Mormont, crossed her arms, and waited for an answer.

"My queen," the big man said slowly, "all you say is true. But Rhaegar lost on the Trident. He lost the battle, he lost the war, he lost the kingdom, and he lost his life. His blood swirled downriver with the rubies from his breastplate, and Robert the Usurper rode over his corpse to steal the Iron Throne. Rhaegar fought valiantly, Rhaegar fought nobly, Rhaegar fought honorably. And Rhaegar *died*."

— *Trading in Dragons*

"*All?*" The slave girl sounded wary. "Your Grace, did this one's worthless ears mishear you?"

Cool green light filtered down through the diamond-shaped panes of the thick windows of colored glass set in the sloping triangular walls, and a breeze was blowing gently through the open terrace doors, carrying the scents of fruit and flowers from the garden beyond. "Your ears heard true," said Dany. "I want to buy them all. Tell the Good Masters, if you will."

She had chosen a Qartheen gown today. The deep violet silk brought out the purple of her eyes. The cut of it bared her left breast. While the Good Masters of Astapor conferred among themselves in low voices, Dany sipped tart persimmon wine from a tall silver flute. She could not quite make out all that they were saying, but she could hear the greed.

Each of the eight brokers was attended by two or three body slaves . . . though one Grazdan, the eldest, had six. So as not to seem a beggar, Dany had brought her own attendants; Irri and Jhiqui in their sandsilk trousers and painted vests, old Whitebeard and mighty Belwas, her bloodriders. Ser Jorah stood behind her sweltering in his green surcoat with the black bear of Mormont embroidered upon it. The smell of his sweat was an earthy answer to the sweet perfumes that drenched the Astapori.

"All," growled Kraznys mo Nakloz, who smelled of peaches today. The slave girl repeated the word in the Common Tongue of Westeros. "Of thousands, there are eight. Is this what she means by *all?* There are also six centuries, who shall be part of a ninth thousand when complete. Would she have them too?"

"I would," said Dany when the question was put to her. "The eight thousands, the six centuries . . . and the ones still in training as well. The one who have not earned the spikes."

Kraznys turned back to his fellows. Once again they conferred among themselves. The translator had told Dany their names, but it was hard to keep them straight. Four of the men seemed to be named Grazdan, presumably after Grazdan the Great, who had founded Old Ghis in the dawn of days. They all looked alike; thick fleshy men with amber skin, broad noses, dark eyes. Their wiry hair was black, or a dark red, or that queer mixture of red and black that was peculiar to Ghiscari. All wrapped themselves in *tokars*, a garment permitted only to freeborn men of Astapor.

It was the fringe on the *tokar* that proclaimed a man's status, Dany had been told by Captain Groleo. In this cool green room atop the pyramid, two of the slavers wore *tokars* fringed in silver, five had gold fringes, and one, the oldest Grazdan, displayed a fringe of fat white pearls that clacked together softly when he shifted in his seat or moved an arm.

"We cannot sell half-trained boys," one of the silver fringe Grazdans was saying to the others.

"We can, if her gold is good," said a fatter man whose fringe was gold.

"They are not Unsullied. They have not killed their sucklings. If they fail in the field, they will shame us. And even if we cut five thousand raw boys tomorrow, it would be be ten years before they are fit for sale. What would we tell the next buyer who comes seeking Unsullied?"

"We will tell him that he must wait," said the fat man. "Gold in my purse is better than gold in my future."

Dany let them argue, sipping the tart persimmon wine and trying to keep her face blank and ignorant. *I will have them all, no matter the price*, she told herself. The city had a hundred slave traders, but the eight before her were the greatest. When selling bed slaves, fieldhands, scribes, craftsmen, and tutors, these men were rivals, but their ancestors had allied one with the other for the purpose of making and selling the Unsullied. *Brick and blood built Astapor, and brick and blood her people.*

It was Kraznys who finally announced their decision. "Tell her that the eight thousands you shall have, if her gold prove sufficient. And the six centuries, if she wishes. Tell her to come back in a year, and we will sell her another two thousand."

"In a year, I shall be in Westeros," said Dany when she had heard the translation. "My need is *now*. The Unsullied are well-trained, but even so, many will fall in battle. I shall need the boys as replacements to take up the swords they drop." She put her wine aside and leaned toward the slave girl. "Tell the Good Masters that I will want even the little ones who still have their puppies. Tell them that I will pay as much for the boy they cut yesterday as for an Unsullied in a spiked helm."

The girl told them. The answer was still no.

Dany frowned in annoyance. "Very well. Tell them I will pay double, so long as I get them all."

"Double?" The fat one in the gold fringe all but drooled.

"This little whore is a fool, truly," said Kraznys mo Nakloz. "Ask her for triple, I say. She is desperate enough to pay. Ask for ten times the price of every slave, yes."

The tall Grazdan with the spiked beard spoke in the Common Tongue, though not so well as the slave girl. "Your Grace," he growled, "Westeros is being wealthy, yes, but you are not being queen now. Perhaps will never being queen. Even Unsullied may be losing battles to savage steel knights of Seven Kingdoms. I am reminding, the Good Masters of Astapor are not selling flesh for promisings. Are you having gold and trading goods sufficient to be paying for all these eunuchs you are wanting?"

"You know the answer to that better than I, Good Master," Dany replied. "Your men have gone through my ships and tallied every bead of amber and jar of saffron. How much do I have?"

"Sufficient to be buying one of thousands," the Good Master said, with a contemptuous smile. "Yet you are paying double, you are saying. Five centuries, then, is all you buy."

"Your pretty crown might buy another century," said the fat one in Valyrian. "Your crown of the three dragons."

Dany waited for his words to be translated. "My crown is not for sale." When Viserys sold their mother's crown, the last joy had gone from him, leaving only rage. "Nor will I enslave my people, nor sell their goods and horses. But my ships you can have. The great cog *Balerion* and the galleys *Vhagar* and *Meraxes*." She had warned Groleo and the other captains it might come to this, though they had protested the necessity of it furiously. "Three good ships should be worth more than a few paltry eunuchs."

The fat Grazdan turned to the others. They conferred in low voices once again. "Two of the thousands," the one with the spiked beard said when he turned back. "It is too much, but the Good Masters are being generous and your need is being great."

Two thousand would never serve for what she meant to do. *I must have them all.* Dany knew what she must do now, though the taste of it was so bitter that even the persimmon wine could not cleanse it from her month. She had considered long and hard last night, and found no other way. *It is my only choice.* "Give me all," she said, and you may have a dragon."

There was the sound of indrawn breath from Jhiqui beside her. Kraznys smiled at his fellows. "Did I not tell you? Anything, she would give us."

Whitebeard stared in shocked disbelief. His thin, spotted hand trembled where it grasped the staff. "No." He went to one knee before her. "Your Grace, I beg you, win your throne with dragons, not slaves. You must not do this thing—"

"*You* must not presume to instruct me. Ser Jorah, remove Whitebeard from my presence."

Mormont seized the old man roughly by an elbow, yanked him back to his feet, and marched him out onto the terrace.

"Tell the Good Masters I regret this interruption," said Dany to the slave girl. "Tell them I await their answer."

She knew the answer, though; she could see it in the glitter of their eyes and the smiles they tried so hard to hide. Astapor had thousands of eunuchs, and even more slave boys waiting to be cut, but there were only three living dragons in all the great wide world. *And the Ghiscari lust for dragons*. How could they not? Five times had Old Ghis contended with Valyria when the world was young, and five times gone down to bleak defeat. For the Freehold had dragons, and the Empire had none.

The oldest Grazdan stirred in his seat, and his pearls clacked together softly. "A dragon of our choice," he said in a thin, hard voice. "The black one is largest and healthiest."

"His name is Drogon." She nodded.

"All your goods, save your crown and your queenly raiment, which we will allow you to keep. The three ships. And Drogon."

"Done," she said, in the Common Tongue.

"Done," the old Grazdan answered in his thick Valyrian. The others echoed that old man of the pearl fringe. "Done," the slave girl translated, "and done, and done, eight times done."

"The Unsullied will learn your savage tongue quick enough," added Kraznys mo Nakloz, when all the arrangements had been made, "but until such time you will need a slave to speak to them. Take this one as our gift to you, a token of a bargain well struck."

"I shall," said Dany.

The slave girl rendered his words to her, and hers to him. If she had feelings about being given for a token, she took care not to let them show.

Arstan Whitebeard held his tongue as well, when Dany swept by him on the terrace. He followed her down the steps in silence, but she could hear his hardwood staff *tap tapping* on the red bricks as they went. She did not blame him for his fury. It was a wretched thing she did. *The Mother of Dragons has sold her strongest child*. Even the thought made her ill.

Yet down in the Plaza of Pride, standing on the hot red bricks between the slavers' pyramid and the barracks of the eunuchs, Dany turned on the old man. "Whitebeard," she said, "I want your counsel, and you should never fear to speak your mind with me . . . when we are alone. But *never* question me in front of strangers. Is that understood?"

"Yes, Your Grace," he said unhappily.

"I am not a child," she told him. "I am a queen."

"Yet even queens can err. The Astapori have cheated you, Your Grace. A dragon is worth more than any army. Aegon proved that three hundred years ago, upon the Field of Fire."

"I know what Aegon proved. I mean to prove a few things of my own." Dany turned away from him, to the slave girl standing meekly beside her litter. "Do you have a name, or must you draw a new one every day from some barrel?"

"That is only for Unsullied," the girl said. Then she realized the question had been asked in High Valyrian. Her eyes went wide. "Oh."

"Your name is Oh?"

"No. Your Grace, forgive this one her outburst. Your slave's name is Missandei, but . . ."

"Missandei is no longer a slave. I free you, from this instant. Come ride with me in the litter, I wish to talk." Rakharo helped them in, and Dany drew the curtains shut against the dust and heat. "If you stay with me you will serve as one of my handmaids," she said as they set off. "I shall keep you by my side to speak for me as you spoke for Kraznys. But you may leave my service whenever you choose, if you have father or mother you would sooner return to."

"This one will stay," the girl said. "This one . . . I . . . there is no place for me to go. This . . . I will serve you, gladly."

"I can give you freedom, but not safety," Dany warned. "I have a world to cross and wars to fight. You may go hungry. You may grow sick. You may be killed."

"*Valar morghulis,*" said Missandei, in High Valyrian.

"All men must die," Dany agreed, "but not for a long while, we may pray." She leaned back on the pillows and took the girl's hand. "Are these Unsullied truly fearless?"

"Yes, Your Grace."

"You serve me now. Is it true they feel no pain?"

"The wine of courage kills such feelings. By the time they slay their sucklings, they have been drinking it for years."

"And they are obedient?"

"Obedience is all they know. If you told them not to breathe, they would find that easier than not to obey."

Dany nodded. "And when I am done with them?"

"Your Grace?"

"When I have won my war and claimed the throne that was my father's, my knights will sheath their swords and return to their keeps, to their wives and children and mothers . . . to their *lives*. But these eunuchs have no lives. What am I to do with eight thousand eunuchs when there are no more battles to be fought?"

"The Unsullied make fine guards and excellent watchmen, Your Grace," said Missandei. "And it is never hard to find a buyer for such fine well-blooded troops."

"Men are not bought and sold in Westeros, they tell me."

"With all respect, Your Grace, Unsullied are not men."

"If I did resell them, how would I know they could not be used against me?" Dany asked pointedly. "Would they do that? Fight *against* me, even do me harm?"

"If their master commanded. They do not question, Your Grace. All the questions have been culled from them. They obey." She looked troubled. "When you are . . . when you are done with them . . . Your Grace might command them to fall upon their swords."

"And even that, they would do?"

"Yes." Missandei's voice had grown soft. "Your Grace."

Dany squeezed her hand. "You would sooner I did not ask it of them, though. Why is that? Why do you care?"

"This one does not . . . I . . . Your Grace . . ."

"Tell me."

The girl lowered her eyes. "Three of them were my brothers once, Your Grace."

Then I hope your brothers are as brave and clever as

you. Dany leaned back into her pillow, and let the litter bear her onward, back to *Balerion* one last time to set her world in order. *And back to Drogon*. Her mouth set grimly.

It was a long, dark, windy night that followed. Dany fed her dragons as she always did, but found she had no appetite herself. She cried a while, alone in her cabin, then dried her tears long enough for yet another argument with Groleo. "Magister Illyrio is not here," she finally had to tell him, "and if he was, he could not sway me either. I need the Unsullied more than I need these ships, and I will hear no more about it."

The anger burned the grief and fear from her, for a few hours at the least. Afterward she called her bloodriders to her cabin, with Ser Jorah. They were the only ones she truly trusted.

She meant to sleep afterward, to be well rested for the morrow, but an hour of restless tossing in the stuffy confines of the cabin soon convinced her that was hopeless. Outside her door she found Aggo fitting a new string to his bow by the light of a swinging oil lamp. Rakharo sat cross-legged on the deck beside him, sharpening his *arakh* with a whetstone. Dany told them both to keep on with what they were doing, and went up on deck for a taste of the cool night air. The crew left her alone as they went about their business, but Ser Jorah soon joined her by the rail. *He is never far*, Dany thought. *He knows my moods too well.*

"*Khaleesi*. You ought to be asleep. Tomorrow will be hot and hard, I promise you. You'll need your strength."

"Do you remember Eroeh?" she asked him.

"The Lhazareen girl?"

"They were raping her, but I stopped them and took her under my protection. Only when my sun-and-stars was dead Mago took her back, used her again, and killed her. Aggo said it was her fate."

"I remember," Ser Jorah said.

"I was alone for a long time, Jorah. All alone but for my brother. I was such a small scared thing. Viserys should have protected me, but instead he hurt me and scared me worse. He shouldn't have done that. He wasn't just my brother, he was my *king*. Why do the gods make kings and queens, if not to protect the ones who can't protect themselves?"

"Some kings make themselves. Robert did."

"He was no true king," Dany said scornfully. "He did no justice. Justice . . . that's what kings are *for*."

Ser Jorah had no answer. He only smiled, and touched her hair, so lightly. It was enough.

That night she dreamt that she was Rhaegar, riding to the Trident. But she was mounted on a dragon, not a horse. When she saw the Usurper's rebel host across the river they were armored all in ice, but she bathed them in dragonfire and they melted away like dew and turned the Trident into a torrent. Some small part of her knew that she was dreaming, but another part exulted. *This is how it was meant to be. The other was a nightmare, and I have only now awakened.*

If I look back I am lost, Dany told herself the next morning as she entered Astapor through the harbor gates. She dared not remind herself how small and insignificant her following truly was, or she would lose all courage. Today she rode her silver, clad in horsehair pants and painted leather vest, a bronze medallion belt about her waist and two more crossed between her breasts. Irri and Jhiqui had braided her hair and hung it with a tiny silver bell whose chime sang of the Undying of Qarth, burned in their Palace of Dust.

The red brick streets of Astapor were almost crowded this morning. Slaves and servants lined the ways, while the slavers and their women donned their *tokars* to look down from their stepped pyramids. *They are not so different from Qartheen after all*, she thought. *They want a glimpse of dragons to tell their children of, and their children's children*. It made her wonder how many of them would ever have children.

Aggo went before her with his great Dothraki bow. Strong Belwas walked to the right of her mare, the girl Missandei to her left. Ser Jorah Mormont was behind in mail and surcoat, glowering at anyone who came too near. Rakharo and Jhogo protected the litter. Dany had commanded that the top be removed, so her three dragons might be chained to the platform. Irri and Jhiqui rode with them, to try and keep them calm. Yet Viserion's tail lashed back and forth, and smoke rose angry from his nostrils. Rhaegal could sense something wrong as well. Thrice he tried to take wing, only to be pulled down by the heavy chain in Jhiqui's hand. Drogon only coiled into a ball, wings and tail tucked tight. Only the red glow of his eyes remained to tell that he was not asleep.

The rest of her people followed; Groleo and the other captains and their crews, and the eighty-three Dothraki who remained to her of the hundred thousand who had once ridden in Drogo's *khalasar*. She put the oldest and weakest on the inside of the column, with nursing women and those with child, and the little girls, and the boys too young to braid their hair. The rest—her warriors, such as they were—rode outrider and moved their dismal herd along, the hundred-odd gaunt horses who had survived both red waste and black salt sea.

I ought to have a banner sewn, she thought as she led her tattered band up across Astapor's meandering river. She closed her eyes for a moment, to imagine how it would look: all flowing black silk, and on it the red three-headed dragon of Targaryen, breathing golden flames. *A banner such as Rhaegar might have borne*. The river's banks were strangely tranquil. The Worm, the Astapori called the stream. It was wide and slow and crooked, dotted with tiny wooded islands. She glimpsed children playing on one of them, darting among elegant marble statues. On another island two lovers kissed in the shade of tall green trees, with no more shame than Dothraki at a wedding. Without clothing, she could not tell if they were slave or free.

The Plaza of Pride with its great bronze harpy was too confined a space to hold all the Unsullied she had bought. Instead they had been assembled in the Plaza of Punishment, fronting on Astapor's main gate, so they might be marched directly from the city once Daenerys had taken them in hand. There were no bronze statues here; only a great wooden platform where rebellious slaves were racked, and flayed, and hanged. "The Good Masters place them so they will be the first thing a new slave sees upon entering the city," Missandei told her as they came to the plaza.

At first glimpse, Dany thought for a moment that their skin was striped like the zorses of the Jogos Nhai. Then she rode her silver nearer and saw the raw red flesh beneath the crawling black stripes. *Flies. Flies and maggots.* The rebellious slaves had been peeled as a man might peel an apple, in a long curling strip. One man had an arm black with flies from fingers to elbow, and red and white beneath. Dany reined in beneath him. "What did this one do?" she demanded of Missandei.

"He raised a hand against his owner."

Her stomach roiling, Dany wheeled her silver about and trotted toward the center of the plaza, and the army she had bought so dear. Rank on rank on rank they stood, her stone halfmen with their hearts of brick; eight thousand and six hundred in the spiked bronze caps of fully trained Unsullied, and five thousand odd behind them, bareheaded, yet armed with spears and short swords. The ones furthest to the back were only boys, she saw, but they stood as straight and still as all the rest.

Kraznys mo Nakloz and his fellows were all there to greet her. Other well-born Astapori stood in knots behind them, sipping wine from silver flutes as slaves circulated among them with trays of olives and cherries and figs. The elder Grazdan sat in a sedan chair supported by four huge copper-skinned slaves. Half a dozen mounted lancers rode along the edges of the plaza, keeping back the crowds who had come to watch. The sun flashed blinding bright off the polished copper disks sewn to their cloaks, but she could not help but notice how nervous their horses seemed. *They fear the dragons. And well they ought.*

Kraznys had a slave help her down from her saddle. His own hands were full; one clutched his *tokar*, while the other held an ornate whip. "Here they are." He looked at Missandei. "Tell her they are hers . . . if she can pay."

"She can," the girl said.

Ser Jorah barked a command, and the trade goods were brought forward. Six bales of tiger skin, three hundred bolts of fine soft silk. Jars of saffron, jars of myrrh, jars of pepper and curry and cardamom, an onyx mask, twelve jade monkeys, casks of ink in red and black and green, a box of rare black amethysts, a box of pearls, a cask of pitted olives stuffed with maggots, a dozen casks of pickled cave fish, a great brass gong and a hammer to beat it with, seventeen ivory eyes, and a huge chest full of books written in tongues that Dany could not read. And more, and more, and more. Her people stacked it all before the slavers.

While the payment was being made, Kraznys mo Nakloz favored her with a few final words of counsel on the handling of her troops. "They are green as yet," he said through Missandei. "Tell the whore of Westeros she would be wise to blood them early. There are many small cities between here and there, cities ripe for sacking. Whatever plunder she takes will be hers alone. Unsullied have no lust for golds or gems. And should she take captives, a few guards will suffice to march them back to Astapor. We'll buy the healthy ones, and for a good price. And who knows? In ten years, some of the boys she sends us may be Unsullied in their turn. Thus all shall prosper."

Finally there were no more trade goods to add to the pile. Her Dothraki mounted their horses once more, and Dany said, "This was all we could carry. The rest awaits you on the ships, a great quantity of amber and wine and black rice. And you have the ships themselves. So all that remains is . . ."

". . . the dragon," finished the Grazdan with the spiked beard, who spoke the Common Tongue so thickly.

"And here he waits." Ser Jorah and Belwas walked beside her to the litter, where Drogon and his brothers lay basking in the sun. Jhiqui unfastened one end of the chain, and handed it down to her. When she gave a yank, the black dragon raised his head, hissing, and unfolded wings of night and scarlet. Kraznys mo Nakloz smiled broadly as their shadow fell across him.

Dany handed the slaver the end of Drogon's chain. In return he presented her with the whip. The handle was black dragonbone, elaborately carved and inlaid with gold. Nine long thin leather lashes trailed from it, each one tipped by a gilded claw. The gold pommel was a woman's head, with pointed ivory teeth. "The harpy's fingers," Kraznys named the scourge.

Dany turned the whip in her hand. *Such a light thing, to bear such weight* "Is it done, then? Do they belong to me?"

"It is done," he agreed, giving the chain a sharp pull to bring Drogon down from the litter.

Dany mounted her silver. She could feel her heart thumping in her chest. She felt desperately afraid. *Was this what my brother would have done?* She wondered if Prince Rhaegar had been this anxious when he saw the Usurper's host formed up across the Trident with all their banners floating on the wind.

She stood in her stirrups and raised the harpy's fingers above her head for all the Unsullied to see. *"It is done!"* she cried at the top of her lungs. *"You are mine!"* She gave the mare her heels and galloped up and down before the first rank, holding the fingers high. *"You are the dragon's now! You're bought and paid for! It is done! It is done!"*

She glimpsed old Grazdan turn his grey head sharply. *He hears me speak Valyrian*. The other slavers were not listening. They crowded around Kraznys and the dragon, shouting advice. Though the Astapori yanked and tugged, Drogon would not budge off the litter. Smoke rose grey from his open jaws, and his long neck curled and straightened as he snapped at the slaver's face.

It is time to cross the Trident, Dany thought, as she wheeled and rode her silver back. Her bloodriders moved in close around her. "You are in difficulty," she observed.

"He will not come," Kraznys said.

"There is a reason. A dragon is no slave." And Dany swept the lash down as hard as she could across the slaver's face. Kraznys screamed and staggered back, the blood running red down his cheeks into his perfumed beard. The harpy's fingers had torn his features half to pieces with one slash, but she did not pause to contemplate the ruin. "Drogon," she sang out loudly, sweetly, all her fear forgotten. "*Dracarys.*"

The black dragon spread his wings and roared.

A lance of swirling dark flame took Kraznys full in the face. His eyes melted and ran down his cheeks, and the oil in his hair and beard burst so fiercely into fire that for an instant the slaver wore a burning crown twice as tall as his head. The sudden stench of charred meat overwhelmed even his perfume, and his wail seemed to drown all other sound.

Then the Plaza of Punishment blew apart into blood and chaos. The Good Masters were shrieking, stumbling, shoving one another aside and tripping over the fringes of their *tokars* in their haste. Drogon flew almost lazily at Kraznys, black wings beating. As he gave the slaver another taste of fire, Irri and Jhiqui unchained Viserion and Rhaegal, and suddenly there were three dragons in the air. When Dany turned to look, a third of Astapor's proud demon-horned warriors were fighting to stay atop their terrified mounts, and another third were fleeing in a bright blaze of shiny copper. One man kept his saddle long enough to draw a sword, but Jhogo's whip coiled about his neck and cut off his shout. Another lost a hand to Rakharo's *arakh* and rode off reeling and spurting blood. Aggo sat calmly notching arrows to his bowstring and sending them at *tokars*. Silver, gold, or plain, he cared nothing for the fringe. Strong Belwas had his *arakh* out as well, and he spun it as he charged.

"*Spears!*" Dany heard one Astapori shout. It was Grazdan, old Grazdan in his *tokar* heavy with pearls. "*Unsullied*! Defend us, stop them, defend your masters! Spears! Swords!"

When Aggo put an arrow through his mouth, the slaves holding his sedan chair broke and ran, dumping him unceremoniously on the ground. The old man crawled to the first rank of eunuchs, his blood pooling on the bricks. The Unsullied did not so much as look down to watch him die. Rank on rank on rank, they stood.

And did not move. *The gods have heard my prayer.*

"*Unsullied*!" Dany galloped before them, her silver-gold braid flying behind her, her bell chiming with every stride. "Slay the Good Masters, slay the soldiers, slay every man who wears a *tokar* or holds a whip, but harm no child under twelve, and strike the chains off every slave you see." She raised the harpy's fingers in the air . . . and then she flung the scourge aside. "*Freedom!*" she sang out. "*Dracarys! Dracarys!*"

"*Dracarys!*" they shouted back, the sweetest word she'd ever heard. "*Dracarys! Dracarys!*" And all around them slavers ran and sobbed and begged and died, and the dusty air was filled with spears and fire.

The Raggle Taggle Gypsy-O

Michael Swanwick

*Michael Swanwick has a wild imagination that manifests itself in a continuous stream of fiction, both short and long. He has won and lost more awards than bear mentioning. His fine novels come out every three or four years—*In the Drift *(1984),* Vacuum Flowers *(1987),* Stations of the Tide *(1991),* The Iron Dragon's Daughter *(1993), and* Jack Faust *(1997). His new novel,* A Feast of Dinosaurs, *will be out in 2002. Each year or so recently he has published a tasty assortment of short stories and has written several delightful series of short-shorts. His new series, The Periodic Table of Science Fiction—one short-short for every known element, will appear once a week at The Infinite Matrix at http://infinite.matrix.net in 2001. In 2000, he had three new collections from small presses:* Moondogs *from NESFA Press,* Puck Aleshire's Abecedary *from Dragon Press, and* Tales of Old Earth *from Frog, Ltd.*

On the origins of this story, Swanwick says he was asked at a signing for a story for an anthology of ballad stories: "If you can come up with two elements that nobody could possibly fit into a ballad story, I'll give it a whack," he said. Driving home from the bookstore, he said to his wife Marianne, "Okay, the first element is dinosaurs. What's the second?" And without an instant's hesitation, she replied, "A picnic hamper full of dead puppies."

"I can WRITE this sucker!" he cried happily. And he did.

"The Raggle Taggle Gypsy-O" is a story reminiscent of the work of Roger Zelazny, particularly "Damnation Alley," with perhaps a bit of Michael Moorcock added. It appeared first in Tales of Old Earth. *Here Swanwick explores archetypes from a science fantasy standpoint, finding a mechanism by which people who are archetypes can live forever.*

Among twenty snowy mountains, the only moving thing was the eye of Crow. The sky was blue, and the air was cold. His beard was rimed with frost. The tangled road behind was black and dry and empty.

At last, satisfied that there was nobody coming after them, he put down his binoculars. The way down to the road was steep. He fell three times as he half pushed and half swam his way through the drifts. His truck waited for him, idling. He stamped his feet on the tarmac to clear the boot treads and climbed up on the cab.

Annie looked up as he opened the door. Her smile was warm and welcoming, but with just that little glint of man-fear first, brief as the green flash at sunset, gone so quickly you wouldn't see it if you didn't know to look. *That wasn't me, babe,* he wanted to tell her. *Nobody's ever going to hit you again.* But he said nothing. You could tell the goddamnedest lies, and who was there to stop you? Let her judge him by his deeds. Crow didn't much believe in words.

He sat down heavily, slamming the door. "Cold as hell out there," he commented. Then, "How are they doing?"

Annie shrugged. "They're hungry again."

"They're always hungry." But Crow pulled the wicker

picnic hamper out from under the seat anyway. He took out a dead puppy and pulled back the slide window at the rear of the cab. Then, with a snap of his wrist, he tossed the morsel into the van.

The monsters in the back began fighting over the puppy, slamming each other against the walls, roaring in mindless rage.

"Competitive buggers." He yanked the brake and put the truck into gear.

They had the heat cranked up high for the sake of their cargo, and after a few minutes he began to sweat. He pulled off his gloves, biting the fingertips and jerking back his head, and laid them on the dash, alongside his wool cap. Then he unbuttoned his coat.

"Gimme a hand here, willya?" Annie held the sleeve so he could draw out his arm. He leaned forward and she pulled the coat free and tossed it aside. "Thanks," he said.

Annie said nothing. Her hands went to his lap and unzipped his pants. Crow felt his pecker harden. She undid his belt and yanked down his BVDs. Her mouth closed upon him. The truck rattled underneath them.

"Hey, babe, that ain't really safe."

"Safe." Her hand squeezed him so hard he almost asked her to stop. But thought better of it. "I didn't hook up with a thug like you so I could be *safe*."

She ran her tongue down his shaft and began sucking on his nuts. Crow drew in his breath. What the hell, he figured, might as well go along for the ride. Only he'd still better keep an eye on the road. They were going down a series of switchbacks. Easy way to die.

He downshifted, and downshifted again.

It didn't take long before he spurted.

He came and groaned and stretched and felt inordinately happy. Annie's head came up from his lap. She was smiling impishly. He grinned back at her.

Then she mashed her face into his and was kissing him deeply, passionately, his jism salty on her tongue and her tongue sticky in his mouth, and he *couldn't see!* Terrified, he slammed his foot on the brake.

He was blind and out of control on one of the twistiest and most dangerous roads in the universe. The tires screamed.

He pushed Annie away from him so hard the back of her head bounced off the rider-side window. The truck's front wheels went off the road. Empty sky swung up to fill the windshield. In a frenzy, he swung the wheel so sharply he thought for a second they were going to overturn. There was a hideous *crunch* that sounded like part of the frame hitting rock, and then they were jolting safely down the road again.

"God damn," Crow said flatly. "Don't you ever do that again." He was shaking. "You're fucking crazy!" he added, more emphatically.

"Your fly is unzipped," Annie said, amused.

He hastily tucked himself in. "Crazy."

"You want crazy? You so much as look at another woman and I'll show you crazy." She opened the glove compartment and dug out her packet of Kents. "I'm just the girl for you, boyo, and don't you forget it." She lit up and then opened the window a crack for ventilation. Mentholated smoke filled the cabin.

In a companionable wordlessness they drove on through the snow and the blinding sunlight, the cab warm, the motor humming, and the monsters screaming at their back.

For maybe fifty miles he drove, while Annie drowsed in the seat beside him. Then the steering got stiff and the wheel began to moan under his hands whenever he turned it. It was a long, low, mournful sound like whale-song.

Without opening her eyes, Annie said, "What kind of weird-shit station are you listening to? Can't you get us something better?"

"Ain't no radio out here, babe. Remember where we are."

She opened her eyes. "So what is it, then?"

"Steering fluid's low. I think maybe we sprung a leak back down the road, when we almost went off."

"What are we going to do about it?"

"I'm not sure there's much we *can* do."

At which exact moment they turned a bend in the road and saw a gas station ahead. Two sets of pumps, diesel, air, a Mini-Mart, and a garage. Various machines of dubious functionality rusting out back.

Crow slammed on the brakes. "*That* shouldn't be there." He knew that for a fact. Last time he'd been through, the road had been empty all the way through to Troy.

Annie finally opened her eyes. They were the greenest things Crow had ever seen. They reminded him of sunlight through jungle leaves, of moss-covered cathedrals, of a stone city he'd once been to, sunk in the shallow waters of the Caribbean. That had been a dangerous place, but no more dangerous than this slim and lovely lady beside him. After a minute, she simply said, "Ask if they do repairs."

Crow pulled up in front of the garage and honked the horn a few times. A hound-lean mechanic came out, wiping his hands on a rag. "Yah?"

"Lissen, Ace, we got us a situation here with our steering column. Think you can fix us up?"

The mechanic stared at him, unblinking, and said, "We're all out of fluid. I'll take a look at your underside, though."

While the man was on a creeper under the truck, Crow went to the crapper. Then he ambled around back of the garage. There was a window there. He snapped the latch, climbed in, and poked around.

When he strolled up front again, the mechanic was out from under the truck and Annie was leaning against one of the pumps, flirting with him. He liked it, Crow could tell. Hell, even faggots liked it when Annie flirted at them.

Annie went off to the ladies' when he walked up, and by the time she came back the mechanic was inside again. She raised her eyebrows and Crow said, "Bastard says he can't fix the leak and ain't got no fluid. Only I boosted two cases out a window and stashed 'em in a junker out back. Go in and distract him, while I get them into the truck."

Annie thrust her hands deep into the pockets of her leather jacket and twisted slightly from foot to foot. "I've got a better thought," she said quietly. "Kill him."

"Say what?"

"He's one of Eric's people."

"You sure of that?"

"Ninety percent sure. He's here. What else could he be?"

"Yeah, well, there's still that other ten percent."

Her face was a mask. "Why take chances?"

"Jesus." Crow shook his head. "Babe, sometimes you give me the creeps. I don't mind admitting that you do."

"Do you love me? Then kill him."

"Hey. Forget that bullshit. We been together long enough, you must know what I'm like, okay? I ain't killing nobody today. Now go into the convenience there and buy us ten minutes, eh? Distract the man."

He turned her around and gave her a shove toward the Mini-Mart. Her shoulders were stiff with anger, her bottom big and round in those tight leather pants. God, but he loved the way she looked in those things! His hand ached to give her a swat on the rump, just to see her scamper. Couldn't do that with Annie, though. Not now, not never. Just one more thing that bastard Eric had spoiled for others.

He had the truck loaded and the steering column topped up by the time Annie strode out of the Mini-Mart with a boom box and a stack of CDs. The mechanic trotted after her, toting up prices on a little pad. When he presented her with the total, she simply said, "Send the bill to my husband," and climbed into the cab.

With a curt, wordless nod, the man turned back toward the store.

"Got any more doubts?" Annie asked coldly.

Crow cursed. He'd killed men in his time, but it wasn't anything he was proud of. And never what you'd call murder. He slammed down the back of the seat, to access the storage compartment. All his few possessions were in there, and little enough they were for such a hard life as he'd led. Some spare clothes. A basket of trinkets he'd picked up along the way. His guns.

Forty miles down the road, Annie was still fuming. Abruptly, she turned and slammed Crow in the side with her fist. Hard. She had a good punch for a woman. Keeping one hand on the wheel, he half-turned and tried to seize her hands in one enormous fist. She continued hitting him in the chest and face until he managed to nab them both.

"What?" he demanded, angrily.

"You should have killed him."

"Three handfuls of gold nuggets, babe. I dug 'em out of the Yukon with my own mitts. That's enough money to keep anybody's mouth shut."

"Oh mercy God! Not one of Eric's men. Depend upon it, yon whoreson caitiff was on the phone the very instant you were out of his sight."

"You don't know that kind of cheap-jack hustler the way I do—" Crow began. Which was—he knew it the instant the words left his mouth—exactly the wrong thing to say to Annie. Her lips went thin and her eyes went hard. Her words were bitter and curt. Before he knew it, they were yelling at each other.

Finally he had no choice but to pull over, put the truck in park, and settle things right there on the front seat.

Afterwards, she put on a CD she liked, old ballads and shit, and kept on playing it over and over. One in particular made her smile at him, eyes sultry and full of love, whenever it came on.

It was upstairs downstairs the lady went
Put on her suit of leather-o
And there was a cry from around the door
She's away wi' the raggle taggle gypsy-o

To tell the truth, the music wasn't exactly to his taste. But that was what they liked back where Annie came from. She couldn't stand his music. Said it was just noise. But when he felt that smile and those eyes on him it was better than three nights in Tijuana with any other woman he'd ever met. So he didn't see any point in making a big thing out of it.

The wheel was starting to freeze up on them again. Crow was looking for a good place to pull off and dump in a few cans of fluid, when suddenly Annie shivered and sat up straight. She stared off into the distance, over the eternal mountains. "What is it?" he asked.

"I have a premonition."

"Of what?" He didn't much like her premonitions. They always came true.

"Something. Over there." She lifted her arm and pointed.

Two Basilisks lifted up over the mountains.

"Shit!"

He stepped on the gas. "Hold tight, babe. We're almost there. I think we can outrun 'em."

They came down the exit ramp with the steering column moaning and howling like a banshee. Crow had to put all his weight on the wheel to make it turn. Braking, he left the timeless lands.

And came out in Rome.

One instant they were on the exit ramps surrounded by lifeless mountains. The next they were pushing through narrow roads choked with donkey carts and toga-clad pedestrians. Crow brought the truck to a stop, and got out to add fluid.

The truck took up most of the road. People cursed and spat at him for being in their way. But nobody seemed to find anything unusual in the fact that he was driving an internal-combustion engine. They all took it in their stride.

It was wonderful how the timelines protected themselves against anachronisms by simply ignoring them. A theoretical physicist Crow had befriended in Babylon had called it "robust integrity." You could introduce the printing press into dynastic Egypt and six months later the device would be discarded and forgotten. Machine-gun the infant Charlemagne and within the year those who had been there would remember him having been stabbed. A century later every detail of his career as Emperor would be chronicled, documented, and revered, down to his dotage and death.

It hadn't made a lot of sense to Crow, but, "Live with it," the physicist had said, and staggered off in search of his great-great-five-hundred-times-great-grandmother with silver in his pocket and a demented gleam in his eye. So there it was.

Not an hour later, they arrived at the Coliseum and were sent around back to the tradesmen's entrance.

"*Ave,*" Crow said to the guard there. "I want to talk to one of the—hey, Annie, what's Latin for animal-wrangler?"

"Bestiarius."

"Yeah, that's it. Fella name of Carpophorus."

Carpophorus was delighted with his new pets. He watched eagerly as the truck was backed up to the cage. Two sparsores with grappling-hooks unlatched the truck doors and leaped back as eleven nightmares poured out of the truck. They were all teeth and claws and savage quickness. One of their number lay dead on the floor of the truck. Not bad for such a long haul.

"What are they?" Carpophorus asked, entranced.

"Deinonychi."

"'Terrible-claws,' eh? Well, they fit the bill, all right." He thrust an arm between the bars, and then leaped back, chuckling, as two of the lithe young carnivores sprang at it. "Fast, too. Oh, Marcus *will* be pleased!"

"I'm glad you like 'em. Listen, we got a little trouble here with our steering column . . ."

"Down that ramp, to the right. Follow the signs. Tell Flamma I sent you." He turned back to the deinonychi, and musingly said, "Should they fight hoplomachi? Or maybe dimachaeri?" Crow knew the terms; the former were warriors who fought in armor, the latter with two knives.

"Horses would be nice," a sparsore commented. "If you used andabatae, they'd be able to strike from above."

Carpophorus shook his head. "I have it! Those Norse bear-sarkers I've been saving for something special—what could be more special than this?"

It was a regular labyrinth under the Coliseum. They had everything down there: workshops, brothels, training rooms, even a garage. At the mention of Carpophorus' name, a mechanic dropped everything to check out their truck. They sat in the stands, munching on a head of lettuce and watching the gladiators practice. An hour later a slave came up to tell them it was fixed.

They bought a room at a tavern that evening and ordered the best meal in the house. Which turned out to be sow's udders stuffed with fried baby mice. They washed it down with a wine that tasted like turpentine and got drunk and screwed and fell asleep. At least, Annie did. Crow sat up for a time, thinking.

Was she going to wake up some morning in a cold barn or on a piss-stained mattress and miss her goose-down comforters, her satin sheets, and her liveried servants? She'd been nobility, after all, and the wife of a demiurge . . .

He hadn't meant to run off with anybody's wife. But when he and some buddies had showed up at Lord Eric's estates, intent upon their own plans, there Annie was. No man that liked women could look upon Annie and not want her. And Crow couldn't want something without trying to get it. Such was his nature—he couldn't alter it.

He'd met her in the gardens out by Lord Eric's menagerie. A minor tweak of the weather had been made, so that the drifts of snow were held back to make room for bright mounds of prehistoric orchids. "Th'art a ragged fellow indeed, sirrah," she'd said with cool amusement.

He'd come under guise of a musician at a time when Lord Eric was away for a few years monkeying with the physical constants of the universe or some such bullshit. The dinosaurs had been his target from the first, though he wasn't above boffing the boss's lady on the way out. But something about her made him want her for more than just the night. Then and there he swore to himself that he'd win her, fair and without deceit, and on his own terms. "These ain't rags, babe," he'd said, hooking his thumbs into his belt. "They're my colors."

They stayed in Rome for a week, and they didn't go to watch the games, though Annie—who was born in an era whose idea of entertainment included public executions and bear-baitings—wanted to. But the deinonychi were by all accounts a hit. Afterwards, they collected their reward in the form of silver bars, "as many," Carpophorus gleefully quoted his sponsor, Marcus, as saying, "as the suspension of their truck will bear."

Marcus was a rich man from a good family and had political ambitions. Crow happened to know he'd be dead within the month, but he didn't bother mentioning the fact. Leave well enough alone, was his motto.

"Why did we wait around," Annie wanted to know afterwards, "if we weren't going to watch?"

"To make sure it actually happened. Eric can't come in now and snatch back his dinos without creating a serious line paradox. As I read it, that's considered bad form for a Lord of Creation." They were on the streets of Rome again, slowed to a crawl by the density of human traffic. Crow leaned on the horn again and again.

They made a right turn and then another, and then the traffic was gone. Crow threw the transmission into second and stepped on the accelerator. They were back among the Mountains of Eternity. From here they could reach any historical era and even, should they wish, the vast stretches of time that came before and after. All the roads were clear, and there was nothing in their way.

Less than a month later, subjective time, they were biking down that same road, arguing. Annie was lobbying for him to get her a sidecar and Crow didn't think much of that idea at all.

"This here's my *hog*, goddamnit!" he explained. "I chopped her myself—you put a sidecar on it, it'll be all the fuck out of balance."

"Yeah, well, I hope you enjoy jerking off. Because my fucking ass is so goddamn sore that . . ."

He'd opened up the throttle to drown out what she was about to say when suddenly Annie was pounding on his back, screaming, "Pull over!"

Crow was still braking the Harley when she leaned over to the side and began to puke.

When she was done, Crow dug a Schlitz out of the saddlebags and popped the tab. Shakily, she accepted it. "What was it?" he asked.

Annie gargled and spat out the beer. "Another premonition—a muckle bad one, I trow." Then, "Hey. Who do I have to fuck to get a smoke around here?"

Crow lit up a Kent for her.

Midway through the cigarette, she shuddered again and went rigid. Her pupils shrank to pinpricks, and her eyes turned up in their sockets, so they were almost entirely white. The sort of thing that would've gotten her burned for a witch, back in good old sixteenth-c England.

She raised a hand, pointing. "Incoming. Five of them."

They were ugly fuckers, the Basilisks were: black, unornamented two-rotor jobs, and noisy too. You could hear them miles off.

Luckily, Annie's foresight had given Crow the time to pick out a good defensive position. Cliff face to their back, rocks to crouch behind, enough of an overhang they couldn't try anything from above. Enough room to stash the bike, just in case they came out of this one alive. There was a long, empty slope before them. Their pursuers would have to come running up it.

The formation of Basilisks thundered closer.

"Pay attention, babe," Crow said. "I'm gonna teach you a little guerrilla warfare."

He got out his rifle from its saddle sheath. It was a Savage 110 Tactical. Good sniper rifle. He knew this gun. He'd packed the shells himself. It was a reliable piece of machinery.

"This here's a trick I learned in a little jungle war you probably ain't never heard of. Hold out your thumb at arm's length, okay? Now you wait until the helicopter's as big as the thumb. That's when it's close enough you can shoot it down."

"Will that work?" she asked nervously.

"Hell, if the Cong could do it, so can I."

He took out three Basilisks before the others could sweep up and around and out of range again. It was damned fine shooting if he did say so himself. But then the survivors set down in the distant snow and disgorged at least thirty armed men. Which changed the odds somewhat.

Annie counted soldiers, and quietly said, "Crow . . ."

Crow held a finger to her lips.

"Don't you worry none about *me*. I'm a trickster, babe. I'm archetypal. Ain't none of them can touch the Man."

Annie kissed his finger and squeezed his hand. But by the look in her eyes, he could tell she knew he was lying. "They can make you suffer, though," she said. "Eric has an old enemy staked to a rock back at his estates. Vultures come and eat his intestines."

"That's his brother, actually." It was an ugly story, and he was just as glad when she didn't ask him to elaborate. "Hunker down, now. Here they come."

The troops came scattershot up the slope, running raggedly from cover to cover. Very professional. Crow settled himself down on his elbows, and raised his rifle. Not much wind. On a day like today, he ought to be able to hit a man at five hundred yards ten times out of ten. "Kiss your asses good-bye," he muttered.

He figured he'd take out half of them before they got close enough to throw a stasis grenade.

Lord Eric was a well-made man, tall and full of grace. He had the glint of power to him, was bold and fair of face. A touch of lace was at his wrist. His shirt was finest silk.

"Lady Anne," he said.

"Lord Eric."

"I have come to restore you to your home and station: to your lands, estates, gracious powers, and wide holdings. As well as to the bed of your devoted husband." His chariot rested in the snow behind him; he'd waited until all the dirty work was done before showing up.

"You are no longer my husband. I have cast my fortune with a better man than thou."

"That gypsy?" He afforded Crow the briefest and most dismissive of glances. " 'Tis no more than a common thief, scarce worth the hemp to hang him, the wood to burn him, the water to drown him, nor the earth to bury him. Yet he has made free with a someat trifle that is mine and mine alone to depose—I speak of your honor. So he must die. He must die, and thou be brought to heel, as obedient to my hand as my hawk, my hound, or my horse."

She spat at his feet. "Eat shit, asshole."

Lord Eric's elegant face went white. He drew back his fist to strike her.

Crow's hands were cuffed behind his back, and he couldn't free them. So he lurched suddenly forward, catching his captors and Eric by surprise, and took the blow on his own face. That sucker hurt, but he didn't let it show. With the biggest, meanest grin he could manage, he said, "See, there's the difference between you and me. You couldn't stop yourself from hurting her. I could."

"Think you so?" Lord Eric gestured and one of his men handed him a pair of grey kid gloves of finest Spanish leather. "I raised a mortal above her state. Four hundred years was she my consort. No more."

Fear entered Annie's eyes for the first time, though nobody who knew her less well than Crow could have told.

"I will strangle her myself," Eric said, pulling on the gloves. "She deserves no less honor, for she was once my wife."

The tiger cage was set up on a low dais, one focus of the large, oval room. Crow knew from tiger cages, but he'd never thought he'd wind up in one. Especially not in the middle of somebody's party.

Especially not at Annie's wake.

The living room was filled with demiurges and light laughter, cocaine and gin. Old Tezcatlipoca, who had been as good as a father to Crow in his time, seeing him, grimaced and shook his head. Now Crow regretted ever getting involved with Spaniards, however sensible an idea it had seemed at the time.

The powers and godlings who orbited the party, cocktails in hand, solitary and aloof as planets, included Lady Dale, who bestowed riches with one hand and lightnings from the other, and had a grudge against Crow for stealing her distaff; Lord Aubrey of the short and happy lives, who hated him for the sake of a friend; Lady Siff of the flames, whose attentions he had once scorned; and Reverend Wednesday, old father death himself, in clerical collar, stiff with disapproval at Crow's libertine ways.

He had no allies anywhere in this room.

Over there was Lord Taleisin, the demiurge of music, who, possibly alone of all this glittering assemblage, bore Crow no ill will. Crow figured it was because Tal had never learned the truth behind that business back in Crete.

He figured, too, there must be some way to turn that to his advantage.

"You look away from me every time I go by," Lord Taleisin said. "Yet I know of no offense you have given me, or I you."

"Just wanted to get your attention is all," Crow said. "Without any of the others suspecting it." His brow was set in angry lines but his words were soft and mild. "I been thinking about how I came to be. I mean, you guys are simply *there*, a part of the natural order of things. But us archetypes are created out of a million years of campfire tales and wishful lies. We're thrown up out of the collective unconscious. I got to wondering what would happen if somebody with access to that unconscious—you, for example—was to plant a few songs here and there."

"It could be done, possibly. Nothing's certain. But what would be the point?"

"How'd you like your brother's heart in a box?"

Lord Tal smiled urbanely. "Eric and I may not see eye to eye on everything, yet I cannot claim to hate him so as to wish the physical universe rendered uninhabitable."

"Not him. Your other brother."

Tal involuntarily glanced over his shoulder, toward the distant mountain, where a small dark figure lay tormented by vultures. The house had been built here with just that view in mind. "If it could be done, don't you think I'd've done it?" Leaving unsaid but understood: *How could you succeed where I have failed?*

"I'm the trickster, babe—remember? I'm the wild card, the unpredictable element, the unexpected event. I'm the blackfly under the saddle. I'm the ice on the O-rings. I am the *only* one who could do this for you."

Very quietly, Lord Taleisin said, "What sureties do you require?"

"Your word's good enough for me, pal. Just don't forget to spit in my face before you leave. It'll look better."

"Have fun," Lord Eric said, and left the room.

Eric's men worked Crow over good. They broke his ribs and kicked in his face. A couple of times they had to stop to get their breath back, they were laboring so hard. He had to give them credit, they put their backs into the work. But, like Crow himself, the entertainment was too boorish for its audience. Long before it was done, most of the partyers had left in boredom or disgust.

At last he groaned, and he died.

Well, what was a little thing like death to somebody like Crow? He was archetypal—the universe demanded that he exist. Kill him here-and-now and he'd be reborn there-and-then. It wouldn't be long before he was up and around again.

But not Annie.

No, that was the bitch of the thing. Annie was dead, and the odds were good she wasn't coming back.

Among twenty smog-choked cities, the only still thing was the eye of Crow. He leaned back, arms crossed, in the saddle of his Harley, staring at a certain door so hard he was almost surprised his gaze didn't burn a hole in it.

A martlet flew down from the sky and perched on the handlebars. It was a little bird, round-headed and short-beaked, with long sharp wings. It eyes were two stars shining. "Hail!" it said.

"Hail, fire, and damnation," Crow growled. "Any results?"

"Lord Taleisin has done as you required, and salted the timelines with songs. In London, Nashville, and Azul-Tlon do they praise her beauty, and the steadfastness of her love. In a hundred guises and a thousand names is she exalted. From mammoth-bone medicine lodges to MTVirtual, they sing of Lady Anne, of the love that sacrifices all comfort, and of the price she gladly paid for it."

Still the door did not open.

"That's not what I asked, shit-for-brains. Did it work?"

"Perhaps." The bird cocked its head. "Perhaps not. I was told to caution you: Even at best, you will only have a now-and-again lady. Archetypes don't travel in pairs. If it works, your meetings will be like solar eclipses—primal, powerful, rare, and brief."

"Yeah, yeah."

The creature hesitated, and if a bird could be said to

look abashed, then it looked strangely abashed. "I was also told that you would have something for me."

Without looking, Crow unstrapped his saddlebag and rummaged within. He removed a wooden heart-shaped box, tied up in string. "Here."

With a glorious burst of unearthly song, the martlet seized the string in its talons and, wings whirring, flew straight up into the sky. Crow did not look after it. He waited.

He waited until he was sure that the door would never open. Then he waited some more.

The door opened.

Out she came, in faded Levis, leather flight jacket, and a black halter top, sucking on a Kent menthol. She was looking as beautiful as the morning and as hard as nails. The sidewalk cringed under her high-heeled boots.

"Hey, babe," Crow said casually. "I got you a sidecar. See? It's lined with velvet and everything."

"Fuck that noise," Annie said and, climbing on behind him, hugged him so hard that his ribs creaked.

He kick-started the Harley and with a roar they pulled out into traffic. Crow cranked up the engine and popped a wheelie. Off they sped, down the road that leads everywhere and nowhere, to the past and the future, Tokyo and Short Pump, infinity and the corner store, with Annie laughing and unafraid, and Crow flying the black flag of himself.

Ebb Tide

Sarah Singleton

Sarah Singleton grew up in rural Northamptonshire and holds an honors degree in English Literature and Language from the University of Nottingham. She traveled in Europe, India, and Nepal, and worked variously with horses, in a chocolate shop, as a factory operative, and a chambermaid in Germany, before becoming a journalist. In 1993 she married Brian Hoare, and they have two young daughters. While Singleton was a full-time parent she wrote a novel, The Crow Maiden, *to be published in 2001, and is also the author of* In the Mirror *(Enigmatic Novellas #4), reprinted in 2001. She has had short stories published in* QWF *magazine,* Enigmatic Tales, *and* Interzone, *and is working on her next novel. Now she lives in Chippenham, "in beautiful, mystic Wiltshire," and works as a senior reporter for the* Wiltshire Gazette & Herald, *campaigns with a local human rights group, and is learning to play the violin.*

"Ebb Tide" she writes, "reflects my abiding curiosity in the ordinariness of the strange, and the strangeness of the ordinary. I am intrigued by the way in which we embroider seemingly random events into the stories that make up our lives." "Ebb Tide" appeared in Interzone, *which publishes much distinguished fantasy fiction as well as SF. It is a complex story of cryptozoology—the study of obscure creatures that may or may not exist—that subtly examines how what people want to see colors their perceptions. It begins in that most primordial and psychologically sugges-*

tive of all settings: on the beach. A young man discovers some fascinating remains that have washed up. We feel a sense of déjà vu: I've had this dream or I've done this. And then the story takes turns into places most of us haven't been.

He ran along the lane, through the gloomy cloister of beech and hawthorn. Up, and up, leaping choked puddles and soft pockets of mud. At the clifftop, he burst from the dim, dank woodland onto bald rock, overlooking the grey sweep of the sea and the blue-grey mantle of sky. The wind rose, a cold tongue on the perspiration soaking his shirt. Then he skipped off again, scrabbling down the stony lane through the rock, to the village folded away at the root of the valley, at the edge of the sea.

At the top of the village, Jake knocked on the door of a cottage.

"Mr. Ainslie. Mr. Ainslie!" He stepped back from the doorstep. The little window was dark. Jake choked on frustration. He stamped his foot on the path, and dug his nails into the palm of his hand.

"Mr. Ainslie!" he shouted again, on the verge of tears. At the side of the cottage, the gate latch clinked. A very tall, white-haired man peered out. He regarded Jake uneasily.

"What do you want? Is something the matter?"

"Mr. Ainslie. I . . . I found something. I thought you might . . ." Jake's face crumpled. The tide of excitement carrying him on the long, hard run to the house, that had prompted him, unthinking, to call on the old man, had ebbed away. Stranded, he struggled for words.

"I found something. On the beach. I came to tell you."

"What? What did you find?" Ainslie shut the gate. His shoulders were stooped, but he towered above Jake. He wore a neat tweed suit and a tie, a flat cap, and brown shoes, expensive and well-polished.

"What did you find?" he repeated.

"I..." Jake drew back. What had he seen? His hands trembled. The image blurred.

"A mermaid," he blurted. "A dead mermaid. On the rocks, in the next cove. I think it was a mermaid. It was. It was, I'm sure." He could hear the drumming of his pulse.

"It was," he repeated. "I ran all the way here. To tell you."

Ainslie didn't speak. Cautiously, Jake raised his eyes from the old man's brown shoes.

"I see," Ainslie said at last. He took off his glasses and pressed his fingers against his eyes. "Will you show me?" he said, with a faint tremor in his voice. A posh accent. An old fashioned, upper class voice, like the English officers in black-and-white war films.

Ainslie collected his waxed jacket. His mind had jammed in a kind of seizure. Outside, the thin purple-haired youth was hopping about like a bird. A gawky, decorated boy, about 19, still a little childish. Ainslie tried to think. How did the boy know? Who had told him? Was this some kind of trick? Ainslie drew his glossy oak walking stick from the coat rack.

The boy led the way, along the footpath to the clifftop, through the wood, and down again the other side into the next cove. Last year's leaves patterned the drab mud underfoot. Although he was fit, Ainslie found it hard to keep pace with the boy, who hurried ahead, waited impatiently, then hurried ahead again.

The cove opened like a mouth in the cliff, a tongue of dun brown boulders licking the hem of the sea. The cliff stepped back unevenly, tenacious shrubs gripping the rock, suspended with roots dangling, as the land fell away, inch by precarious inch.

"This way, this way," the boy called, a crow in black, against the greys of the sea, sky and stone. He jumped lightly from rock to rock.

"Over here! It's here!" The boy waved his arms in the air. Ainslie looked about warily.

"Here. Look. See? I told you."

The mermaid had washed up into a rockpool, scooped like a bowl in a mound of glistening limestone, with leathery bladderwrack, soft pink anemones and pebbles. She lay half-submerged, face down, torso bobbing gently in the cold salt water, tail draped heavily across the rough stone. Ainslie took a deep breath. He stepped closer. He clapped his hand across his nose and mouth.

"Stinks, doesn't she?" the boy grinned. "Rotten fish. Been in the air too long."

Ainslie inhaled carefully, but he couldn't avoid the stench. He took out a white handkerchief from his pocket, to hold against his face. A large, round chunk had been bitten from the mermaid's tail. Inside the wound, the flesh was the colour of pearl, bloodless, jutting curved slivers of transparent bone. Suspended in the pool, the dark green streamers of her hair drifted in the seaweed.

"What's your name?" Ainslie asked the boy, who had picked up a curved antler of driftwood, smooth and brittle from the sea.

"Jake," the boy said. "Jake the Rake." He prodded the dense, inert mass of the mermaid's body with his stick.

"Don't do that!" Ainslie shot out.

Jake recoiled. Then he rallied. "She can't feel it. She's dead," and then sulky, "anyway, she's not yours, Mr. Ainslie. I found her."

Ainslie frowned. "Have you seen her face?"

Jake shook his head. His ears glittered with metal hoops. And he had a ring in his nose, and another in his eyebrow. Half a dozen pendants hung around his neck. Ainslie grimaced, despite himself. For a moment, the hapless boy with his distasteful body-piercings and coloured hair disturbed him far more than the fish-woman rotting at his feet.

"Will you help me turn her over?" Ainslie asked.

Jake pulled a face, suddenly squeamish. "Touch her? She's all smelly and slimy." Then he changed his mind. He hopped down from the rock.

"Grab her shoulders. Carefully. She's slippy. Don't bruise her on the rock." Ainslie stooped and slid his hands beneath her hips, where her body swelled into the fish-tail. His hands found no purchase, so he pushed against her with his chest and shoulders. The body flopped over. Patches of silver skin had torn from her tail, dried and stuck to the rock where she had lain so long. The boy cooed, gazing at her face.

"Let me see," Ainslie said. He leaned over, looking through the glinting surface of the pool to the face beneath the water. The eyes were gone. Pale flesh sockets, holes in her head where the fish had nibbled. A thin nose. Her mouth hung open, lipless, tongueless, a straight tunnel down into her body, lined with narrow barbs. Her breasts were very shallow, scales about the nipples. Torn, translucent fins jutted from her sides below the ribs. Her fingers were webbed, bleached white.

They sat upon the rocks near the body. The waves rose and fell. Jake fiddled with his stick, pattering a rhythm on the pebbles. What now? Mr. Ainslie gazed at the mermaid, lost in thought.

What now?

The question echoed in Jake's head. He assumed Mr. Ainslie would know the procedure—what should be done in such a case, who to contact. Mr. Ainslie collected curiosities from the beach. He walked for miles, everyone knew, looking for driftwood, shaped stones, fragments of coloured glass worn smooth by the sea. And other stuff too, which he gave to the village museum. Old fishing equipment, antique floats, ships in bottles, Ainslie's name inscribed on the information card underneath, "Kindly donated by . . ." But Mr. Ainslie seemed at a loss. He was staring out to sea, squinting in the sunshine.

"What now?" Jake said aloud, the words repeated in his mind so often they sounded absurd, spoken out.

Mr. Ainslie shifted, recalled to the present.

"Shouldn't we tell someone?" Jake said.

But Mr. Ainslie shook his head. "No such thing," he said. "Mermaids, that is. If we talk about it—we'll have the newspapers here, gawping and taking pictures. Then the police, the authorities. They'll take her away and they'll discover she's a fake. A hoax. The papers will explain, the fuss will die down, and that will be end of it."

Jake bit his lip. "So that's it?" he said. "A waste of time, me finding her?"

Mr. Ainslie turned impatiently. "No. Why is it a waste of time? You saw her. So did I. We know she's real. What does it matter about anyone else?"

"So what shall we do?"

"I think we should cover up the body. Protect it from seabirds. Make sure nobody else finds her. Then tomorrow morning, on the ebb tide, I'll bring a boat round, and we can take her out from the coast, a long way, and let the sea have her back."

Jake nodded, disappointed. He had expected something more. But what? Miraculous, this creature, lying on the rock, and he had discovered her. He wanted some kind of recognition. A party, or a celebration, events to flower out from the seed of his find. He wanted to explain, but Mr. Ainslie seemed gruff and distant.

So they moved the mermaid, working in concert, lifting her in the cradle of their arms, further away from the sea. Mr. Ainslie draped his coat upon the body, and this they carefully covered with stones. The burial took some time, and when at last the mermaid was obscured to the old man's satisfaction, the sun was low above the sea. They walked heavily back to the village. At the cottage, Mr. Ainslie paused on the doorstep, and asked Jake if he would like to come in for a drink and a wash. Jake hesitated, suddenly shy.

"No, it's okay. Thanks. I'd better be off. I'll see you tomorrow, yes?"

Then he was off, along the steep cobbled path, where the houses tottered down to the sea.

Ainslie shut the door. He washed his hands thoroughly, removing the rotten-fish taint from his skin. He splashed warm water onto his face. The cottage was very dim and quiet. Outside he could hear a gull's solitary screech and, distantly, the murmur of the sea.

He was shaken, deep down, to the roots. Time cheated. He had put so many years behind him and still the distant event rose up, as close as ever, like yesterday. Sitting by the sea he had wanted to speak—to tell Jake—but the words shrivelled in his throat, self-containment a habit of years. Too old to change. Not like the brazen, modern people, baring their souls, without dignity, tumbling out secrets and pains to their self-help groups, counsellors, television chat-show hosts.

He poured himself a whisky, and sat in the evening twilight. Fifty years, it had been. Half a century. Before even Jake's mother was born. And still, the memory was like a sore spot, to be poked.

He had been 28, not so much older than Jake, and lieutenant commander of *HMS Triton*, a submarine prowling the Norwegian coast, confined in the rumbling, metallic cold, stretches of sombre boredom salted with intervals of fighting and fear. Surfaced one morning, in the leached, bitter pre-dawn light, Ainslie was standing on the bridge when the *Triton* was fired on unexpectedly. A salvo of four. When the first torpedo passed, Ainslie recognized the hot shale-oil smell from the exhaust.

"That's one of ours!"

Another British submarine had mistaken the *Triton* for a German U-boat. The second and third torpedoes ploughed into the *Triton*, tearing a wound in its side. The greedy, icy water filled the submarine.

Ainslie fell into the sea's cold embrace, and the shock

knocked the sense from his body. Waves thrust salt fingers in his mouth and throat. Then—uncanny, lightless silence, the water closed above his head. Down, and down, into the sea's unfathomable darkness. His bright consciousness flared, a blaze of sunlit memories, then dwindled, close to snuffing out, when he heard a thin, unearthly singing. Long, arching strains, like the calling of whales. The echoes ribboned eerily through the water, almost tangible. Then Ainslie was lifted, his head thrust above the surface into the light and noise. He choked and coughed, gulping the burning air into his body. The waves beat him down, but something held him free of the sea's ravenous grip. Then he heard a shout. The other British sub. He'd been spotted. He was pulled from the water. The only survivor. When he looked back, a blurred white face appeared beneath the waves. A thin pearly hand lifted briefly, and then a glimpse of emerald, the smooth, shining flanks.

He was granted four weeks' leave. He stayed in the village, visiting his godfather who owned the run-down manor house at the top of the valley. A blazing June, the sunburnt children running and screeching by the sea, possible, almost, to forget about the war, with the fishing boats working as usual, and the food plentiful. But Ainslie wasn't ready for a holiday, watching women chatting and laughing in the dappled, rosy light beneath the trees, while the bodies of his comrades still drifted in the black Norwegian Sea. He walked for miles along the coast, by the sea's deceitful, tranquil blue, eyes upon the horizon, as though he might see the submarines, far out. He felt a peculiar hollow in his chest. Maybe in the final drowning moments, the sea had taken a part of him. Guilt needled, for allowing the *Triton* to be caught on the surface. For surviving.

Ainslie wandered in the heat across the shingle, a light breeze tugging the sleeves of his white shirt. She was sitting on a rock, combing her hair.

She had her back to him—a naked, slender back, skin white as milk. And curious silver-blonde hair, very long and thick, blowing in strands. Taken back, Ainslie halted and coughed decorously. He turned away, kicked noisily at a pebble, so the girl would be able to cover herself. But the image burned like a brand. He heard a laugh. He turned again. She was regarding him over her shoulder. The moment stretched. He knew he was reckoned handsome, with his heroic height and bright blue eyes. Once his photo had been printed on the front page of *The Times*. "*Triton* does it again!" He had found it hard to connect with the grave, clear-eyed young man in the picture. Now, seeing through the girl's eyes, he took possession of himself.

"Just a moment," she called. She bent over, retrieving a blouse which she buttoned on carelessly. She swung round two long legs, feet bare on the sunburnt beach. An unexpected desire flickered.

Julia was a London exile, working on a farm for a dour farmer and his hostile, suspicious wife. She told Ainslie about the heavy, physical toil, and the loneliness. The farm was four miles away from the village, so her valiant effort for the war had amounted to an indefinite sentence of utter isolation. Clearing ditches, cutting back the dense, overgrown hedgerows, and shovelling the stinking litter from the cowsheds. Ainslie didn't mention the *Triton*, and Julia did not elaborate upon her home life in London. For a few weeks, the shingle cove was an enchanted place, an enclosure cordoned away from the stream of life, and from the war. Whenever she could get away, Julia would meet him there. She shocked and delighted him, peeling off her clothes to spring into the sea. She flexed her muscles, boasting of her new strength. Her skin, sun-hot, tasted of stone and salt. When he lay upon her, his back burning and his face against her throat, her hair brushed against his shoulders, soft as feathers. Almost, he could forget the hollow space in his chest. Almost, the cold black seawater running in his veins warmed through.

Then abruptly, the charmed space closed. He was called back, to take charge of a new submarine, another iron coffin to bury him beneath the sea. He couldn't find Julia, to tell her he was leaving.

He took too many risks, and decorations. At the end of the war, visiting his godfather, he heard the tittle-tattle about the former land girls and their immoral ways. One locally, he learned, had been sent home in disgrace after giving illegitimate birth to a deformed child. A little boy, with his toes and fingers webbed like a fish. Stricken with horror, Ainslie tried to find her—Julia the needle in London's inestimable haystack. But Julia and his son had disappeared, just like the *Triton* and her crew. Obscurely Ainslie was afraid that the sea was exacting its due, that Julia had paid for his escape. He stayed in the navy. When he retired, nearly 20 years ago now, he moved to the village, waiting patiently at the ocean's hem.

Jack went to the Black Ship, half way down the cobbled street. In the bar, half a dozen weathered, grey-haired men had called in for a drink. The fishing trade had died away. In high season, the remaining seamen ran tourist pleasure trips around the coast, or tended the weekenders' brightly-coloured yachts. They stood at the bar, diminished and dispirited, resigned to their place at the tattered tail end of a fishing history.

"Who's this, then? What daft colour d'you call that?" one of the men gestured to Jake's hair. The others grinned. Jake had grown up around them. His efforts to alter and adorn himself amused rather than shocked, and Jake winced as he hurried past into the lounge where his own peers gathered. Jake the fake. He had to leave this godforsaken nowheresville, indeed he did, to forge a separate self, an individuality. Here he was a child still, a joke for the old fools. He heard them laugh again, from the far side of the bar.

Two fledgling bikers, kids in leather jackets and Iron Maiden t-shirts, sipped lager at a table in the lounge. In an alcove by the empty fireplace, a skinny, black-haired girl of 17 was gazing blankly about the room. She fiddled with a beer mat, turning it over and over. Then she drew out a packet of cigarettes and lit up, breathing out smoke in a long, bored sigh. She leaned forward, propping her elbows on the table. Silky, ebony tresses fell forward across her cheek.

"Hey, Jake," she said.

"Dawn, you okay?"

Dawn shrugged heavily. "Fed up. You know."

"You meeting someone?"

She shrugged again. Then some thought occurred, for momentarily her face brightened. She rummaged in the pocket of her velvet jacket.

"Look," she said, thrusting a creased flyer towards Jake. "The Dead Girls. They're playing in town tonight. Have you got any money? If you could lend me some, we could hitch in."

Briefly Jake's hopes rose, but he'd squandered his last coins on a half pint of beer.

"No," he said. "I'm broke."

They lapsed into silence, in the curls of cigarette smoke. Dawn folded the flyer. From a pool of shadow, she fixed her gaze on the window, as though it might open onto some more tempting prospect. Absent-minded, she brushed flecks of ash from her skirt. She ran her fingers through her hair, bored, but studiously elegant. And Jake was entranced, as ever.

The secret burned.

Like a hot coal in his pocket, like a treasure he'd foolishly agreed to cast back down into the earth and cover. The promise chafed. Somewhere, somehow, Ainslie's plan had a rightness, a dignity. But . . . but . . . what a gem, what a prize, to lay at the feet of the princess. Jake wrangled with his conscience. Dawn drew out another cigarette.

Finally, she stood up. On the brink of tears.

"I'm going home," she said, in a kind of violence. Jake hesitated for a moment. Then he dashed out after her, down the cobbled street. The houses rose darkly each side, the vista of the leaden sea filling the U in between.

"Dawn, Dawn, are you okay?" He caught her easily.

"What apart from being bored witless? Apart from feeling everything's happening without me? Well, yes, apart from that I am okay." Her voice was choked, and she looked away from him, to the sea.

"Dawn, I . . ." Jake began. He quivered. Something caught in his chest, an impediment he had to breach.

"Dawn, I . . ." he repeated.

"What?" she said sharply. She took a step away, her face now hostile, anticipating some unwelcome revelation of feelings.

"I found something you might want to see," he said in a rush. "Something exciting. And weird. You won't be bored, no, it's amazing. I'll show you."

"What?" she said again, curious now.

"A mermaid." He forced the words. For a moment, they hung in the air. The dim, deserted street seemed to tense, straining to hear. A flicker of hope in Dawn's face, then:

"Yeah. Sure, Jake. Go away, will you? Leave me alone." She turned away, scuffing the cobbles.

"Dawn, it's true. It's true, honestly, I swear. I'll take you there right now, I'll show you. A dead mermaid, we covered her with stones." He seized her arm, pulling her to a halt. Again, he was conscious of the words ringing out, the eerie sense of unseen listeners, and his own treachery.

"Where is it?" she said cautiously.

"In the next cove. Get a torch, I'll show you."

"You'd better be telling the truth Jake, or I'll never speak to you again."

But she hurried home and found a torch.

In the cove they could hear the boom of the waves, the rocks smooth and grey like mushrooms, in the torch's beam. Dawn moaned, about her soiled clothes, cold feet, twisted ankle. Jake hurried here and there, tense and anxious, trying to find the burial mound. In the isolated patches of illumination the cove was a puzzle of disconnected pieces. He hopped about, from stone to stone, frantically pulling at the pebbles.

Then—at last—he found it. A corner of Ainslie's waxed coat peeped from a pile of stones.

"Yes, yes, yes," he murmured, hefting the stones away.

"Dawn! Dawn! I've found it! Over here."

She hurried over. Reverently, Jake folded back the coat. The fetid stink rose from the body, the white face bleached in the torchlight. Jake pulled the coat right off, exposing the battered fish tail. Tiny beetles scuttled from the wound, in the electric glare.

"Well?" he said, at last. "I told you. Didn't I?"

Dawn crouched beside the mermaid. She stretched out her hand. Not quite daring to touch, the hand hovered above the dead face. Then, gingerly, she brushed the white cheek with her fingertips.

"Cold," she said gently. "She's beautiful. But very fishy too. A mermaid. A real mermaid." She repeated the phrase a few more times, as though she was nailing it down for herself, so it shouldn't slip away.

"We should've brought a camera," she said. "So people'll believe us. Just wait till we tell them!"

Jake felt a chill in his heart. The secret was leaking away.

"No," he said suddenly. "No, we mustn't tell anyone else. You mustn't. Tomorrow morning. Commander Ainslie and me, we're going to give her back to the sea."

Jake flicked the torch's beam from the mermaid to Dawn's face.

She shaded her eyes, blinded. "Don't! Stop it!"

He lowered the light.

Her face, half-lit, was puzzled and annoyed. "You can't," she said. "A real mermaid! We've got to tell people, so they'll believe too. We discovered her. We'll be in the papers. We'll be famous!"

Sensing her thoughts, Jake shared them. An unrolling sequence, of interviews, press photographs (he and Dawn together), a television appearance, hanging out with the Dead Girls . . . Being where it was at. Whatever "it" was. Life, the world. The Elsewhere everything seemed to happen.

Jake covered the mermaid. He replaced the stones carefully.

A milky mist drifted above the still, slaty surface of the sea. Ainslie rowed steadily, the dip and rise of the oars disturbing the silky water. Droplets glistened.

On the shore he could see the red flash of Jake's hairy

jumper. The boy was jumping up and down, impatient at the water's edge. He waved his arms and shouted, but Ainslie couldn't hear what he said. The tide was sinking, almost at its lowest point. Between the rocks in the cove and the sea's edge a stretch of sleek brown sand had opened. In the shallows, Ainslie jumped from the boat and heaved it out of the water.

"She's gone, Mr. Ainslie, she's gone." Jake danced about him, getting in the way.

Ainslie stood up slowly. "What?"

"The mermaid. She's gone. And it's all my fault. Oh my god, it's all my fault, I'm so sorry, Mr. Ainslie, you told me not to tell and I did, I'm sorry." Jake sat upon a rock with his head in his hands and wept, an unmanly, undisciplined, wretched little boy.

Unwilling as yet to digest this piece of news, Ainslie walked up the beach. Four metal stakes had been thrust into the ground, an orange plastic ribbon threaded between them. The mermaid had disappeared. Ainslie regarded the scene with chilly incomprehension, a kind of frozen grief. The empty space in his chest began to hurt.

High up, on the cliff-top, two uniformed figures looked down.

"Jake," Ainslie said quietly. "Get the boat in the water. They'll want to talk to us. To me. They'll have found my coat. I'm not ready, not right now. Get in."

"Oy! Wait there!" Seeing them make for the sea, a policeman called down. Ainslie jumped in the boat, and grabbed the oars. They pushed off and headed out to sea.

He rowed in silence for a while, till the shore receded, and the cove was one among many. Jake rubbed his eyes with his knuckles, his cheeks shiny with tears.

"I'm sorry," he said. Ainslie nodded. He felt very old and tired, just then, too weary to be angry. No wonder the boy had been so evasive and subdued, in the pale of dawn, when he'd bidden him walk to the cove, while he rowed the boat from the harbour.

The sun burned away the mist. The sea shone a dull silver, like a tarnished mirror.

The mermaid. A sign, a revelation. What had it proved? He remembered the long descent into the Norwegian Sea, the heat sucked from his body, the darkness. A mermaid had slipped her arms around him.

He shut his eyes, recalling the pressure of her hard, sinuous body against his chest and the seaweed drift of her hair on his face. She had borne him up, to the turbulent face of the sea. In the intervening years he had doubted this to be true. A dream of some kind, a fantasy conjured in the far reaches of his sinking mind, the vision of a drowning man. And then it had become an obsession, finding a proof of the mermaid, as though this improbable, inexplicable event was the key to all the other happenings—the sinking of the *Triton*, the wasted lives of the crew, the loss of Julia and his son. If a mermaid had risen from the depths to save his life . . . perhaps a providence of sorts was at work. Maybe a pattern could be drawn.

Except that it hadn't worked out that way. He had seen the dead mermaid, the unambiguous cold flesh. The eyeless face, the tail, the bones. And he hadn't been given an answer.

He looked up at Jake, who was sitting up straighter now, looking out at the sea in wonderment.

"Once, a mermaid kissed me," Ainslie said. Jake regarded him, eyes wide.

"When?"

And Ainslie told him. About the submarine, the attack from their own side, the breach in the *Triton*. As he spoke, he couldn't stop his eyes watering. Hot tears, burning his face.

"I bet it was frightening, trapped in a submarine. I'd hate it," Jake said.

Ainslie assented.

"You know," Jake went on, "old people—they're always saying we're no good. That they fought the war for us, and how ungrateful we are, and all that. It's not true. It isn't." His voice wavered, he struggled for the right words.

"It's like—those wars are in our bones. And there hasn't been a day of my life when there hasn't been a war going on, and every night on the news I see wars, and children killed, and cities bombed and all that. Sometimes I think we're always in the war. Sometimes I think it must have been good to know what side was the right one, to know what to fight for."

Ainslie looked at Jake, in his scarlet jumper, the jewellery twinkling in his nose and ears. He looked again, with a curious sense of compassion.

Peculiar, to be sitting in the little boat like this, adrift upon the spreading sea. The oars dipped, and lifted.

"I thought she'd poisoned me somehow, the mermaid," Ainslie said. "Some kind of pollution. I had a son once, you see. I never met him. I lost him. But they told me he had webbed fingers and toes."

To Ainslie's surprise, Jake erupted with laughter. Unsettling how quickly his mood could change, flitting from gravity to levity. Changeable, indeed, as the sea.

"Don't be silly!" Jake said. "Quite a few babies are born like that—some kind of development not working out properly before the baby's born. It runs in families. Look!" He held up his hand, displaying thin pink scars, like seams, running between his fingers.

"And my dad was the same," he added brightly. "Don't you know anything?"

Ainslie was taken aback. He thought for a moment, shaking his head. "There is a great deal I don't know," he admitted. "I'm an old man, Jake. And I'm worn out. Perhaps you could row?"

Jake jumped to his feet, rocking the boat. He fooled with the oars, splashing and making little headway. When Ainslie offered advice, Jake argued flamboyantly.

They made slow progress to the shore.

The Hunger of the Leaves

Joel Lane

Joel Lane lives in Birmingham, England, and is one of the more promising and accomplished fantasy writers to emerge in the UK in the 1990s. His short stories have appeared in a number of magazines and anthologies, including The Third Alternative, Fantasy Tales, Darklands, Little Deaths, Dark Terrors 4 and 5, White of the Moon, *and* Hideous Progeny. *His collection* The Earthwire and Other Stories *(1994) won a British Fantasy Award and was nominated for a World Fantasy Award. Lane's first novel,* From Blue to Black, *a post-punk music novel set in England in the early 1990s, was published in 2000. Lane is also the editor of* Beneath the Ground, *an anthology of subterranean horror stories to be released by Alchemy Press this year, and is currently working on a second novel,* Your Broken Face.

"The Hunger of the Leaves," a Zothique story after Clark Ashton Smith, appeared in the anthology Swords Against the Millennium, *edited by Mike Chinn and published by Alchemy Press—a nostalgic and dark-edged anthology of weird fantasies. He says the anthology "gave me an opportunity to pay tribute to the genius of Clark Ashton Smith, whose Zothique stories appeared in* Weird Tales *in the 1930s." In this innovative and uncanny story, atmospheric details become the antagonist.*

The forest realm of Yhadli occupied many miles of unpopulated terrain within the central lowlands of Zothique, the last of Earth's continents. It was rumoured to include the barren remains of towns and garrisons, abbeys and cemeteries, which the forest had reclaimed. None knew its full extent, since there were no longer any maps. No man living had seen its infamous ruler, the aged sorcerer Niil; if he still lived, he and his subjects had no need of the outside world. Like Zothique itself, the forest realm lived in a silence bound by the shadows of the past.

The three men passing from the twilit fields to the deeper gloom of the forest canopy were possessed of no desire to escape into a bygone time. Nor had they rejected such convivial pleasures as the violent towns of Ultarn and Acoxgrun had to offer to embrace the austere life of a hermit. Passing through these towns, they had heard tales of the great wealth of the sorcerer Niil: a wealth that must have been hoarded, since it had never been spent. It was a permanent harvest, with gold for wheat and jewels for berries. That harvest had been gathered through deeds of blood and terror that were already the stuff of grim legend. They intended to reap some portion of it through kidnap, robbery or simple theft. All three were experienced villains, with an acquired lack of scruples and imagination. Their evil repute in the regions of Tasuun and Xylac had forced them to come to a place where they were unknown—and thus, one which was unknown to them.

The forest was as quiet and still as a vast underground vault. In places, the faint red light of the Earth's dying sun played on complex traceries of black twigs, jagged leaves and bark mottled with pale lichen and mould. Cobwebs hung everywhere, fine and translucent like shrouds; but no spiders could be seen. Nor could any bird or beast be discerned in the tangled branches or the shadowy, yielding undergrowth. The dead leaves beneath the robbers' feet were of an unfamiliar kind: clawlike, with three hooked points and hard, reddish veins. As the thieves continued, the shadows thickened; soft tatters of cobweb clung unpleasantly to their sleeves. Soon they were forced to light torches in order to see where they were going. The paths were twisted, overgrown and impossible to follow. The torchlight distorted the shapes of the overhanging branches, made them resemble the faces of starving creatures or the intertwined bodies of human lovers in the grip of desire.

After nightfall, they took their direction from the northern star (which an ancient myth told them was a world much like their own). The nocturnal life of the forest seemed oddly subdued. No owl cried in the darkness; no bat swooped overhead. Even the lonely baying of wild hounds, thin demons that preyed on their former masters, was absent. The only sound was a faint, dry rustling, like the sand on a desert shore, only just distinguishable from silence.

At length, they came upon a small clearing where they might pause for the night. Jharscain and Dimela cut some twigs and branches; while Medarch prepared a small fire. By its light, they saw that another traveller had reached this place. Hanging from the twisted branches of a squat black tree was the wide, hooded robe of a monk. It was full of dead leaves, from which the pale glimmer of bones indicated the presence of a long-decayed cadaver. No rope held the skeleton in place, and the cause of death was not evident. His skull was packed with leaves, like the black thoughts of a madman; leaves clung to his ribs and pelvis, and to the inner surface of his ample robe. Beneath the dangling bones of his feet lay the dull shards of a broken wine flagon.

More imaginative souls might have deemed such grisly company unwelcome; but the thieves had lit a fire, and were loth to delay their rest. They ate of their spiced provisions, and drank deeply from a flask of the thrice-distilled spirit of grain. Jharscain raised his cup in ironic salute to their silent companion: 'Wilt thou not share a drink with us? Hath Mordiggian taken thy thirst along with thy throat and belly? But know this: we too are of his realm. We are merely in that earlier phase of death which we please to call life. What thou seest tonight, we too shall see in the red light of morning.'

They slept that night the deep sleep of drunkards, each man soaked in the light of his own visions. Jharscain dreamed of finding the house of the sorcerer Niil untenanted, and of gaining access to the treasures of his wine-cellar: wines so rich and fragrant, spirits so fiery and evocative, that they would shame even the abbeys of Puthuum. The dreaming soul of Dimela visited not the cellars of Niil, but his comfortable bedchamber, where it was entertained by the seven young women of the sorcerer's harem on sheets of the finest black silk. The dreams of Medarch had less of actual theft about them: he saw himself beside the ageing sorcerer as a valued servant, entrusted with the patient torture and execution of his master's enemies. And among those dying in blind, limbless, voiceless ruin were Dimela and Jharscain, wearing bright skins of blood.

In the morning, all three men had the furtive and bloodshot eyes of villains who had not slept well. Under the vacant gaze of the monk, they partook of a hasty breakfast and continued on their way. The ebon trees and their harvest of pale cobwebs showed no sign of thinning out; every step of the way had to be forced through damp undergrowth and drifts of leaves as brittle as fired clay. Repeatedly they passed the hanging skeletons or withered corpses of men in the trees, their loose clothing snagged on branches, dead leaves clamped to their skulls like sleeping bats; and this convinced them that the house of the sorcerer Niil could not be far away.

It was a day of twilight, fatigue and silent horror. The three men forged onward, certain that the house of Niil must be surrounded by widespread farming and habitation. However, they found no occupied houses, fields or gardens. The black trees and their spectral veils of cobweb held dominion over all. Yet this region had once been tenanted. Crumbling walls and broken flagstones could be glimpsed through the undergrowth. And everywhere, human skulls stared whitely from hoods of dead leaves. A house stood with its roof and front wall in ruins, three skeletons sitting at a table covered with the smaller bones of rats. A temple of carven stone lay in fragments, the skeleton of a small child on a rust-stained altar bearing witness to the sacred rituals of the priests of Thasaidon. Among the surface roots of a great tree, two almost fleshless cadavers lay in a permanent embrace that was no longer restrained by the boundaries of skin; a fine layer of cobweb surrounded them, like the sheet of a marriage bed. Most strange of all was a great well, ringed with black stone and deeper than Medarch could discern, yet full almost to the brim with clean-picked human bones.

This domain, Medarch realised, was more than abandoned: it was the scene of some terrible annihilation, and had been preserved as a bleak reliquary of the human race. The hideous soul of a mad poet had created this roofless vault as a symbol of the Earth and its place in a blind cosmos. What the people of Zothique knew in their fearful hearts was here proven. Medarch thought this and smiled within himself, but said nothing. For his soul was deeper than those of his companions. He was a murderer, where they were merely thieves. His parents had lived and died on the accursed isle of Uccastrog; and he had been delivered from his mother's womb by the jaws of a hound.

When the haze of reddish light beyond the trees turned

to illimitable blackness, clouds obscuring even the brightest stars, the three men stopped to light a fire and rest once more. They ate little, unsure of their destination; but drank deep of the spirit of grain, since a certain unease had come upon them. Jharscain, who was the most afraid, drank most deeply. They spoke little, but stared thoughtfully into the heart of the fire, where the twigs and branches were charred to a bonelike white. At length, they stamped out the fire and gave themselves up to sleep.

Jharscain slept poorly, troubled by a thirst that his previous intake had served only to intensify. The darkness itched at his eyes like a coarse fabric. Silently, he reached for the bag containing the vessel of grain liquor; with infinite care, he tilted it above his gaping mouth. Only a few precious mouthfuls remained. He fancied he could see the creeping denizens of the cobwebs, spinning fine threads to reach him; when he shut his eyes, he saw them still. A death-mask of perspiration covered his face. Then he heard a voice close by: 'Wilt thou not drink with us?' When he opened his eyes, he saw lights flickering just beyond the nearest trees.

As he staggered through the undergrowth toward the blurred lights, Jharscain heard the faint sounds of some terrific revel; wine was poured and gulped, voices were raised in drunken litany to Thasaidon. The very air seemed hazy with the fumes of wine. Around him, pale hands raised drinking-vessels and tipped them into faces of mist. The leaves shifted underfoot, and he fell to his knees. Dead leaves rose and drifted around him, their veins swollen with sweet-scented wine. But when a leaf touched his face, its thin flesh was dry as the driest paper. It stuck to his lips; as he raised a hand to pull it away, more leaves settled on his face. Where they touched him, his skin dried out; it shrivelled and broke, as if burned by the cold flame of sobriety. However much blood the leaves took from him, they remained as dry as bones in the desert.

Later in the night, Dimela stirred from his uneasy slumber. Was that a laugh he had heard: a sound bright with youthful vigour, yet strangely curdled with desire? Perhaps a hanging cobweb had fallen on him; it had felt as soft and clinging as a maiden's long hair. He had last savoured the pleasures of carnal love three nights before, at a debauched inn of the town known as Acoxgrun. Now loneliness rode on his back, and the darkness was faintly scented with the perfume of roses. A figure moved between the nearest trees, backlit by a distant fire: a silhouette whose contours were drawn by the hand of his needs. And now he could hear the crackling of the fire, and the voices of those who writhed and danced around it: whispering, pleading, laughing, sobbing, gasping. He could not see them clearly; yet he heard their message of joy and anguish. 'Wilt thou not dance with us?'

Tearing at his clothes, Dimela stumbled towards the blood-red fire. Though it appeared close, his steps brought it no closer. Eventually he stopped, confused; and a cloud of dead leaves rose gently around him, evading his outstretched arms to drift like patches of lonely skin upon his body. So overwhelming were his sensations that the loss of blood went unnoticed. The leaves that floated before Dimela's fading gaze bore the reddened imprint of faces transfigured by the secret fire of ecstasy. As his flesh joined with theirs, the night exposed the keen nakedness of bone. And so it began over again.

Medarch slept like a child until Dawn, twining about his thin fingers a cloth formerly used for strangling. The rumour of light that was sunrise in Zothique roused him and told him he was alone. His first thought was that the other two villains had abandoned him to continue their search for the house of Niil together. Then he saw that their shoulder-bags remained. Had they been taken by some wild beast of the nighted forest? But there was no sign of struggle, no blood on the dead leaves. Besides, what animal life had they seen in this crypt of shadows? Then a faint sound, as of choking breath or waterlogged footfalls, came from beyond the trees on the other side of the dead fire. Medarch gripped his dagger and crossed the ashes. Some cobwebs, he saw, had been torn aside; he stepped through the gap.

The body of Jharscain lay in a drift of leaves that half-covered him. The skin of his face was stretched like parchment over his skull, and was so dry that the corners of his mouth had torn into a hideous thin grimace. As Medarch watched, the cadaver's sere hands twitched mindlessly; and from the stretched parody of a mouth, a pale tongue emerged to lick the cracked and bloodless lips. A dead leaf moved on his throat with a horrible purpose, cutting into skin that was already as ravaged as that of a desiccated corpse in the deep catacombs of Naat. Despite his long and pleasurable experience of horror, Medarch felt a shiver pass through him. Raising his eyes, he saw a red blur through the veil of cobweb that linked two branches: a brighter red than that of the crepuscular daylight.

The body in the next glade was not recognisable as that of Dimela. It was a scattering crimson ruin, flayed and dismembered, at its centre a mound of leaves the size of a human head. A few items of clothing lay torn on the ground. Hands, eyes, lungs, bones and patches of skin crawled among the black leaves, somehow unable to die. They shuddered as if still infused by a common pulse. The three-pointed leaves clung to them in a terrible embrace, a slow dance that was truly the pleasure of the flesh. The odour of blood and decay was like a cloud in the chill air. Medarch was no innocent; but he was human, and this was an alien horror beyond his comprehension. Madness laughed and danced within his brain as he rushed on through the twilit forest, crashing through drifts of leaves and shrouds of tenantless cobweb, blind instinct driving him first in one direction and then in another. He no longer remembered what it was that he was searching for.

After hours of insane stumbling and circling, he came upon a part of the forest realm where the trees were bare and brittle like stone. The hanging cobwebs were corpse-grey, stained with the imprints of tormented faces. It was so cold here that Medarch's ragged breath formed tissue in the air. Memories floated before his eyes, random and meaningless: the dead and dying victims of his career. He had known many trades: mercenary in Tasuun, torturer in Naat, executioner in Cincor, jailer in Xylac. Among the scattered and frightened peoples of Zothique, warfare was vicious and perpetual. Crime and punishment were lucrative parallel trades, and the fate of prisoners was rarely a matter of public concern. It was not distressing for Medarch to recall the men, women and children he had mutilated; indeed, he kept a trunk full of dried souvenirs to help him remember his most cherished atrocities. Many times, when unable to torture within the law, he had found other means to procure young victims; and his knowledge of the ways of villains had opened many a secret and nighted door to him.

Yet, alone in the bleak forest realm of Yhadli, his sense of status deserted him; he could scarcely remember his own name. The ruined faces of his victims swam in a grey mist before him: nameless, voiceless, eyeless, hopeless. Their silence felt like mockery.

Eventually, sheer exhaustion brought the torturer to a standstill. His body was gashed and bruised from a thousand small injuries, and he had with him neither food nor water. The stark trees about him felt as cold as stone. The ground beneath his feet was slimy with leaf-mould and buried decay. Before him stood another ruined house, one different from the others they had passed: this one was made of wood, and had no windows. The black, dead twigs of the surrounding trees were woven into its dense roof. The walls were coated with layers of cobweb that glistened, rotting from within. He could discern no door in this unearthed tomb, until it opened.

The figure in the lightless doorway was like a monk, though thinner than any monk that Medarch had ever seen. He was clad in a black gown that clung to his bony frame. His hooded face was a shadow without features or skin; it was broken by countless fine cracks and wrinkles. It was a visage of dead leaves. Within it, two crimson eyes glowed with the cold distant fire of alien suns. Medarch felt those frozen eyes stare through him, dismissing him as if he were a ghost. A misshapen hand with three hooked fingers reached up to the door. And then the creature had gone, back into the darkness of its sealed house.

At once, Medarch knew that he had found the house of the sorcerer Niil, and that his offer of service had been rejected as of no value. A terrible breath of loneliness passed through him. At last, he understood why only the *dead* leaves were hungry. If Niil had ever been human, he was so no more. He was one with his realm of stillness and decay.

For a long time, the man who had dedicated his life to pain stood before the windowless abode of the creature for whom pain had no meaning. Then, as the weak sun bled into the western sky, Medarch set his face toward the distant towns of Ultarn and Acoxgrun. No longer running, but with steady and relentless steps, he made his way back to the abodes of men. The marks cut on his face by leaves and twigs bled freely, and decaying cobwebs tangled in his hair. It no longer mattered. Half-naked, filthy, bloody and red-eyed, Medarch strode forward to his destiny: to be the silent emissary of Niil throughout the continent of Zothique, and any other lands that might remain, until the legions of the dead lay scattered on the dying Earth like the fallen leaves of a splendid and fertile autumn.

Greedy Choke Puppy

Nalo Hopkinson

Nalo Hopkinson says, "I've lived in Toronto, Canada, since 1977, but spent most of my first 16 years in the Caribbean, where I was born. My writing reflects my hybrid reality." She studied with Judith Merril in Canada and attended the Clarion writing workshop in 1995. After publishing a few short stories, her first novel, Brown Girl in the Ring *(1998), won the Warner Aspect First Novel Contest and established her reputation as an important new fantasy writer. Her second novel,* Midnight Robber, *was published in 2000. Hopkinson recently edited the anthology* Whispers From the Cotton Tree Root: Caribbean Fabulist Fiction; *the anthology contains another fine story by Hopkinson, "Glass Bottle Trick." Her Web site is located at www.sff.net/people/nalo.*

This story appeared in Dark Matter, *a distinguished anthology of speculative fiction by black writers edited by Sheree Thomas. Hopkinson says: "I wrote the first draft of the story 'Greedy Choke Puppy' at Clarion in 1995. I've always been fascinated by the vampiric Caribbean tales of women who can turn into blood-sucking balls of fire. There's something I find tragic about those women. Some of my classmates thought the title sounded like it could be the name of a punk band, but it actually comes from a proverb, Craven choke puppy (A puppy that's greedy will choke)."*

"*I see a* Lagahoo last night. In the back of the house, behind the pigeon peas."

"Yes, Granny." Sitting cross-legged on the floor, Jacky leaned back against her grandmother's knees and closed her eyes in bliss against the gentle tug of Granny's hands braiding her hair. Jacky still enjoyed this evening ritual, even though she was a big hard-back woman, thirty-two years next month.

The moon was shining in through the open jalousie windows, bringing the sweet smell of Ladies-of-the-Night flowers with it. The ceiling fan beat its soothing rhythm.

"How you mean, 'Yes, Granny'? You even know what a Lagahoo is?"

"Don't you been frightening me with jumby story from since I small? Is a donkey with gold teeth, wearing a waistcoat with a pocket watch and two pair of tennis shoes on the hooves."

"Washekong, you mean. I never teach you to say 'tennis shoes.'"

Jacky smiled. "Yes, Granny. So, what the Lagahoo was doing in the pigeon peas patch?"

"Just standing, looking at my window. Then he pull out he watch chain from out he waistcoat pocket, and he look at the time, and he put the watch back, and he bite off some pigeon peas from off one bush, and he walk away."

Jacky laughed, shaking so hard that her head pulled free of Granny's hands. "You mean to tell me that a Lagahoo come all the way to we little house in Diego Martin, just to sample we so-so pigeon peas?" Still chuckling, she settled back against Granny's knees. Granny tugged at a hank of Jacky's hair, just a little harder than necessary.

Jacky could hear the smile in the old woman's voice. "Don't get fresh with me. You turn big woman now, Ph.D. student and thing, but is still your old nen-nen who does plait up your hair every evening, oui?"

"Yes, Granny. You know I does love to make mako 'pon you, to tease you a little."

"This ain't no joke, child. My mammy used to say that a Lagahoo is God horse, and when you see one, somebody go dead. The last time I see one is just before your mother dead." The two women fell silent. The memory hung in the air between them, of the badly burned body retrieved from the wreckage of the car that had gone off the road. Jacky knew that her grandmother would soon change the subject. She blamed herself for the argument that had sent Jacky's mother raging from the house in the first place. And whatever Granny didn't want to think about, she certainly wasn't going to talk about.

Granny sighed. "Well, don't fret, doux-doux. Just be careful when you go out so late at night. I couldn't stand to lose you, too."

She finished off the last braid and gently stroked Jacky's head. "All right. I finish now. Go and wrap up your head in a scarf, so the plaits will stay nice while you sleeping."

"Thank you, Granny. What I would do without you to help me make myself pretty for the gentlemen, eh?"

Granny smiled, but with a worried look on her face. "You just mind your studies. It have plenty of time to catch man."

Jacky stood and gave the old woman a kiss on one cool, soft cheek and headed toward her bedroom in search of a scarf. Behind her, she could hear Granny settling back into the faded wicker armchair, muttering distractedly to herself, "Why this Lagahoo come to bother me again, eh?"

The first time, I ain't know what was happening to me. I was younger them times there, and sweet for so, you see? Sweet like julie mango, with two ripe tot-tot on the front of my body and two ripe maami-apple behind. I only had was to walk down the street, twitching that maami-apple behind, and all the boys-them on the street corner would watch at me like them was starving, and I was food.

But I get to find out know how it is when the boys stop making sweet eye at you so much, and start watching after a next younger thing. I get to find out that when you pass you prime, and you ain't catch no man eye, nothing ain't left for you but to get old and dry-up like cane leaf in the fire. Is just so I was feeling that night. Like something wither-up. Like something that once used to drink in the feel of the sun on it skin, but now it dead and dry, and the sun only drying it out more. And the feeling make a burning in me belly, and the burning spread out to my skin, till I couldn't take it no more. I jump up from my little bed just so in the middle of the night, and snatch off my nightie. And when I do so, my skin come with it, and drop off on the floor. Inside my skin I was just one big ball of fire, and Lord, the night air feel nice and cool on the flame! I know then I was a soucouyant, a hag-woman. I know what I had was to do. When your youth start to leave you, you have to steal more from somebody who still have plenty. I fly out the window and start to search, search for a newborn baby.

"Lagahoo? You know where that word come from, ain't, Jacky?" asked Carmen Lewis, the librarian in the humanities section of the Library of the University of the West Indies. Carmen leaned back in her chair behind the information desk, legs sprawled under the bulge of her advanced pregnancy.

Carmen was a little older than Jacky. They had known each other since they were girls together at Saint Alban's Primary School. Carmen was always very interested in Jacky's research. "Is French creole for werewolf. Only we could come up with something as jokey as a were-donkey, oui? And as far as I know, it doesn't change into a human being. Why does your Granny think she saw one in the backyard?"

"You know Granny, Carmen. She sees all kinds of things, duppy and jumby and things like that. Remember the duppy stories she used to tell us when we were small, so we would be scared and mind what she said?"

Carmen laughed. "And the soucouyant, don't forget that." She smiled a strange smile. "It didn't really frighten me, though. I always wondered what it would be like to take your skin off, leave your worries behind, and fly so free."

"Well, you sit there so and wonder. I have to keep researching this paper. The back issues come in yet?"

"Right here." Sighing with the effort of bending over, Carmen reached under the desk and pulled out a stack of slim bound volumes of *Huracan*, a Caribbean literary journal that was now out of print. A smell of wormwood and age rose from them. In the 1940s, *Huracan* had published a series of issues on folktales. Jacky hoped that these would provide her with more research material.

"Thanks, Carmen." She picked up the volumes and looked around for somewhere to sit. There was an empty private carrel, but there was also a free space at one of the large study tables. Terry was sitting there, head bent over a fat textbook. The navy blue of his shirt suited his skin, made it glow like a newly unwrapped chocolate. Jacky smiled. She went over to the desk, tapped Terry on the shoulder. "I could sit beside you, Terry?"

Startled, he looked up to see who had interrupted him. His handsome face brightened with welcome. "Uh, sure, no problem. Let me get . . ." He leapt to pull out the chair for her, overturning his own in the process. At the crash, everyone in the library looked up. "Shit." He bent over to pick up the chair. His glasses fell from his face. Pens and pencils rained from his shirt pocket.

Jacky giggled. She put her books down, retrieved Terry's glasses just before he would have stepped on them. "Here." She put the spectacles onto his face, let the warmth of her fingertips linger briefly at his temples.

Terry stepped back, sat quickly in the chair, even though it was still at an odd angle from the table. He crossed one leg over the other. "Sorry," he muttered bashfully. He bent over, reaching awkwardly for the scattered pens and pencils.

"Don't fret, Terry. You just collect yourself and come and sit back down next to me." Jacky glowed with the feeling of triumph. Half an hour of studying beside him, and she knew she'd have a date for lunch. She sat, opened a copy of *Huracan*, and read:

> **Soucouyant/Ol'higue** (**Trinidad/Guyana**)
> Caribbean equivalent of the vampire myth. "Soucouyant," or "blood-sucker," derives from the French verb "sucer," to suck. "Ol' Higue" is the Guyanese creole expression for an old hag, or witch woman. The soucouyant is usually an old, evil-tempered woman who removes her skin at night, hides it, and then changes into a ball of fire. She flies through the air, searching for homes in which there are babies. She then enters the house through an open window or a keyhole, goes into the child's room, and sucks the life from its body. She may visit one child's bedside a number of times, draining a little more life each time, as the frantic parents search for a cure, and the child gets progressively weaker and finally dies. Or she may kill all at once.

The smell of the soup Granny was cooking made Jacky's mouth water. She sat at Granny's wobbly old kitchen table, tracing her fingers along a familiar burn, the one shaped like a handprint. The wooden table had been Granny's as long as Jacky could remember. Grandpa had made the table for Granny long before Jacky was born. Diabetes had finally been the death of him. Granny had brought only the kitchen table and her clothing with her when she moved in with Jacky and her mother.

Granny looked up from the cornmeal and flour dough she was kneading. "Like you idle, doux-doux," she said. She slid the bowl of dough over to Jacky. "Make the dumplings, then, nuh?"

Jacky took the bowl over to the stove, started pulling off pieces of dough and forming it into little cakes.

"Andrew make this table for me with he own two hand," Granny said.

"I know. You tell me already."

Granny ignored her. "Forty-two years we married, and every Sunday, I chop up the cabbage for the saltfish on this same table. Forty-two years we eat Sunday morning breakfast right here so. Saltfish and cabbage with a little small-leaf thyme from the back garden, and fry dumpling and cocoa-tea. I miss he too bad. You grandaddy did full up me life, make me feel young."

Jacky kept forming the dumplings for the soup. Granny came over to the stove and stirred the large pot with her wooden spoon. She blew on the spoon, cautiously tasted some of the liquid in it, and carefully floated a whole ripe Scotch Bonnet pepper on top of the bubbling mixture. "Jacky, when you put the dumpling-them in, don't break the pepper, all right? Otherwise this soup going to make we bawl tonight for pepper."

"Mm. Ain't Mummy used to help you make soup like this on a Saturday?"

"Yes, doux-doux. Just like this." Granny hobbled back to sit at the kitchen table. Tiny graying braids were escaping the confinement of her stiff black wig. Her knobby legs looked frail in their too-beige stockings. Like so many of the old women that Jacky knew, Granny always wore stockings rolled down below the hems of her worn flower print shifts. "I thought you was going out tonight," Granny said. "With Terry."

"We break up," Jacky replied bitterly. "He say he not ready to settle down." She dipped the spoon into the soup, raised it to her mouth, spat it out when it burned her mouth. "Backside!"

Granny watched, frowning. "Greedy puppy does choke. You mother did always taste straight from the hot stove, too. I was forever telling she to take time. You come in just like she, always in a hurry. Your eyes bigger than your stomach."

Jacky sucked in an irritable breath. "Granny, Carmen have a baby boy last night. Eight pounds, four ounces. Carmen make she first baby already. I past thirty years old, and I ain't find nobody yet."

"You will find, Jacky. But you can't hurry people so. Is how long you and Terry did stepping out?"

Jacky didn't respond.

"Eh, Jacky? How long?"

"Almost a month."

"Is scarcely two weeks, Jacky, don't lie to me. The boy barely learn where to find your house, and you was pestering he to settle down already. Me and your grandfather court for two years before we went to Parson to marry we."

When Granny started like this, she could go on for hours. Sullenly, Jacky began to drop the raw dumplings one by one into the fragrant, boiling soup.

"Child, you pretty, you have flirty ways, boys always coming and looking for you. You could pick and choose until you find the right one. Love will come. But take time. Love your studies, look out for your friends-them. Love your old Granny," she ended softly.

Hot tears rolled down Jacky's cheeks. She watched the dumplings bobbing back to the surface as they cooked; little warm, yellow suns.

"A new baby," Granny mused. "I must go and visit Carmen, take she some crab and callaloo to strengthen she blood. Hospital food does make you weak, oui."

I need more time, more life. I need a baby breath. Must wait till people sleeping, though. Nobody awake to see a fireball flying up from the bedroom window.

The skin only confining me. I could feel it getting old, binding me up inside it. Sometimes I does just feel to take it off and never put it back on again, oui?

Three A.M. *'Fore day morning. Only me and the duppies going to be out this late. Up from out of the narrow bed, slip off the nightie, slip off the skin.*

Oh, God, I does be so free like this! Hide the skin under the bed, and fly out the jalousie window. The night air cool, and I flying so high. I know how many people it have in each house, and who sleeping. I could feel them, skin-bag people, breathing out their life, one-one breath. I know where it have a new one, too: down on Vanderpool Lane. Yes, over here. Feel it, the new one, the baby. So much life in that little body.

Fly down low now, right against the ground. Every door have a crack, no matter how small.

Right here. Slip into the house. Turn back into a woman. Is a nasty feeling, walking around with no skin, wet flesh dripping onto the floor, but I get used to it after so many years.

Here. The baby bedroom. Hear the young breath heating up in he lungs, blowing out, wasting away. He ain't know how to use it; I go take it.

Nice baby boy, so fat. Drink, soucouyant. Suck in he warm, warm life. God, it sweet. It sweet can't done. It sweet.

No more? I drink all already? But what a way this baby dead fast!

Childbirth was once a risky thing for both mother and child. Even when they both survived the birth process, there were many unknown infectious diseases to which newborns were susceptible. Oliphant theorizes that the soucouyant lore was created in an attempt to explain infant deaths that would have seemed mysterious in more primitive times. Grieving parents could blame their loss on people who wished them ill. Women tend to have longer life spans than men, but in a superstitious age where life was hard

> and brief, old women in a community could seem sinister. It must have been easy to believe that the women were using sorcerous means to prolong their lives, and how better to do that than to steal the lifeblood of those who were very young?

Dozing, Jacky leaned against Granny's knees. Outside, the leaves of the julie mango tree rustled and sighed in the evening breeze. Granny tapped on Jacky's shoulder, passed her a folded section of newspaper with a column circled. *Births/Deaths.* Granny took a bitter pleasure in keeping track of who she'd outlived each week. Sleepily, Jacky focused on the words on the page:

> *Deceased: Raymond George Lewis, 5 days old, of natural causes. Son of Michael and Carmen, Diego Martin, Port of Spain. Funeral service 5:00 p.m. November 14, Church of the Holy Redeemer.*

"Jesus. Carmen's baby! But he was healthy, don't it?"

"I don't know, doux-doux. They say he just stop breathing in the night. Just so. What a sad thing. We must go to the funeral, pay we respects."

> Sunlight is fatal to the soucouyant. She must be back in her skin before daylight. In fact, the best way to discover a soucouyant is to find her skin, rub the raw side with hot pepper, and replace it in its hiding place. When she tries to put it back on, the pain of the burning pepper will cause the demon to cry out and reveal herself.

Me fire belly full, oui. When a new breath fueling the fire, I does feel good, like I could never die. And then I does fly and fly, high like the moon. Time to go back home now, though.

Eh-eh! Why she leave the back door cotch open? Never mind; she does be preoccupied sometimes. Maybe she just forget. Just fly in the bedroom window. I go close the door after I put on my skin again.

Ai! What itching me so? Is what happen to me skin? Ai! Lord, Lord, it burning, it burning too bad. It scratching me all over, like it have fire ants inside there. I can't stand it!

Hissing with pain, the soucouyant threw off her burning skin and stood flayed, dripping.

Calmly, Granny entered Jacky's room. Before Jacky could react, Granny picked up the Jacky-skin. She held it close to her body, threatening the skin with the sharp, wicked kitchen knife she held in her other hand. Her look was sorrowful.

"I know it was you, doux-doux. When I see the Lagahoo, I know what I have to do."

Jacky cursed and flared to fireball form. She rushed at Granny, but backed off as Granny made a feint at the skin with her knife.

"You stay right there and listen to me, Jacky. The soucouyant blood in all of we, all the women in we family."

You, too?

"Even me. We blood hot: hot for life, hot for youth. Loving does cool we down. Making life does cool we down."

Jacky raged. The ceiling blackened, began to smoke.

"I know how it go, doux-doux. When we lives empty, the hunger does turn to blood hunger. But it have plenty other kinds of loving, Jacky. Ain't I been telling you so? Love your work. Love people close to you. Love your life."

The fireball surged toward Granny. "No. Stay right there, you hear? Or I go chop this skin for you."

Granny backed out through the living room. The hissing ball of fire followed close, drawn by the precious skin in the old woman's hands.

"You never had no patience. Doux-doux, you is my life, but you can't kill so. That little child you drink, you don't hear it spirit when night come, bawling for Carmen and

Michael? I does weep to hear it. I try to tell you, like I try to tell you mother: Don't be greedy."

Granny had reached the back door. The open back door. The soucouyant made a desperate feint at Granny's knife arm, searing her right side from elbow to scalp. The smell of burnt flesh and hair filled the little kitchen, but though the old lady cried out, she wouldn't drop the knife. The pain in her voice was more than physical.

"You devil!" She backed out the door into the cobalt light of early morning. Gritting her teeth, she slashed the Jacky-skin into two ragged halves and flung it into the pigeon peas patch. Jacky shrieked and turned back into her flayed self. Numbly, she picked up her skin, tried with oozing fingers to put the torn edges back together.

"You and me is the last two," Granny said. "Your mami woulda make three, but I had to kill she, too, send my own flesh and blood into the sun. Is time, doux-doux. The Lagahoo calling you."

My skin! Granny, how you could do me so? Oh, God, morning coming already? Yes, could feel it, the sun calling to the fire in me.

Jacky threw the skin down again, leapt as a fireball into the brightening air. *I going, going, where I could burn clean, burn bright, and allyou could go to the Devil, oui!*

Fireball flying high to the sun, and oh, God, it burning, it burning, it burning!

Granny hobbled to the pigeon peas patch, wincing as she cradled her burnt right side. Tears trickled down her wrinkled face. She sobbed, "Why allyou must break my heart so?"

Painfully, she got down to her knees beside the ruined pieces of skin and placed one hand on them. She made her hand glow red hot, igniting her granddaughter's skin. It began to burn, crinkling and curling back on itself like bacon in a pan. Granny wrinkled her nose against the smell, but kept her hand on the smoking mass until there was nothing but ashes. Her hand faded back to its normal cocoa brown. Clambering to her feet again, she looked about her in the pigeon peas patch.

"I live to see the Lagahoo two time. Next time, God horse, you better be coming for me."

The Golem

Naomi Kritzer

Naomi Kritzer grew up in Madison, Wisconsin ("a domed lunar colony populated mostly by Ph.D.s"), and has lived in London and Nepal. Still in her twenties, she now resides in Minneapolis with her husband and daughter, Molly (born in September 2000). Before having a baby, she worked at the University of St. Thomas in St. Paul as a technical writer. For the time being, she opts for the more important job of parenting. Her first published story, "Faust's SASE," appeared in Scavengers Newsletter *in 1999. She has since published several stories, in* Tales of the Unanticipated *and in* Realms of Fantasy, *where this story appeared, including (in* Realms*) "Spirit Stone," an excellent fantasy about a teenage nomadic midwife. She is perhaps the most interesting and talented new fantasy writer to emerge in 2000. For Hanukkah, her husband bought her the domain name www.naomikritzer.com, where you can now find her Web site.*

"The Golem" is a meditation on fate, predestination, and loyalty. One of the themes that emerges from Holocaust literature is the importance of recognizing that people have choices even under the worst of circumstances. This story, with its resonant ending, extends that tradition. The golem of this story relies upon supernatural knowledge rather than supernatural strength. A lesser writer would perhaps have begun this story where Kritzer ends it.

The golem woke on December 1, 1941 to a cold wind. Prague smelled different than she remembered. She lay on the earth from which she'd been made, breathing in the scent of the new century—mud and sour garbage and gasoline fumes. Prague surrounded her like a machine that turned on a thousand notched wheels, spinning in the night toward a future that she could see like an unrolled scroll.

"Hanna, are we almost done? I think I hear someone coming."

"One more minute, Alena."

Her creators—women. How strange. That was, of course, why the golem was a woman as well. Hanna Lieben was the golem's creator; Alena Nebesky was Hanna's assistant. Hanna had seven months to live, the golem saw—she would die with Alena in June, in the vicious purges after the assassination of Reinhard Heydrich. The police would knock on their door at 4:17 P.M.; Hanna would shout, "Where are you taking her?" and be shot dead on the doorstep, one less Jew to deport to Terezin.

Which would mean that the golem should be free, if she could persuade Hanna not to destroy her before then.

It was time to sit up. She hoped that Hanna and Alena wouldn't run—she'd be able to find them, of course, but it was always a bad sign when her creator ran. Creators who were that fearful typically destroyed the golem within a week. At least she could take this slowly. No patrol would pass the Old Jewish Cemetery for one hour, six minutes, and forty-three seconds.

She tested her muscles and quietly cleared her throat. Everything seemed to work as expected; Hanna hadn't done anything stupid, like forgetting to give her a tongue.

Alena swung her head toward the golem. "What was that?"

The golem sat up slowly.

Alena sucked in her breath. Hanna stepped forward, as if to protect the taller woman. The golem could hear Hanna's heart beating like the wings of a trapped bird, but Hanna's face showed no trace of fear.

Good.

The golem stood up, a little unsteadily. She was Alena's height—a head taller than Hanna. Since her creators hadn't run, she took a moment to study them. Alena was not unusually tall, but Hanna was very short. She had vast dark eyes and tiny hands, like a child. A yellow Star of David was sewn to the left breast of her coat. Alena had ash-blonde hair and no star. The golem remembered that the two women had spoken Czech, not Yiddish, and realized with surprise that Hanna was Jewish, but Alena was not.

A gust of wind blew through the cemetery, and the golem felt the skin on her body rise into gooseflesh. Alena winced at the sight. Stepping around Hanna, she took off her coat. "Here," she said, holding it out.

The golem took the coat and stared at Alena, unsure what she was supposed to do with it.

"You're supposed to put it *on*," Alena said, slipping it around the golem's shoulders. "If we run into the police, we'll be in enough trouble with Hanna being out after curfew, never mind walking around with a naked woman."

The golem put the coat on and buttoned it. "Thank you," she said. Hanna started a little at the sound of the golem's voice.

Alena glanced at Hanna. "You could have suggested that I bring clothes for the golem."

Hanna blinked. "It's not in any of the stories."

Alena snorted and shook her head. "Weren't you the one who complained that all the stories were written by men?" She studied the golem again. "There's something familiar about your face," she said.

"Look in a mirror," Hanna said. "She could be your sister."

Alena looked again, and recoiled slightly. "Did you do that on purpose?"

"No," Hanna said. "I was working so quickly, she's lucky she has a nose."

There was a rustle somewhere in the darkness behind them, and Alena glanced over her shoulder. "Do we need to have this conversation in the cemetery?" she asked.

"No one will come here for one hour, one minute, and twenty-one seconds," the golem said.

"Maybe," Alena said. Her tone was doubtful. "But it's cold out here." She turned brusquely and strode toward the cemetery gate.

The gate was locked, of course; it was well after closing hours. Alena and Hanna had scrambled over the fence to get in, and they scrambled over it to get out. The golem helped them as well as she could; her previous bodies had been better suited to this sort of thing. Always before, she had possessed strength without knowledge; this time, she had knowledge, and little else. So she told them what she could—that they could take their time.

Hanna and Alena shared an apartment on Dlouhá street. They lived at the edge of Josefov, the old Jewish ghetto, in one of the oldest parts of Prague. Alena led the way up the stairs to the apartment, locking the door behind them quickly once they were inside. The front room was immaculate, without so much as an old newspaper on the floor. The two women actually lived in the back bedroom and the kitchen; the front room, the golem knew instantly, was for others to see.

"We tell people that Hanna is my maid," Alena said,

with a gesture toward the room. "Jews aren't supposed to share apartments with gentiles, unless they're married to one."

The back room was where all the clutter was—all of Hanna's possessions, and most of Alena's. Suitcases were stacked in the corner; one had burst open, spilling books onto the floor. An antique copy of the Talmud had been placed carefully on top of the stack; a copy of Freud's *The Future of an Illusion* lay beside a copy of Martin Buber's *I and Thou*. Tucked half-under the bottom suitcase was a copy of *The Autobiography of Alice B. Toklas*, by Gertrude Stein. There was another stack of books in the corner, all in Hebrew—the lore of the golem. The windows were covered with dark, heavy curtains.

Hanna checked the curtains as Alena lit the lamp, to be certain that they still covered the windows securely. Then Hanna hung up her coat and sat down. Alena rummaged through a heap of clothing draped over a chair, looking for a dress suitable for the golem.

The golem took off Alena's coat and hung it up beside Hanna's. "You called me, and I woke," she said. "For what purpose have you created me?"

Hanna turned to her, meeting her gaze without flinching. "For the same purpose as all the golems: to protect the Jews of Prague."

The golem felt the impossibility of the request sweep over her like rising floodwater. The machinery of death was already in motion around her. The Protectorate of Bohemia and Moravia was run by Reinhard Heydrich, the man who had built Dachau and enshrined the words *Arbeit Macht Frei* (work will set you free) over the gates. He had already begun deporting the Czech Jews to Terezin; the deportations would continue, taking 1,200 Jews each week until only a handful—the spouses or children of gentiles—remained. From Terezin, nearly all would ultimately be taken to Auschwitz or Treblinka to die.

The golem's voice was flat when she answered. "No one can protect the Jews of Prague." Hanna's eyes showed disbelief, so the golem continued. "Some will survive, but most will die. Terezin is just the pen outside the slaughterhouse."

"There must be something that can be done," Alena whispered. She had selected a dress from the pile; now it slipped from her hands.

The golem had opened her mouth to tell her no, there was nothing, but as the dress fluttered to the floor she hesitated. "There are things that can be done. Perhaps they will even do a little good. But there is nothing I can do to protect *all* the Jews of Prague, or even most. Or even many."

Four hundred years ago, Rabbi Löw had created the golem to protect the Jews against pogroms. Pogroms, in Prague and elsewhere, were typically fueled by blood libel—the story that the Jews murdered gentile children to make unleavened bread with their blood. When a young Christian woman disappeared, the hideous stories had surfaced like scum on a pond. Rabbi Löw had sent the golem out to look; the golem had hunted through the night, and found the girl alive, hidden away in a cellar. The golem had broken down the door and brought the girl to the Town Square for all to see. And so the Jews had been saved.

Unfortunately, Rabbi Löw had destroyed his creation shortly afterward. But at least that miracle had been relatively easy to accomplish.

Hanna picked up Alena's dress from where it had fallen. "Put this on," she said. "Even if you can't save us, there's plenty of work you can do."

The golem pulled the dress over her head and began to fasten the buttons.

"She needs a name," Hanna said. "We're going to have to introduce her to other people."

Alena looked her over. "We'll tell them she's my cousin, Margit."

"Doesn't Margit live in England?"

"Canada," Alena said. "But nobody in Prague knows that."

"Do you think Pavlik can arrange false papers for her?" Hanna asked.

"Papers won't be necessary," the golem said, straightening the skirt of the dress. "I will not be asked for them."

Hanna and Alena exchanged looks.

"Are you *sure*?" Alena asked.

"The police will pass by on the street outside in nine minutes and forty-three seconds," the golem said. "Watch, if you don't believe me."

Alena checked her watch and went to the front room to wait. Ten minutes later, she returned, raised one eyebrow, and nodded once.

"I guess she may be useful, after all," Hanna said.

Alena sent the golem to sleep on the couch in the unused living room. The golem did not need sleep, but lay down obediently and closed her eyes for the duration of the night. Very early, she heard footsteps and a faint, faint male voice, speaking Czech. She rose and went into the back bedroom. The voice was coming from the kitchen; she realized after a moment that it was a radio, turned down so as to be almost inaudible. "This is Radio Free Prague," the voice said.

Alena sat at the kitchen table, transcribing the radio broadcast in shorthand. Hanna cooked breakfast, making enough noise to cover the sound of the radio for any ears but the golem's. Alena nodded a greeting as the golem came in, then bent her head over her notes again.

The broadcast lasted for 45 minutes, then switched over to a different language. Hanna gave Alena a bowl of porridge, and Alena pushed the paper aside with a sigh, picking up her spoon. Hanna sat down, took out a separate piece of paper, and quickly transcribed the shorthand into a neat, readable script.

Alena looked up from her porridge to study the golem. "Do you eat?"

The golem shrugged. "I can eat, but I don't have to."

"Are you hungry?"

"No."

Alena still hesitated, and Hanna looked up from the transcript. "Don't be silly," Hanna said. "She doesn't need anything, so why waste the rations?"

Alena shrugged, and went back to eating. A few minutes later, Hanna finished the transcription. She blew on the ink to dry it, then folded the letter, put it in an envelope, sealed the envelope, and addressed it as if it were an ordinary letter. Then she held it out to the golem. "Take this to Vltavská 16. Do you know where that is?"

"Yes."

"Take this there and put it into the mail slot. If anybody asks your name, say that you're Margit Nebesky. Come back here when you're done."

"She should take my papers," Alena said. "My photo's not that good. She could pass as me, easily."

"I won't need them," the golem said.

"Take them anyway," Alena said. "I'll stay here until you get back." Alena handed the golem her purse, then looked at her again and laughed. "Hanna, were you really going to send her out like that? Barefoot, without a hat?"

Hanna looked at the golem and blushed. "Sorry," she said.

Alena took out a hat and pair of shoes, as well as her winter coat, and the golem put them on. Everything fit. "We'll have to get another coat somewhere," Alena said. "Even if she can get by without papers, sending her out with no coat in December seems a bit cruel, and I don't want to be stuck in the apartment."

"At least that should be easier than false papers," Hanna said. She tucked the envelope into Alena's purse and handed it back to the golem. "Do you have any questions?"

"No."

"Then get going."

The golem headed out. Hanna called after her, "If you see anything *helpful* you could do while you're out—do it."

The December sky was as gray as cement; it was not raining or snowing as the golem left the apartment, but it would start soon. Nobody glanced twice at the golem, and she strode quickly through the streets toward her destination.

Vltavská 16 was on the other side of the Vltava River. It would have been fastest to take the streetcar, but Hanna had not specifically *told* the golem that she *had* to take the fastest route. Despite the cold, the golem was in no particular hurry to return to the apartment. Besides, Prague had changed a lot since her last visit; she wanted to see the city.

From the house on Dlouhá street, she passed through the Old Town Square. It was no longer the commercial center of the city, but there were plenty of people here, and plenty of commerce. A few police officers swaggered through the crowd, but she avoided any who might have asked to see her papers. They had finished Tyn Church, she noticed; also, they had put up a huge statue of Jan Hus. It was the biggest thing in the square.

Continuing toward the Vltava, she passed the National Theatre; that was new. It was huge and boxy and ornate, with a silvery roof and carvings along the sides. She skipped that bridge and continued along the river to the bridge that would take her directly to the Smíchov district.

Vltavská 16 was a small house, new since her last visit, but not that new. The Nazi informant who lived a few doors down would be coming out to water her plants in a minute, so the golem slipped the transcript through the mail drop quickly and was on her way before the woman came out. The Resistance member who lived at Vltavská 16 had a printing press; by evening, handbills with the transcript would be passed hand to hand in the markets and squares of Prague.

The golem decided to cross at the Charles Bridge on the way back. The Charles Bridge was old even when she'd last lived in Prague, although it had a different name then. The bridge had statues now, saints and angels looming over the people as they crossed. She was passing the Church of Saint Nicholas, most of the way there, when she saw a patch of yellow through the jostling crowd. A Jewish family, struggling with suitcases and two small children. The golem made her way toward them. Hanna had told her to help, if she could.

The woman had set down her suitcase, trying to rebalance the child on her hip, when the golem reached them. They were already tired, she could see, and ashamed to be seen struggling on foot through Prague like this. The golem didn't really want to know who they were or what fate awaited them, but the knowledge was there as soon as it occurred to her to wonder: Shayna and Mandel Feinbaum, and their children—Selig, age three, and Reise, age six months. Shayna and Reise would die at Terezin during one of the typhoid outbreaks. Mandel and Selig would live to be murdered at Treblinka, in 18 months.

"Excuse me," the golem said. "You look a bit overwhelmed, with the children and the suitcases. May I carry something for you?"

They looked nervous when she first approached, but Shayna's face broke quickly into sweet relief. "Oh, thank you," she said. "Yes, please, if you'd be so kind. Thank you."

Mandel would not let the golem take both suitcases, but she lifted one easily, freeing the woman to carry just the child. "We're going to the Trade Fair grounds," Shayna said.

The golem nodded. The Trade Fair grounds was where the Jews of Prague would be assembled, one thousand at a time. Like the others, Mandel and Shayna would be stripped of their documents and any items of value, then deported to Terezin in the dark hours of night.

Shayna introduced herself and her husband and children; the golem introduced herself as Margit. "You're so kind to help us," Shayna said, in a tone that asked *why* any Czech woman would help Jews.

"It's nothing," the golem said.

The Trade Fair grounds were in Holesovice, north and east along the curve of the Vltava. In coming weeks, the Jewish teenagers of Prague would organize to assist families like this one, oiling the machinery that would ultimately devour them. Not that they knew that, of course; all they knew was that they were helping people who needed help, carrying bags for people who would have to struggle alone across Prague in the cold.

The golem knew, of course. She considered this, as she carried the suitcase, but it seemed to her that to tell this family their fate would only increase their suffering—if they believed her. As she had told Hanna, there was very little that could be done; she could carry their suitcases, and ease their suffering, but she couldn't save them.

"Here we are," Mandel said as they reached the edge of the Trade Fair grounds. "Thank you so much for your help."

"It was nothing," the golem said, and turned to go.

"Wait," Shayna said. "I want to give you something."

"I don't need any payment," the golem said.

"Not payment," Shayna said. "Just a gift." She opened one of the bags and drew out a small silver case, which she pressed into the golem's hand. "Just to say thank you."

The golem closed her hand over the gift and watched as the families went to join the other families queuing in a jostling mass. When they were gone, she opened her hand and looked; Shayna had given her a silver cigarette case, with five cigarettes inside, and a book of matches. Looking more closely, the golem realized that a pearl had been hidden inside the cigarette case, as well. It was a single perfect pearl, set into a pendant, with a thin gold chain. She wondered if Shayna had meant to give her the pearl, or just the cigarettes, but it hardly mattered—in a few hours, the rest of the family's valuables would be confiscated by the Nazis, even the gold jewelry that they had so carefully sewn into the lining of their coats. Better the golem have the pearl than the Nazis.

The golem touched the pearl, then smiled and closed the cigarette case with a click, slipping it into the pocket of her dress. The cigarettes might also be useful, and Hanna would not think to ask whether the golem had received any gifts.

When the golem reached the apartment, she could hear someone weeping. She slipped in quietly, stepped out of her shoes, and crossed the floor to listen at the door. It was Hanna who was weeping, and for a chill moment the golem thought she had decided to destroy her. But she was crying for a friend—a young man she'd known, Jewish, shot for failure to report for deportation to Terezin. Alena sat beside Hanna at the kitchen table, one arm around Hanna's waist.

After a long time, Hanna raised her head. "What are we going to do if I get called for deportation?" she whispered through her tears.

Alena pulled a handkerchief out of her pocket. "Why don't you ever have a handkerchief in your own pocket, Hanna? Blow your nose."

Hanna wiped her nose and her eyes. "You didn't answer my question."

Alena took the handkerchief back. "You're not going anywhere I can't go," she said. "I'll hide you if it comes to that."

"They'll look here."

"We'll hide you with a member of the Resistance, then. I have connections."

"But if they find me—"

"If I have to, I'll get false papers that say I'm Jewish—those should be easy enough to come by—and go with you."

Hanna laughed through her tears. "Your Resistance friends would think you were crazy."

"I don't care," Alena said. "We'll do what we have to do. For now . . ." She leaned her forehead against Hanna's shoulder. "Don't worry yourself."

It was ironic, the golem thought, that in the end it would be Alena who put Hanna in danger, rather than the other way around. Hanna would probably have died regardless, but there was no way to know. The golem retraced her steps through the parlor, slipped her shoes back on, and banged the door shut as if she'd just come in.

The women's voices stopped. "Who is it?" Alena called.

"It's me—Margit," the golem said.

Alena threw open the door to the back rooms, a welcoming smile on her face. "How did it go?"

"Fine." The golem followed Alena back into the kitchen. Hanna hastily wiped her nose again, this time on her sleeve, and straightened up. "I delivered the letter where you told me," the golem said to her.

"Did anyone ask for your papers?" Alena asked.

"No."

"You can go out without them tomorrow, then. But I'm going to try to get a false set for you, just in case."

In the meantime, Alena had bartered with someone in her building for an extra coat; it was shabby but reasonably warm, and it fit.

"There's something else I'd like to know," Hanna said. "What happens if you get arrested?"

The golem knew what she was asking. The golem was made of clay, brought to life with faith and magic. Hanna could destroy the golem with a quick gesture across the golem's forehead, changing the word *emet*—truth—to *met*—death. But if she were shot—could a bullet stop a heart of clay?

"Bullets will not stop me," the golem said. "But a hot enough fire can consume even clay."

Hanna nodded.

"However, I cannot be coerced to reveal your secrets," the golem said. Her clay body could feel pain, but she was as indifferent to pain as she was to cold.

Alena raised an eyebrow. "That's useful to know."

"What did you do today after you delivered the letter?" Hanna asked.

"I helped a Jewish family that was walking to the Trade Fair grounds," the golem said.

Hanna's eyes softened. "Good. That was the sort of thing I'd hoped you'd do."

The golem shrugged. For the Germans to deport the Jews from Prague, it was necessary that the deportations be clean and quiet. The Czechs were not an unkind people; on the one occasion that the Germans marched them to the train station by day, the Czech witnesses were horrified at the spectacle. The men ostentatiously doffed their hats, and the women wept. To the extent that the golem had made the deportation cleaner—more painless—she had served the Germans that day, and not the Jews of Prague.

It didn't matter. Nothing she did would matter.

"Do you have anything else you want me to do today?" she asked.

But Alena had no more messages that needed to be delivered, and hadn't yet made contact with the Resistance to tell them about their new volunteer—her cousin Margit, who had an almost supernatural ability to avoid attracting the attention of the authorities. They passed the evening in companionable discomfort, the golem watching the two women eat. She did *enjoy* eating, when she had the opportunity. Hanna's cooking smelled delicious, defying the limits of the ration book. Well. It was understandable that they wouldn't want to share, and the fact that the golem didn't have to eat would come in handy in seven months, when she was free.

The Prague Resistance was initially suspicious of Alena's claims regarding Margit's abilities. But after a few close calls (easy enough for the golem to produce), they accepted their good fortune. After that, the golem spent most of each day delivering messages, walking from one end of Prague to the other.

One day in early spring, the golem's duties took her beyond the Trade Fair grounds and farther toward the edge of Holesovice. Afterward, as she walked home along the curving roadway, she realized that she was standing somewhere that would be important. Looking around, she realized this was the spot where Heydrich would be assassinated at the end of May. The assassins had trained in England, and had been dropped by parachute in December. On the evening of May 27, the first assassin would fire his gun only to have it jam; another would see that the gun had misfired and hurl a grenade. The shrapnel from the grenade would severely wound Heydrich, though he would cling to life for several days. Thousands would die in the reprisals that would follow—in addition to wiping out every trace they could find of the Resistance, the Germans would execute the entire male population of a town called

Lidice, then send the women to concentration camps and the children to German families.

The golem was standing where the assassin would stand. A chill rippled through her body. Shuddering, she turned and walked back the way she had come, then took a fork in the road and headed away from Prague.

She had been walking for 20 minutes when she realized what she'd done.

Hanna had not told her to do this. Hanna had told her to deliver the message and return.

She sat down abruptly by the roadway. She had disobeyed—she hadn't meant to, but she had been able to, nonetheless. *If I don't have to obey Hanna, then I don't have to wait for her to die. I can go anywhere.* The Czech countryside stretched out before her; she could see it like a map. Warton, yes, but she knew where the bombs would fall and which buildings would stand through the war. I'll go to Litomĕrice, she thought. I've never seen it. I'll find a job—but for that she really *would* need papers, and Alena hadn't gotten them for her yet. Well, it didn't matter—she'd come up with something.

First, though, she would celebrate her freedom. She took out a cigarette from Shayna's cigarette case. Hanna would not want her to do this—Hanna would want her to hand over the cigarettes, so that they could be used for small bribes. The golem struck a match and lit the cigarette, breathing in the bitter smoke. The cigarette made her feel a little lightheaded, and her lungs burned, but even the pain was exhilarating. She didn't have to wait until June; she was free now.

As the golem finished her cigarette, she heard footsteps behind her and turned around. There was a young woman, Jewish, carrying a suitcase. No doubt she was headed for the Trade Fair grounds. The information clicked in like the snap of a purse opening: Dobre Kaufman, 24 years old, single. Blonde enough to pass as Czech, but without the connections to get false papers. Besides, she believed what the Germans had told her about Terezin, that she would be safe there. She'd survive Terezin, then be shipped out to

Auschwitz in one of the last transports. The golem realized with depressed astonishment that Dobre would die only a week before the Red Army would arrive to liberate her.

"Excuse me," the golem said.

Dobre looked up.

The golem took out the cigarette case and opened it; Shayna's pearl was still there. There was a man in Holesovice who made false documents; he'd be executed in the purges after Heydrich's assassination, but that was months away. And he worked cheap. "If you go to Terezin as you've been ordered, you will not survive the war," she said. She put the pearl in Dobre's hand. "Take this to Vysebrad 2. Tell the man who answers the door that Stépan sent you, and give him the pearl. Have him make you false papers that say you're Catholic. Go somewhere where nobody knows you and don't tell *anyone* that you're Jewish, not until the end of the war. If you do as I say, you *might* survive."

Dobre stared at her in silent wonder.

"Do you understand me?" the golem asked impatiently.

"Yes," Dobre said. "Who are you? Why are you helping me?"

"Don't ask questions. Just do as I tell you." The golem walked away before the girl could ask her anything else. Let the girl think what she wanted—the golem had done what she could.

She realized after a few minutes of walking that she had automatically headed back toward Prague. Well, it hardly mattered. She knew that Hanna would die in June, and the golem would be free. Perhaps in the meantime Alena would get her the false papers. Maybe if she arranged to have a close call or two, that would encourage Alena to take care of it. Or if she came up with something she'd *definitely* need papers for, like rail travel or a job. She could go back to Prague for now; it wouldn't hurt anything.

First, though, she thought she'd spend the night outside—just because she knew she could. It was still cold out, but the cold didn't bother her. She crossed the river, then settled down under the bridge where it was dry. She smoked two more cigarettes as she waited for the dawn to come. As she finished the second, she found herself thinking about Dobre, and she realized with a shock that she no longer *knew* Dobre's fate—it was as if the page she'd been looking at was now simply missing. She found herself poking at it mentally, like the tongue pokes a missing tooth. Still gone.

Dobre must have taken her advice. She might or might not live, but she would no longer die from typhus and starvation one week before liberation.

It occurred to her suddenly that something she had done might also have changed Hanna's fate, but no, that was still there. Relieved, she headed back to the apartment.

The golem expected Alena and Hanna to be angry, and had invented a story. Alena was watching for her out the window, but when she arrived, Alena pulled her into a hug. "Thank God you're safe," she said. After a moment, she closed the apartment door. "Hanna has gone out to look for you. She has this crazy idea you're in the Old Jewish Cemetery. I was sure you'd been arrested, and I was so terrified—we'd never be able to raise bribe money."

"Arrested?" the golem said. *"Me?"*

Alena led the golem back to the kitchen and started water for tea. Hanna arrived a few minutes later.

"She's here," Alena said.

Hanna almost burst into tears. "We were so worried," she said. "Where were you?"

"I heard a patrol coming and hid," the golem said. "I figured they'd be on their way in a few minutes, but then they stood around smoking cigarettes for hours. There were a lot of patrols around—I ended up waiting until morning, and then they thinned out."

It was a pathetic story; of course, the golem would know exactly when the patrol would leave, just as she would know when they were coming. She could not be trapped like that. But Hanna wanted to believe her, and she did.

"You did exactly the right thing," Alena said. "You're one of the most valuable members of the Resistance right now. We can't afford to lose you."

Hanna rose and spooned out a bowl of porridge for the golem. "Have something to eat," she said.

The golem had errands to run on May 27, the day that Heydrich would be shot, but fortunately none of them took her anywhere near Holesovice. She didn't tell Hanna or Alena about the assassination before it happened; they had lectured her several times on need-to-know, and this definitely qualified. Still, she took the streetcar to deliver her messages, and returned home as quickly as she could.

Heydrich was shot in the evening. The crackdowns began within hours. The assassins had hidden well and would not be found until June 18, but the Germans recovered enough evidence at the scene of the attack to identify certain key members of the Resistance. They were arrested and interrogated; the wheels of the Nazi machine turned, crushing their bodies beneath it, and moved outward from there.

Radek, who appeared on Alena and Hanna's doorstep at two in the morning on June 14, was not a leader of the Resistance but a friend of Alena's. Alena yanked him into the parlor without a word, closed the door, and took him to the back room.

"You shouldn't have taken me in," he said. "I'm putting you both in danger."

"That's for us to decide," Alena said. "So hush. Are you hurt?"

"No. I got a warning five minutes before they arrived." Radek looked like he'd left home in a hurry—unshaven, he wore his nightshirt tucked into trousers, with an overcoat thrown on over the top, despite the summer heat.

Alena settled Radek in her bed, to get a few hours' rest. At dawn, she would go out to get a razor and less conspicuous clothes for him—and, if she could, false papers. *This is it*, the golem thought. The man who would sell her the papers would be arrested later that day; when interrogated, he would implicate Alena. The mistake was hers, going to someone who knew her name and address, but so many members of the Resistance had already been arrested that she had nowhere else to go. Ironically, the golem realized, thanks to the false papers that Elsa would obtain. Radek would survive the war, although Alena would die, and Hanna with her.

And the golem would be free.

Alena was gone for several hours. Radek slept peacefully. Hanna cleaned, holding the broom in fists clenched so tight her knuckles were white. Alena returned without incident and with everything she'd gone for. She work Radek, and he quickly dressed and shaved. Hanna went to let him out through the back stairs.

"Margit." Alena said, once Hanna was gone. "I'm sorry this took so long. I got you your papers."

The golem looked down at the documents. The photo was of Alena, but as Hanna had observed that first night, they were close enough to pass for each other. The name was not Margit, though.

Alena shook her head. "If Margit hasn't been fingered as a member of the Resistance yet, she will be."

The golem looked up. "So will Alena."

Alena shrugged. "My contingency plan is to cause them enough trouble when they come for me that they just shoot me down then and there, and spare myself torture."

"Why didn't you get false papers for yourself?" the golem asked. "You could hide, too."

"Between what Radek gave me and what I had saved, I had money for two sets. One of those had to go to Radek. And I'm not leaving Hanna. I'd rather die with her than lose her."

When Alena spoke of Hanna, her face twisted oddly, almost as if she were in pain. The golem studied Alena's eyes, wondering what that would be like, to feel that way for another.

"You know how to stay out of trouble," Alena said. "You'll be able to use those papers well."

The golem tucked them into her purse. Hanna had errands for her—messages that needed to be delivered. The golem knew, however, that all of the recipients had already been arrested, or would by the time she made it across Prague—even if she could fly. If she did complete the errands, Hanna and Alena would both be dead by the time she returned. Just as she'd been waiting for.

So she took the papers and went to the Old Jewish Cemetery.

Despite the crackdown, the cemetery was not empty. The Jews were gradually being banned from more and more of the parks and streets of Prague; the Old Jewish Cemetery was the closest thing to a recreation area that they still had. There were families picnicking there, among the 1,200 tombstones stacked like books on an over-crowded shelf.

The tomb that the golem was looking for was near the main entrance. Paired marble tablets linked by a roof marked the grave of Rabbi Löw. She sat down in the shade of the slabs and lit a cigarette.

"So I'm back," she said softly.

She heard a peal of laughter from one of the women picnicking in the cemetery.

"This time, nobody is going to destroy me. There won't be anyone to do it. I can live forever—I'll just avoid anyone who could hurt me. I know everything I need to know to stay alive."

She thought of the expression on Alena's face as she spoke of Hanna. *I'd rather die with her than lose her.*

"I've even got papers now," she said. "Alena bought them for me, finally." Instead of buying them for herself.

"I have freedom." She was even freer than Alena. Alena was trapped here, tied to Hanna. The golem was tied to nobody.

Again, she saw the expression on Alena's face, thinking of Hanna.

"All I need to do is walk away," she said.

She could do that, she knew. Even if she had been bound to her creator's will, her creator would be dead within hours. She was free to choose any fate she desired. This time, finally, she would survive. Alone, but alive.

I'd rather die with her than lose her.

The golem realized suddenly that the cigarette had burned away in her hand, and she hadn't even inhaled any of the smoke. Disgusted, she stubbed out the last of it on the ground. Then she stood: the sun was warm on her shoulders. "This is my choice," she said to the Rabbi's grave. "This is my decision."

The golem returned to the apartment at 3:10 P.M. "Alena!" she called. "Hanna. Gather your valuables. Leave everything else, or you'll arouse suspicions. You need to go, now, or you'll both be killed in just over an hour."

The women obeyed her without hesitation. They put on several layers of clothes, though it would be hot, and each filled a purse and a shopping bag with food and the valuables they had left. The golem followed them through the apartment, talking. "Go to Kutná Hora," she said. It was one of the larger towns in Bohemia. She gave them an address for another apartment. "They have a vacancy right now; the landlord isn't nosy, and he won't care who lives in the apartment aside from Alena. Don't waste time: in a week, he'll rent the place to a Nazi sympathizer who will later betray his next-door neighbor for sheltering Jews. It's much better that the landlord rent to you."

There was room in Hanna's shopping bag for her *Talmud*—it was an antique, a family heirloom. She took it, although there were other things that would have been more practical. She left the books of golem lore.

The golem stopped Alena at the door. "Give me your papers," she said, and handed Alena the false papers that Alena had bought for her. "Now go."

As Alena and Hanna headed down the stairs to the street, the golem felt their fate vanish from her mind. She was certain that they would live or die together, whatever happened. In the meantime—the Germans would come to arrest Alena Nebesky, and they would find her. The golem picked up Hanna's book of golem lore, lit the last of Shayna's cigarettes, and sat down in the immaculate parlor to wait.

The Devil Disinvests

Scott Bradfield

*Scott Bradfield is the respected contemporary author of three novels—*The History of Luminous Motion, What's Wrong with America, *and* AnimalPlanet*—and a volume of collected stories,* Greetings From Earth. *He attended Clarion in the early 1970s, and his short fiction has appeared occasionally in SF and fantasy venues ever since. He taught for five years at the University of California, Irvine, where he received his doctorate in American Literature, and currently teaches English at the University of Connecticut at Storrs. He has published a work of nonfiction entitled* Dreaming Revolution: Transgression in the Development of American Romance, *and reviews regularly for* The Times *(London),* The New York Times Book Review, *and* TLS. *This year he was Samuel Fischer Guest Professor in Comparative Literature at the Free University in Berlin. He teaches a class titled "Literature and Crap in American Pop Culture—What We Like To Read and What We're Supposed To." He just finished writing two scripts for Roger Corman at Concorde–New Horizons, entitled "The Enchantment," a modern fairytale set in Ireland, and "Shakedown," an LA thriller.*

"The Devil Disinvests," a wry satire on celebrity and executive biographies, appeared in the airline magazine for Swissair, and also in F & SF, *which had another distinguished year in its long history of publishing fantasy fiction. The Devil sounds very like all those billionaires who are profiled in the business magazines these days, and is certainly a moral comment on them.*

"I don't think of it as laying off workers," the Devil told his Chief Executive Officer, Punky Wilkenfeld, a large round man with bloodshot eyes and wobbly knees. "I think of it as downsizing to a more user-friendly mode of production. I guess what I'm saying, Punky, is that we can't spend all eternity thinking about nothing more important than the bottom line. Maybe it's finally time to kick back, reflect on our achievements, and start enjoying some of that well-deserved R&R we've promised ourselves for so long."

As always, the Devil tried to be reasonable. But this didn't prevent his long-devoted subordinate from weeping copiously into his worsted vest.

"What will I *do*?" Punky asked himself over and over again. "Where will I *go*? All this time I thought you loved me because I was really, really evil. Now I realize you only kept me around because, oh God. For you it was just, just, it was just *business*."

The Devil folded his long forked tail into his belt and checked himself out in the wall-sized vanity mirror behind his desk. He was wearing a snappy handmade suit by Vuiton, gleaming Cordovan leather shoes, and prescription Ray-Bans. The Devil had long been aware that it wasn't enough to be good at what you did. In order for people to know it, you had to look good, as well.

Roger "Punky" Wilkenfeld lay drooped over the edge of the Devil's desk like a very old gardenia. The Devil couldn't help himself. He really loved this guy.

"What can I tell you, Roger?" the Devil said, as gently as he could. "Eventually it comes time for everybody to move on, and so in this particular instance, I'll blaze the trail, and leave you and the boys to pack things up in your own good time. Just be sure to lock up when you leave."

The Devil went to California. He rented a beachfront cottage on the Central Coast, sold off his various penthouses and Tuscan villas, and settled into the reflective life as easily as an anemone in a tide pool. Every day he walked to the local grocery for fresh fruits and vegetables, took long strolls into the dry amber hills, or rented one of the Nouvelle Vague classics he'd always meant to watch from Blockbuster. He disdained malls, televised sports, and corporate-owned franchise restaurants. He tore up his credit cards, stopped worrying about the bottom line, and never once opened his mail.

In his heyday, the devil had enjoyed the most exotic pleasures that could be devised by an infinite array of saucy, fun-loving girls named Delilah. But until he met Melanie, he had never actually known true love.

"I guess it's because love takes time," the Devil reflected, on the night they first slept together on the beach. "And time has never been something I've had too much of. Bartering for souls, keeping the penitents in agony, stoking the infernos of unutterable suffering and so forth. And then, as if that's not enough, having to deal with all the endless constant whining. Oh *please*, Master, *please* take my soul, *please* grant me unlimited wealth and fame and eternal youth and sex with any gal in the office, I'll do *any*thing you ask, please *please*. When a guy's in the damnation game, he never gets a moment's rest. If I'd met you five years ago, Mel? I don't think I'd have stopped working long enough to realize what a wonderful, giving person you really are. But I've got the time now, baby. Come here a sec. I've definitely got lots of time for you now."

They moved in together. They had children—a girl and a boy. They shopped at the Health Food Co-Op, campaigned for animal rights, and installed an energy efficient Aga in the kitchen. They even canceled the lease on the Devil's Volvo, and transported themselves everywhere on matching ten-speed racing bikes. These turned out to be the most wonderful and relaxing days the Devil had ever known.

Then, one afternoon when the Devil was sorting recyclable materials into their appropriate plastic bins, he received a surprise visitor from his past. Melanie had just taken the kids to Montessori. The Devil had been looking forward all day to catching up with his chores.

"How they hanging, big boy? I guess I imagined all sorts of comeuppances for a useless old fart like yourself, but certainly never this. Wasting your once-awesome days digging through garbage. Cleaning the windows and mowing the lawn."

When the Devil looked up, he saw Punky Wilkenfeld climbing out of a two-door Corvette. Clad in one of the Devil's old suits, he looked slightly out of place amidst so much expensive retailoring. Some guys know how to hang clothes, the Devil thought. And some guys just don't.

"Why, Punky," the Devil said softly, not without affection. "It's you."

"It sure is, pal. But they don't call me Punky anymore."

"Oh no?" The Devil absently licked a bit of stale egg from his forepaw.

"Nope. These days, people call me *Mr.* Wilkenfeld. Or better yet, the Eternal Lord of Darkness and Pain."

* * *

"It's like this, Pop," Punky continued over Red Zinger tea in the breakfast room. "When you took off, you left a trillion hungry mouths to feed. Mouths with razor-sharp teeth. Mouths with multitudinously forked tongues. Frankly, I didn't know what to do, so I turned the whole kit-and-kaboodle over to the free-market-system and just let it ride. We went on the Dow in March, and by summer we'd bought out two of our closest rivals—Microsoft and ITT. I even hear Mr. Hot-Shot Heavenly Father's been doing a little diversifying. Doesn't matter to me, either. Whoever spends it, it's all money."

"It's always good to see a former employee make good, Punky," the Devil said graciously. "I mean, excuse me. *Mr.* Wilkenfeld."

Punky finished his tea with a long, parched swallow. "*Ahh,*" he said, and hammered the mug down with a short rude bang. "I guess I just wanted you to know that I haven't forgotten you, Pops. In fact, I've even bought this little strip of beach you call home, and once we've finished erecting the new condos, we'll move on to offshore oil rigs, docking facilities, maybe even a yachting club or two. Basically, Pop, I'm turning your life into scrap metal. Nothing to do with business, either. I just personally hate your guts."

The Devil gradually grew aware of a dim beeping sound. With a sigh, Punky reached into his vest pocket and deactivated his digital phone with a brisk little flick.

"Probably my broker," Punky said. "He calls at least six times a day."

The Devil distantly regarded his former *chargé d'affaires*, whose soft pink lips were beaded with perspiration and bad faith. Poor Punky, the Devil thought. Some guys just never learn.

"And wanta know the best thing about this shoreline redevelopment project, Pop? There's absolutely nothing you can do about it. You take it to the courts—I own them.

You take it to the Board of Supervisors—I own *them.* You organize eight million sit-down demonstrations and I pave the whole damn lot of you over with bulldozers. That's the real pleasure of dealing dirt to you born-again types, Pop. You gotta be *good.* But I don't."

The Devil watched Punky stand, brush himself off, and reach for his snakeskin briefcase. Then, as if seeking a balance to this hard, unaccommodating vision, he looked out his picture window at the hardware equipment littering his back yard. The Devil had been intending to install aluminum siding all week, and he hated to see unfulfilled projects rust away in the salty sea air.

"One second," the Devil said. "I'll be right back."

"Sorry, Pop, but this is one CEO who believes in full-steam-ahead, toot toot! Keep in touch, guy. Unless, that is, I keep touch with *you* first—"

But of course before Punky reached the front door the Devil had already returned from his back yard with the shearing scissors. And Punky, who had belonged to the managerial classes for more eons than he cared to remember, was slow to recognize any instrument used in the performance of manual labor.

"Hey, Pop, that's more like it," Punky said slowly, the wrong sun dawning from the wrong hills. "I could use a little grooming if only to remind us both who's boss. Here, see, at the edge of this cloven hoof? What does that look like to you? A hangnail?"

Punky had crouched down so low that it almost resembled submission.

At which point the Devil commenced to chop Punky Wilkenfeld into a million tiny bits.

"Seagulls don't mind what they eat," the Devil reflected later. He was standing at the end of a long wooden pier, watching white birds dive into the frothy red water. "Which is probably why they remind me so much of men."

The Devil wondered idly if his life had a moral. If it did, he decided, it was probably this:

Just because people change their lives for the better doesn't mean they're stupid.

Then, remembering it was his turn to do bouillabaisse, the Devil turned his back on the glorious sunset and went home.

A Serpent in Eden

Simon Brown & Alison Tokley

Alison Tokley is Head of English at an Anglican school; "A Serpent in Eden" is her first fiction sale. Tokley and Brown are married and live with their two children on the New South Wales south coast. Simon Brown is the author of the novels Privateer *(1995) and* Winter *(1997), and a collection of short stories,* Cannibals of the Fine Light *(1998). He won an Aurealis Award for the story "Atrax," a collaboration with Sean Williams. His new fantasy novel* Inheritance, *the first volume in his Keys of Power trilogy, is being published by HarperCollins Australia. He has had several stories and articles published in Australia and overseas in magazines and anthologies such as* Eidolon, Aurealis, *and* Dreaming Down Under. *He worked as a journalist with the University of Western Sydney, and is now a full-time writer. His Web site can be found at www.eidolon.net/simon_brown.*

"A Serpent in Eden" appeared in Eidolon: The Journal of Australian Science Fiction and Fantasy. *This story of a family troubled by a snake in their garden in urban Australia (where there are more kinds of poisonous snakes than anywhere else on Earth) accents the differences in perception between a small child and the surrounding adults.*

After Frances had seen to Rowan's leg, which needed a fresh bandage twice a day, she found their four-year-old daughter Phoebe standing by the loungeroom window and looking out over the front garden. When Phoebe heard her mother behind her she turned around and said: "He's coming."

"Who's coming, lovely?" Frances asked, following her daughter's gaze. There was no one outside.

Phoebe frowned in thought, then said again: "He's coming."

Frances nodded, pretending to understand. She noticed that the foxgloves were being crowded by weeds. "We should do some gardening," she told Phoebe.

Together they went outside and, while Frances tended to the weeds, Phoebe, equipped with her own bucket and spade, determinedly moved as much dirt as possible from one corner of the yard to another and then moved it all back again.

It was early spring, and already Frances was sniffing back the symptoms of hay fever. After digging up the weeds, she started clearing a patch under the Cypress pines for the next planting of azaleas. One rock in particular gave her a hard time, but with a crowbar and a brick fulcrum she was able to loosen it and lift it onto one edge. She stopped suddenly and backed away. Phoebe noticed that something was wrong and ran up to have a look.

"Stay away, sweetheart," Frances ordered her.

"Is it spiders?"

Frances shook her head, pointed with her crowbar at the thick, reptilian cord that had been hiding under the sandstone. Grey with faint blue stripes, the muscular length curled like a knot around a second, half-submerged stone. She could see neither head nor tail.

"A snake!" Phoebe cried, clapping her hands.

Frances nodded. She was tossing up whether or not to explore a little further. Last summer they had come across a similar find and immediately called the local snake catcher, Mr. Wilosz. Over the phone, Mr. Wilosz had thought it was a young brown snake, but when he arrived he laughed and gently eased out a harmless and hibernating blue tongue lizard. Frances didn't want to call out Mr. Wilosz again on a false alarm. Still, what she could see of the reptile suggested at least a *very* large blue tongue.

She eased the rock back, and carefully lifted a second one nearby.

"More snakes!" Phoebe exclaimed. Frances took her daughter's hand and moved her away. *This is no lizard*, she told herself.

After moving several other rocks, Mr. Wilosz wasn't sure what to make of it.

"You see, Ms. West, it's like this. If there was something there for me to actually *look* at, then I could tell you what it was. As it is . . ."

He let the sentence hang. Frances, trying vainly not to be embarrassed, could only apologize again for calling him out on a false call.

"I really did see something."

"Me, too," Phoebe chipped in.

Mr. Wilosz sighed. "From your description it sounds like either a blue tongue or a young brown snake. If it was as big as you think it was, then it *could* have been a tiger snake, but no one's seen one of those around here for donkey's years."

"So what do we do?" Frances demanded. "I don't want Phoebe exposed to any danger."

Mr. Wilosz looked sideways at Phoebe. She returned his look with a cool gaze that seemed far too old for her four years. Rowan joined them, favouring his bandaged leg.

"What's going on?" he demanded. "Where's the snake?" Phoebe went to hold her father's hand.

"It's gone," Frances said.

"Not another bloody false alarm," Rowan said angrily.

Frances shook her head. "It was a snake."

"I need another bandage. This one is weeping."

Frances looked at Rowan, her expression tired. "I can't do that, honey. You know you can only have the ointment applied twice a day. The cortisone is too strong—"

"Fuck the cortisone," Rowan spat, and Phoebe backed away from him. It was Mr. Wilosz's turn to look embarrassed.

"Shouldn't say that," Phoebe said.

Rowan closed his eyes. "Sorry, sweetheart." He gently put a hand on his daughter's head. "Sometimes I lose it, that's all. I don't mean anything by it." He nodded in apology to Mr. Wilosz. Frances got nothing.

"Go back to bed, Rowan," Frances said. "You shouldn't be putting weight on your leg. That's probably why the sores are weeping."

Rowan nodded. "Yeah." He turned to leave, dejected. Frances wanted to say something to make him feel better, but over the long months of his illness all her kind words had somehow become blandishments.

Mr. Wilosz made to leave. "Whatever it was, Ms. West, obviously didn't like its hibernation being disturbed and moved off to find somewhere safer. It'll probably go some distance and settle down again."

"So you think it's left my garden?" Frances wanted assurance.

"More than likely," Mr. Wilosz said. "But if you see it again, let me know."

The next day, Frances set up a banana chair on the front porch for Rowan. He wasn't keen on sitting in the sun, but his doctors had said the sun was good for his sores, so Frances was firm. She carefully unwrapped his bandage, and made sure he had a good book and a long cool glass of fruit juice.

Phoebe joined her in the garden as Frances planted some sweet peas along the side trellis. Things were going well until Maisie O'Day made an appearance. Frances thought of her as the neighbour from hell.

"Not enough sun for the sweet peas," Maisie declared, sniffing, coolly regarding Frances' efforts.

"Oh, I think it will be alright," Frances replied politely, wishing she had the courage to punch Maisie on the nose. She looked over her neighbour's front yard, across the dying crab grass to the withered acacias. *What you know about gardening, Maisie O'Day, wouldn't fill a match box.*

"What was all the fuss about yesterday?" Maisie asked.

At first, Frances wasn't sure what Maisie was on about, then remembered the snake. She explained what had happened.

"I saw a snake once," Maisie said indifferently.

Yeah, in your mirror, Frances thought.

"Must have been six foot long. Brown thing. Wicked looking."

Frances kept on digging, planting, hoping Maisie would go away. Then Phoebe came up. "Hello, Mrs. O'Day."

Maisie's face softened. Her only saving grace, as far as Frances was concerned, was that she had time for Phoebe.

"Hello, little darling. Did you see the snake yesterday?"

Phoebe nodded vigorously, and stretched her arms to their greatest extent. "It was that long."

Maisie's mouth formed a wide 'o'. "Were you scared?"

Phoebe shook her head. "He went away."

"Well, thank goodness for that."

"But he will come back again," Phoebe declared.

Frances stopped what she was doing. "Probably not, lovely. The snake catcher said it went a long way away."

Phoebe looked calmly at her mother. "No. He's coming back." Having made her statement, she walked off.

Maisie watched her for a moment. "Those sweet peas would be better off against the house," she said firmly, then left before Frances could reply. Frances turned to her husband to exchange a weary and knowing look, but he had gone back inside. She sighed heavily and returned to her gardening.

Frances made a light supper, then left Phoebe in the loungeroom reading her picture books while she tended to Rowan's leg. The sores were less angry than usual and seemed to be causing him less trouble. She carefully applied the cortisone ointments, rewrapped the bandage and made him swallow a couple of Panadeine. When it was done he rested back and closed his eyes, relieved it was done for another few hours.

Frances went to check up on her daughter. She noticed a picture book on the floor, opened up on a photo of a rock python, but there was no Phoebe. She checked in the bathroom, then in her bedroom.

"Phoebe?" she called out softly. "Where are you, honey?"

Frances went back to the loungeroom, noticed the front door was ajar.

"Oh, shit." She went outside, called out her daughter's name more loudly, heard a giggle coming from the front.

"Phoebe, don't play games. It's getting dark. Come back inside immediately." She walked to the front garden, saw her daughter standing near the foxgloves, looking into the shadows. Frances felt a cold shiver pass through her.

"Darling, what are you doing?"

"He's here!" Phoebe called out, delighted, and pointed.

Frances ran to her daughter, picked her up in her arms. Phoebe didn't complain. And there, curled in the gloom, Frances saw again the thick body of . . . whatever it was. *Hell, what's going on here?*

She heard Rowan calling out to them from the front door. "Is everything okay? Did you find Phoebe?"

"I've got her," Frances answered. "The snake's come back."

Rowan stumped his way to his wife and child, saw the thing for the first time. "God." He swayed a little, and Frances leant against his shoulder to steady him. "Take Phoebe inside, love. I'll try and move it."

Frances looked appalled. "You'll do no such thing! We don't know what it is."

"Well, we can't leave it there," he said weakly.

Frances put Phoebe down behind her and moved to a rock about a metre from their discovery. She edged it over with her shoe. "It's under here, too."

"Well, if it's that long, it's not a blue tongue. Gotta be a snake."

"We have to call Mr. Wilosz again," Frances said.

"He won't see it," Phoebe said with certainty.

Rowan sighed. "Now, honey, just because he didn't find it this morning—"

"He's a *snake* catcher," Phoebe said impatiently. "This isn't a snake."

Frances and Rowan exchanged glances. "What do you mean?" Rowan asked.

Phoebe shrugged. "I'm cold," she said. "Go inside now?"

Frances nodded. "Okay. It's probably too late to phone Mr. Wilosz, anyway. Besides, Phoebe's right. It is getting cold, and snakes don't move unless it's warm."

She took Rowan's arm and helped him back to the house, Phoebe leading the way. Frances patted Rowan's hand. "I should check your bandage after all this excitement," she said calmly.

"Yes," Rowan said evenly, and unexpectedly leaned across to kiss his wife's cheek. "Thank you."

Rowan was up first the next morning. His leg was hurting less than it had for months, and he woke feeling almost refreshed. He got out of bed without disturbing Frances and went outside. The snake was still there. He moved a few more rocks experimentally, and under each was another length of the creature. He should have been afraid, but instead all he felt was an absurd sense of wonder. He never saw head nor tail, only a thick, scaled body that seemed to twist into the ground like an anchor for the garden's soil and rocks. He tried to estimate its length, but not knowing where it started or finished made that a frustrating exercise.

"Well, what *are* you?" he asked aloud.

"Rowan? Should you be up and around on that leg of yours?"

Rowan turned in surprise to see Maisie O'Day. *Oh, God, what does she want?*

She came across, stopped when she saw what was under the rocks. "Goodness."

"Have you ever seen anything like this before?" Rowan asked her.

Maisie shook her head solemnly. "No. Seen a snake once, but nothing like . . . like this." She looked up and down the garden. "It seems to extend right to our boundary." She went to her own garden, then, and turned over the first rock she came to. "Oh, dear!"

Rowan hobbled over to where she was standing, openmouthed. Whatever this thing was, it was *huge*. Maybe a python?

"Well, I'd better go in and call the snake catcher again," Rowan said. "Won't he be surprised?"

By the time Mr. Wilosz arrived, Frances and Phoebe had joined Rowan and their neighbour. The snake catcher parked on the curb, banging his car door shut with impatience. The sound made everyone look around at him.

"You won't believe this . . ." Rowan began, then turned back to point at the snake.

But it was gone.

* * *

The four of them sat in Maisie's kitchen eating some of her sponge cake. Frances studied the kitchen, surprised it was almost as disorganized as her own; she had somehow imagined Maisie as so fastidious that a stain on a tea spoon would give her apoplexy.

"Do you think Mr. Wilosz will *ever* forgive us?" Rowan asked, smiling. The snake catcher's perplexed fury was, in hindsight, almost hilarious.

"Probably not," Frances said, pleased to see her husband's face without a frown. "But I'm more worried about our occasional visitor. A snake that large shouldn't be able to move that quickly without us at least hearing—well, *something*."

"A rustling sound," Maisie said, gazing out through the kitchen window, her eyes unfocused. "Like wind blowing leaves across a roof."

"That's it exactly!" Frances said. "Not slithering so much, as making its way."

Phoebe, who had spent the first ten minutes in Maisie's house concentrating on demolishing her generous portion of cake, looked up at the adults with something like curious frustration. "He didn't make a sound because he's still there," she said simply.

"Is she asleep?" Rowan asked.

Frances pulled the quilt up over her daughter's slender shoulders. "Yes." She stood there for a moment, looking down on Phoebe, resisting the urge to pick her up and hold her close. She quietly closed the door as she left the bedroom and joined Rowan on the lounge.

"She seems to understand more than she lets on," Frances said.

"What do you mean?"

"Well, she's not fussed at all about the mystery, is she? It's not that she doesn't care, more like she knows what it's all about. We're the ones in the dark."

Rowan sighed. "A child's imagination."

"Time for your fresh bandage."

Rowan shook his head. "No. Just take the old one off. I think I can go without the ointment tonight."

Phoebe woke not long after her parents had fallen asleep. She crept out of her bed and went to her window, pushing back the curtains and opening the sash. There were high clouds in the sky that turned the stars into white blurs, and diffused the moonshine so evenly that everything she saw seemed to glow with an inner light. The old ironbark just outside her window looked vibrantly alive. Phoebe dropped from the window and sat on the ground. She stared at the branches and thin grey leaves for a long while, patient as Job. After a time, a head formed from the patterns in the moonlight, slender and scaled, jaws grinning. Yellow eyes noticed the girl and turned to her.

"You should be asleep," said the deepest voice she had ever heard.

"They don't know what you are," Phoebe said.

"Do you?"

Phoebe thought about the question. "Yes."

The creature seemed amused. "And you are not afraid of me?"

"Some things are scarier than dragons," Phoebe answered.

The creature feigned surprise. "Not many, surely?"

"Like giants."

The dragon laughed, a sound like rustling leaves. "Have you imagined them as well?"

"Not yet," Phoebe said.

Wrong Dreaming

Kain Massin

"Kain Massin" is the pseudonym of a high school math and science teacher who lives with his wife, teenage daughter, and a menagerie of two cats and a beleaguered dog, in suburban Adelaide, South Australia. The reason for the pseudonym, he explains, is that "my real name is too difficult for any English-speaking person who hasn't got an extra epiglottis." He migrated to Australia from Hungary when he was seven. He says: "I had the handicap of learning a new language and a new culture. I was pleased to find that I could compete in English, as I felt compelled to write fiction. Although high school, University studies, and factory work interrupted my writing, I came back to it when I purchased my first computer." He has been published in Harbinger, Altair, On Spec, *and the Polish magazine* Nowa Fantastyka.

Massin has received an Honorable Mention from the Writers of the Future contest, and has been short-listed for the Aurealis Awards for Australian science fiction and fantasy. He is also co-editor of Tesselations, *a collection of short stories from the Blackwood Writers Group.*

"Wrong Dreaming," a story of supernatural vengeance in the age of mechanical reproduction, took first place in a short story contest in On Spec, *the leading Canadian magazine of fantasy, SF, and horror, in their special issue devoted to the winners of their short story contest. It is a particularly effective use of aboriginal magic systems.*

RAINBOW RIVER, BLACK RIVER;
Young girl, little spirit;
Fire sun, salmon moon;
Little spirit, black river;
Crow man, come soon.

The old man's body ached with the effort of leaning over and drawing in the fine silt. He stopped the chant, sat back and waited for the pain to ease. A breeze sprang up and danced along the gorge, bouncing off the steep cliffs and tickling the leaves of the gum trees that clung to the rocks. The old man smiled in gratitude as tongues of air licked the perspiration off his face and back.

After some time the strain lessened, and he looked back down at the picture. He stayed that way, his resolve waning, but his eyes strayed to the stick figure he had included, the figure of the little girl, and his jaws clenched. His anger smoldered, again, and he leaned forward, carefully bringing the point of his sharp stick down on the surface. He drew a line to cut off the river, to mark its boundary.

Rainbow river, black river.

Perspiration again ran through his beard, but he ignored it; the picture would send another breeze soon. His brows furrowed in concentration, and he was barely aware of the creep of shadows along the ground.

A soft sound caught his attention, its dissonance magnified by the silence in the gorge. Somewhere in the cliffs above him, a stone had been dislodged, and he heard its progress downward, a series of clatters punctuated by silence as it fell free. He would have scrambled to his feet, but his limbs were too stiff.

The stone clattered closer, and he felt it whisper past his head and land in the silt with a soft thud. He scanned the ancient rocks above him, but there was nothing else to disturb the quiet.

The stone was lying in the picture. It was thin and long as a finger and had landed on its side in the one space he had left free and he immediately saw that it would leave an indentation like a crow's beak.

Willing his hands to calmness, he reached over and plucked the stone up. Quickly, before he lost the fury that had driven him, he drew the rest of the crow's head around the indentation.

Muscles stretching and tendons groaning, he stood up and walked carefully around the picture. He saw that it was perfect, even better than he'd planned. He did not smile. Instead, he turned his back and walked up the gorge, deeper into the ancient and eroded mountains, past a bend and out of sight of the picture.

The sun was setting, its golden light shining full in his face, and he welcomed the warmth. Ahead, a kangaroo sipped from the stream, its ears up and turning in all directions. It heard his quiet step, and stood up, tall and alert. The two of them regarded each other.

The old man grew uneasy: there was something in the animal's gaze. He thought he read disapproval, but tried to ignore it.

Can't trust kangaroos; they don't know everything.

"You don't know everything," he said, but the kangaroo stood its ground, its gaze unrelenting and implacable.

The old man nodded. He turned and walked back down the gorge.

Someone else had been down there; there were the marks of shoes in the silt, but the picture was as he remembered and he didn't have the time to worry about intruders. He scooped some mud out of the stream and smeared it over his chest and down his arms. He was much more careful with the designs he drew on his face.

He clapped his hands at the cliff faces in acknowledgment. His feet moved in response, and he launched into a dance, his back straight as he slapped his feet down on the sand. His chant echoed off the walls to provide a beat. After some minutes, he stepped onto the picture, his feet ramming down like piledrivers.

The sun was gone, and his feet were bleeding, before the surface finally yielded under the stamping.

The old man's face was a mask of rigid control, his lips pressed firmly together, his black fists balled, his eyes hard. Around him was a sea of grief, with people weeping openly. One old woman had collapsed onto the coffin, her mouth open in a wail. But the old man was detached from them.

The next photograph, however, showed his face contorted in an effort to keep back tears that had sneaked past his control. His eyes were shut, their defiance quelled, and his fingers were clutching at the shoulder of the woman on the coffin.

Campbell watched as Worrell casually dropped the photograph and looked at the next one, his face mirroring the disinterest evident in his posture. Worrell glanced at the next photo before flipping it onto the growing pile of discarded pictures.

"You might remember the story," Campbell continued. "A young Aboriginal girl came from the Flinders Ranges to do her Year 12 in Adelaide? She was abducted on the way from school? Murder-rape?"

"Oh yes," Worrell replied, with no effort to put any interest in his voice. Campbell hadn't really expected him to remember, or even to try. What happened in the world outside his immediate sphere was of no consequence to Worrell. His only interests lay in the field of art and artists; all else belonged in someone else's world.

"Her body was returned to her people," Campbell went on, "and it was picked up by them in Hawker. The paper sent me up there to get some pictures, try to inject some human interest."

"Oh yes," Worrell repeated, casually flipping over another photo. He paused.

Campbell smiled, knowing which picture had stopped Worrell. It was the old man again. The girl's uncle . . . at least that was all the information he'd been able to get out of the locals. (Although, to be exact, the locals had described him as the uncle for everyone in the tribe.) In this picture, he had changed: his face was determined, as if he'd reached a decision that he'd wanted to avoid. There was an aura of dignity that shone out of the photo. Campbell was proud of the shot.

"Yes, Quentin," Campbell said, "that face of his . . . it got my attention. I decided to follow him, see what he did. I had the feeling there was another story here."

Worrell moved on to the next photo, then slipped back into his bored routine. This next batch consisted mostly of landscapes, shot while he'd driven his rented car after the old man. They'd left Hawker and headed into the Flinders Ranges, Campbell keeping well back. When the old man left his car, Campbell had followed on foot, along the trickling waterways, deeper into the ancient hills. Followed him to an isolated gorge, where the old man had sat down next to a stream and started drawing in the sand.

Campbell watched Worrell carefully, and saw him freeze at the photo. His eyes raced over the surface. "Wayne," he said, "what's this?"

Campbell felt a smile tug at his lips. "The old man drew it in the sand. He took about an hour to do it. Then, he got up and left."

Worrell actually turned to face him. *"He left?"*

Now, Campbell smiled freely. "Yes. Just left it there. As soon as he was out of sight, I scooted over and snapped it."

He leaned forward and pointed at the markings. "Luckily, it was near sunset, so the shadows highlight every line."

"Yes." Worrell was only half listening, his eyes avidly caressing the photograph. "Just left it?" He shook his head. "It's a strange design. Never seen it before. He seems to have divided into two: the normal world and . . . something else." He shook his head again, then he looked at Campbell. "He really just left it?"

Campbell's smile widened. "Just walked away."

"With nothing to protect it," Worrell finished. "No ring of stones, no warding sticks." He swallowed, a deliberate act. "No copyright."

Campbell, wondering how long it would take Worrell to think of this, smiled complacently.

Mark Dewling had a dead goat draped over his shoulder as he entered the wide gorge. He walked over to the four-wheel-drive he'd left parked in the shade of some gum trees.

"Uncle!" he called, heaving the goat's carcass up to the roof racks. Although summer had not yet set in, the shade was refreshingly cool. He pulled a rag out of the boot and rubbed away the worst of the dried blood that had dripped onto his legs.

Then he stopped. There had been no answer from the old man.

Bags had been placed near the vehicle, and he looked inside. As he'd expected, they contained ochre powder, eight or ten different colors, which the old man used for painting. He raised his eyes to the slopes, quickly picking out the spots where the old man had scraped his powders from the rocks.

The old man was sitting near a deep mauve rock, his collecting bag discarded next to him, his gaze unfocused. Dewling climbed up quickly, heart racing with fear. The old man did not look around, but sat immobile like the rocks.

"Uncle," Dewling whispered as he knelt next to him. He

reached out a tentative hand and dared to touch the old, dry skin. There was a coldness to the touch, and Dewling's heart skipped a beat, but the old eyes regained their focus and a sere smile was turned to him.

"Ah, little lizard, you've come back." The old man's voice was as dry as the land, crackling with the effort. The eyes drifted away, again. "I had a feeling—something I thought was all finished. Bloody near buggered my feet trying to stop it." The grey mane shook. "Help me to the car. You have to take me somewhere."

Dewling helped the old man to his feet. He seemed unsteady, as if he'd aged suddenly, not at all like the sprightly man Dewling knew him to be. They slid and crawled down the slope, and walked slowly to the car. He helped the old man into the front seat and strapped him in.

"Where are we going, Uncle?" he asked.

The eyes turned on him, shining with moisture. "I'll show you," whispered the reedy voice.

Dewling nodded, not daring to ask more. He drove out of the gorge and turned onto the dirt road, turning the vehicle towards Hawker. He was unsettled by the old man's apparent weakness. Although no one knew his true age, he had never been fragile. Dewling just thought of him as *being*, an immortal who never seemed to age.

"Turn here." The order was whispered, as if with effort. Dewling turned the wheel, although his heart gave a thump.

"No, Uncle," he pleaded, "please don't go there!"

The old man said nothing, his eyes lost in the distance, ignoring Dewling's outburst. The young man bit his lip and drove on. As they neared the parking area, he kept his eyes on the road, hoping that the old man wanted to go past.

"Stop here."

Dewling pulled off the road and into the carpark. There were already two cars there, and he groaned at the thought of meeting white tourists.

"Bring my paints," came the whispery voice.

The old man's hand and arm felt light, as if he had withered during the short drive. His back was stooped, and he leaned on the young man when they walked along the pathway. Dewling picked him up and carried him when they walked over a dry creek bed; there was almost no weight.

A middle-aged couple met them coming the other way. As Dewling had expected, they dropped their voices and pretended to ignore the two Aboriginals, even though they stepped off the path to let them by.

"You leave my goat alone," Dewling muttered as he walked by them, and was gratified to see their faces drop in shock.

He stopped on the bank of the dry river. Ahead, the bed was strewn with rocks, a bold testament to the river's strength on the rare occasions when it ran. Now, there wasn't even a trickle. The only water lay in the permanent pool that his gaze was trying to avoid.

"Take me there." This time, he could hear a reluctance in the tone, but the determination was clear.

Dewling carried the old man down to the riverbed and over to the pool. Beyond it rose a rock, dark and silent. He put the old man down and stepped back, his heart pounding.

Death Rock.

"Tourist attraction," the old man said, a soft derision in his voice. "This is a bloody sacred place. Bloody rock was pulled out of the ground, long time ago, and the water filled its hole. There's always water here. The elders used to come here when it was their time to die."

Dewling wanted to shout: *I know that!* However, he kept quiet and nodded in acknowledgment. The old man turned around until he was facing the water and the rock.

"I did a bad drawing," he whispered, his voice so quiet that Dewling had to sit in front of him. "Back then, couple weeks ago, when they brought the body of the little sparrow, I got very angry." He looked over at Dewling, his face soft, although his words were harsh. "How could they do that to my little sparrow? Those white bastards! I'd show them." The eyes closed. Tightly. "I did a drawing. A bad drawing."

A bad drawing? Dewling tried to understand, but it was beyond him.

"I'll get it back for you."

The old head shook with some effort. "I destroyed it. But somebody stole it, first. Some poor bloody white fella doesn't understand."

The printing process had worked beyond their expectations. The picture had been transferred to blank canvas, every dot and line and scrape standing out clearly. Campbell set it on an easel and stood back to admire it. He and Worrell had thought long and hard about their enterprise, deciding on the best course of marketing the picture. Eventually, Worrell had come up with the idea.

"You know, Wayne," he had said, still holding the photograph, "we could have this transferred to canvas and sell it as an uncolored painting. Let them paint it to their liking."

Campbell had snorted. "That's like selling a coloring-in book to children."

Worrell's face had taken on a look that indicated Campbell could well be an infidel. "No, Wayne. Aboriginal art is *very* mode. Something like this, that people can personalize . . . well, let's just try it. What say we make up a small run, say about a hundred, and see how they sell?"

Campbell had shrugged; he was not an expert on art, or its market, but he was willing to go along with the suggestion.

"Needs color," he said to himself as he studied the canvas. He turned and walked over to the package that Worrell had sent to him. In it were tiny pots of paint: ochre in a range of colors, all collected from the Flinders ranges. Worrell had even made sure that the powders were fixed with egg-white, so that they were as authentic as possible.

Campbell opened some of the pots and selected a brush. Where to start?

The river? He shrugged and stepped over to the picture. What color?

Rainbow river.

The thought just came to him, as if whispered into his mind, but he absorbed the idea.

"All right," he addressed the picture, "which color?"

Blue.

Again the idea insinuated itself in his mind, and he chuckled quietly: this was going to be easy.

The blue waters of the gulf shimmered and danced on his right, but Dewling glanced over to his left. The Flinders Ranges rose up from the plain a bare ten kilometers away. He could never get over how old they were. They had endured so many millions of years of erosion that anything sharp had long been leveled by the hammering of weather. In fact, they looked like a blanket thrown over a sleeping form.

He looked back at the road. Adelaide was four hours in front of him, and the old man had pressed him to hurry.

"You got to go to Adelaide," he had said, his eyes rheumy. "There's a poor white bastard, there, and he don't know what he's doing."

"Adelaide's a big place," Dewling had pointed out, careful to not appear to be rejecting the task. "I won't know—"

"You'll know." The words, although whispered, had the tone and finality of a command. He could not argue.

"How'm I going to find him?" Dewling repeated, to himself, as his car droned down the road.

The old man started awake, blinking rapidly as he tried to take in his surroundings. The shadows had lengthened and there was a babble of voices. He looked around and winced: a group of schoolchildren was climbing over the river's banks, laughing and giggling, ignoring the instructions of their teachers. Then he was spotted, and the noise level dropped. He was aware of hurried whispers and quiet giggles, but chose to ignore them. Instead, he listened to the sounds of the rocks and the whispers of the grass.

Time passed, although he did not pay attention to it. He was marginally aware that the schoolchildren were gone, when a deep sound reached out to him. A silent sound, rising from the rock, but resonating in all the objects around him.

Slowly, he raised his eyes to the silhouette of the rock. It was aware of him, but regarded him with a studied indifference. It raised its voice, louder now, although still silent, and the surface of the water shivered.

So, his little lizard had not made it in time. He'd known it would be left to him, although he'd tried to avoid it.

He opened some of his paints, took off his shirt and began painting designs on his face and chest.

Little magpie, little mischief;
Fast wings, cheeky beak;
Be brave, fly quick.

By the time he was finished, the water in the pool was swirling, gripped in an eddy of forces that even he could not understand. With a final look around at his surroundings, he stepped into the icy air that now bordered the water.

Dewling only noticed the building darkness after he had entered Adelaide. Up until then, he'd been too concerned with the traffic along the Port Wakefield Road. However, when he pulled over to the side to flip through the street directory, he had to turn on the cabin light. It was only four in the afternoon, but it was as dark as night. A quick glance at the other cars showed that their headlights were all off, as were the streetlights. People walking seemed to have no trouble with the lighting: he could see shoppers moving through shops, children on bikes, old people walking. No one noticed.

Strange. Am I the only one who can see?

He lifted his eyes above the surrounding buildings and looked at the green hills that ring Adelaide. The air in his chest froze.

There, on the hill's face, he could see a wound in the hill, and, like blood pouring from a wound, a black cloud was spurting out of the hillside, covering the city and blocking the sun.

Against every instinct in his body, Dewling put his car into drive and moved off in that direction, the old man's words swirling eerily in his mind.

I did a bad drawing.

You'll know.

I did a bad drawing.

Campbell blinked. His eyes were watery, and he could hardly see. He rubbed his eyes with the heels of his hand, but it didn't help. With a reluctance he couldn't understand, he laid his brush to one side and walked to the bathroom to splash water on his face. The water was cool and refreshed him; he hadn't realized how tired he'd become.

"Coffee," he muttered aloud.

A crow cawed. Close.

He looked out the window, and stepped forward. The outside was dark. No, not dark; it was black. From up here, in Belair, he should have been able to see the Adelaide Plains and the setting sun over the gulf. He couldn't even see the trees in his front yard. He ran his tongue over his lips, drawing in some water, moistening a mouth that had suddenly gone dry. He turned and walked toward the front door.

Black.

The thought rose in him as he passed the painting, and he stopped. All that remained was to finish the part that looked like a crow's head, only a few strokes with the brush. Just the beak and the head; a simple swirl, just the outline, with one color. The idea was seductive, to the point of being compelling, and he picked up the brush.

There was a noise, a distant sound, tantalizingly familiar, but just beyond his grasp. It added a rhythm to his action, a segue from inactivity to creation. He didn't even have to concentrate; he almost closed his eyes. His hand moved easily, and the crow's head was finished.

Now, he recognized the sound, as it flared around him, and swelled into being: it was a didgeridoo, played with anger. The crow's head in the picture turned and faced him. It wasn't a crow's head, but a headdress, and the Aboriginal face below it was painted white, the streaks of white ochre barely covering the black skin beneath. The eyes glared at him, bored into him, and the mouth opened.

The Figure cawed, a crow's voice filled with triumph and fury.

Campbell stepped back, his eyes opening wide. *This is not happening!!*

The painting went black. Every bit of its uncolored surface suddenly turned jet black. The rainbow colors faded, and the black captured all the animals and river, the sun and the moon, even the Figure. Campbell tried to turn and run, but the changing picture held him mesmerized.

The black spread. Like a growing shadow, it climbed over the walls, the floor, the ceiling. Campbell closed his eyes, trying to clear his head. When he opened them, he gasped.

His study was gone, and he was standing amongst tumbled boulders. The light of a campfire beyond the boulders threw a shimmering glow in his direction; he could hear the chirp of crickets and feel a cool breeze on his skin.

Something moved in the glow from the fire, the shadow of an approaching man.

His heart beating, he backed away.

"Bloody hell!" The voice came from behind Campbell. He whirled around to see a young Aborigine standing near him, his face openly shocked. "What's this?" The Aborigine took a step forward. "I just stepped into your house, but—" He looked around, eyes wide, then faced Campbell. "You should sue the decorators."

Campbell took a step backward, before realizing that it was towards the fire, towards the approaching Figure. He half-turned, looking wildly from the young Aborigine to the boulder that blocked his view of the fire.

The Figure stepped in view. The crow's headdress was still in place, glassy eyes staring at him with malice. Feathers had been sewn onto a cape draped over its body; more feathers padded its feet. It held a long spear in its hands. The Figure stopped and looked at them, eyes sharp and quick.

"You're in deep shit." The young Aborigine breathed the words, fear making his voice shake. He looked down to avoid the piercing gaze, and swallowed. "I hope it's you, anyway."

The fear in the other's voice bonded Campbell to him; he hoped that they had a common purpose. "What is it?" he asked from between teeth he had clenched together.

"Kadaicha," the young man said. "A bad spirit. Come to kill someone."

Campbell tried to turn, but his legs were frozen. The Kadaicha screamed again, then turned sideways, lifted the spear and took a slow, exaggerated step toward Campbell. And another, as slow and deliberate. In a macabre dance, the Kadaicha moved inexorably closer and the spear remained pointed at Campbell's heart. He managed to back away a step, then another, before a boulder blocked his retreat. The Kadaicha screamed, and all hope disappeared. Campbell watched the tip of the spear touch the front of his shirt.

The Kadaicha stabbed once, and the point slid through Campbell's chest. He felt the coldness of its passage, felt it slide out his back and into the rock behind him. He looked down at the shaft in shock.

There was no pain!

The spear was insubstantial. Campbell cried in relief, a sound dying on his lips when he saw the tight smile on the Kadaicha's face. Very slowly, the spear began to solidify, and Campbell felt pain in his chest. He clutched at the spear.

"Help!" he screamed, trying to pull the shaft out.

A hand grabbed the Kadaicha from behind and dragged it back. The spear slid free, and Campbell slipped to the ground, his lungs painfully grabbing air.

"Oh, shit," the young Aborigine muttered. "What have I done?" Taking a deep breath, he stepped between Campbell and the Kadaicha.

A wind started from nowhere, going nowhere, and a maelstrom of dust and rocks swirled around them. An old man, Campbell recognized him at once, stepped out of the air, and threw his hands up. He chittered wildly, like an angry bird, and faced the Kadaicha, who regarded him with annoyance, but did not back away.

Another shape stepped out of the air, a young girl with heavy sadness about her. She walked up to the Kadaicha and spoke softly to it. Campbell couldn't hear her words, but they were quiet and pleading. The Kadaicha looked at her, its head cocked to one side. Then, its face twisted with anger, it walked forward, brushing the girl and the old man aside.

Campbell barely managed to throw himself sideways. The spear hissed past him and sparks flew off the rock. He saw the point withdrawn and the mighty arm prepared for another thrust. The old man shrieked in the voice of a bird, a magpie, and moved forward.

The Kadaicha also screamed, this time in irritation, and strode past Campbell. The Aborigines followed it around the boulders and disappeared. Moments passed in silence, and he was starting to realize that he didn't feel safe on his own, when he heard a scream. Scared to follow the Kadaicha, but more scared to stay, Campbell followed the others.

He walked into another clear area, and stopped in shock.

The Aborigines were watching three white men in the middle of the cleared area. The three men huddled together, naked fear on their faces. The Kadaicha circled them, its spear weaving through the air. It saw Campbell enter from the rocks, and gave him a deadly, mirthless smile. With casual speed, it thrust its spear first into one, then another, and then the third man. They grabbed at their wounds and collapsed wordlessly. Campbell knew with absolute certainty that they were dead. The girl turned a stricken gaze on Campbell.

The Kadaicha walked from the area, its back defiantly straight.

"They the ones who killed the girl?" Campbell asked.

The old man gave him a hard stare, and followed the Kadaicha.

"Come on," the young Aboriginal pulled on Campbell's arm. The two of them returned to the cleared area where Campbell had first seen the Kadaicha. Only the old man waited for them.

"You bloody stole my bloody picture."

When Campbell nodded, the old man sighed. "You should leave things alone. That was a picture I drew when I was stupid angry. I drew it to call a Kadaicha. I called him to kill white fellars. All white fellars. All Kadaichas are bad. Can't control them. They do what they want. You shouldn't touch what you don't know."

Campbell could only nod and look down. "I'm sorry. You can have it back."

"I don't bloody want it, you stupid bastard. Pictures like this got to be destroyed." The old man leaned close. "I have to paint my body, to protect me, and then dance on the picture. Only way to get rid of picture. You stay 'way from things you don't understand, 'cause this not your Dreaming. We're lucky to get rid of this Kadaicha."

The old man turned. "Little lizard, you did good today."

"Thanks, Uncle." The young man looked deferentially at the ground.

"Only one thing," the old man said. His voice grew distant. "You got a phone there? You call up the tribe. Tell 'em to get me from Death Rock. I'm bloody hungry."

Campbell blinked. He and the young man were back in his study, and light from the setting sun streamed through the window.

"Did all that really happen?"

The young man looked closely at him. "No. Your imagination played silly-buggers with you. Nothing happened." His eyes bored into Campbell's.

The painting was still on the easel, its surface a featureless black. Nodding with agreement and uncertainty, Campbell turned from him and walked to the front door. The view over Adelaide was clear. He rubbed a tired hand over his tired eyes.

Nothing happened.

A strange sound caught his attention, and he looked up at the trees just as the other man joined him. They both stared up, a cold fear gripping their chests.

The tree was alive with crows.

As they watched, one of the crows gave a squawk, and all the birds took off, scattering in different directions.

"What was that about?" the young man asked.

Campbell groaned and sagged against the doorframe, his eyes closed tightly. "Quentin's sold another hundred of those paintings."

Mom and Dad at the Home Front

Sherwood Smith

Sherwood Smith lives in Westminster, California, has been married twenty years (two kids, two dogs, and a house full of books), and is currently a part-time teacher as well as a writer. She says she began making books out of taped paper towels when she was five years old, and at eight began writing stories about another world full of magic and adventure—and hasn't stopped yet. She studied history and languages in college, lived in Europe one year, and has worked at tending bar in a harbor tavern and at various jobs in Hollywood. She began publishing in the late 1980s and really took off in the 1990s. She now has over a dozen books out in the last decade, ranging from space opera (five volumes of the Exordium series, in collaboration with Dave Trowbridge, and three novels in collaboration with Andre Norton) to children's fantasy (seven novels). She has also published numerous short stories.

"Mom and Dad at the Home Front," published in Realms of Fantasy, *explores the familiar fantasy trope: children who escape to a marvelous fantasy world at night, as in* Peter Pan *and many others before and since. There were several fantasy stories published this year on this very theme, but the others were, as usual, from the children's point of view. This is from the parents' point of view and struck us as an interesting twist.*

Before Rick spoke, I saw from his expression what was coming.

I said the words first. "The kids are gone again."

Rick dropped onto the other side of the couch, propping his brow on his hand. I couldn't see his eyes, nor could he see me.

It was just past midnight. All evening, after we'd seen our three kids safely tucked into bed, we'd stayed in separate parts of the house, busily working away at various projects, all of them excuses not to go to bed ourselves—even though it was a work night.

Rick looked up, quick and hopeful. "Mary. Did one of the kids say something to you?"

"No. I had a feeling, that was all. They were so sneaky after dinner. Didn't you see Lauren—" I was about to say *raiding the flashlight and the Swiss Army Knife from the earthquake kit* but I changed, with almost no pause, to "—sneaking around like . . . like Inspector Gadget?"

He tried to smile. We'd made a deal, last time, to take it easy, to try to keep our sense of humor, since we knew where the kids were.

Sort of knew where the kids were.

How many other parents were going through this nightmare? There had to be others. We couldn't be the only ones. I'd tried hunting for some kind of support group on the Internet—*Seeking other parents whose kids disappear to other worlds*—and not surprisingly the e-mail I got back ranged from offers from psychologists for a free mental exam to "opportunities" to MAKE $ IN FIVE DAYS.

So I'd gone digging again, this time at the library, rereading all those childhood favorites: C.S. Lewis, L. Frank Baum, Joy Chant, Ruth Nicholls, and then more recent favorites, like Diana Wynne Jones. All the stories about kids who somehow slipped from this world into another, adventuring widely and wildly, before coming safely home via that magic ring, or gate, or spell, or pair of shoes. Were there hints that adults missed? Clues that separated the real worlds from the made-up ones?

"Evidence," I said, trying to be logical and practical and adult. "They've vanished like this three times that we know about. Doors and windows locked. Morning back in their beds. Sunburned. After the last time, just outside R.J.'s room you saw two feathers and a pebble like nothing on Earth. You came to get me, the kids woke up, the things were gone when we got there. When asked, the response was, and I quote, 'What feathers?' "

But Rick knew he had seen those feathers, and so we'd made our private deal: Wait, and take it easy.

Rick rubbed his hands up his face, then looked at me. And broke the deal. "What if this time they don't come back?"

We sat in silence. Then, because there was no answer, we forced ourselves to get up, to do chores, to follow a normal routine in hopes that if we were really, really good, and really, really normal, morning would come the same as ever, with the children in their beds.

I finished the laundry. Rick vacuumed the living room and took the trash cans out. I made three lunches and put them in the fridge.

I put fresh bath towels in the kids' bathroom.

At one o'clock we went to bed and turned out the light, but neither of us slept; I lay for hours listening to the clock tick, and to Rick's unhappy breathing.

Dawn. I made myself get up and take my shower and dress, all the while listening, listening . . . and when I finally nerved myself to check, I found a kid-sized lump in each of the three beds, a dark curly head on each pillow. R. J.'s face was pink from the Sun—from *what* Sun?—and Lauren had a scrape on one arm. Alisha snored softly, her hands clutching something beneath the bedclothes.

I tiptoed over and lifted the covers. Her fingers curled loosely around a long wooden wand with golden carving on its side. If it wasn't a magic wand, I'd eat it for breakfast.

Alisha stirred. I laid her covers down and tiptoed out.

"A magic wand?" Rick whispered fiercely. "Did you take it?"

"Of course not!" I whispered back. "She'd have woken up, and—"

"And what?" he prompted.

I sighed, too tired to think. "And would have been mad at me."

"Mad?" Rick repeated, his whisper rising almost to a squeak. "Earth to Mary—*we* are the parents. *They* are the kids. We're supposed to keep them safe. How can we do it if they are *going off the planet every night?*"

I slipped back into Alisha's room. She had rolled over, and the wand had fallen off the mattress onto her blue fuzzy rug.

I bent, my heart thumping so loud I was afraid she'd hear it, closed my fingers round the wand, and tiptoed out.

"Hmm." Rick waved it back and forth. It whistled—just like any stick you wave in the air—but no magic sparks came out, no lights, no mysterious hums.

"This has got to be how they get away," Rick murmured, holding the wand up to his nose and sniffing. "Huh. Smells like coriander, if anything."

"Except how did they get away the first time?"

"Good question."

I felt my shoulders hunch, a lifetime habit of bracing against worry.

Rick grimaced. "I know what you're thinking, and I'm thinking it too, but maybe it's OK. Maybe the other world isn't a twisted disaster like ours."

"But—why *our* kids?"

Rick shrugged, waving the wand in a circle. "Found by a kid from another world? Some kid who knows magic, maybe?" His voice suspended, and he gave me a sort of grinning wince. "Kid magician?" He laughed, the weak, unfunny laugh that expresses pain more than joy. "Listen to me! Say those words to any other adult and he'll dial 1-800-NUTHOUSE."

I gripped my hands together, thinking of my kids, and safety. I said, "Touch it on me."

"What?" Rick stared.

"Go ahead. If it sends me where they go—"

Rick rubbed his eyes. "I'm still having trouble with the concept. Right. Of course. But we'll go together." His clammy left hand closed round my equally damp fingers, and with his right he tapped us both on our heads.

Nothing happened.

Rick looked hopeful. "Maybe it's broken."

"I don't think we're that lucky," I muttered, and went down to fix breakfast.

The kids appeared half an hour later, more or less ready for school. The looks they exchanged with each other let me know at once that they were worried—desperately—about something.

Then three pairs of brown eyes turned my way.

"Um, Mom?" R.J. said finally, as he casually buttered some toast. "Did you, uh, do house cleaning this morning? You know, before we woke up?"

"No," I replied truthfully, watching his toast shred into crumbs. He didn't even notice.

"Did you, like, find any, um, art projects?" Lauren asked.

"Art projects?" I repeated.

R. J. frowned at his toast, then pushed it aside.

Alisha said, "Like a stick. For a play. A play at school. Uhn!" This last was a gasp of pain—someone had obviously kicked her under the table. Her eyes watered, and she muttered to Lauren, "What did you do that for?"

"The play was last month, remember?" Lauren said in a sugary voice, rolling her eyes toward me. "Mom helped paint scenery!"

I fussed with my briefcase, giving them sneakier looks than they were giving me, as I watched them trying to communicate by quick whispers and pointing fingers. Rick came in then, looked at us all, and went out again—and I could hear him turning a laugh into a cough.

"You all reminded me of a bunch of spies in a really bad movie," Rick said later, when I was driving us to our respective workplaces. He grinned. "All squinting at each other like—"

"Rick." I tried not to be mad. "It is *our kids* we're spying on. Lying to. I feel terrible!"

He said, "I don't. At least they're home—"

"They're not at home. They're at school."

"They're safe. The wand's in the trunk of the car, by the way. And as soon as I can, I'm going to take the damn thing out and burn it, and make sure the kids *stay* safe."

I sighed as I drove past palm trees and billboards—the once-reassuring visual boundaries of mundane reality. Mundane made sense. It was safe, because there were no reminders in that everyday blandness that the rules we make to govern our lives are not absolute, and that safety is an illusion.

I dropped Rick off at his printshop. Sighed again when I parked the car.

And I sighed a third time when I sat down at my computer, punched up Autocad, and stared at the equations for the freeway bridge I was supposed to be designing.

When we got home, the first sign that Something Was Up was the house—spic and span. Usually housecleaning is something that gets done when Rick and I feel guilty, or when it's gotten so cluttered and dusty I turn into the Wicked Bitch of the West and dragoon everyone into jobs.

I knew, of course, that they'd given the place a thorough search—but at least they hadn't made a mess. I considered this a Responsible Act, and brought it up to Rick later, when we got ready for bed. And didn't a Responsible Act deserve one in return?

"Very responsible," he agreed. "Won't it be a pleasant, refreshing change to sleep the entire night, knowing they are safely in their beds?"

"Did you destroy the wand?" I asked.

He studied the ceiling as though something of import had been written there. "No. Not yet. But I will."

Home life was normal for about a week.

At least on the surface.

The kids tried another surreptitious search, more oblique questions, and then finally they just gave up. I know the exact hour—the minute—they gave up because they really gave up. Not just their secret world, but everything. Oh, they ate and went to school and did their homework, but the older ones worked with about as much interest and enthusiasm as a pair of robots, and Alisha drifted about, small and silent as a little ghost.

I hated seeing sad eyes at dinner. We cooked their favorite foods. Rick made barbequed ribs and spaghetti on his nights, and I fixed Mexican food and Thai chicken on my nights—loving gestures on our part that failed to kindle the old joy. R.J. and Lauren said "Please" and "Thank you" in dismal voices, and picked at the food as though it were prune-and-pea casserole.

Alisha didn't talk, just *looked.*

I avoided her gaze.

Eight days later I passed by Lauren's room with a stack of clean sheets and towels, and heard soft, muffled sobs. Her unhappiness smote my guilty heart and I was soon in our room snuffling into my pillow, the clean laundry laying on the carpet where I'd dropped it.

We're the parents. They are the kids.

That's what Rick had said.

I got up, wiped my face on one of those clean towels, and went back—not sure what I'd say or do—but I stopped when I heard all three kids in Lauren's room.

"I can't help it." Lauren's voice was high and teary. "Queen Liete was going to make me a maid of honor to Princess Elte—my very best friend! Now we've missed the ceremony!"

"You can't miss it, not if you're the person being ceremonied." That was Alisha's brisk, practical voice. Even though she's the youngest, she's always been the practical one.

"Celebrated," R.J. muttered. "How much time has passed there? What if they think we don't want to come back? That we don't care any more? Brother Owl was going to teach me shape-changing on my own, without his help!"

Lauren sniffed, gulped, and cried, "I wish you hadn't picked up that stupid wand, Alisha. I wish we'd never gone. It's so much worse, being stuck here, and *remembering.*"

"I don't think so." That was R.J.'s sturdy voice. "Somebody got the wand, but nothing can take away what I remember. Riding on the air currents so high, just floating there. . . ."

"Learning a spell," Alisha put in, "and seeing it *work.* Knowing that it had to be us, that we made all the difference."

"You're right," Lauren said. The tears were gone. "Only

for me the best memory was sneaking into the Grundles' dungeon. Oh, I hated it at the time—it was scarier than anything I'd ever done—but I knew I *had* to get Prince Dar out and, being a girl, and an outworlder, and a very fast runner, I was the *only one* who could get by those magic wards. I liked that. Being the only one who could do it."

"Because of our talents," Alisha murmured longingly.

"Because we saw the signs, and we believed what we saw," R. J. added, even more longingly.

Gloomy silence.

I tiptoed away to pick up the towels and sheets.

Rick was in the garage, supposedly working on refinishing one of the patio chairs, but I found him tossing the sander absently from hand to hand while he stared at R. J.'s old bicycle.

"You haven't burned the wand," I guessed.

He gave his head a shake, avoiding my eyes. "I can't."

"I think we ought to give it back," I said.

He looked up. His brown eyes were unhappy, reminding me terribly of R. J.'s sad eyes over his untouched dinner.

"They're our kids," I said. "Not our possessions." I told him what I'd overheard.

"Talents," he repeated when I was done.

I said, "What if Alisha had been born with some incredible music talent? She'd be just as lost to us if she were at some studio practicing her instrument eight hours a day, or being taken by her music coach to concerts all over the country."

"She'd be safe," Rick said.

"Not if some drunk driver hits her bus—or a terrorist blows up her concert hall. We taught them to be fair, and to be sensible. But to be totally safe in this world we'd have to lock them in a room. The world *isn't* totally safe. I wish it were."

Rick tossed the sander once more from hand to hand, then threw it down onto the workbench. "They lied to us."

"They didn't lie. Not until the wand disappeared. And we lied right back."

"That's love," Rick said. "We did it out of love. Our duty as parents is to keep them safe, and we can't possibly protect them in some world we've never even seen!"

"Think of Lauren, making friends. For five years we've worried about her inability to make friends—she's never fit in with the kids at school."

"She needs to learn to fit in," Rick said. "In this world. Where we live."

I felt myself slipping over to his way of thinking, and groped for words, for one last argument. "What if," I said. "What if those people from the other world find their way here, but they only have the one chance—and they offer the kids only the one chance to go back? Forever? What if we make them choose between us and that world? They've always come back, Rick. It's love, not duty, that brings them back, but they don't even know it, because they've never been forced to make that choice."

Rick slammed out of the garage, leaving me staring at R. J.'s little-boy bike.

I was in bed alone for hours, not sleeping, when Rick finally came in.

"I waited until Alisha conked off," he said, and drew in a shaky breath. "Damn! That kid racks up more under-the-covers reading time than I did when I was a kid, and I thought I was the world's champ."

"You put the wand back?" I asked, sitting up.

"Right under the bed."

I hugged my knees to my chest, feeling the emotional vertigo I'd felt when Lauren was first born, and I stared down at this child who had been inside me for so long. Now a separate being, whose memories would not be my memories. Whose life would not be my life.

And Rick mused, "How much of my motivation was jealousy, and not just concern for their safety? I get a different answer at midnight than I do at noon."

"You mean, *why didn't it ever happen to me?*"

His smile was wry.

They were gone the next night, of course.

It was raining hard outside, and I walked from room to silent room, touching their empty beds, their neatly lined-up books and toys and personal treasures, the pictures on their walls. Lauren had made sketches of a girl's face—Princess Elte? In R. J.'s room, the sketches were all of great birds, raptors with beaks and feathers of color combinations never seen in this world. He'd stored in jewelry boxes the feathers and rocks he'd brought back across that unimaginable divide.

Alisha's tidy powder-blue room gave nothing away.

The next morning I was downstairs early, fixing pancakes, my heart light because I'd passed by the three rooms and heard kid-breathing in each.

I almost dropped the spatula on the floor when I looked up and there was Alisha in her nightgown.

She ran to me, gave me a hug round the waist. "Thanks, Mom," she said.

"Thanks?" My heart started thumping again. "For pancakes?"

"For putting it back," she said. "I smelled your shampoo in my room that day, when the wand disappeared. But I didn't tell the others. I didn't want them to be mad."

I suddenly found the floor under my bottom. "Your dad put it back," I said. "We were in it together. We didn't mean to make you unhappy."

"I know." Alisha sat down neatly on the floor next to me, cross-legged, and leaned against my arm, just as she had when she was a toddler. "We didn't tell you because we knew you'd say no. Not to be mean. But out of grownup worry."

"We just want to keep you safe," I said.

She turned her face to look up at me, her eyes the color of Rick's eyes, their shape so like my mother's. "And we wanted to keep you safe."

"Ignorance is not real safety," I pointed out. "It's the mere illusion of safety."

Alisha gave me an unrepentant grin. "How many times have you said about us, *they're safer not knowing?*" she retorted, and then she added, "That's why we always go at midnight, and we're only gone a couple of hours. We can do that because the time there doesn't work like here."

"But another *world.* How can we set safety rules? We don't know what happens." I held her tightly against me.

"You send us to school," Alisha said, pulling away just a little, so she could look at me again. "You don't know what happens there. Not really."

I thought back to my own school days, and then thought of recent media orgies, and felt my heart squeeze. "True. But we're used to it. And habit and custom are probably the strongest rules we know. Can we go with you to the other world? Just to see it?" I asked.

Alisha shook her head. "There's a big spell. Prevents grownups, because of this big war in the past. Only kids can cross over—not even teenagers. One day we'll be too old. I know you'll be real sorry!"

I tried to laugh. It wasn't very successful, but we both smiled anyway. "It's not every set of parents who have kids who cross worlds—you'll have to give us time to get used to it."

She hugged me again, and flitted away to get dressed.

"R. J. has taken to telling me stories," Rick said a few days later. "Not—quite—admitting anything, just offering me these stories instead of me reading to him."

Only Lauren went about as if nothing were different, everything were normal. Keeping the other world secret was important to her, so we had to respect that, and give her the space to keep it.

"Alisha told me more about magic," I said that next week.

The kids were gone again. A spectacular thunderstorm raged like battling dragons outside. We didn't even try to sleep. We sat in the kitchen across from each other, hands cradling mugs of hot chocolate. Rick had put marshmallows in it, and whipped cream, and just enough cinnamon to give off a delicious scent.

"Magic." He shook his head.

"The amazing thing is, it sounds a lot like the basic principles of engineering."

"I think R.J. has learned how to turn himself into a bird," Rick said, stirring the marshmallows round and round with his finger. "They fly in a flock, and watch for the Grundles, who I guess have a bad case of What's-yours-is-mine as far as other kingdoms are concerned." His smile faded, and he shook his head. "Nothing will be the same again, Mary—we can't even pretend to be a normal family."

"Is anybody?" I asked. "I mean, really?"

What *is* normal?

We live in our houses and follow schedules and pick jobs that are sensible and steady and keep the bills paid, but in my dreams I fly, as I did when I was small.

"The universe is still out there just beyond the palm trees and malls and freeways," I said. "And the truth is we still don't really know the rules."

What we do know is that we love our children, will always love them, until the stars have burned away to ash, and though parents are not issued experience along with our babies' birth certificates, we learn a little wisdom and a lot of compromise as the children grow.

Rick said slowly, "Well, I hope Lauren and her sword-swinging princess pal are kicking some serious Grundle butt."

We remember how to laugh.

The Fey

Renee Bennett

Renee Bennett was born near Seattle and raised there, and in Alaska, and in Alberta, Canada, and acquired a Bachelor's degree in Linguistics from the University of Calgary, after forays into General Studies and Fine Arts. She has had the usual wide array of jobs, including salesperson, office worker, movie extra, and beaded fringe maker, of which the first has been the most constant and the last the most peculiar. Her fiction has appeared in Marion Zimmer Bradley's Fantasy Magazine, TransVersions, *and* Dreams of Decadence; *she has also sold work to CBC Radio's* Alberta Anthology.

"The Fey" appeared in Marion Zimmer Bradley's Fantasy Magazine, *one of several magazines in the field to close its door this year. About this story, she says, "The idea first came to me in a dream, which is not how I usually get ideas. Dreams are so disjointed that, enjoyable as they are to experience, they lose far too much in the retelling. What I kept from this one was the intense feeling of disconnection that Morgwenna suffers under, in the shadows of the trees, and the rest of the story flowed from there." Arthurian fantasy is one of the mainstreams of the fantasy story these days, and we found this an usually interesting example.*

As a child, clumsy was a curse I feared, as I feared the shadows I saw in bricks and railings, leaves swaying like ghosts all around me. Vines that clutched, twigs that stabbed, the thick boles of trees that blocked my way and hid the sane world from my desperate searching.

My mother thought me mad, banned all television to me, then spent long years consulting doctors and psychiatrists. I spent those years describing trees, drawing chalk lines on floors where the trunks thrust up, describing new buds in spring, stark branches in winter. Listened, as learned men and women spoke of my delusions, of that wood that was there for me, in rooms where I was treated as if I were not there for them.

School was not a possibility, of course. How could I attend a school, where ghostly brambles infested doorways, where a fresh-running stream coursed across a hallway without a ford to cross it, where a deep green chasm opened up beneath my feet on the edge of the playground?

Another child, laughing, pushed me into that. I dashed to the rocks, broke my arm in two places and my head in one, and left teachers wondering how so many bruises came to me in a fall from my feet to my face.

But I remember falling farther than that.

Tutors after that, who thought me odd. One, who thought me whimsical, gave me pencils and papers and asked me to draw what I saw.

Leaves and twigs and the trunks of trees, marching into phantom distances. "

Where are the spiders?" he said, touching one drawing, then another. "Where are the birds?"

I looked at my work, pencil still. "I don't see spiders or birds," I said, and lay my hand flat on the face of the page. "I don't see animals or people. I see flowers sometimes," and I looked up into his face.

He blinked at me several times from behind his glasses.

"Trees," he said.

He brought a book of Audubon to the next session, a book full of watercolor plates of trees and shrubs. I had never heard of Audubon. I was enchanted.

"This one," I said, pointing to a graceful drawing of a beech. "I see them on the hilly places. And these," pointing to a page of hemlocks, "these on the slopes." I was eight years old. I had never seen a hemlock, nor a beech. My childish drawings were full of beech twigs and hemlock leaves.

He rubbed his nose where his glasses sat, and frowned. He made notes in a little book about it, which I did not mind, not so much as I minded the doctors. My tutor had given me what the doctors had not—names. A sense of belonging to my world of trees. I could forgive him his notes for that.

Thus I discovered botany, and painting. Years passed within the pages of books, eight to eighteen to twenty-eight, a lifeline between where I lived with people and where I lived with trees, Trees that sometimes were shadows in silence, sometimes so solid I bruised myself on roots or scratched myself on brambles. The world passed around me, great and small events, the deaths of parents and pets, the fighting and winning of wars and governments. I paid little attention, because of trees.

There was a border, an arm of sea that guarded my island home from the mainland. Navies fought back and forth and back again to possess the waterway until, finally, the mainlanders won it. I knew this dimly, heard in scattered reports between the whispers of leaves and the tap of twig on twig. Grown, I had inherited my mother's house, had found a comfortable living for myself with paintbrushes and canvas and images of forest. In wartime my paintings sold remarkably well. Glimpses of serenity.

And then the mainlanders landed, and our unready army shattered under the new advance. I looked up and out my window, between a maple seedling and the knuckled root of its mother, and found black uniforms marching past in the street.

A knock on the door. I got up, pushed the panel open, faced an officer with red piping on his trousers and dogwood blooms shining pale around his face. He spoke stiffly, his mouth wooden around the consonants and vowels of my language.

"This town is now a garrison," he said, taking his hat off to me and holding it in front of him like some diminutive shield. "You will have guests, soldiers, living with you. I must see your premises, we will determine how many you will service."

I misliked his choice of words, but then, he was not here by choice. I let him in, and the two soldiers who followed, who stared at me and made lewd gestures behind the officer's back after the introductions. I stared at them until the shape of the dogwood became clear behind them, and they fell to muttering between themselves.

I had three bedrooms upstairs, all unused. I myself slept in the little den off the parlor, which was my studio. The officer looked like he could not decide if I were mad or merely odd, and told the two with him to choose rooms.

"I would rather have you, sir officer," I said, watching the taller of the two soldiers loss his bag onto my mother's bed. "These two have few manners around women."

The officer turned red, and muttered something about finding another soldier for the other room. He escaped my presence with that, while the two soldiers snickered behind his back.

I went down the stairs to the kitchen. The taller of the two soldiers followed me, while the other tried the taps in the bathroom upstairs. I pulled vegetables out of the icebox with the sound of running water above my head.

"I am Luth. Corporal Luth," said the man in my kitchen. He sauntered over and leaned over me as I took a peeler to a carrot. "You will like me. Won't you?"

He was trying to frighten me. He knew nothing about trees. "You are a poor fortune-teller," I told him, and picked up the big knife. He looked at that and sauntered back over to the door. I chopped the carrot, got the biggest pot out and put the pieces in.

"We are winning," he said, sounding sulky. I picked an onion out of my pile of vegetables and cut it into eighths. He shifted against the door. I lifted the onion pieces into the pot, then chose a potato. He shifted again. "You don't believe me."

"Belief is over-rated," I said, and discarded the potato. It had a black hollow in it.

A third soldier arrived, a woman, yellow-haired and bluff. I disliked her at first sight, a rare thing for me. She stood out solid among my trees, an even rarer thing. I served her vegetable soup, frowning, trying to remember the last time that had happened.

"I don't bite, Mistress Morgana," she said, and grinned as I startled out of thought.

"Too bad," Luth said, and grinned at her glare.

She and I stared at him, until he fell to muttering into his soup bowl. The other man slurped, and pronounced me a good cook.

"I am Jan. Jannivar," said the yellow-haired soldier. She followed me to the sink after supper, watched me run water and soap over the dishes there. I looked at her and saw oak leaves shadowing her hair. The oaks are dignified trees—they come to my sight only for special occasions.

"Jannivar," I said, rolling the syllables in my mouth. Then, "Gwenivere."

She caught her breath. Then something thumped and crashed upstairs. Gwen looked up and swore. "I'll deal with them," she said, and ran. I finished the dishes and opened the back door onto my garden, let the night into my kitchen. Ghost leaves flittered around my feet, driven by a ghost breeze. Ghost oaks.

"Gwenivere," I said into the black beyond the door, and a white moth fluttered drunkenly across the light. Its wings were translucent—it belonged to the trees.

I have no sons. Perhaps the old tragedy won't play this time.

Gwenivere. It was too much to ask; fate has no mercy.

I got my shawl and headed for the street. Luth met me at the door. "Where do you think you're going? There's a curfew."

I stared at him, recognizing him now that Gwenivere had stirred up the old memories, other lives, other times. "You've never been able to hold me, Lot, even when you should." There was a broken pine behind him; I flicked a corner of my shawl into his eyes and stepped around it when he blinked.

Brambles scratched my hands. The soft earth of the forest road took me through the door while Lot shouted in confusion. I had not done all of my exploring of trees between the pages of books in the decades after my broken arm.

Tragedy. I am a painter now, and happy in it. I refuse to be part of ancient feuds, ancient curses, ancient wars that repeat themselves endlessly, uselessly through lifetimes. If I must, I will strangle Arthur with my bare hands to stay out of it this time. I went looking for my brother.

The streets were full of fair-haired soldiers, black uniforms marching together, the red stripes on the trousers flickering in the dark like pale flames. Tall, men and women both, their voices raised sometimes in orders and sometimes in question. They paid me no heed, small dark-haired, dark-eyed woman that I am, as they paid no heed to the trees I sheltered under.

At a corner, a man in grey pants and a green sweater

knelt on the pavement, his hands clasped behind his neck. A neighbor; he had bought painted lilies from me, for his wife. His face was bleak. The men around him conferred in low tones in their own language, sounding angry, perhaps frustrated.

I stayed among my trees. Whatever they had caught him at, I could not help him now.

"You there! Who are you, and where are you going?"

Someone else caught. There was a lightening over the roofs of the houses, toward the town square; I headed in that direction. Then a man's hand fell on my wrist and he pulled me around, out of the trees. He shook me and I blinked upward . . . into Lancelot du Lac's blue eyes.

He shook me again. "I said, who are you, and where are you going?"

He's at least half fey himself—where else would he have got his black hair? Or that power coursing through him, that can see through trees, to snatch me out from among them? But he is blind to his deeper self, and for all his usually pretty manners, I sometimes wonder who Lancelot du Lac's real mother was, and why he never speaks of her.

His manners were not pretty now. His grip tightened on my wrist and he shouted something over his shoulder to one of the men around my neighbor. The man nodded and pulled something steel-glittery out of a belt pouch. Lancelot reached for the handcuffs.

I should have strangled Gwenivere. Stabbed her in her sleep, poisoned her soup—and Lot's too, while I was at it. That would have broken the curse of us past mending. That would have stopped her meeting Arthur, and Lancelot, and the whole bloody mess blowing up again, to exaltation and ruin.

Inevitable, now. And all my fault.

As a child, clumsy was a curse I feared, tripping over roots that no one else saw. As an adult, clumsy is a curse I fear, tripping over feelings more complex to map than any forest, real or ghost.

Well. Perhaps the time is past for fear.

I lifted my chin as he put the first cuff on. "Take me to Arthur," I said, and watched the blue eyes narrow in puzzlement.

There is still a way. "Tell him . . . Merlin is come."

Golden Bell, Seven, and the Marquis of Zeng

Richard Parks

Richard Parks is a Mississippi native. He says, "Whether it's something in the environment or the local gene pool, Mississippi has always produced more than its share of scoundrels, myth-makers, and storytellers. I don't know why, but we can't help it." He sold his first story to Amazing *back in 1980. After a hiatus, he sold his second to* Asimov's *in 1993. Since then he's had stories in* Science Fiction Age, Asimov's, Dragon, Realms of Fantasy, *and* Weird Tales, *as well as in numerous anthologies. He published a number of fantasy stories this year, giving us several fine ones to choose from for this anthology.*

This story is a love story in a fantasy Orient, another of the traditional settings of fantasy. It appeared in the premier issue of the expensively produced new magazine Black Gate. *Of this story Parks says: "on my daily walk yesterday I saw a flying Chinese dragon. I could clearly see its whiskers, mouth and eyes. Its body was long and gray-white and it blew smoke across half the sky. Now, I've studied science. I've flown in jet planes through the clouds and I know they're nothing but water vapor, ice crystals, and drifting bits of dust. Yet, every now and then and despite all that I know to be true, I will still look at the clouds and see dragons. Golden Bell from 'Golden Bell, Seven, and the Marquis of Zeng' brazenly appeared to me in a dream and whispered, 'I have a fever of poetry that consumes me, a malady of song that wears me down.' I told myself the story to figure out why she was there. Sooner or later I'll have to do the same for that dragon."*

In the province of Zeng, in the time before the First Emperor QinShiHuang, there lived a bright young lad of a large family. By the time the boy was born his parents had run out of both patience and imagination, so the child was simply called "Seven." He was actually the tenth child, but that didn't seem to matter.

In those days Zeng was ruled by the Marquis Yi, but Zeng itself was under the protection of the more powerful state of Chu and at peace for the first time in many years. As a further blessing, the Marquis' love of music and wine and concubines kept him in his palace most of the time and not out and about causing mischief for his subjects. It was a good time.

Still, if people can sometimes be content, time and the fates never are. In the forty-fifth year of the Marquis Yi's time under Heaven, Seven came into the city of Leigudun on an errand for his father and there, to his everlasting delight and sorrow, he fell in love.

Seven had just counted out three bronze coins to the potter's wife for the new jar his father needed when there arose a commotion on the main street. Gongs, bells, and whistles collided in a divine racket; reed flutes and stone chimes added a softer counterpoint. Seven carried his jar from the side street where the potter had his shop to the main avenue of the city.

People lined the way like a living hedge, eyes turned toward the south entrance to the city gates. The street itself was clear, and two of Yi's mounted guards walked their horses up and down the cobbled road to make sure it remained that way. It was hard to see with all the people in his way, but Seven finally found a spot closer to the street. He turned and saw the vanguard of a procession, and now the shouts and cheers of the people added to the din.

The Marquis' personal bodyguard led the way walking four abreast, resplendent in their bronze and leather brigandines and red sashes, carrying shining spears. Next came two court officials wearing silk and high headpieces. Each carried a jade tablet with the letters of greeting and wishes for happiness to the Marquis from the King. Next came servants, and more guards, and dancers, and more guards, and musicians, and more guards, and then a wagon containing the most beautiful girl Seven had ever seen or even imagined.

"By the Circle of Heaven . . ." was all Seven could say, for several long moments.

She sat on a red cushion placed in a gilt chair. Her hair was long and fell down her back like a flow of black jade, shining with an inner light that had nothing to do with the glaring sun. She was dressed in a robe of red silk with Bat and Dragon motifs appliquéd in yellow and black, and she wore red silk slippers on her dainty feet. She looked at the people thronged around her with a mixture of bewilderment and fear; she did not look happy, and it hurt Seven with a pain of fire that such a girl could be so sad when there might be something, anything, he could do for her.

Seven tugged on the sleeve of a well-dressed man of the *shih* class standing near to him. "Your pardon, High One, but is this girl a princess? I'm sure she must be."

The man managed to look down his nose at Seven, a remarkable skill considering that he was a good three fingerwidths shorter than Seven himself. "You're a foolish, ignorant boy to even ask such a question," he said.

"Certainly what you say is true, for I have asked," Seven said agreeably.

The man sighed. "Of course she is not a princess! She is a gift from Marquis Yi's overlord; do you think the great Hui, King of Chu, would give a princess away for a mere concubine? There are royal marriages and alliances going wanting! No. Her family were artisans at best or perhaps even of the peasant *nung*; she is barely adequate as a gift even under the circumstances." The man shook his head in disgust.

Seven merely shrugged. "She is very beautiful," he said.

"In a rough sort of way," the man conceded. "And the Marquis must surely accept her with appearance of gladness or admit the insult and lose face. He must have offended our overlord in some small regard."

"Insult?" Seven said wistfully, "My fondest hope would be to have someone insult me so agreeably."

"You are a foolish boy, as I said, and cannot hope to understand these things. In any other circumstances the Marquis would be compelled to send her back and pretend it no more than a jest on the part of his lord, and diplomacy would flourish for months. But there's no time for such courtly games now."

"No time? You are certainly correct that I do not understand. It would honor me past expression if you would agree to enlighten me."

For a moment the man's haughty demeanor faded. "You have truly not heard?" When Seven assured the man that he had not, the man became somber. "It is sad to relate, but here it is—the Marquis Yi is very ill. His physicians do not expect him to live to see the new year. This is King Hui's parting gift to his royal servant."

"This is most distressing," Seven said, "but a concubine is certainly an odd gift under the circumstances."

"Not at all. She'll at least serve to increase the Marquis' entourage in the underworld. The larger the better, as befits his exalted station."

"The underworld?" Seven suddenly felt very ill himself.

"Of course. She and those who came before her are for

the Marquis Yi's perpetual service. Their places in his tomb are already prepared."

"It's a great honor," Seven's father said, shaving a lintel post with his chisel. Though they lived in the country, Seven's family were not farmers. They grew flowers and vegetables for their own use, but Seven's father was a skilled carver and woodworker, a very worthy position. More worthy, perhaps, than Seven had realized. "I've been summoned to help finish the funerary buildings."

"Upon the Marquis' death, she's to be strangled!" Seven said.

Seven's father looked up. "Along with the rest of his concubines and servants, that they continue to serve their master in the Court of Heaven. That, too, is a great honor."

Seven shook his head. "I don't think she sees it that way."

If Seven's father's patience was exhausted, at least it allowed him to speak frankly above all. "You speak of things you do not understand. Seek wisdom or be silent. Better yet, do both."

Seven bowed and took his leave. His older brothers were his father's main helpers; Seven had neither his father's talent nor any interest in woodworking. He did have some skill at singing and metalworking, but there was no one to teach him the finer points of either. In truth, much of Seven's time lately had been occupied in consideration of what course his life should take, or had been until he saw the King of Chu's gift. Now all his time was spent in consideration of how he might spare the King of Chu's gift the great honor she was to receive.

He sought the answer at shrines and temples. It was not there. He sought it in the teachings of the ancients, available in some small measure in the city, and it was not there. Seven spent as much time as he could in the city, near to the palace and the treasure of beauty he knew to be within, waiting in vain for a glimpse of his love, listening to the daily rumors of the Marquis Yi's health. They were not good. The one thing Seven did manage to learn was the name of the King of Chu's "poor" gift: Jia Jin.

As the day of Marquis Yi's departure from the earth drew ever closer, Seven was overtaken with despair. He wandered the streets of Leigudun until he could wander no more, and finally sat down to rest on the side of a broad road on the outskirts of the city.

"Forgive me, Jia Jin, but what I want is not possible . . ."

WHAT IS IT YOU WANT?

Seven looked around him. "Who said that?"

I DID.

Seven looked around again, and again he saw no one. He finally noticed something a bit strange about the road he was on—except for himself, it was deserted, and it was lined with immense creatures of stone. They were placed in pairs at wide intervals along the road, each creature staring at its counterpart across the broad flat avenue. There were dragons and serpents and strange animals that Seven could not identify at all.

This is a spirit road!

PRECISELY SO.

There was still no sound to the voice, but now Seven had a hint of its direction. He looked up into the face of a stone creature of immense size. Its body was like an elephant's, its head like a crocodile, though the jaws were shorter, the teeth larger. It had not moved, it could not speak, its visage was turned toward an identical creature across the way. And yet Seven was as sure that the creature had spoken to him as he was of his own, albeit unusual, name.

"Did you speak to me?" he asked, looking up into the cool stone features.

I DID. AND YOU HEARD ME, WHICH IS WORTH REMARKING. MOST PEOPLE DO NOT, EVEN WHEN THE VEILS BETWEEN EARTH AND THE SPIRIT REALM ARE THIN, AS THEY ARE NOW.

"My name is Seven. Who are you, Master?"

I AM NO ONE'S MASTER. I AM A *BIXIE*, ONE OF THE SPIRIT GUARDIANS OF THE TOMB OF MAR-

QUIS YI'S RENOWNED ANCESTOR, YUAN FEN. I WATCH FOR EVIL SPIRITS.

"Are there many such?"

SO FEW THAT EVEN A STONE CAN BE MOVED TO BOREDOM. SO I SPOKE. WILL YOU BE KIND ENOUGH TO ANSWER MY QUESTION? I HAVE SO FEW CHANCES TO CONVERSE.

"I—I wish to marry the girl called Jia Jin. But she belongs to the Marquis Yi, who will soon pass from my domain to yours, taking Jia Jin with him."

AH. THAT IS WHY THE VEILS BETWEEN MY WORLD AND YOURS ARE SO THIN; MARQUIS YI IS ABOUT TO CROSS. THAT IS UNFORTUNATE FOR YOUR LADY.

"Everyone says it's a great honor for her," Seven said. "I suppose I must content myself with that, for her sake."

I SUPPOSE YOU MUST, said the *bixie*. The silence that followed seemed an empty one, empty in that it wished to be filled. But the creature remained silent.

"I feel there is something else you wish to say," observed Seven. "I would be grateful to hear it."

YOU HAVE BEEN KIND TO ME. I WOULD NOT DO YOU EVIL AND ROB YOU OF YOUR COMFORT.

Seven shrugged. "It was a poor sort of comfort," he said. "Perhaps the truth would be better."

The creature's sigh was like a breeze. LOOK TO YOUR LEFT, DOWN THE SPIRIT ROAD. WHAT DO YOU SEE?

Seven peered down the *shendao* as the creature asked, past the paired *bixies*. "I see a wall of stone," he said.

BEYOND THAT WALL IS THE TOMB OF YUAN FEN. INSIDE THAT TOMB WAIL THE SPIRITS OF THE SEVENTEEN UNFORTUNATE LADIES HONORED BY YUAN FEN. THEY HAVE NO PEACE AND, THANKS TO THEM, NEITHER HAS HE. I'VE ALWAYS THOUGHT IT SERVED HIM RIGHT, BUT IN TRUTH THE REASON MY BROTHERS AND I HAVE SO LITTLE TO OCCUPY US IS THAT EVIL SPIRITS WON'T GO NEAR THE PLACE. THEY'RE MORE AFRAID OF

YUAN FEN'S CONCUBINES THAN ANY OF MY FOLK, AND IN THE SPIRIT REALM WE ARE QUITE FIERCE.

Seven looked at the creature's great teeth. "I can well imagine . . ." The *bixie's* words and meaning took a moment to settle in to Seven's brain, but settle they did. "Oh, poor Jia Jin! But this is so far beyond my skill or understanding." Seven sat back down on the ground, nestled beneath the spirit guardian's massive paws. "What shall I do?"

I AM ONLY A GUARDIAN AND NOT FULLY OF THIS WORLD; THE STONE YOU SEE IS BUT A MARKER OF MY PRESENCE. I CAN NOT HELP YOU. BUT I KNOW OF SOMEONE WHO MIGHT. HER PRICE, I FEAR, IS VERY HIGH.

"I don't care. Please tell me who she is, if there is any sense of kindness about you in my regard!"

VERY WELL. IN THE MOUNTAINS TO THE NORTH THERE IS A LADY NAMED GOLDEN BELL. SHE IS OF THE HEAVENLY COURT, A MISTRESS OF POETRY, AND HAS GREAT WISDOM AND POWER IN YOUR WORLD. IF SHE GRANTS YOU COUNSEL THERE MAY BE A WAY. BUT YOU MUST HURRY. FOR THE BARRIERS TO BE SO LOW BETWEEN OUR WORLDS THE MARQUIS YI'S TIME MUST BE VERY SHORT INDEED.

Seven thanked the spirit guardian profusely and went home to make provision for the trip. His mother wept bitterly and tried to dissuade him; his father merely shrugged. "He will return to his senses or he will die in the mountains; in either case I fear it is out of our hands."

So it was decided. Seven took food and blankets and a stout walking stick and headed for the mountains, visible only as a gray line to the north. He walked until his first pair of shoes fell to scraps and he was forced to put on another. By the time these were almost worn out, Seven passed into the foothills. He kept a wary eye out for bandits, but the years of the Marquis Yi's rule had reduced their number greatly and Seven reached the first plateau unhindered.

He saw his first ghost on the second night. It was a poor thing, little more than a few wisps of mist spiraling slowly among the stones, silent and lost. The next evening Seven saw two others, more substantial. They sought through the mountain passes with blind eyes, and Seven counted himself fortunate that they did not find *him*. It was as if where living bandits had been driven out, ghosts had sought a refuge. Seven passed an abandoned bandit village, saw the white, vaporous forms gathered in shadowed corners and empty windows. After that, he was careful to leave a little food and beer some distance from his campfire, to distract them. On the morning of the fourth day, he found something besides ghosts and ruins.

A small stone house nestled into the base of a cliff in a narrow valley, one so insignificant-seeming that Seven had almost passed it by, but the sound of a waterfall had drawn him in. He had taken ease of his thirst at the spring near the entrance before he saw the house. Seven thought it strange that such a perfectly fine, ordinary-looking little house should be in that place. It was clearly no bandit-hovel, but the weeds and vines seemed near to choking it, for all that it appeared to be intact. There was even a wisp of smoke from its chimney.

"Perhaps whoever lives here knows of Golden Bell. I shall ask."

As Seven approached the house, his eyes tricked him, or so it seemed. First he saw a perfectly ordinary little cottage, then it wasn't a cottage at all—the windows were dark niches in the rocks of the cliff, the doorway merely a pattern of shadow where the massive roots of an ancient tree were exposed near the cliff face. Each image seemed to blend, one into the other until it was impossible for Seven to guess which he would see after the next blink.

This is very strange, Seven thought, *but until I find Golden Bell, I can't ignore any possibility*.

"Hello?" Seven said aloud when the house—as indeed it did presently resemble a house—was about forty paces distant. "I'm searching for Golden Bell."

A woman sat on a stone bench in a small patch of garden just in front of the dwelling, under the shade of a crab apple tree. Seven would have sworn, had there been anyone else about to inquire, that neither woman nor bench nor tree had been there just moments before.

"Who seeks Golden Bell?" the old woman demanded. Her tone was imperious, her manner impatient. She was, Seven decided then and there, the ugliest person he had ever seen. Her face was wrinkled, blackened, and shrunken in, like an apple gone rotten. Her teeth were yellowed and sparse, her eyes were like two black stones.

"I am Seven, son of a humble craftsman of Zeng province. A spirit guardian told me to seek Golden Bell assistance."

"I am Golden Bell," the old woman said. "And I have no assistance to give."

Seven was stunned into honesty. "Such a beautiful name, I expected . . ." He managed to stop himself.

The old woman cackled, her eyes shining like dark fire. "Did you think I was born like this? I was more beautiful than my name, Seven, but that was long ago."

"I meant no insult, Lady. Forgive me for slandering the burden of your years."

"Surprisingly well spoken, but my years have little to do with the sorry state you find me in. I have a fever of poetry that consumes me, a malady of song that wears me down, and, sadder still, I have had nothing to eat or drink to sustain me for the past eight hundred years. I am famished."

A woman aged over eight hundred did not seem so impossible to Seven now, after talking with a spirit masked in stone. In truth, looking at Golden Bell, Seven could well accept that she was far older. "I have some food in my pack, Lady. I will gladly share."

She smiled at him. "It is kind of you, but I need a special sort of food that only my servants know how to prepare, and the wretched girls are hiding from me. They forget their duties."

"Then I will find them and remind them."

"You are welcome to try. They are hiding in my garden."

Seven's spirits sank. He feared that his easy acceptance of the unusual had misled him, and that Golden Bell was simply a crazy old woman. He looked about the small patch of ground. It was barely fifteen paces square, with small beds of pink and white peonies joined by paths formed of red paving stones. "Lady, there is no one here besides myself and you."

"Have you looked?" she asked mildly.

There seemed nothing for it but to humor her. Seven sighed, got down on his knees, and started poking about the flower beds and walkways. "I can't seem to—" Seven stopped, his eyes growing wide in wonder. "Oh, my."

Nestled among the peonies was a perfectly formed little cottage of twigs, roofed with broad leaves. Golden Bell nodded. "So that's where they'd gotten off to. Pick it up."

Seven carefully picked up the little hut, and underneath it he found a miniature bed, and hearth, and two small snails in delicate spiral shells.

"What have you to say for yourselves?" Golden Bell asked. The snails, being snails, did not answer. She nodded. "Stubborn things. Even now they will hide from me."

Seven felt obliged to point out the obvious. "These are snails, Lady," he said.

"Or such they would choose, rather than take their rightful places in my service. But as long as they remain in their shells I suppose it matters little. You might as well return them."

Seven thought about it. "Suppose they could be coaxed from their shells?"

Golden Bell looked at them. "And how would you persuade them?"

"My father is a craftsman, but my mother is a gardener, and I learned a thing or two from her. Let me try."

Seven reached into his pack and pulled out a small bottle of the rice beer his mother had given him. He removed the cork and held the bottle over the snails. Seven fancied he could hear them protesting in high, piping voices. He poured several drops on each and they merely closed themselves tighter within their shells, hiding behind their iridescent doors. Seven poured more beer until the snails were nearly afloat. He heard a faint sound that might have been cursing or laughter, he wasn't sure. Then one after the other the snails opened their doors and crawled out, and kept crawling until they were clear. In a moment where there had been two garden snails there now stood two young women in brown robes with dark hair falling in braids down their backs. They glared at Seven fiercely and after a moment began to shrink and change, turning back toward their shells as the last of the beer soaked into the earth. Seven stepped in front of them and crushed the two empty shells to powder.

"Fool of an ill-born goat! How dare you—" wailed the first.

Golden Bell interrupted. "Wretched, wicked girls! To let your Mistress starve for so long! Get to your duties at once!"

As one, the two forgot their quarrel with Seven and bowed deeply to Golden Bell. "It was *her* fault," each began, pointing at the other. "A lark, a jape, that was all. An outing! I wanted to return, but she—" So intent were they on their explanations that it was a few moments before they noticed the gathering storm on Golden Bell's wrinkled brow. "We go at once, Mistress!" they said in unison, and scrambled off toward the cottage.

Seven watched them go. "They were very close, though transformed. Surely you could have found them before now."

"And scrabble about in the dirt like a peasant, to my humiliation and their laughter? I could no more do what you've done than you could call down the moon. I am grateful. Perhaps, after I've eaten, I will consider your problem."

"It would be my fondest wish," Seven said, bowing.

Presently one of the servant girls returned, looking very uncomfortable. "We've searched high and low, Mistress. There is no food in the house."

Golden Bell nodded, resigned. "I suspected as much.

Shrink to the sum of your wretched worth and grow new shells, for all the good in you. Tell your sister."

The girl looked more than ready to obey—indeed, eager—but Seven spoke up. "Perhaps I can find you some food."

"Finding it is easy enough, but will you give it to me? That's the decision before you."

Seven frowned. "I don't understand."

"It's simple enough," said the servant girl. "The food our mistress requires is the human heart." The smile she turned on Seven then was not pleasant.

"Ah, then you are a demon after all, Golden Bell. Well, if it is to be that way, then alas for Jia Jin." Seven closed his eyes.

Golden Bell laughed, and the sound was much more melodious and delicate than Seven would have fancied coming from a demon. "Silly boy. You confuse a blood bellows with the heart? You speak of meat, Seven. I speak of sustenance. Men give their hearts away every day and live to see their grandchildren play. The especially wise or the especially foolish give them to me."

"But . . . how can I give my heart to you when it is already promised to Jia Jin?" Seven asked.

"You do not know Jia Jin. You have not spoken to her, touched her, tasted her wit or known her heart. You are in love with the idea of Jia Jin, and it is your mind that fills you with longing, not your heart. Perhaps that will come later, and your heart will grow again to encompass us both. Even I do not know that for certain. I only know that it is your decision to make."

"If I fail, Jia Jin is lost for certain. Whatever needs to be done, I will do it."

"So be it." Golden Bell reached out and took Seven's heart from him. He got a glimpse of it and she held it like some caged bird; it glowed as if with fire, and was many-faceted like a gem. Golden Bell handed the prize to the servants, who scurried away into the house.

Seven rubbed his chest, looking thoughtful. "In truth, I feel no different than before."

"Men don't always notice when their heart is given. You

will in time, but how it will feel to you then is something I won't presume to tell you."

In a moment the servant girl returned, or perhaps, since Seven could not tell one from the other, it was her sister. "We have searched high and low, Mistress. There is no drink in your house."

"Well, then there's nothing for it. Food without drink sticks in the throat and inflames the belly." Golden Bell turned to the girl, "You and your sister may as well be snails, for all your worth to me."

Seven shook his head. "You know I will not allow that. Tell me what you need to drink."

"A human soul," said the girl, with a look of vengeful satisfaction on her face. "Only this can cool the throat and soothe the belly of our mistress."

"If I lose my soul, then the afterlife is denied me," Seven said, aghast. "I will be as nothing!"

Golden Bell smiled her yellow and black smile. "The soul is a shadow, an echo of the noise of life within. It is no more the sum of all you are than your heart is the sum of all you feel. Life always casts a shadow. Lose one, and there will be another in time."

Seven sighed. "I'd listen to my heart in this matter if I still had one. All I know is that, if I fail, Jia Jin is doomed. Do as you will."

So Golden Bell took Seven's soul from him, pouring it into her cupped hands, then letting it trickle into a crystal goblet the servant girl provided. There it pooled and sparkled like smoky wine.

The other servant emerged from the house carrying a steaming bowl on a small tray. The bowl glittered in the sun, casting sparks of light like a fire. Inside the bowl were red oblong jewels no larger than grains of rice. They filled the bowl. Golden Bell fed herself from the bowl with ebony chopsticks, and sipped the cloudy soul-wine.

She is not so ugly as I thought at first, Seven thought. *Perhaps I'm getting used to her appearance.*

Golden Bell ate some more, and drank again. The bowl and the goblet were both half empty.

Her form is not so bent and misshapen as I'd thought before, Seven thought now. *Strange that my eyes were so deceived . . .*

When the food and the wine were gone, Seven came to understand just how completely his eyes had been deceived. That day in the marketplace in Leigudun, Seven would have sworn before any god who cared to witness that Jia Jin was the most beautiful girl on earth. Now he thought that, perhaps, he had been mistaken. Perhaps the most beautiful girl in the world was Golden Bell.

Seven tried to find the old hag in the vision that stood before him now and his imperfect memory was the only place in which he still found her. Golden Bell wore robes of yellow silk, and her long black hair was braided with golden cord. Her eyes were bright as a summer day, her form long and ethereally graceful.

Seven bowed low. "I was told you were of the Heavenly Court but it is only now that I come to believe it. Forgive my lack of vision."

"It's a common failing for which you bear no blame. For my recovery I thank you. Your soul was sweet and your heart brave and good. I will give you fair trade for them."

"You are most beautiful," Seven said plainly.

She smiled again, showing dimples. "You gave me your heart and soul, Seven. How could I be less in your eyes now? Is it still your wish to wed Jia Jin?" There was a hint of mischief in her eyes.

As Seven gazed at Golden Bell a shadow of doubt fell where there had not been before. Seven was ashamed. "I am not worthy of her, yet that is still my wish, Lady."

"Well then, Seven, I must tell you what to do. Sit beside me and listen."

Seven did as Golden Bell directed, and Golden Bell, in a voice sweeter than the singing of birds, told him a marvelous secret.

When Seven left Golden Bell's house, he went in the direction she specified, deeper into the valley until the ground turned stony again and grass withdrew. He walked as far as he could until the base of a massive cliff rose above him. There was no break in the stone, nothing to climb that he could see, no openings of any kind that he could touch.

Seven shrugged. "It is here, or it isn't. There is only one way to be certain." He sat down on a rock for a few minutes' rest and then sang a song to the stone wall, a short rhyme that Golden Bell taught him. "It's not a very good rhyme," she had said. "But it must suffice." Seven's voice rose high and clear on the still mountain air:

Golden Bell, Chime of Jade,
This narrow path is one I made.
Seventh Son, heart and soul,
Traded for a bandit's gold.
Seventh Son, soul and heart,
Sings a song that stone will part.

He thought a moment, then added. "Golden Bell requests it."

The stone cracked with a sound like thunder, splitting cleanly in front of Seven to a height of thirty feet, then on either side at about ten feet distant from the first crack. These twin fissures spread up the stone cliff until they turned together like travelers greeting one another and joined with the first split. Now what had been solid stone moved aside, two massive doors on hinges of stone. Inside all was dark, and a faint mist flowed from inside like the breath of some beast on a cold morning.

Seven sniffed the air and corrected himself. Not mist. Smoke. Golden Bell had told him what to expect, and that was enough to tell him he should be terrified, or at least very fearful as he followed her directions, but he felt neither terror nor even simple fear. In fact, Seven felt little of anything.

Giving up heart and soul is a great sacrifice, but I can see there are advantages.

He understood now that he followed his quest still as an act of will, and that, perhaps, Golden Bell was right when she said he was in love with the idea of Jia Jin rather than a flesh and blood woman. Still, if love was gone, the idea remained firmly rooted. Seven pressed forward into the cave. It took him only a moment to locate the source of the smoke.

Two strange creatures flanked the passageway about ten feet inside the cave, and for a moment Seven could do nothing but stare at them. They were about four feet tall, with heads that looked somewhat like the pictures of dragon's heads that Seven had seen from time to time. Their bodies were bird-like, their necks long and feathered like a crane's. Their feet had claws like a turtle's, only much larger. The creatures were secured to the wall on either side by golden leashes fixed to massive rings of bronze. Their leashes were just long enough for the creatures to meet each other in the center of the passageway and block admittance. They hissed and strained at their leashes as Seven drew near. Smoke and jets of flames spewed from their nostrils and mouths, their tongues tasting the wind as if searching for him.

Seven tried to keep his voice steady, and mostly succeeded. "Golden Bell commands: Be you submissive."

They were. The hissing stopped. They still strained at their leashes, but now their attitude was that of faithful dogs eager to greet their master. Seven found himself scratching each on the head as it rolled its large eyes and whined gently. He left them there and ventured deeper into the cave. The way was lit with torches as if the bandits—for this was their secret hideout—had just departed a moment or two before, rather than the twenty or so years since the hills had been scoured clean.

Seven passed bags of gold and silver lining the way and, as Golden Bell had commanded, took only one handful of each and placed it in the pouch on his belt. It was still a considerable amount. He left the gold and silver behind and came to chests of rare jewels and stores of lapis, jade, and amber. These, too, he took for himself in carefully restrained amounts. There were side corridors containing beds, rooms of weapons and armor, and the remains of cooking fires, but Seven ignored these. He kept to the main way until it opened into a large chamber, and there Seven found another marvel.

At the far end of the chamber stood a rack holding robes of silk trimmed with gold thread, and belts and pendants of jade. In the center of the room was a table. At each of the four corners of the table stood a pottery statue of a soldier in full armor, holding a spear of bronze. Just before the table was a statue of a dwarf made of the same clay, painted with a three-color glaze of green and yellow and blue. Around the statue was a belt of jade, and two long smooth sticks were hung from that belt on the right side. On the table was a cage of bronze, and in that cage were a multitude of songbirds with glistening feathers of various shades of green, like all the known shadings of green jade. At Seven's approach they began to sing at once and the cave was filled with a sound sweeter than any Seven had heard before.

Seven spoke to the statue of the dwarf first. "Live," he said. "Golden Bell requests it."

The statue changed color like oil floating on a puddle, and then the dwarf was a living man who bowed to Seven and then stood, waiting.

Seven spoke to the four soldiers. "Live. Golden Bell requests it." As one the four statues went through the same changes and stood in their positions, waiting.

Seven walked to the back of the cave, dropped his poor garments and donned the silken robes. His belt and cloth pouch he replaced with one of jade and fine leather, transferring the wealth he had taken from the corridor. He now stood before the transformed statues like a prince before his retainers. He instructed the dwarf to carry the songbirds' cage and all to follow him, and they obeyed silently. They followed Seven back to where the two guardian animals waited. Seven unhooked their leashes from the rings, and the two creatures waddled along beside him like two hounds at heel.

As Seven marched out of the cave with his new retainers, the cliffs closed tight behind them. He passed the place where Golden Bell's home had been, but he saw nothing, no house and no sign that there had ever been such at that place. Seven bowed once toward the place where it had stood, as best he remembered, and, dressed as a prince and with retainers finer and a menagerie more wondrous than any in the province of Zeng—or any other, come to that—Seven returned to Leigudun.

The Marquis Yi passed his shortening days with music, wine, and women for comfort, and the contemplation of eternity for a mystery. He thought it good to consider the mysteries of Heaven and Earth now that he was soon to know the answers to a few of them. It seemed to him a shame and a waste if he didn't at least know some of the questions. On this particular day, after the music was played and the wine consumed and the women—for this was the limit of his interest now—openly admired, the Marquis Yi sought to turn his attention to contemplation of the Immortals. Under the circumstances it was easier thought than accomplished.

"What is that noise? Why am I disturbed thus in my shortening hours? Put a stop to it at once!"

The Marquis' minister hurried from his presence and out to a window that opened over the main gate to the palace. After a moment the minister returned, looking bewildered. He whispered to a servant and the man bowed low and sped away.

"Well?" the Marquis demanded. "What is it?"

"I think, Heavenly One, you should see this for yourself," said the minister. "It is quite beyond my power to describe."

The Marquis frowned in annoyance but allowed two of his concubines to help him rise. He walked with slow, brittle steps to the window.

"Minister, this is indeed a marvelous sight."

A man in princely robes led two fantastic animals on leashes of gold, followed by a dwarf carrying a cage full of birds singing sweetly. Behind them were four fierce spearmen in armor that glittered like gold. Following and flanking the entire procession were the people of Leigudun, murmuring in low voices and staring.

"Who is this man? What does he want?"

The minister could only spread his hands in defeat until the servant reappeared and whispered something to the minister. The minister nodded and bowed low to the Marquis. "Son of Heaven, the young man below calls himself 'Seven,' and he wishes an audience with you."

The Marquis considered this. "I should refuse," the Marquis said. "I do not know his lineage, and he may be a sorcerer bent on doing me harm. Still, I see no reason to miss seeing what is plainly a Wonder of the Earth so soon before I must leave it. Bring him to me."

The young man called "Seven" came into the Marquis Yi's presence leading the two strange animals. He was followed by the dwarf carrying the cage of marvelous birds, and the four splendid guards. All bowed low. Even the birds bobbed their heads in unison at the Marquis. As amazing as this was, the Marquis Yi found all his attention drawn to Seven.

He has the calmest demeanor I have ever seen.

Even long-time retainers at his court always showed a bit of uneasiness in his presence, perhaps understandable since he had undisputed power of life and death over all in Zeng and had been known to exercise that power from time to time. If there was a trace of worry or fear in that young man's smooth features, the Marquis could not detect it.

"Young man," said the Marquis, "I think there is something missing in you."

"My heart and my soul," Seven answered frankly. "These I have traded for these things I bring before you. You have something I desire, Highness, and I seek a trade. Or, if it please you more, call it an exchange of gifts."

There was much murmuring and whispering in the court. The Marquis raised a hand for silence and then smiled grimly. "If you lack heart and soul, you certainly have no shortage of confidence to be so bold before me. I should be offended by your impudence."

"Forgive my coarseness, for such is my nature," Seven

said. "I state clearly for all to hear that I mean no insult to your greatness and, indeed, wish to add to it. It may please you to see what I have to offer." The Marquis was intrigued despite himself. "Show me."

Seven indicated the guards first. "When you pass from this earth, these men will go with you to guard your peace in the next."

"They are very passable," the Marquis agreed, "but I have enough guards of my own."

Seven shrugged. "Then these are not needed." He turned to the soldiers. "Return to what you were."

In an instant there were not four living men standing there but four pottery statues. In another moment they began to crack as if the weight of many centuries had suddenly descended upon them. Another moment and there was nothing left of them but four piles of dust.

The Marquis and all his court stared in open astonishment. Now the Marquis regretted his words, not out of fear of Seven but because the four soldiers had been the most splendid he had ever seen and his pride had led him to speak slightingly of them.

"This is indeed sorcery," the Marquis said, and that was all he said.

"It would be sorcery in your behalf, if it please you," Seven said. "I have one more gift to show you."

The Marquis nodded, not speaking, but his eyes missed nothing. Seven led the two dragon-headed beasts to a position about ten paces in front of the Marquis and had them stand about four feet apart. They kept those positions obediently, their long necks spiraling up like vines, their small leaf-shaped tongues lolling like cheerful dogs.

Seven clapped his hands. "For the Perpetual Use of the Marquis Yi!"

At once the animals stood very, very still. Their color slowly changed, darkening until they were almost black. Seven approached them and rapped the rightmost on the neck like a man knocking at a door. The creature echoed with the faint ring of bronze.

The audience chamber was suddenly very quiet. Even

the birds in the cage stopped singing. Seven went to the cage and opened the door. The jade-colored birds flew out and immediately settled in the rafters. Seven lifted the cage and repeated the command: "For the Perpetual Use of the Marquis Yi!"

The bars of the cage changed in his hands like potter's clay, reshaping as if under his direction into a two-tiered rack of bronze, with small hooks set at precise intervals along the upper and lower bars. Seven approached the two bronze animals and set either end of the rack down firmly on their heads so that the whole structure was now a very beautiful stand for a set of musical stone chimes. Only there were no chimes.

Seven looked to the birds in the rafters and repeated his command. The birds flew down in one great flock, and each one found its place on a hook on the rack and perched there. One by one they let themselves slip on their perches until they hung upside down and then began to grow and change. Each bird was now an exquisite curved chimestone of jade.

Seven turned to the dwarf. "Play for our Lord."

The dwarf took his sticks from his belt, bowed low again, and began to play the chimes. The Marquis Yi and everyone else present knew beyond question that it was the most beautiful music they had ever heard, or ever would hear again.

It was several minutes before the Marquis could bring himself to disturb the music with mere words. "Seven, what is it you wish of me?"

It was a simple question. Once the answer had been simple, too. Now Seven realized that, besides Jia Jin, he would spare all the Marquis Yi's concubines the "honor" of that worthy's perpetual service if he could. But ask the Marquis of Zeng to forego all his servants, and come to his ancestors alone and humbled? Seven almost wished that he was now as big a fool as he was when he began, to believe in one more impossible thing, but that time was past and had taken his heart and his soul with it.

Seven answered the Marquis and, if he did not speak the

whole truth, what he spoke was true as far it went. "I wish for the life and freedom of the girl called Jia Jin."

Thc Marquis Yi frowned. "Jia Jin . . . ?" His minister appeared at the Marquis' elbow and whispered a reminder. "Oh, yes. The gift of my Lord of Chu. How can I agree without dishonoring his show of affection?"

"If she is truly a gift, you may do with her as you will," Seven said.

The Marquis considered this. "Jia Jin, please step forward."

There was a rustling and shuffling among the group of the Marquis' concubines present, and then one girl robed in brocaded yellow silk emerged from the rear of the group and came forward, looking hesitant and frightened. She was exactly as Seven remembered, except, perhaps, even more lovely. She might still have been the most beautiful woman Seven had ever seen, if he had not met Golden Bell.

The more he remembered of Golden Bell the more that memory was of the beautiful woman she had become, and less of the crone he had first met. Yet both were the same, and it was still hard to separate them in his mind. Seven looked at Jia Jin, and for the first time he was able to see beyond the surface to what she might look like one day, and perhaps would if she ever had the chance to be free of youth. That was still to be decided, but Seven saw a woman now, and not an idea. He thought that would make a difference, but somehow it did not. He smiled at her and she returned the smile, hesitant but without guile.

"Jia Jin," Seven said. "If I were to rob you of the honor of the Marquis Yi's company for eternity, could you forgive me?"

The Marquis looked stern. "Young man, what are you doing?"

"I'm asking a question," he said. "Would you be kind enough to allow her to answer?"

The Marquis said nothing, and Jia Jin took a deep breath, then she fixed her gaze on Seven's face as if it were the one candle in an abyss. "How can I answer," she said, "without insulting either my Lord or you, noble sir?"

Seven smiled. "It's answer enough." He turned to the Marquis. "I await yours."

"Why would you trade such a treasure for this poor thing? She is nothing."

"Then you lose nothing, Lord. And gain very much indeed."

"Suppose my Lord of Chu hears of this and is not pleased?"

"At this point in your life's journey, is it really a concern?" Seven asked.

"True enough. Still, do you see this *yue*?" He pointed to a massive ax of bronze borne by a guard. "This is the symbol of the power of life and death, entrusted to me by King Hui of Chu. It is within my rights to have you slain," the Marquis said musingly, "and keep all. Then I would have even less concern."

Seven shrugged. "If that is your wish, then of course it will be done. Forgive me for imposing on your notice, my Lord." He turned to Jia Jin. "And forgive me for offering you a choice you lacked the freedom to make." Seven spoke to the dwarf. "Return," he said, "to what you were."

There was another pile of dust. Seven opened his mouth to speak again, but the Marquis stood up so quickly he almost fell down again in his weakness. "Stop, I command you!" There was more desperation than anger in his voice.

Seven bowed. "You may kill me, Lord," he said. "It is your right. But not before I return this heavenly instrument to dust as well. In this one small matter I cannot obey you."

The Marquis Yi considered, but not for long. "Take her," he said. "And leave Zeng if you value your life."

"As you command, I will do both," Seven said, and he bowed again. "May it please you to remember that I can speak the words wherever I am, and the effect is the same. I am honored by your gift, Marquis Yi. I know you have the wisdom to be honored by mine."

Seven took Jia Jin's hand and led her from the Marquis' palace. No one followed them. They were not even well away before they heard someone else playing the wondrous music on the jade chimes at the request of the Marquis Yi.

Seven bought a rich farm in the province of Chu with the treasure from the cave. The Marquis Yi died soon after and that chapter in Seven and Jia Jin's life was closed. Jia Jin remained with Seven, perhaps out of gratitude at first but love followed soon enough. Golden Bell had spoken truly and Seven's heart and soul, like pruned vines, did grow again and mostly restore themselves with Jia Jin's help. Seven knew fear again but he also knew love. Love for Jia Jin, and for the living woman instead of his perception of her, but the memory of Golden Bell remained too. No man can freely give both heart and soul to another and remain unchanged; Seven was never completely whole again.

Two years after the Marquis' death, Seven made a solo pilgrimage to the valley of the bandits. He did not find Golden Bell's house. He repeated the rhyme at the cave, but he could not bring himself to say that Golden Bell requested it, for he knew it was not true, and the cave did not open. He returned to Chu and Jia Jin and learned to write songs and poetry attempting to heal the parts of his heart and his soul that were still missing. He became quite well known for a time writing under the name Chu Yuen, but that time quickly passed as all time does and, after long and fairly happy lives, both Seven and Jia Jin followed the Marquis Yi from this world to the next.

The Marquis' tomb was soon forgotten and lost for many years, but eventually—and quite by accident—it was found again and his splendid treasures put in a museum. One especially is worth notice: a bronze rack of stone chimes, supported by two creatures with the heads of dragons, the bodies and necks of birds, and the feet of turtles. The one on the right lost his long, puckish tongue sometime in the past three millennia, but the one on the left still retains his. A visitor who looks closely at the tip will still find the following words written there in flowing white characters:

"For the Perpetual Use of the Marquis Yi of Zeng."

Making a Noise in This World

Charles de Lint

Charles de Lint was born in the town of Bussum in the Netherlands, and emigrated to Canada with his family four months later. He now lives in Ottawa, Ontario, with his wife, Mary Ann Harris, an artist and musician. DeLint pioneered the subgenre of urban fantasy in the 1980s with such books as Moonheart, *and continues to tell tales of his trademark city, Newford. He's been a full-time writer for eighteen years now, with forty-six books published (novels, collections, novellas, etc.) and more on the way. Additionally, for twenty-some years now, he's been playing Celtic music in one band or another, and more recently has begun to study fine art. He says: "I've taken to calling my writing 'mythic fiction,' because it's basically mainstream writing that incorporates elements of myth and folktale, rather than secondary world fantasy." He also writes a monthly book review column for* F & SF. *His Web site is excellent and informative—www.cyberus.ca~cdl.*

"Making a Noise in This World" appeared in the anthology Warrior Fantastic, *edited by Martin H. Greenberg and John Helfers, but is more concerned with matters of social justice than warfare. The title of the story, says de Lint, was taken from a song on Robbie Robertson's CD,* Contact from the Underworld of Redboy. *This story is about an artist and a ghost. It is an interesting contrast to the Kain Massin story.*

I'm driving up from the city when I spot a flock of crows near the chained gates of the old gravel pit that sits on the left side of the highway, about halfway to the rez. It's that time of the morning when the night's mostly a memory, but the sun's still blinking the sleep from its eyes as it gets ready to shine us into another day.

Me, I'm on my way to bed. I'm wearing gloves and have a take-out coffee in my free hand, a cigarette burning between the tobacco-stained fingers of the one holding the wheel. A plastic bag full of aerosol paint cans, half of them empty, rattles on the floor on the passenger's side every time I hit a bump. Behind me I've left freight cars painted with thunderbirds and buffalo heads and whatever other icons I could think up tonight to tell the world that the Indians have counted another coup, hi-ya-ya-ya. I draw the line at dream catchers, though I suppose some people might mistake my spiderwebs for them.

My favorite tonight has become sort of a personal trademark: a big crow, its wings spread wide like the traditional thunderbird and running the whole length of the boxcar, but it's got that crow beak you can't mistake and a sly, kind of laughing look in its eyes. Tonight I painted that bird fire engine red with black markings. On its belly I made the old

Kickaha sign for *Bín-ji-gú-sân*, the sacred medicine bag: a snake, with luck lines radiating from its head and back.

I've been doing that crow ever since I woke one morning from a dream where I was painting graffiti on a 747 at the airport, smiling because this time my bird was really going to fly. I opened my eyes to hear the crows outside my window, squawking and gossiping, and there were three black feathers on the pillow beside me.

Out on the highway now, I ease up on the gas and try to see what's got these birds up so early.

Crows are sacred on the rez—at least with the Aunts and the other elders. Most of my generation's just happy to make it through the day, never mind getting mystical about it. But I've always liked them. Crows and coyotes. Like the Aunts say, they're the smart ones. They never had anything for the white men to take away and they sure do hold their own against them. Shoot them, poison them, do your best. You manage to kill one and a couple more'll show up to take its place. If we'd been as wily, we'd never have lost our lands.

It's a cold morning. My hands are still stinging from when I was painting those boxcars, all night long. Though some of that time was spent hiding from the railroad rent-a-cops and warming up outside the freight yard where some hobo skins had them a fire burning in a big metal drum. Half the time the paints just clogged up in the cans. If I'd been in the wind, I doubt they'd have worked at all.

The colors I use are blacks and reds, greens and yellows, oranges and purples. No blues—the sky's already got them. Maybe some of the Aunts' spirit talk's worn off on me, because when I'm trainpainting, I don't want to insult the Grandfather Thunders. Blue's their color, at least among my people.

My tag's "Crow." I was born James Raven, but Aunt Nancy says I've got too much crow in me. No respect for anything, just like my black-winged brothers. And then there's those feathers I found on my pillow that morning. Maybe that's why I pull over. Because in my head, we're kin. Same clan, anyway.

There's times later when maybe I wished I hadn't. I'm still weighing that on a day-to-day basis. But my life's sure on the road to nowhere I could've planned because of that impulse.

The birds don't fly off when I get out of the car, leaving my coffee on the dash. I take a last drag on my cigarette and flick the butt into the snow. Jesus, but it's cold. A *lot* colder here than it was in the freight yards. There I had the cars blocking the wind most of the time. Out here, it comes roaring at me from about as far north as the cold can come. It must be twenty, thirty below out here, factoring in the wind chill.

I start to walk toward where the birds have gathered and I go a little colder still, but this time it's inside, like there's frost on my heart.

They've found themselves a man. A dead skin, just lying here in the snow. I don't know what killed him, but I can make an educated guess considering all he's wearing is a thin, unzipped windbreaker over a T-shirt and chinos. Running shoes on his feet, no socks.

He must've frozen to death.

The crows don't fly off when I approach, which makes me think maybe the dead man's kin, too. That they weren't here to eat him, but to see him on his way, like in the old stories. I crouch down beside him, snow crunching under my knee. I can see now he's been in a fight. I take off my paint-stained gloves and reach for his throat, looking for a pulse, but not expecting to find one. He twitches at my touch. I almost fall over backwards when those frosted eyelashes suddenly crack open and he's looking right at me.

He has pale blue eyes—unusual for a skin. They study me for a moment. I see an alcohol haze just on the other side of their calm, lucid gaze. What strikes me at that moment is that I don't see any pain.

Words creep out of his mouth. "Who . . . who was it that said, 'It is a good day to die'?"

"I don't know," I find myself answering. "Some famous chief, I guess. Sitting Bull, maybe." Then I realize what I'm doing, having a conversation with a dying man. "We've got to get you to a hospital."

"It's bullshit," he says.

I think he's going to lose his hands. They're blue with the cold. I can't see his feet, but in those thin running shoes, they can't be in much better condition.

"No, you'll be okay," I lie. "The doctors'll have you fixed up in no time."

But he's not talking about the hospital.

"It's never a good day to die," he tells me. "You tell Turk that for me."

My pulse quickens at the name. Everybody on the rez knows Tom McGurk. He's a detective with the NPD that's got this constant hard-on for Indians. He goes out of his way to break our heads, bust the skin hookers, roust the hobo bloods. On the rez they even say he's killed him a few skins, took their scalps like some old Indian hunter, but I know that's bullshit. Something like that, it would've made the papers. Not because it was skins dying, but for the gory details of the story.

"He did this to you?" I ask. "Turk did this?"

Now it doesn't seem so odd, finding this drunk brave dying here in the snow. Cops like to beat on us, and I've heard about this before, how they grab some skin, usually drunk, beat the crap out of him, then drive him twenty miles or so out of town and dump him. Let him walk back to the city if he's up for some more punishment.

But on a night like this . . .

The dying man tries to grab my arm, but his frozen fingers don't work anymore. It's like all he's got is this lump on the end of his arm, hard as a branch, banging against me. It brings a sour taste up my throat.

"My name," he says, "is John Walking Elk. My father was an Oglala Sioux from the Pine Ridge rez and my mother was a Kickaha from just up the road. Don't let me be forgotten."

"I . . . I won't."

"Be a warrior for me."

I figure he wants his revenge on Turk, the one he can't

take for himself, and I find myself nodding. Me, who's never won a fight in his life. By the time I realize we have different definitions for the word "warrior," my life's completely changed.

I remember the look on my mom's face the first time I got arrested for vandalism. She didn't know whether to be happy or mad. See, she never had to worry about me drinking or doing drugs. And while she knew that train-painting was against the law, she understood that I saw it as bringing Beauty into the world.

"At least you're not a drunk like your father's brother was," she finally said.

Uncle Frank was an alcoholic who died in the city, choking on his own puke after an all-night bender. We've no idea what ever happened to my father, Frank's brother. One day we woke up and he was gone, vanished like the promises in all those treaties the chiefs signed.

"But why can't you paint on canvases like other artists do?" she wanted to know.

I don't know where to begin to explain.

Part of it's got to do with the transitory nature of painting freight cars. Nobody can stand there and criticize it the way you can a painting hanging in a gallery or a museum, or even a mural on the side of some building. By the time you realize you're looking at a painting on the side of a boxcar, the locomotive's already pulled that car out of your sight and farther on down the line. All you're left with is the memory of it; what you saw, and what you have to fill in from your own imagination.

Part of it's got to do with the act itself. Sneaking into the freight yards, taking the chance on getting beat up or arrested by the rent-a-cops, having to work so fast. But if you pull it off, you've put a piece of Beauty back into the world, a piece of art that'll go traveling right across the continent. Most artists are lucky to get a show in one gallery. But trainpainters . . . our work's being shown from New York City to L.A. and every place in between.

And I guess part of it's got to do with the self-image you get to carry around inside you. You're an outlaw, like the chiefs of old, making a stand against the big white machine that just rolls across the country, knocking down anything that gets in its way.

So it fills something in my life, but even with the trainpainting, I've always felt like there was something missing, and I don't mean my father. Though trainpainting's the only time I feel complete, it's still like I'm doing the right thing, but for the wrong reason. Too much me, not enough everything else that's in the world.

I'm holding John Walking Elk in my arms when he dies. I'm about to pick him up when this rattle goes through his chest and his head sags away from me, hanging at an unnatural angle. I feel something in that moment, like a breath touching the inside of my skin, passing through me. That's when I know for sure he's gone.

I sit there until the cold starts to work its way through my coat, then I get a firmer grip on the dead man and stagger back to my car with him. I don't take him back to the city, report his death to the same authorities that killed him. Instead, I gather my courage and take him to Jack Whiteduck.

I don't know how much I really buy into the mysteries. I mean, I like the idea of them, the way you hear about them in the old stories. Honoring the Creator and the Grandfather Thunders, taking care of this world we've all found ourselves living in, thinking crows can be kin, being respectful to the spirits, that kind of thing. But it's usually an intellectual appreciation, not something I feel in my gut. Like I said, trainpainting's about the only time it's real for me. Finding Beauty, creating Beauty, painting her face on the side of a freight car.

But with Jack Whiteduck it's different. He makes you believe. Makes you see with the heart instead of the eye. Everybody feels that way about him, though if you ask most people, they'll just say he makes them nervous. The corporate braves who run the casino, the kids sniffing glue and gasoline under the highway bridge and making fun of the elders, the drunks hitting the bars off the rez . . . press them hard enough and even they'll admit, yeah, something about the old man puts a hole in their party that all the good times run out of.

He makes you remember, though what you're remembering is hard to put into words. Just that things could be different, I guess. That once our lives were different, and they could be that way again, if we give the old ways a chance. White people, they think of us as either the noble savage, or the drunk in the gutter, puking on their shoes. They'll come to the powwows, take their pictures and buy some souvenirs, sample the frybread, maybe try to dance. They'll walk by us in the city, not able to meet our gaze, either because they're scared we'll try to rob them, or hurt them, or they just don't want to accept our misery, don't want to allow that it exists in the same perfect world they live in.

We're one or the other to them, and they don't see a whole lot of range in between. Trouble is, a lot of us see ourselves the same way. Whiteduck doesn't let you. As a people, we were never perfect—nobody is—but there's something about him that tells us we don't have to be losers either.

Whiteduck's not the oldest of the elders on the rez, but he's the one everybody goes to when they've got a problem nobody else can solve.

So I drive out to his cabin, up past Pineback Road, drive in as far as I can, then I get out and walk the rest of the way, carrying John Walking Elk's body in my arms, following the narrow path that leads through the drifts to Whiteduck's cabin. I don't know where I get the strength.

There's a glow spilling out of the windows—a flickering light of some kind. Oil lamp, I'm guessing, or a candle. Whiteduck doesn't have electricity. Doesn't have a phone or running water either. The door opens before I reach it and Whiteduck stands silhouetted against the yellow light like he's expecting me. I feel a pinprick of nervousness settle in between my shoulder blades as I keep walking forward, boots crunching in the snow.

He's not as tall as I remember, but when I think about it, that's always been the case, the few times I've seen him. I guess I build him up in my mind. He's got the broad Kickaha face, but there's no fat on his body. Pushing close to seventy now, his features are a road map of brown wrinkles, surrounding a pair of eyes that are darker than the wings of the crows that pulled me into this in the first place.

"Heard you were coming," he says.

I guess my face reflects my confusion.

"I saw the dead man's spirit pass by on the morning wind," he explains, "and the manitou told me you were bringing his body to me. You did the right thing. After what the whites did to him, they've got no more business with this poor dead skin."

He steps aside to let me go in, and I angle the body so I can get it through the door. Whiteduck indicates that I should lay it out on his bed.

There's not much to the place. A pot-bellied cast-iron stove with a fire burning in it. A wooden table with a couple of chairs, all of them handmade from cedar. A kind of counter running along one wall with a sink in it and a pail underneath to catch the runoff. A chest under the counter that holds his food, I'm guessing, since his clothes are hanging from pegs on the wall above his bed. Bunches of herbs are drying over the counter, tied together with thin strips of leather. In the far corner is a pile of furs, mostly beaver.

The oil lamp's sitting on the table, but moment by moment, it becomes less necessary as the sun keeps rising outside.

"Mico'mis," I begin, giving him the honorific, but I don't know where to go with my words past it.

"That's good," he says. "Too many boys your age don't have respect for their elders."

I'd take offense at the designation of "boy"—I'll be twenty-one in the spring—but compared to him, I guess that's what I am.

"What will you do with the body?" I ask.

"That's not a body," he tells me. "It's a man, got pushed off the wheel before his time. I'm going to make sure his spirit knows where it needs to go next."

"But . . . what will you do with what he's left behind?"

"Maybe a better question would be, what will you do with yourself?"

I remember John Walking Elk's dying words. *Be a warrior for me.*

"I'm going to set things right," I say.

Whiteduck looks at me and all that nervousness that's been hiding somewhere just between my shoulder blades comes flooding through me. I get the feeling he can read my every thought and feeling. I get the feeling he can see the whole of my life laid out, what's been and what's to come, and that he's going to tell me how to live it right. But he only nods.

"There's some things we need to learn for ourselves," he says finally. "But you think on this, James Raven. There's more than one way to be a warrior. You can, and should, fight for the people, but being a warrior also means a way of living. It's something you forge in your heart to make the spirit strong and it doesn't mean you have to go out and kill anything, even when it's vermin that you feel need exterminating. Everything we do comes back to us—goes for whites the same as skins."

I was wrong. He does have advice.

"You're saying I should just let this slide?" I ask. "That Turk gets away with killing another one of us?"

"I'm saying, do what your heart tells you you must do, *no'cicen*. Listen to it, not to some old man living by himself in a cabin in the woods."

"But—"

"Now go," he says, firm but not unfriendly. "We both have tasks ahead of us."

I leave there feeling confused. Like I said, I'm not a fighter. Whenever I have gotten into a fight, I got my ass kicked.

But there's something just not right about letting Turk get away with this. Finding the dying man has lodged a hot coal of anger in my head, put a shiver of ice through my heart.

I figure what I need now is a gun, and I know where to get it.

"I don't know," Jackson says. "I'm not really in the business of selling weapons. What do you want a gun for anyway?"

That Jackson Red Dog has never been in prison is an ongoing mystery on the rez. It's an open secret that he has variously been, and by all accounts still is, a bootlegger, a drug dealer, a fence, a smuggler, and pretty much anything else against the law that's on this side of murder and mayhem. "I draw the line at killing people," he's said. "There's no percentage in it. Today's enemy could be tomorrow's customer."

He's in his fifties now, a dark-skinned Indian with a graying ponytail, standing about six-two with a linebacker's build and hands so big he can hold a cantaloupe the way you or I might hold an apple. He lives on the southern edge of the rez and works out of the back of that general store on the highway, just inside the boundaries of the rez, where he can comfortably do business with our people and anybody willing to drive up from the city.

"I figure it's something I need," I tell him. "You got any that can't be traced?"

He laughs. "You watch too much TV, kid."

"I'm serious," I say. "I've got the money. Cash."

I'd cleaned out my savings account before driving over to the store. I found Jackson in the back as usual, holding court in a smoky room filled with skins his age and older, sitting around a pot-bellied stove, none of them saying much. This is his office, though, come spring, it moves out onto the front porch. When I said I needed to talk to him, he took me outside and lit a cigarette, offered me one.

"How much money?" Jackson asks.

"How much is the gun?" I reply.

I'm not stupid. I tell him what I've got in my pocket—basically enough to cover next month's rent and a couple of cases of beer—and that's what he'll be charging me. He looks me over, then gives me a slow nod.

"Maybe I could put you in touch with a guy that can get you a gun," he says.

Which I translate as, "We can do business."

"Just tell me," he adds. "Who're you planning to kill?"

"Nobody you'd know."

"I know everybody."

All things considered, that's probably true.

"Nobody you'd care about," I tell him.

"That's good enough for me."

There's laughter in his eyes, like he knows more than he's letting on, but I can't figure out what it is.

The gun's heavy in my pocket as I leave the store and drive south to the city. I don't know any more about handguns than I do fighting, but Jackson offers me some advice as he counts my money.

"You ever shoot one of these before?" he asks.

I shake my head.

"What you've got there's a .38 Smith and Wesson. It's got a kick and to tell you the truth, the barrel's been cut down some and it's had a ramp foresight added. Whoever did the work, wasn't exactly a gunsmith. The sight's off, so even if you were some fancy shot, you'd have trouble with it. Best thing you can do is notch a few crosses on the tips of your bullets and aim for the body. Bullet goes in and makes a tiny hole, comes back out again and takes away half the guy's back."

I feel a little sick, listening to him, but then I think of John Walking Elk dying in the snow, of Turk sitting in his precinct, laughing it off. I wonder how many others he's left to die the way he did Walking Elk. I get to thinking about some of the other drunks I've heard of that were supposed to have died of exposure, nobody quite sure what they were doing out in the middle of nowhere, or how they got there.

"You planning to come out of this alive?" Jackson asks when I'm leaving.

"It's not essential."

He gives me another of those slow nods of his. "That'll make it easier. You got the time, tell Turk it's been a long time coming."

That stops me in the doorway.

"How'd you know it was Turk?" I ask.

He laughs. "Christ, kid. This is the rez. Everybody here knows your business before you do. What, did you think you were excused?"

I think about that on the drive down to the city, how gossip travels from one end of the rez to the other. It's like my paintings, traveling across the country. I don't plan where they go, how they go, they just go. It's not something you can control.

I'm not worried about anybody up here knowing what I'm planning. I can't think of a single skin who would save Turk's life if they came upon him dying, even if all they had to do was toss him a nickel. I'm just hoping my mom doesn't hear about it too soon. I'd like to explain to her why I'm doing this, but I'm not entirely sure myself, and I know if I go to her before I do it, she'll talk me out of it. And if that doesn't work, she'll sit on me until the impulse goes away.

There are crows lined up on the power lines and leafing the trees for miles down the road. Dozens of them, more than I've ever seen. I know their roost is up around Pineback Road, near Whiteduck's cabin. A rez inside the rez. But they're safe there. Nobody on the rez takes potshots at our black-feathered cousins.

When I come up on the entrance to the gravel pit, I see the crows are still there as well. I stand on the brakes and the car goes slewing toward the ditch. I only just manage to keep it on the road. Then I sit there, looking in my rearview mirror. I see a man standing there among the crows, John Walking Elk, leaning on the gate at the entrance and big as life.

I back up until I'm abreast the gates and look out the passenger window at him. He smiles and gives me a wave. He's still wearing that thin windbreaker, the T-shirt and chinos, the running shoes without socks. The big difference is, he's not dead. He's not even dying.

I light a cigarette with shaking hands and look at him for a long moment before I finally open my door. I walk around the car, the wind knifing through my jacket, but Walking Elk's not even shivering. The weight of the gun in my pocket makes me feel like I'm walking at an angle, tilted over on one side.

"Don't worry," he says when I get near. "You're not losing it. I'm still dead."

And seeing a walking, talking dead man isn't losing it?

"Only why'd you have to go leave me with that shaman?" he adds.

My throat's as dry and thick as it was when I did my first two vision quests. I haven't done the other two yet. Train-painting distracted me from them.

"I . . . I thought it was the right thing to do," I manage after a long moment.

"I suppose. But he's shaking his rattle and burning smudge sticks, singing the death songs that'll see me on my way. Makes it hard not to go."

I'm feeling a little confused. "And that's a bad thing because . . . ?"

He shrugs. "I'm kind of enjoying this chance to walk around one last time."

I think I understand. Nobody knows what's waiting for us when we die. It's fine to be all stoic and talk about wheels turning and everything, but if it was me, I don't think I'd be in any hurry to go either.

"So you're going to shoot Turk, are you?" the dead man says.

"What, is it written on my forehead or something?"

Walking Elk laughs. "You know the rez . . ."

"Everybody knows everybody else's business."

He nods. "You thinks it's bad on the rez, you should try the spiritworld."

"No thanks."

"You try and kill Turk," he says, "you might be finding out firsthand, whether you want to or not." He gives a slow shake of his head. "I've got to give it to you, though. I don't think I'd have the balls to see it through."

"I don't know that I do either," I admit. "It just seems like a thing I've got to do."

"Won't bring me back," Walking Elk says. "Once the shaman finishes his ceremony, I'll be out of here."

"It's not just for you," I tell him. "It's for the others he might kill."

The dead man only shakes his head at that. "You think it starts and stops with Tom McGurk? Hell, this happens anyplace you got a cold climate and white cops. They just get tired of dealing with us. I had a cousin who died the same way up in Saskatchewan, another in Colorado. And when they haven't got the winter to do their job for them, they find other ways."

"That's why they've got to be held accountable," I say.

"You got some special sight that'll tell you which cop's decent and which isn't?"

I know there are good cops. Hell, Chief Morningstar's brother is a detective with the NPD. But we only ever seem to get to deal with the ones that have a hard-on for us.

I shake my head. "But I know Turk hasn't got any redeeming qualities."

He sighs. "Wish I could have one of those cigarettes of yours."

I shake one out of the pack and light it for him, surprised that he can hold it, that he can suck in the smoke and blow it out again, just like a living man. I wonder if this is like offering tobacco to the manitou.

"How come you're trying to talk me out of this?" I ask him. "You're the one who told me to be a warrior for you."

He blows out another lungful of smoke. "You think killing's what makes a warrior?"

"Now you sound like Whiteduck."

He laughs. "I've been compared to a lot of things, but never a shaman."

"So what is it you want from me?" I ask. "Why'd you ask me to be a warrior for you?"

"You look like a good kid," he says. "I didn't want to see you turn out like me. I want you to be a good man, somebody to make your parents proud. Make yourself proud."

I've no idea what would make my father proud. But my mom, all she wants is for me to get a decent job and stay out of trouble. I can't seem to manage the first and here I am, walking straight into the second. But he's annoying me all the same. Funny how fast you can go from feeling awed to being fed up.

"You don't think I have any pride?" I ask.

"I don't know the first damn thing about you," he says, "except you were decent enough to stop for a dying man."

He takes a last drag and drops his butt in the snow. Studies something behind me, over my shoulder, but I don't turn. He's got a look I recognize—his gaze is turned inward.

"See, someone told me that once," he goes on, his gaze coming back to me, "except I didn't listen. I worked hard, figured I'd earned the right to play hard, too. Trouble is I played too hard. Lost my job. Lost my family. Lost my pride. It's funny how quick you can lose everything and never see it coming."

I think about my uncle Frank, but I don't say anything.

"I guess it was my grandma told me," the dead man says, "how there's no use in bringing hurt into the world. We do that well enough on our own. You meet someone, you try to give them a little life instead. Let them take something positive away from whatever time they spend with you. Makes the world a better place in the short and the long haul."

I nod. "Putting Beauty in the world."

"That's a warrior's way, too. Stand up for what's right. Ya-ha-hey. Make a noise. I can remember powwow dancing, there'd be so many of us out there, following the drumbeat and the singing, you'd swear you could feel the ground tremble and shake underfoot. But these last few years, I've been too drunk to dance and the only noise I make is when I'm puking."

I know what he means about the powwows, that feeling you can't get anywhere else except maybe a sweat and that's a more contemplative kind of a thing. In a powwow it's all rhythm and dancing, everybody individual, but we're all part of something bigger than us at the same time. There's nothing like it in the world.

"Yeah," the dead man says. "We used to be a proud people for good reason. We can still be a proud people, but sometimes our reasons aren't so good anymore. Sometimes it's not for how we stand tall and honor the ancestors and the spirits with grace and beauty. Sometimes it's for how we beat the enemy at their own game."

"You're starting to sound pretty old school for a drunk," I tell him.

He shakes his head, "I'm just repeating things I was told when I was growing up. Things I didn't feel were important enough to pay attention to."

"I pay attention," I say. "At least I try to."

He gives me a considering look. "I'm not saying it's right or wrong, but what part of what you were taught has to do with that gun in your pocket?"

"The part about standing up for ourselves. The part about defending our people."

"I suppose."

"I hear what you're saying," I tell him. "But I still have to go down to the city."

He gives me a nod.

"Sure you do," he says. "Why would you listen to a dead drunk like me?" He chuckles. "And I mean dead in the strictest sense of the word." He pushes away from the gates. "Time I was going. Whiteduck's doing a hell of a job with his singing. I can feel the pull of that someplace else getting stronger and stronger."

I don't know what to say. Good luck? Good-bye?

"Spare another of those smokes?" he asks.

"Sure."

I shake another one free and light it for him. He pats my cheek. The touch of his hand is still cold, but there's movement in all the fingers. It's not like the block of ice that tried to grab my sleeve this morning.

"You're a good kid," he says.

And then he fades away.

I stand there for a long time, looking at the gate, at the crows, feeling the wind on my face, bitter and cold. Then I walk back to my car.

Before I first started trainpainting, I thought graffiti was just vandalism, a crime that might include a little creativity, but a crime nonetheless. Then one day I was driving back to the rez and I had to wait at a crossing for a freight train to go by. It was the one near Brendon Road, where the tracks go uphill and the freights tend to slow down because of the incline.

So I'm sitting there, bored, a little impatient more than anything else, and suddenly I see all this art going by. Huge murals painted on the sides of the boxcars and all I can do is stare, thinking, where's all that coming from? Who did these amazing paintings?

And then just like that, there's this collision of the synchronicity at seeing those painted cars and this feeling I've had of wanting to do something different with the iconology I grew up with on the rez—you know, like the bead patterns my mom sews on her powwow dresses. I turn my car back around and drive for the freight yards, stopping off at a hardware store along the way.

I felt a kinship to whoever it was that was painting those boxcars, a complete understanding of what they'd done and why they'd done it. And I wanted to send them a message back. I wanted to tell them, I've seen your work and here's my side of the conversation.

That was the day Crow was born and my first thunderbird joined that ongoing hobo gallery that the freights take from city to city, across the country.

It's a long ride down to the city. I leave the crows behind, but the winter comes with me, wind blowing snow down the highway behind my car, howling like the cries of dying buffalo. It's full night by the time I'm in the downtown core. It's so cold, there's nobody out, not even the hookers. I drive until I reach the precinct house where Turk works and park across the street from it. And then I sit there, my hand in my pocket, fingers wrapped around the handle of the gun.

Comes to me, I can't kill a man, not even a man like Turk. Maybe if he was standing right in front of me and we were fighting. Maybe if he was threatening my mom. Maybe I could do it in the heat of the moment. But not like this, waiting to ambush him like in some Hollywood Western.

But I know I've got to do something.

My gaze travels from the precinct house to the stores alongside the street where I'm parked. I don't even hesitate. I reach in the back for a plastic bag full of unused spray cans and I get out of the car to meet that cold wind head on.

I don't know how long I've got, so I work even faster than usual. It's not a boxcar, but the paint goes on the bricks and glass as easy as it does on wooden slats. It doesn't even clog up in the muzzle—maybe the Grandfather Thunders are giving me a helping hand. I do the crow first, thunderbird style, a yellow one to make the black and red words stand out when I write them along the spread of its wings.

TOM McGURK KILLS INDIANS.

I add a roughly rendered brave with the daubed clay of a ghost dancer masking his features. He's lying faceup to the sky, power lines flowing up out of his head as his spirit leaves his body, a row of crosses behind him—not Christian crosses, but ours, the ones that stand for the four quarters of the world.

HE HAULS THEM OUT OF TOWN, I write in big sloppy letters, AND LEAVES THEM TO DIE IN THE COLD.

I'm starting a monster, a cannibal windigo all white fur and blood, raging in the middle of a winter storm, when a couple of cops stop their squad car abreast of where I parked my own. They're on their way back to the precinct, I guess, ending their shift and look what they've found. I keep spraying the paint, my fingers frozen into a locked position from the cold.

"Okay, Tonto," one of them says. "Drop the can and assume the position."

I couldn't drop the can if I wanted to. I can barely move my fingers. So I keep spraying on the paint until one of them gives me a sucker punch in the kidneys, knocks me down, kicks me as I'm falling. I lose the spray can and it goes rattling across the sidewalk. I lose the gun, too, which I forgot I was carrying.

There's a long moment of silence as we're all three staring at that gun lying there on the pavement.

They really work me over then.

So as I sit here in county, waiting for my trial, I think back on all of this and find I'm not sorry that I didn't try to shoot Turk. I'm not sorry that I got busted in the middle of vandalizing a building right across the street from the precinct house either. But I do regret not getting rid of the gun first.

The charges against me are vandalism, possession of an unlicensed weapon, carrying a concealed weapon, and resisting arrest. I'll be doing some time, heading up to the pen, but I won't be alone in there. Like Leonard Peltier says on that song he does with Robbie Robertson, "It's the fastest growing rez in the country," and he should know, they've kept him locked up long enough.

But something good came out of all of this. The police

didn't have time to get rid of my graffiti before the press showed up. I guess it was a slow news day because pictures of those paintings showed up on the front page of all three of the daily papers, and made the news on every channel. You might think, what's good about that? It's like prime evidence against me. But I'm not denying I painted those images and words, and the good thing is, people started coming forward, talking about how the same thing had happened to them. Cops would pick them up when the bars closed and would dump them, ten, twenty miles out of town. They identified Turk and a half-dozen others by name.

So I'm sitting in county, and I don't know where Turk is, but he's been suspended without pay while the investigation goes on, and it looks like they've got to deal with this fair and square because everybody's on their case now, right across the city—whites, blacks, skins, everybody. They're all watching what the authorities do, writing editorials, writing letters to the editor, holding protest demonstrations.

This isn't going away.

So if I've got to do some jail time, I'm thinking the sacrifice is worth it.

My cousin Tommy drives my mom down from the rez on a regular basis to visit me. The first time she comes, she stands there looking at me and I don't know what she's thinking, but I wait for the blast I'm sure's coming my way. But all she says is, "Couldn't you have stuck with the boxcars?" Then she holds me a long while, tells me I'm stupid, but how she's so proud of me. Go figure.

Some of the Creek Aunts have connections in the city and they found me a good lawyer, so I'm not stuck with some public defender. I like him. His name's Marty Caine and I can tell he doesn't care what color my skin is. He tells me that what I did was "morally correct, if legally indefensible, but we'll do our damnedest to get you out of this anyway." But nobody's fooled. We all know that whatever happens to the cops, they're still going to make a lesson with me. When it comes to skins, they always do.

* * *

I see Walking Elk one more time before the trial. I'm lying on my bunk, staring up at the ceiling, thinking how, when I get out, I'm going on those last two vision quests. I need to be centered. I need to talk to the Creator and find out what my place is in the world, who I'm supposed to be so that my being here in this world makes a difference to what happens to the people in my life, to the ground I walk on and the spirits that share this world with us.

I hear a rustle of cloth and turn my head to see John Walking Elk sitting on the other bunk. He's still wearing the clothes he died in. I assume he's still dead. This time he's got the smokes and he offers me one.

I swing my feet to the floor and take the cigarette, let him light it for me.

"How come you're still here?" I ask.

He shrugs. "Maybe I'm not," he says. "Maybe Whiteduck sent my spirit on and you're just dreaming."

I smile. "You'd think if I was going to dream, I'd dream myself out of this place."

"You'd think."

We smoke our cigarettes for a while.

"I'm in all the papers," Walking Elk finally says. "And that's your doing. They wrote about how Whiteduck sent my body down to the city, how the cops drove me up there and dumped me in the snow. Family I didn't even know I had anymore came to the funeral. From the rez, from Pine Ridge, hell, from places I never even heard of before."

I wasn't there, but I heard about it. Skins came from all over the country to show their solidarity. Mom told me that the Warriors' Society up on the rez organized it.

"Yeah, I heard it was some turnout," I say. "Made the cover of *Time* and everything."

Walking Elk nods. "You came through for me," he says. "On both counts."

I know what he's talking about. I can hear his voice against the northern winds that were blowing that day without even trying.

Don't let me be forgotten.

Be a warrior for me.

But I don't know what to say.

"Even counted some coup for yourself," he adds.

"Wasn't about that," I tell him.

"I know. I just wanted to thank you. I had to come by to tell you that. I lived a lot of years, just looking for something in the bottom of a bottle. There was nothing else left for me. Didn't think anybody'd ever look at me like I was a man again. But you did. And those people that came to the funeral? They were remembering me as a man, too, not just some drunk who got himself killed by a cop."

He stands up. I'm curious. Is he going to walk away through the wall, or just fade away like he did before?

"Any plans for when you get out?" he asks.

I think about that for a moment.

"I was thinking of going back to painting boxcars," I say. "You see where painting buildings got me."

"There's worse places to be," he tells me. "You could be dead."

I don't know if I blinked, or woke up, but the next thing I know, he's gone and I'm alone in my cell. But I hear an echo of laughter and I've still got the last of that cigarette he gave me smoldering in my hand.

"Ya-ha-hey," I say softly and butt it out in the ashtray.

Then I stretch out on the bed again and contemplate the ceiling some more.

I think maybe I was dead, or half-dead, anyway, before I found John Walking Elk dying in the snow. I was going through the motions of life, instead of really living, and there's no excuse for that. It's not something I'll let happen to me again.

Magic, Maples, and Maryanne

Robert Sheckley

Robert Sheckley lives in Portland, Oregon. A satirist even better known for his short stories than his novels, he has been writing since the early 1950s and is one of the classic SF writers of the last five decades. His hundreds of wild, ironic, and stylistically graceful stories over the years tend to combine elements from a variety of genres: fantasy, science fiction, detective, and even conspiracy theory. He is known as a master of the plotted story, the kind that ends with a satisfying turn of events.

He wrote "The Seventh Victim," which was the basis for the '60s movie The Tenth Victim, *starring Marcello Mastroianni and Ursula Andress. Many of his stories are collected in* Citizen in Space, Can You Feel Anything When I Do This?, *and seven other books. He has been selected as Author Emeritus for 2001 by the SFFWA. His most recent books are the fantasy novel* Godshome *(1999), and a "soft-boiled" detective series* Soma Blues *(1997),* Draconian New York *(1996), and* The Alternative Detective *(1997). His Web site is at www.sheckley.com.*

This light-hearted allegory appeared in F & SF. *In it, a young man trying out the possibilities of magic discovers appealing possibilities beyond magic, happily shedding the identity of magician for another role, yet to be discovered. Most writers would compel a character who figured out how to make magic make money, to continue making money (and find happiness that way). Sheckley, however, is fond of playing, to use the current phrase, "outside the box." It is also an interesting comparison to the Scott Bradfield story.*

A few years ago I was working at Sullivan's department store in Manhattan. In the evenings, I returned to my one room apartment on New York's Lower East Side and practiced magic.

Magic exists. But once you write down your methods, magic stops working. And once you start asking for specific things, instead of taking what magic is willing to give, you are letting yourself in for trouble. I kept my secrets to myself.

It is not a utilitarian thing, this matter of magic. Once you enter it, you move into realms where things happen in accord with a logic that becomes clear only in retrospect. The elusiveness, the contrariness of magic explains what happened to those magicians of old who produced gold and counted kings among their patrons, rose to power and influence, only to be proven frauds and mountebanks and have everything taken away from them.

But the best of them weren't frauds. They had compromised their powers by revealing them to kings and learned men, and by asking for wealth for themselves. They had brought the inscrutable wrath of magic down on their heads.

I had a sense of the purity of the matter, but I wasn't

completely convinced of it. That's how I got the Donna Karan jackets.

My job at Sullivan's was to take the old stuff off the racks and display dummies and put out the new stuff. My researches in magic were going well for me at that time. I had discovered the principle of the *temenos*; the importance of creating a sacred space. I learned for myself the words and combinations of words, sounds, and gestures that seemed to hold magical possibilities. And sometimes, things appeared overnight in my *temenos*, my sacred space.

Once, magic gave me a small elephant carved in mellow old ivory. I was able to sell it to a curio shop for two hundred dollars, even without being able to say where it came from. The productions of magic provide no provenance. But mainly, my investigations didn't bring me anything tangible.

I wondered if I could specify something and ask magic to make me a copy of it, or bring me another one like it. That didn't seem too much to ask.

Working alone late one night, I set up a portion of the stock room as a sacred space. I drew the magical lines. I put in a Donna Karan jacket for the spirit to look over.

Early next morning, I was gratified to find four copies of this jacket. That, plus the original, made five. I never knew which was the original. They were all identical, even down to the tiny flaw in an inner seam.

I didn't know at the time that magic had plans for me. I didn't know I was being watched by no less a person than Phil, the floor manager.

Phil walked in while I was putting away the extra jackets in my backpack. "What have we here?" he asked.

"These four jackets are mine," I told him.

He smiled his superior smile. "Don't happen to have a sales slip, do you?"

"You don't understand," I said. "These jackets don't belong to the store. I made them."

Phil looked at the jackets more closely. "I know this model. It's what we have in the display space."

"That's the original," I said. "These others are my copies."

Phil looked them over, frowned, and said, "Well, let's go to my office and straighten this out."

Phil had an office on the mezzanine above Sullivan's main floor. After checking the floor model, he went to his computer and called up the item number. He was surprised to find it was one of a kind.

"That must be wrong," he said. "We must have ordered five of these."

But a phone call to our distributor told him he had indeed ordered only one. The other four could not be accounted for.

"I really don't understand," Phil said.

"It's my fault," I said.

"You? How could that be?"

"I did it," I told him. "I'm sorry about this, sir. I don't want to cause any trouble. I need this job. Look, you can have the jackets. I promise I won't do it again."

"Let me try to follow your reasoning. How did you do it?"

"I just did it," I said, still not wanting to tell him about the magic.

"But what did you do, specifically? You must have done something. These jackets didn't just fall out of the air."

"As a matter of fact, that's exactly what happened. Or so I believe. I didn't see it myself. We're not supposed to."

"We?

"Magicians, sir." I knew I'd have to come out with it sooner or later.

Phil looked at me, his eyes narrowed, brows wrinkled. "Explain."

"I do magic," I told him.

"I see," Phil said.

"I do it in a *temenos*, a sacred space," I babbled, as if that would make it all clear.

Phil stared at me and frowned and looked like he was going to fire me on the spot. Then his face took on a thoughtful look, and he stared at the jackets for a while. At last he said, "Can you make something appear here on the table in front of me?"

"Oh, no! Magic doesn't work in the open. It doesn't like anyone watching. It's not like science, you know. It's magic, it loves to hide."

"So what do you do if you want to get something?"

"I do the magic, in the *temenos*. But usually I don't wish for anything specific. I don't think magic likes that."

"Okay, sure, whatever. But when you do this magic of yours, something always turns up in your sacred space?"

"Not every time. But surprisingly often."

Phil stared at me for a long time. Finally he said, "This is crazy, you know."

"I know," I said.

"But I'm interested. I'd like you to demonstrate for me."

"I could do that," I said, "but not here in the store. I don't think magic liked me doing that. But in my own apartment . . ."

"Sure. I don't care where you do it. I just want to see it."

We met two nights later. Phil was good enough not to sneer outright at my small, cramped slummy apartment. But I knew what he was thinking: *this guy can do magic? I must be crazy to be here.*

Still, here he was. He had brought something for me to duplicate. A very small gold coin. Phil said it wasn't worth much—just twenty dollars.

"It's not a good idea to ask magic for any particular thing," I said.

"Then how do we know it works?" he said.

I couldn't answer that.

"I'll want it back," he said, handing me the coin. "Hopefully, with a couple of others like it."

"You'll probably get it back. As for getting more, we'll have to see what magic decides."

I put the coin in the sacred space I had created in my closet. I asked Phil to stay in the front room while I did the formulas and gestures. I don't like people to see me doing magic. I think it works against the success of the enterprise.

Phil sat down on the bed while I went into the closet and closed the door. In magic, moments are not all alike. You have to guess which kind of Power you're working with, and what its mood is. I did what I thought would work for that particular moment.

When I came out, Phil asked, "So what happens now?"

"Tomorrow night at this same time," I said, "I open the door to the *temenos*."

"You mean the closet?"

"For now, it's a *temenos*."

"Couldn't we take a peek now? Maybe whatever it's sending is there already."

I shook my head. "I won't open that door until tomorrow evening. Impatience is very bad form when you're dealing with magic. You can't rush the Powers. Twenty-four hours is a minimum time. A couple of days would be better."

Phil looked like he had a few things to say about that, but finally he shrugged and said, "See you here tomorrow," and left.

Next evening, after Phil arrived, I opened the closet door, and there were seven gold coins in the *temenos*. They all looked the same.

I handed them to Phil. "I think this is what the Power or the spirits or magic or whatever wanted you to have."

"I thought you said the spirits don't like to be asked for anything specific."

"The spirits are unpredictable," I said.

Phil jingled the coins in his hands. Then he held out one to me. "You might as well get something out of this."

"No thanks," I said.

"Suit yourself." Phil put the coins in his pocket. He was

thinking hard. Finally he said, "Might you be open to a business proposition?"

"I'd have to hear it first."

"I'll get back to you," Phil said, and left.

About a week later, Phil asked me to meet him and a couple of friends at an expensive restaurant not far from Sullivan's. He indicated that they had talked the previous night and had a proposition to put to me.

I could imagine how his meeting with his friends had gone. I could hear Phil saying, "I don't want you fellows to laugh at me, but I know we're all interested in far-out investments."

"Sure," Jon said. "What have you got?"

"I've got a guy who does magic, or some damned thing."

And he would have explained what happened. He would have said, "Hey, I don't know what he's doing, but it looks good enough to invest a few bucks in."

So we sat in the restaurant in a comfortable haze of smoke and beer smell and dim golden lights and hurrying waitresses with twinkling legs, and we had drinks and they all stared at me.

Finally, one of them, a fat, complacent-looking guy named Haynes, said to me, "so what exactly do you do in this magical closet of yours?"

"It's not the closet that's magical, it's the *temenos*, the sacred space I create within it."

"And what do you do with this sacred place?"

"I perform certain procedures."

"Such as?"

"I can't tell you. Telling destroys the magic."

"Convenient, if you want to keep your secret."

I shook my head. "Necessary, strictly necessary."

I didn't tell him how I had deduced that magicians in the past like Cagliostro and the Comte de St.-Germain had grown rich and famous, but finally their powers had deserted them and they ended badly. I think their downfall came from telling, and from demanding too much.

They held a whispered consultation. Then Jon, a tall, thin, balding guy in a three-piece business suit, said to me, "Okay, we're interested."

"It's a far-out kind of thing," I told him.

"We're not scared of far-out investments," Phil said. "We've got a share in a shaman's school in Arizona. Is that far enough out for you?"

"How could you invest in me?" I asked.

"Oh, we weren't thinking of anything fancy. But we could set you up with a place to practice your magic. A place where you wouldn't be disturbed. We'd supply your food and pocket money. You could give up that lousy day job at Sullivan's. You could live on your magic."

I said, "Looks like there's a lot you could do for me. But what could I do for you?"

"Split the take with us fifty-fifty."

"Take?"

"Whatever you produce in that sacred space of yours."

"But that might be nothing."

Phil said, "Then we're stuck with fifty percent of nothing. But we like a gamble. We can get this facility in Jersey for free. Feeding you for a couple weeks won't cost much. And we can drive out and see how you're doing."

"Interesting," I said.

"And don't forget," Haynes put in, "you get to keep fifty percent of what you wish for."

It struck me as a pretty good deal at the time.

Phil had rented this place in northern Jersey to use as a software lab. But then the bottom went out of that business. Or they found it wouldn't be profitable under present conditions. They still had a couple months' rent paid for, so they set me up in the place. It was a small, isolated facility with a two-room apartment in back. I moved in, and Phil drove out from New York every few days with some frozen dinners.

I lived alone, saw no one—the nearest town was two miles away, I didn't have a car, and besides, what would I do there? I had books to read when I wasn't working on magic. I had a collection of Marsilio Ficino's letters. His nobility made me ashamed of myself. I knew I was being too self-seeking. But I went on anyhow. I figured, what's the sense of being a magician if you can't prove it to anyone?

A week later, on a late afternoon on a golden day in late October, the maples were just starting to turn colors. I could see birds overhead, flying south, away from the dark winter that was waiting for me. The little lawn in front of the facility was set back from the road. No one ever came by here, but she came. She came with an easel and a folding chair and a big straw purse in which she had watercolors and a bicycle bottle filled with water. She was sitting on my front lawn.

I came outside, and she got up hastily. "I didn't know anyone lived here. I hope I'm not trespassing."

"Not at all. I live here, but I don't own the place."

"But I'm intruding on your privacy."

"A welcome intrusion."

She seemed relieved. She sat down again in front of her easel.

"I'm a painter," she said. "A watercolorist. Some say that's not real painting, but it pleases me. I noticed this place a long time ago. I wanted to paint it, but I wanted to wait until the maples were in just the stage of bloom they're in now."

"Are they at their peak?" I asked.

"No, they're still one or two weeks from their full color. But I like them as they are right now, with the brilliant reds and oranges showing, but merging with the green leaves. It's a time of change, very fragile, and very precious. Anyone can paint a tree in full autumn foliage. But it's something else to paint one just before it explodes from cool green to hot red."

"And after that comes winter," I said.

"Exactly."

"You're very welcome to paint my trees or anything else.

Perhaps it would be better if I went inside and left you undisturbed?"

"It doesn't bother me if you want to stay," she said. "I'm Maryanne Johnson, by the way."

Maryanne set up her brushes and set to work. She sketched in the tree in hard pencil, mixed her washes, and began. She worked very quickly. Her painting was like a dance. I enjoyed watching her work. And I liked looking at her. She was not pretty, but her features were delicate, and I already knew she saw more than I did. She was a small, comfortable woman, about the same age as I, maybe a year or so younger. We talked about painting and trees and magic. At the end of two hours, the painting was done.

"I just need to give it a few minutes to dry," she said. "Then I'll spray it with an acrylic fixative and I'm out of your hair."

"Do you really have to go?"

"It's time for me to go," she said, not answering me directly.

"All right," I said. "I told you that I do magic."

"Yes. It sounds wonderful."

"Let's go in and see if the *temenos* has anything for you."

"I really don't think I should go in," Maryanne said.

"Then I'll run in and see if it's left you anything."

She hesitated, then said, "Never mind, I'll go in with you. I'd like to see where you live."

Inside we walked quickly through the cold, polished laboratory space, to the closet. I opened the door. In the shrine, under the red light, there was something oval-shaped and made of metal. I picked it up. It appeared to be of silver.

I led her outside into the fading afternoon light and said, "I think it's a pendant of some sort. Magic meant it for you. Please accept the gift."

Gravely Maryanne took it and turned it over and over in her fingers.

"Well," she said, "I didn't expect the day to turn out like this."

"Nor did I. May I see you again?"

"You know the Albatross Restaurant in town? I'm a hostess there."

And then she was gone and the gloom of my laboratory closed in on me. I walked up and down the silent room, between the work stations, with the last light of the late afternoon sun slanting in. It was quiet in here, always quiet, a sort of concrete tomb. And I had put myself into it.

I thought about magic and its practitioners. What kind of lives had they had? Lonely, boring, and dangerous. The only happily married magic-worker from the past I could think of was Nicholas Flamel and his precious Perrenelle. And he was very much the exception. In my rush to join the ranks of magicians, to be counted among them, I hadn't really considered what I was getting into.

Suddenly magic seemed to me a poor enterprise indeed, one that excluded the human dimension. At that moment, I made up my mind.

That evening, in response to my telephone calls, they all assembled at the facility. There was Phil and Jon, and Haynes, and two others I hadn't met before. They had cassette recorders with them, and even a video camera. I felt strangely calm. I knew this was going to be the last act, good or bad, fair or foul.

I took them with me into the closet with its *temenos*. It was small and narrow, but it held all of us, with the partners strung out in the narrow space behind me, and Phil at my shoulder with the video camera.

"You're actually going to let us watch?" Phil said. "Will wonders never cease!"

"You'll get the whole show," I said. "For better or worse."

"What should we ask for?" Haynes asked.

I shrugged. "Whatever you want."

"A million dollars in gold sounds pretty good to me," Phil said.

"You think the spirit or whatever it is can do that?" Jon asked.

"Magic can do anything," I said. "The question is whether it wants to or not. If this works, the wished-for matter will appear before your very eyes, here in the space of the *temenos*."

"You always gave it overnight before," Phil said.

"I'm in a hurry now."

I turned to the *temenos*. I began my incantations and my gestures.

There's no need to talk here about what I did. Phil's friends have a complete record—if they dare look at it after what happened.

At the end of my ceremony, there was a growing darkness in the middle of the shrine. It started as a stillness, but there was a fury within that stillness. You could feel the presence of something malevolent and strange. A cold wind came up inside the closed dark room, and the partners began to edge away.

"What have you done?" Haynes asked.

"Merely asked for what you want."

Now the darkness in the middle of the *temenos* was a spinning top of dark and luminous lines. It gave off a disturbed emanation, as though some creature had been called into being and didn't like it at all.

The darkness formed up into a crouched, dark creature in the middle of the shrine, its luminous eyes slanted and strange.

"Who is calling me?" the dark creature said.

"It's me," I said. "My friends here would like a million dollars in gold."

"You bother me for a trivial matter like that? Very well, they can have it. But it must be paid back."

"Paid back?" Phil said. "I didn't know it worked like that."

"We have to get our investment back," the dark creature told him. "Our resources are not without limit. But our terms are easy: five years to repay, no interest or carrying charges."

Phil held a hasty consultation with his partners. It was obvious to them that they'd earn considerable interest on a million dollars over five years. It made this a paying proposition.

"Yes, sir," Phil said to the creature. "We'd like to take you up on that. That would be very acceptable, sir."

"Who will be personally responsible for repaying this debt?" the dark creature asked.

"My backers and I, sir."

"Your backers?" the dark creature said scornfully. "To hell with that! I need one person! Who will hold himself *personally* responsible for this debt?"

"I will, sir," Phil said.

"And who are you?"

"I'm Phil."

"Fine. Then I'll take you as collateral."

"Hey, just a minute," Phil said. "I didn't intend—" Then he was pulled into the darkness so fast he was cut off in mid-scream. One moment he was there, the next moment he was gone.

"I'll expect repayment in five years," the darkness said. "Then you get Phil back. Or what's left of him."

Like a wisp of smoke, the dark creature was gone. But now there was a pile of gold in the shrine. A pile that looked like a million dollars' worth.

The partners stared at it uneasily.

Finally Haynes said, "It's a lot of money."

"Sure," Jon said, "but how about Phil?"

"Well, it *was* his idea."

"But we can't leave him wherever that thing has taken him. And certainly not for five years!"

"No, that wouldn't be fair," Haynes said thoughtfully. "But what do you think about thirty days?"

They looked at each other. Then Jon said, "Phil himself

wanted to make a profit on this. And besides, what the hell, he's there already."

Haynes nodded. "Thirty days wherever he is can't be so bad. I'm sure he'll have quite a story to tell when he gets back." He turned to me. "What do you think?"

"I'm finished with magic," I said. "But I'll be available when you need me to bring Phil back."

"You get a share of this," Haynes said, pointing to the gold.

"No thanks, I don't want any."

"Phil said you had some funny ideas. He'll be amused by this when he gets back."

"True. If you get him back alive."

"Damn, that's right," Jon said.

"Sure hope he's okay," Haynes said. "Hey, where are you going!"

"The Albatross Restaurant. I understand they have the best food available anywhere." And I walked out the door.

It seemed to me that both the partners and I had profited. They had gotten a million dollars at the possible cost of Phil. I had maybe gotten a chance at a life with Maryanne. At what price I was still to learn.

The Prophecies at Newfane Asylum

Don Webb

Don Webb has a new book out in the mystery/thriller field, Endless Honeymoon, *which, he says, "aptly describes his life with filmmaker and artist Guiniviere Webb." He lives in Austin, Texas, where he occasionally gives fascinating tours of the State Capitol building. A licensed fireworks operator, he is also known locally for his culinary expertise; and he is an expert on the magical practices of Late Antiquity. His most recent occult book is* The Seven Faces of Darkness: Practical Typhonian Magic, *from Runa Raven Press. For several years he wrote a weekly Internet column entitled "Letters to the Fringe." His collection,* Uncle Ovid's Exercise Book, *won the Illinois State University/Fiction Collective book contest in 1988. An unsung hero of the small press, Webb has a strong literary streak, as is seen in his books from Black Ice and Fiction Collective, and promises to do a breakthrough novel soon to complement his already 2000+ published pieces of short fiction.*

"The Prophecies at Newfane Asylum," a Lovecraftian tale of monsters in the 18th-century American colonies, was published in Interzone. *There has been a strong resurgence of fantasy in the manner and tradition of H.P. Lovecraft's Cthulhu mythos stories in recent years, of which this story is a particularly fine example. In this story and other recent stories, Webb takes on the topic of the sense of humor of the Elder Gods and other unnatural entities; their jokes are, needless to say, at the expense of poor mortals.*

For the price of a Spanish dollar the asylum would allow visitors to enjoy the entertainments of the mad. This form of entertainment had disgusted me in Britain, but out of sheer boredom I decided to try this stimulation in America. I had found New Connecticut to be the least interesting of the new republics, lacking in both Wit and Coffee. I had written to His Majesty suggesting that there was little hope of returning the country to British rule, and despite its slate mines and forests primeval, little reason in doing so. But King George was mainly daubing the walls of his room with spit, and not wanting to hear my prediction that New Connecticut was bound to join in ever-closer ties to the rest of the Colonies.

Another man sat and stared catatonically at the lanthorns, slowly defecating on himself. I saw very little in these men and women's actions that indicated they were in fact much different than those we allow to run on the streets. There were more entertaining madmen in the Coffee Houses of Pittsburgh and upon the streets of New York. I saw one rather sad-looking specimen that sat by himself in the furthermost corner of the asylum. He clearly did not relish being the source of another's amusement. His eyes seemed clear and his face untroubled when he glanced at us.

I was beginning to believe the man was sane, when a raven or another large bird landed on the roof of the building with a great clatter. The man began to scream that "they" had found him and begged the guards to go outside and see to shooting it off the roof, before it could talk to him.

As we left the Asylum I enquired of one of the guards as to the identity of the man so terrified by the raven.

"He's Mr Jeremiah Brewster."

This was one of those coincidences that makes us wonder at the workings of Providence. Jeremiah Brewster had been King George's agent before me. His disappearance had been a matter of great speculation.

"How," I asked, "does one obtain an audience with one of the patients? I would like to meet Mr Brewster."

Brewster, not having a history of violence, could be seen at any time. I was cautioned to go during the day, as his "fits" occurred only at night.

"I don't want to talk to you," said Mr Brewster.

"I am not particularly interested in your wants. I am interested in why after five years of sterling service, you stopped writing your reports. How did you land in this hell-hole?" I asked.

His cell was littered with straw, it being a curative for the mad to sleep in the manner of animals. It was lit by a single lanthorn and it smelled bad, the chamber pot being emptied but once every two days. He had a few books stacked nicely along the wall, and a portrait of King George. He maintained (I had discovered) an active correspondence with the Observatory at Greenwich, but otherwise wrote to no one, nor had any visitors.

"I came here to seek protection," he said.

"Protection from what?" I asked.

"Didn't they tell you? My particular hobbyhorse is that I believe the night sky is filled with demons under Satan's great majesty that wish to torment me for my wickedness."

This was set in such a tone of biting sarcasm, that I knew not to believe it.

"You know who I am, I've given you the password, I can get you back to England. Who is it, the Green Mountain Boys? The Spaniards? The Jesuits?" I asked.

"You cannot give me protection. I might be safe in London for awhile, but they have human agents."

"Tell me what you know, and I will make sure the proper authorities know."

"Certainly. I'll tell you what you I know. You'll see just how far you can get with your knowledge. I came to New Connecticut, or as our French friends call it, Vermont, in 1770. The land had opened up after the French and Indian War, government wasn't settled, different colonies claimed the land, and the Crown wanted to know which faction they should back. There were treaties being negotiated with the Pennacook and the Hurons. You saw Mr James Maskelyne? The man who threatened to scalp you when you came for your night's entertainment?"

"Yes."

"Better if he had, I'm going to do something worse to you. Mr Maskelyne negotiated the Crown's first treaty with the Pennacook. Settlers paid it no mind, and there was war. It quite unhinged him. The Pennacook aren't forgiving on this point, a quick way to die is to walk in our thick pine forests with a red coat. My advice to the Crown was to back Ethan Allen and his Green Mountain Boys. My advice was ignored. I don't know why His Majesty sends out his spies, when he listens so little to them. I imagine you have wondered on the same issue, much of late. Oh just because I am in an asylum does not mean that I don't know what is going on in the world. I filed my reports and I awaited my next assignment, and I drank and whored to the extent that either of these occupations could be well pursued in this uncivilized land, and I met Taylor Mason.

"A learned man, he had settled with his family from Salem in the Massachusetts colony. He had a lovely little wife, Charlotte, a son, Monck and a daughter, Sarah. He was an intense man full of knowledge on topics as diverse as Chinese philosophy, Marcilio Ficino and Pico della Mirandola, Dr Franklin's experiments, codes and ciphers, waterworks, and above all astronomy. I had been mentioning the discovery of the new planet called the Georgium Sidus by Herschel. A great Symbol for our age, I called it, the widening of man's world by pure science, when he remarked on two things. Firstly that Herschel's discovery would not be the ending of our solar system, that there were planets beyond, and secondly it wasn't due to Herschel's ingenuity that the planet had been discovered.

"I expressed my surprise at his notions. Surely the Georgian planet, being twice the distance from the sun as Saturn, must be the true limit. But Mr Mason assured me that Uranus, using the name that the Germans called the planet, had at least three other planets beyond it. One of which he said was inhabited. Now you may wonder at the fact that I didn't run from this man at that moment since he was clearly one of those madmen who believe in extraterrestrial life, a hobbyhorse of many a Mystic, but Mr Mason had been so clear in his dialogue otherwise and so full of fascinating facts, I thought to keep his company.

"Our conversations ranged on many topics, and at one point he began to speak of the future. He had some very definite opinions on the way the future would unfold, and I placed many bets with him of the newly-minted New Connecticut pine-tree schillings on the topics. He won with uncanny accuracy. I made the mistake of mentioning this in my report, and the order came from King George himself that I discover the secret of this man's uncanny accuracy.

"I dedicated myself to this task, first by beginning to act as though everything he said was sensible, for I indeed expected him to be in the service of some supersensible entity that had knowledge of the future. I would in all things act as his disciple in the hopes that I would be of service to King George as well as answering to my own overweening curiosity.

"He told me that he had been in contact with a hidden race that dwelt in the deep hills engaged in mining. I expected that he meant some sort of Indian, for America as you know has seen its share of older races that have erected such curiosities as the Mounds near the Ohio river. He said that this race possessed great secrets of travel, and that he would be Initiated into them at a certain time. He said they were seldom open to the human race except at certain times of instability, when they used mental accelerants in the form of magical symbols to move the human race into something more useful for them.

"I believed very little of this, but pleaded whole-heartedly to be allowed to attend the secret conclaves of this group, so that I too might be useful to the group. He agreed that I might go to one of their gatherings. I was expecting some kind of witches' Sabbat. But I found something infinitely more horrible."

At this point Mr. Brewster's voice began to tremble, and he began acting like a madman again—possessed of fears and giving many terrified glances at the ceiling of his cell.

"We went to a deep forest gorge in the unsettled Vermont woods, near Townshend. We approached dramatically at twilight from a rising path ending in a cleft boulder. A buzzing like the swarm of many bees could be heard, and I saw or thought I saw some large shape fly overhead as it passed along a magnificent terraced waterfall that frothed over the sheer bedrock. Above the tumbling stream rose high rock precipices crusted with strange lichens and honeycombed with alluring caves. We waited till night fell and then they came forth from the cave mouths, while others of their number flew down from the skies. There were a dozen or so of them. They were not human. They were like a great crab with six to twelve pairs of pincers not unlike a lobster, and great chitinous wings like a beetle's, and for heads there was a pulsing mass of pyramidal entrails. I saw them briefly in Mason's lanthorn's light, which he quickly doused. He spoke to them saying, 'This is the one who will tell much to Him in the Gulf, and will utter our spells at the correct time. He will tell the world of men of the World-of-the-Must-Be. He can not do otherwise, for he is a spy for one of mankind's kings.'

"I did not know that Mason knew I was a spy—I had

pretended to be a veteran from Washington's army. I moved to run, but one of the creatures grabbed my arm. It had great strength in its pincer, much greater than I would have suspected its body had. Their bodies looked soft and brittle like a puffball, and they smelled of something long-dead. A dust or spore seemed to drift from its body from time to time. I began a violent coughing spell as the dust entered my lungs. I became dizzy and lost consciousness. I had a sort of Dream of great lucidity.

"I saw a series of scenes that made little sense to me. At first I saw the creatures in completely black rooms—in fact I can not say in truth that I 'saw' them for a new sense wholly different than sight was mine. They were playing with globes, putting little pins in them in the manner a witch is said to torment a doll, then they would tie strings between these pins, which they could do with great spider-like ease. When they had tied the globe up they would pass it to a creature whose form I could not make out who swallowed the globe. Some had many strings and others few.

"The next scene I saw was on Earth, at least I believed it to be Earth. There were great roads of tar being busily laid everywhere, and fast-moving carriages of metal speeding about these roads with men and women inside of them. There were great cities being built, but their pattern resembled the string models I had seen in the black chamber.

"Then I saw large metal cylinders with wings like birds, but these wings did not flap and they were moving through the air and their movement was charted on big maps and corresponded with one of the globes' string pattern.

"Then I saw men and women talking into small devices connected to the walls of their homes and businesses, and these devices were connected with wires that likewise resembled one of the globes.

"Then I saw vast numbers of men and women labouring in front of glowing boxes, their fingers flying over a usually silent array of keys, and a look of growing anxiety on their faces. These too were linked together. I could not understand the extreme—shall I say hellish?—agitation of these scenes. These men and women were working for some goal, but I could not begin to guess what goal could furrow so many brows. The world was filling with billions of men and women, they were everywhere like maggots on a ripe corpse, and they were all tied with strings to one another.

"Then I saw the world as from a great height, and it seemed that the world disappeared except for the netting. It was roughly round, and it squirmed in the darkness of space. The creatures visited it at certain nodes, taking away from it some yellowish substance, that seemed to serve as food for another creature that lay in a dark hole of space, which was blacker than black.

"The great round net grew tighter and tighter, until it began to resemble nothing less than an eyeball, at which point the creatures flew to it in the millions and attached themselves to it and began to move it entire through space. As it passed by me I tried to read its expression: it seemed divided between anger and fear. The creatures carried it to the great dark hole where some vast creature oozed forth and attached the eyeball to what might have been its face.

"Then I saw a series of practical designs for things called *telephone* and *telegraph*, and information on better surveying techniques and new forms of mathematics. Although I am untrained in these fields, these things burned themselves on my mind, I could draw any of them today.

"I came to lying in a different glen, my feet being washed by (what I later discovered to be) the Wantastiquet. There was no sign of Mason, nor of the hellish flying beings. I followed the stream downward and came upon some human habitation in a few hours, a pair of Scott hunters that fed me and escorted me to the village of Athol.

"I eventually made my way back to Concord, where I discovered that Mr Mason had gone missing. I said nothing in my reports about my encounter with Mason, but then a more horrifying discovery came in a month's time. Mason's body had been found near Townshend. It had signs of being frozen, and most peculiarly the top of the skull had been sawn off and his brains had been eaten by wild animals.

"It was a month later still that one of the creatures began visiting my house on moonless nights. I heard it land and gave a general alarum, but it possessed a power akin to the Mesmerism so recently a fashion in France. It could make my servants sleep. It told me that Mason was alive and well on a planet beyond the Georgian, which it called Yuggoth. The special mode of travel that Mason had spoken of was accomplished by surgically removing his brain and placing it in a metal cylinder. A similar cylinder was reserved for me when I completed my mission. I must write my visions and send them to King George.

"I resisted this demonic request, but on every night of the new moon, or on nights when clouds held the lunar radiations at bay, the creatures came to me again and again. They delighted in telling me secrets, each more horrible than the one before. They spoke of Purposes so alien to mankind that such things as we poor worms find significant such as organic life, good and evil, love and hate, are but local attributes of a race both negligible and temporary. And as I learned these things, I became less and less human and more caught up in thinking of the Cosmos, so that I cared not for my servants' trouble, nor the essentials of my spying mission, nor even for things like nation and church. I could have stopped listening at any time, I guess, but my life had always been based on the collecting of secrets.

"In the end I sent my notes to King George. I explained that such inventions could vastly empower the nation which had them, but that some time would have to pass before suitable materials could be made to produce the inventions. In the meantime a series of international protocols would need to be worked out to allow such inventions to come into being and link the world.

"I never received an answer from him."

I asked Mr Brewster what happened then, why was he so afraid of the entities that he had so willingly served.

"After I had sent the packet to King George, I went to the woods ready to seek out the creatures from Yuggoth. Some nights I heard them flying overhead, but they would not come to me. I lived for half a year in the woods, and I came to worry about the coming of the Vermont winter. I did not know why they had forsaken me, but on a frosty night in October they came to my tent. They thanked me for having played my part in their prank. What I had done was very funny, it fit the purpose of Him in the Gulf. The joke, they explained to me, was the supreme Purpose of the One they served, a joke that led to screaming and ecstasy, a joke that was of the same Essence as the playing of the blind flute-players at the Throne of the Laughing One Who Doth Cry. It was the same sort of joke as the Great Ones played, calling their jokes matter and energy, time and dimension. They were very, very thankful. They would play a last little joke on me. They would show me such sights as were too strong to be seen by a human mind. They would show the great tedium of trans-stellar travel, where I would see nothing for aeons, they would show me the horrors of the bodies of the creatures that lived on the Georgian planet, they would take me to a place beyond the Rim of Space and Time. And they would eat my thoughts as they did this. It would be very, very funny.

"Then they left me. For some months I contemplated suicide, but they had done something to me that rendered me incapable of the act. I tried to aim a pistol at myself, or claim myself with a hangman's rope, but a strange paralysis would overtake me at the crucial moment.

"I lost not only the will to live, but such simple wills as the desire to eat or keep myself clean. I merely lay about, sleeping wherever I fell, until the good people of New Connecticut placed me in this asylum. They will come for me some day. I have been thinking a great deal about what that will be like. It won't be the heaven that religions promise for discarnate intelligences—maybe that whole myth comes from mankind's interactions with the creatures from Yuggoth, a sort of supreme jest. No, it will be like when you scrape your thumb. A rawness like when your crotch has been turned red from riding hard all day long. Except it will be all over, extending in infinite length from my naked brain, and it will go on forever, through the long spaces of time as I drift from star to star in one of their metal cylinders, with them flying beside me in the infinite night, their vast wings catching an aether so fine as to be unknown to our senses.

"And then there will be the other scenes. Not just Yuggoth and Yaddith, but worlds that I will need special senses even to see, senses that were never meant for mankind. It won't be all terror, it will be ecstasy too, torment sublime that will melt my humanity away like a candle stub thrown in the fire by a wilful child. And they will laugh in their voice like the buzzing of a thousand bees."

He told many other things, things I thought too horrid to write down, even in this my private journal.

I thought of asking whether his prophecies had ever been received in London, but I decided it would not be a wise thing to inquire of. If such scientific ideas had been received, they would be too valuable to mention to anyone. My mere knowledge would make me a candidate for death. I tried very hard to dismiss Mr Brewster's warnings. Certainly after my one visit I never returned to the Newfane Asylum.

I did however send Christmas packages to him, German *stollen* and jams and cheeses. Even a small brandy, although I am sure that was consumed by the guards.

Three years later when New Connecticut changed its name to Vermont and became the 14th state in the fledgling United States, I received some distressing news. It seemed that one moonless night Mr James Maskelyne, the would-be Indian, did manage to get an axe from the guards and scalp Mr Brewster in what my informant called "a novel and repulsive manner," and that furthermore Mr James Maskelyne, with the cleverness of the truly mad, had been able to hide the axe from the guards when they sought it.

I must believe that this is the case, for otherwise I would look at the sky when it is dark and think that somewhere so many thousands of airless dark miles above, something, something that would smell of rot if I met it in the clean air of Earth, is laughing in a voice like a million bees.

For Ramsey Campbell

The Window

Zoran Zivkovic

translated from the Serbian by Alice Copple-Tosic

Zoran Zivkovic was born in Belgrade, Yugoslavia, in 1948. In 1973 he graduated from the University of Belgrade, and received his Master's degree in 1979 and his doctorate in 1982 from the same school. He lives in Belgrade, across the street from the Chinese Embassy. Of the U.S. planes' bombing of the embassy in 1999, he says, "All our windows and doors to the balcony facing the street were blasted out, together with their frames. It was incredible luck that nobody was injured, although we all—myself, my wife, Mia, and our twin boys of 18—found ourselves on the floor, amid overturned furniture and broken glass." He is the author of Contemporaries of the Future *(1983),* Starry Screen *(1984),* First Contact *(1985),* Encyclopedia of Science Fiction *(1990),* The Fourth Circle *(1993),* Essays on Science Fiction *(1995),* Time Gifts *(1997, the US edition 2000),* The Writer *(1998),* The Book *(2000), and* Impossible Encounters *(2000; also English translation 2000). He has translated more than fifty books, mostly from English. He looks to be a major figure in world SF, though not widely published outside his native language until last year.*

"The Window" appeared both in Interzone *and in* Impossible Encounters, *a collection of fantasy stories which was published in English by Polaris Press.* Interzone*'s edi-*

tor David Pringle had the editorial acumen to publish all six stories from Impossible Encounters *over the course of the year 2000, giving Zivkovic a strong debut for English language readers. The story is a classic literary fantasy, in which the manager of reincarnation appears, as a likeable but rather ordinary clerk. It is an interesting contrast to Scott Bradfield's story about the Devil.*

I died in my sleep.

There wasn't anything special about my death. I hardly even noticed it. I dreamed I was walking down a long hallway closely lined with doors on both sides. The end of the corridor was invisible in the distance, and I was alone. On the wall next to each door hung a framed portrait, slightly larger than life, and lit from above by a lamp.

I looked at the paintings as I passed by them. What else could I do? Only the portraits disturbed the endless monotony of the corridor. There seemed to be male and female portraits in approximately equal numbers, but randomly distributed. The people were mostly of advanced age, and some were very old indeed, but here and there was a younger face, or even a child, though these were quite rare. The images were formal studio-portraits, and the people were all elaborately, even ceremonially dressed. They looked conscious of their own importance, and that of the occasion. Most of them were smiling, but some faces were simply not suited to smiling. They looked grimly serious.

I was not overly surprised when I finally saw my own portrait next to one of the doors. I hadn't actually expected it, but it didn't seem out of place. After all, if so many others had their portraits hanging there, why shouldn't I?

Where else can one hope for a privileged position if not in one's own dream? The only thing that momentarily confused me was that I could not remember when the portrait had been painted. I must have posed for it, I supposed. But maybe that hadn't been necessary. It's hard to say. I don't pretend to understand much about portrait-painting.

Regardless of its origin, I liked the portrait. It did me full justice—more, it showed me in exceptional form. Although I was depicted at my current age, the painter had skillfully diminished some of the more unpleasant aspects of aging: he had slightly smoothed the wrinkles on my forehead and around my eyes, tightened my double chin, removed the yellowness and blotches from my cheeks, darkened some of the gray streaks in my hair. This was not to make me look younger. The years were still on the painting, but I bore them with greater élan. And most important of all, there was no sign of the debilitating disease that had taken such heavy toll of my looks. No effort on the part of a photographer could ever have produced the same effect, however great his skill.

I stood in front of my portrait for a long time, gazing in satisfaction. But all things have their measure, even vanity. I couldn't stand there forever. Someone might pass by sooner or later and find me in this unbecoming position, which would certainly be embarrassing. But where could I go? Continue down the corridor? That did not seem promising; it appeared to extend endlessly before me, with no destination to make for.

Should I go back? That possibility hadn't crossed my mind before. I turned around and immediately understood I could not count on going back. Just a few steps behind me the hallway disappeared, turning into deep darkness, as though all the lamps above the paintings had turned off as soon as I passed them. Maybe the lights would go on again if I headed in that direction, but I had no desire to find out.

I turned around facing forward again—and suffered a new surprise. The same thing had happened to the corridor in front of me. It had turned into a dark tunnel that began at the edge of the small, conical beam of light illuminating my portrait from above. This sole remaining source of light covered the painting, the door beside it and myself in front of it—a tiny island of existence bounded by an opaque, black sea of nothingness.

I had lost the right to choose; there was only one path before me. The moment I touched the doorknob, I was overcome by the feeling that something important was about to happen, but I had no immediate inkling of what it could be. It was only after I opened the door and entered the room that I realized I had died. It happened in the middle of raising and lowering my foot as I crossed the threshold. I was still alive when I started the step outside, and already dead when I finished it inside. I barely felt the transition itself. Something streamed through me, a wave resembling a light trembling or momentary shiver. It lasted a split second, then passed, leaving behind no other trace than the certainty of death.

I was not afraid. Fear of death has meaning before one dies, and not afterward. The only thing I felt was confusion. I naturally knew nothing about this state. How could I, after all? I had not even tried to picture it in my mind. That had always seemed a pointless exercise to me, and as the disease got the upper hand, such thoughts had come to fill me with revulsion—to be avoided as much as possible.

First of all, I wondered if I was still asleep. It is said that the deceased rest in eternal peace, but that is probably a metaphor, not meant be taken literally. In any case, the sight before me did not resemble in the least any that I had seen in my dreams. There was nothing unreal or strange. On the contrary. The room I entered was some sort of study, elegantly furnished to be sure, but otherwise not the least bit unusual. There was no one inside. Feeling a bit uncomfortable, I started to inspect it, without stepping away from the door, which I had closed behind me.

To my right stood a large, black, wooden desk. A lamp with an arching neck and green shade illuminated numerous objects, arranged in an orderly fashion upon it: a wide, leather-bound desk-pad; a decorative brass inkwell with a heavy maple-wood blotter; a rose-wood cube, drilled with holes to make a pen and pencil holder; a shallow lacquer paper tray; an ivory-handled magnifying glass; a double silver candlestick (without any candles); three identical little boxes covered in dark velour whose purpose I could not make out; a white flowerpot containing a flowerless plant with long, thin leaves; an engraved pipe stand with three pipes of different shapes.

Across from the desk, on the left side, were two large brown leather armchairs with a small, round coffee table between them. On the table was a lamp with a tasselled yellow shade and an oval tray containing a lidded jug of water and two glasses placed upside down on round paper coasters. Behind the armchairs rose shelves full of books that covered the entire wall. The volumes were of uniform height and thickness, and their spines were bound in a limited range of sombre tones. A vertical ladder rose along the edge of the shelves, its ends firmly anchored to guide-rails on the floor and ceiling.

The middle of the wall facing the door was covered by a large painting in a simple rectangular frame, shorter side down, brightly illuminated from bellow. It depicted an area of clear, blue sky seen through a double window. The deep blue was portrayed so convincingly that for a moment I even took it for a real window.

The window was closed, but there was a certain tension in the otherwise tranquil scene that indicated it might open at any moment—through a draft, perhaps, or by someone going up to open it, someone who was still not visible, but whose presence was hinted at by a shadow that flickered just inside the frame. The only thing that disturbed the harmony of the straight lines and uniform shades was a colourful butterfly that had already tired from its efforts to fly outside, clearly unable to understand the existence of a completely invisible, but still impenetrable obstacle such as glass.

To the right of the picture, in the semi-darkness, stood a grandfather clock in a tall mahogany case. The glass door was decorated with geometric designs in the corners, and a disproportionately small key protruded from the keyhole. At first I thought I saw only one hand pointing straight up, but when I had a better look I discerned the small hand hidden under the big one. I stared at them for some time, but when they failed to change position I lowered my eyes suspiciously; only then did I notice that the pendulum was resting in the middle, motionless.

To the left of the painting, hard by the bookshelves, was another door. It was the same colour as the wall around it and could only be distinguished by its edges, which appeared somewhat darker. It had an unusual characteristic that I did not notice at first glance. There was a lock, but no doorknob. If the door could be opened, then it was only possible from the other side.

Just as I was looking at it, that happened, quite without sound. Part of the wall seemed simply to arch forward, and a figure appeared in the emptiness left behind. I stared at it fixedly. Had I not been dead, I am sure that my heart would have jumped, and pins and needles would have run up and down my spine.

The man who appeared in front of me seemed unassuming, almost like a clerk: in late middle age, not very tall, balding, with a thick, narrow moustache that covered only the line under his nose, small, round, wire-rimmed glasses, and wearing a dark suit of classic cut that did not quite succeed in hiding his extra pounds. The smile that appeared on his round, ruddy face seemed guileless and unaffected.

He hastened brightly to greet me, his hand stretched out. I had no recourse but to accept it.

"Welcome! Welcome!"

I didn't know what to say in return, so I smiled too, although mine was somewhat forced. We stood there like that for some time, gripping each other's hands, eyeing each other curiously, like friends meeting after a long separation.

He was the first to break the silence. "Please, make yourself comfortable." He indicated one of the armchairs in front of the bookshelves, waited for me to sit down, and then sat down in the other, hitching up his trouser legs a bit. He was still smiling.

"I was expecting you earlier. You stayed a bit longer than planned."

His voice seemed to contain a touch of reproach, but that might have been my imagination. He looked at me in silence for several moments, perhaps expecting me to say something. As I remained silent, he finally waved his hand dismissively.

"Well, it's all the same. Some are late, some are early. There are very few who arrive on time. They all come, however, sooner or later. How do you feel?"

I cleared my throat before answering uncertainly. "Fine, I think."

He nodded his head in satisfaction. "Nothing is bothering you, there is no discomfort?"

I paused briefly. "No, everything's all right."

The man's smile broadened. "I'm glad to hear that. You're just a bit confused, right?"

"Yes," I admitted after a moment's hesitation, "a little."

"You mustn't reproach yourself for that. You're no exception in this regard. They're all confused when they arrive. It's quite normal. Would you like a glass of water?" He indicated the jug on the table between us.

"No, thank you," I replied. I had the ghostly impression that my throat was dry, but somehow it didn't seem appropriate to drink water in this new position. Maybe later, when I got used to it.

"People are really quite full of questions," continued the man. "They are dying of curiosity. I'm sure that you are, too."

There was no reason to pretend. "I hope that's normal, too."

"Of course, of course. You are certainly interested in where you have arrived, what awaits you here, and who I am, as well."

"Certainly," I agreed in a faltering voice.

"There is a little difficulty in this connection. I, naturally, can answer all these questions. And many others that you might like to ask. But if I do that, I will deprive you of the possibility of going back."

"Going back?"

"Yes. You can return. To life."

I stared fixedly at the stranger in the other armchair. His tiny eyes returned my glance good-naturedly through his round glasses.

"But I'm dead," I said finally, in a half-questioning voice.

"Yes, that's clear. Otherwise you wouldn't be here."

"Well, then, how . . ."

"I can't explain it to you. Unless you decide to stay."

Now my throat felt not only dry, but tight. I tried to swallow, without success. As I poured water from the jug into one of the glasses, my hand trembled a bit. I hoped this clumsiness had not been too conspicuous. The water was cold, but it tasted a little stale.

"Do you mean to say I'm the one who decides—whether I go back or stay?"

"You, of course. Who else?"

"I mean, it doesn't depend on my behaviour in . . . my previous life? I might be someone really bad, for example."

The man gave a short laugh. "Yes, you could. But it makes no difference. There is no punishment or reward here. This is not the Last Judgment."

"So, it's enough for me to decide to go back. Do I understand that correctly?"

"You understand correctly. You can even choose the shape in which you will return."

I put the glass back on the coaster. Several drops that had spilled from the jug sparkled in the yellow light on the silver surface of the tray.

"I wouldn't change my shape. I'm used to this one."

The smile disappeared from the man's lips. "I'm afraid that's the only thing that's impossible. Your old shape has been used up, it is no longer serviceable. You can't go back to it. And it would not be wise. Disease has completely destroyed you, isn't that so? But you can choose something completely new. The choice is almost unlimited."

"Be someone else?"

"You would not be someone else, because you would have no memory of your earlier life. It would be a new beginning for you."

"I would be born again?"

"Most assuredly. You would return to the world as a newborn child, as is fitting. To live a new life. With the characteristics that you want."

"You mean, I can choose what I'll look like, or how tall I'll be?"

"And much more than that. You could change the colour of your skin, your sex . . ."

"Sex?"

The look of amazement that appeared on my face caused the stranger to smile once again. "That is one of the most frequent changes. In both directions. I think it's not so much dissatisfaction with one's original sex as much as curiosity about trying the opposite sex."

I shook my head. "Well, I'm not curious."

"I understand. Would you perhaps be interested in going back as something other than a human being? That is also possible."

I squinted my eyes in disbelief. "What do you mean?"

"There are other forms of life on earth besides humans. There are countless numbers, in fact. They are all at your disposal."

"What, for example?"

"Oh, anything. Of course, it all depends on the inclinations of the one going back. People usually choose an animal."

I paused a bit before answering. "Why would someone want to be an animal, and not a human, in his new life?"

"Well, it doesn't have to be at all as bad as you might think. The life of a pure-bred cat or thoroughbred horse, for example, could be much more comfortable and carefree than many human lives. And if you prefer excitement, there are few human experiences that can compare to what a lion, an eagle or a shark experiences every day."

I thought it over briefly. "I still don't think I want to be an animal."

"Whatever you want. There are other possibilities as well. You could be a plant."

"A plant?"

"Yes, that is not such a rare choice."

"But plants don't have any . . . any consciousness."

"That's true, but this drawback is compensated by other advantages. A long life, for example. Almost every type of tree lives considerably longer than a man. Sequoias are highly valued in this regard. Also, they are protected, which makes them additionally attractive. But even short-lived flowers have their admirers. People sometimes decide to go back as an orchid or a rose-blossom, even though they know they will only live one short season."

"But that's absurd. Getting the chance for a new life and wasting it on some flower . . ."

"They don't look at it like that. Beauty means everything to them. That is something we must accept. But there are truly some decisions that are hard to understand. Even for me. What would you say to going back as a salamander, a worm, as a sagebrush, a stinging-nettle or a spider?"

"A spider?" I repeated. My face twisted into a disgusted grimace.

"Yes, quite unpleasant, wouldn't you say?"

"I would not change at all," I rushed to say, shaking my head. "I would like to stay as similar as possible to myself in my previous life. If that's possible."

"Of course it is. The great majority choose just that. So this means you have decided to go back?"

I did not answer at once. A multitude of confusing questions swarmed inside me. Finally, one outweighed all the others. "If I returned, I would live out another lifetime, right?"

"Yes."

"And in the end I would die again?"

"That is inevitable, unfortunately."

"After that would I . . . come back here again?"

"No, you only come here once. After your second life all that remains is death. You are given no further choice."

He said this with an even voice, as though it were something banal. I looked at him for a few moments without talking.

"But what is that choice all about, anyway? On one side there is a new life. I understand that. But what's on the other side? What am I supposed to choose between?"

The stranger removed his glasses, took a large white handkerchief from the inside pocket of his jacket and started to wipe them. He did it patiently and with extreme care, and in the end lifted them against the table-lamp to check them. Without them his face seemed somehow bare. He put them back on slowly, pressing them onto the bridge of his nose.

"They rarely get around to that question," he said at last. "Almost all of them immediately grab the chance to return. They're not interested in anything else."

"What do you say to the others?"

"Nothing specific. The most I can do is give them a hint. Anything more than that would endanger their return, if they decided to go back after all."

"A hint?"

"Yes," replied the man. "Please come with me."

He got up, waited for me to do the same, and then took me cordially by the arm and led me. At first I thought we were heading for the door through which he had entered, but we stopped in front of the large picture in the middle of the wall.

His voice dropped almost to a whisper. "Look at it carefully."

My eyes were filled with the sight of the blue heavens seen through the closed window. The moments passed by slowly. Nothing happened. When the change finally happened, it first affected my sense of hearing and not my sight. Suddenly, as though from a great distance, I started to hear an even, steady drumming. I didn't recognize it at first. It was only when it got louder in the surrounding silence that I realized it was the dull ticking of the clock. I did not need to turn my eyes towards the large mahogany case in the right corner to know that the pendulum was no longer motionless.

As though in answer to this awakening sound, the picture came to life. The butterfly fluttered once, sluggishly, without the hope of finally breaking out, and slid down a bit lower. The shadow moved because the hand outside the frame moved. The hand entered the frame and made for the middle of the window. It tried to beat its own shadow, but they reached the handle at the same time and turned it.

The moment the window opened, I was almost stunned by a rush of dizziness. The man's firm clasp on my arm was a welcome support without which I would have lost my balance and fallen. But the butterfly had no one to help it. The gust of wind easily whisked it off the smooth glass surface and sent it rushing into the blue infinity.

That very instant everything disappeared: the picture frame, the wall, the stranger, the entire study. I was in the middle of nothing and started to fall. I knew that I had to move my wings, that I was supposed to fly, and not sink headlong, but I suddenly no longer knew how. Many flashes of an eternity filled with icy horror passed before I once again mastered this simple, instinctive skill. First my sinking slowed down, then stopped, and when I finally started to climb on an ascending stream of air, I didn't have to move my wings at all. I just kept them spread out like two enormous, colourful twin sails in the middle of the vast open sea of air that surrounded me.

Fear turned into the rapture that always accompanies flying. I could have stayed there forever, surrendering to this tide of joy. Then, at an unspecified distance ahead of me, I caught sight of something wrinkled on the uniform fabric of blue. Something had started to thin the air, dissolve it, something that appeared from underneath. It was bright, radiant, inviting. I flapped my wings energetically, wrenching myself away from the main airstream. The call that drew me, the radiance coming from the other side of the firmament, was irresistible: the flame of a candle attracting a moth in the dark.

But I was not allowed to reach the light. The airstream suddenly changed direction. I tried to resist it feverishly, realizing in despair that I was being borne away from where I longed to go. The strength of my wings, however, was nothing compared to that powerful pull. I rushed backwards faster and faster, filled with a painful feeling of futility and helplessness. The window slammed shut after me when I flew back in, and the same moment I was swallowed up in darkness.

The darkness was not completely empty; it was filled with the beating of a colossal heart. It was a regular, uniform sound, but somehow I knew it would soon stop. That happened all at once, without any premonitory slowing. Dropping to the lowest point, the pendulum did not continue on the other side; it stopped there, having nothing else to measure. In the silence it left behind, my sight slowly returned. I was still standing in front of the picture, staring at it, although there was no longer anything moving in it. The butterfly was drooping in one of the corners again, and the shadow was patiently waiting for the unseen hand to move. Another hand slightly increased its pressure around my arm.

"This way. You'll feel more comfortable if you sit down again."

I wanted to tell him that everything was all right with me, but I staggered at the very first step and was grateful for the support he offered. When we were settled in the armchairs, he poured some more water from the jug into my glass. I wasn't thirsty, but I still took a long drink.

The man did not speak right away, just watched me with his customary grin. He was clearly giving me the chance to collect my wits. And I was grateful for that, too.

"An exceptional painting, wouldn't you agree?" he said at last.

"Yes," I agreed after a brief hesitation, a little hoarse. "Exceptional."

We stopped talking once again. Just then a thought crossed my mind, one completely inappropriate to the decisive moment at hand. The other glass was still turned upside-down on the tray, unused. I wondered if it was there incidentally, just like the multitude of other objects in the room, or if the stranger sometimes drank a little water from it.

"So? Have you chosen?" There was no impatience in his voice, and I felt under no pressure. He could have asked me something quite trivial in the same tone.

"A butterfly," I replied softly. "I would like to be a butterfly, of course."

He looked at me wordlessly several moments, and then gave a brief nod. "Of course." His smile grew broader. He indicated the door with his hand. "After you."

I got up, a little unsteady, and headed in that direction, but stopped after a few steps, confused. The door had no handle on this side. How could I open it? I thought about turning around and asking the man. But that very instant I realized there was no need, for there was no longer any door in front of me.

And Still She Sleeps

Greg Costikyan

Greg Costikyan lives in New York City and works as Chief Design Officer for Unplugged Games, a wireless games venture he co-founded. He has designed a slew of games over the years, writes frequently about the games and the game industry, and has written three fantasy novels and a number of short stories. His fourth novel (and first SF), First Contract, *appeared in 2000 from Tor Books. His essay entitled "New Front In the Copyright Wars: Out-of-Print Computer Games" was recently published in the* New York Times. *He was recently inducted into the Adventure Games Hall of Fame. He can be found on the Web at www.costik.com.*

"And Still She Sleeps," which appeared in Black Heart, Ivory Bones, *edited by Ellen Datlow and Terri Windling, is an interesting collision of science and magic: a sleeping beauty from the time of the Picts is found on an archeological dig in Northumberland. Costikyan says the story is "in some sense, an attempt to grapple with the nature of love . . . a subject I still can only claim to have the haziest grip on. The story of Sleeping Beauty is one of the ur-stories that shapes our society's notion of Romantic love—and thinking about it, and what's wrong with the image of love it presents, was the proximate cause of the urge to write it."*

"*'Ow'd ye like* to kiss them smackers, eh?" said the fellow in the queue ahead of me—cloth cap, worn tweed trousers, probably his only shirt. I gave him a stern look, and he, suitably chastened, turned away.

There she stood in her glass case; they had dressed her in someone's idea of Medieval garb, a linen dress at least four centuries wrong. Slowly, her breast rose and fell; slowly enough to show that this was no mortal slumber.

I forbore from saying that I had indeed kissed her, poor dear. To no avail, to no avail.

I found her, after all. Well, to be literal about it, one of von Stroheim's diggers found her, but von Stroheim was away at the time. I was in charge of the excavation.

We were in the Cheviot Hills, not far from the village of Alcroft in Northumberland. It was a crisp October day, a brisk breeze off the North Sea some miles to our east, the sky pellucid; a good day to dig, neither cold enough to stiffen the fingers nor hot enough to raise a sweat. I had been with von Stroheim in Mesopotamia, and this was far more pleasant—though the stakes were surely smaller, a little Northumbrian hill fort, not a great city of the Urartu.

Still, it was a dig; while many of my profession prefer less strenuous scholarship—days and nights spent with cuneiform and hieroglyphs—I enjoy getting out in the field, feeling the dust of ages between my fingers, divining the magics and devices the ancients used.

This, indeed, is my dear Janet's despair: that I am forever, so she says, charging off to Ionia or Tehran or the Valley of the Kings, places where a woman of refinement is unlikely to find suitable accommodation. Ah, but the homecomings after such forays are sweet; and truthfully, they are not so common, a few months out of each year. And between times, there is our little Oxford cottage, the rose garden, the faculty teas; a pleasant enough life for a man of scholarly bent and a woman of intelligence, a serene and healthful environment for our children. Far better this than the life of many of my classmates, amid the stinks and fumes and poverty of London, or building the Empire amid ungrateful savages in some tropical hell a thousand miles from home.

When I told Janet that von Stroheim proposed to excavate in Northumberland, she was pleased. She and the children could accompany us; after all, it was in England. What was the difficulty?

So I had let a little house in Alcroft, and rode up each morning to join von Stroheim and his men.

I brought Clarice with me that morning, she riding behind me, small arms about my waist, a picnic lunch in the panniers. I doubted she would want to come with me often, as there is not much to excite a child at a dig; but she could play on the lea, pet the sheep, wander about and plague us with questions.

The encampment made me glad that I had taken the house in Alcroft; the tents were downwind from the jakes, today, the sheep browsing amid them. The diggers were breaking their fast on eggs and kippers, while our students dressed in their tents. De Laurency was missing, I saw—my prize pupil, but a bit of a trial, that man.

While Clarice happily chased sheep, I went up the hill. The diggers—rough men in work shirts and canvas trousers—and such of the students as had completed their toilet came with me. They resumed excavation along the lines von Stroheim had marked out with lengths of twine, while I pottered about with a surveyor's level, an enchanted pendant, a dowsing rod of ash.

It was while I was setting up my equipage that de Laurency appeared, striding up the hill, burrs in his trouser legs, his hair windblown and wild, a gnarled old walking stick in one hand. "Where the devil have you been?" I asked him.

He smiled vaguely. "Communing with the spirits of the moor," he said.

"Damme, fellow," I told him. "There's work to be done. And hard work, too; you can't expect to gad about the countryside all night and—"

"Bosh, Professor," he said gently. "I'll dig like a slavey, never you fear."

I returned to my equipment; if it weren't for his brilliance, I'd shuck de Laurency off on some other don. Dig like a slavey indeed; the man was slight and prone to sickness. He'd be exhausted by midday, I had no doubt, and wandering Northumberland in a mid-October night is a good way to become consumptive.

But to work. My task was to delineate the ley lines, the lines of magical force that converged on this site. They were the reason we had chosen to dig here; in this part of Northumbria, there was no site so propitious for ritual. That, no doubt, was one reason a fort had been built here; another was its defensibility and its capacity to dominate the region. From the hilltop, one could see as far as Woolet to the north, to the peak of the Cheviot to the west.

There was not much left of the old hill fort: a hummock of sod marking where walls had run. It was one of a series of forts built by the Kings of Northumbria along these hills, defenses against the Picts, though by the eighth century it was well within the Northumbrian borders, for the kingdom stretched north as far as the Firth of Forth.

Still, it was the prospect of magic that had drawn us here. We knew so little about the period, really; we knew the Romans had bound the Britons with powerful spells, had tamed the wild Celtic magic of their precursors. We knew the Anglo-Saxons had brought with them their own pagan power; and we knew the Church preserved much Roman knowledge through the fall, magic well used by the Carolingians in their doomed attempt to re-create the Empire. But how much exactly had survived, here in Britain? What was the state of the art in the eighth century? We could not ask the question in the south, for modern works have masked so much of the past, but here in sparsely inhabited Northumberland we had a better chance to find some answers.

My first surprise of the morning was to discover that the ley lines were active; power was drawing down them, from a line up the Cheviot in the direction of Glasgow. A spell or spells were active still, buried somewhere in this fort.

Lest this sound everyday to you, let me emphasize that the fort was eleven centuries old. The last mention of it—Castle Coelwin, it was called—was in the chronicles of the reign of Eadbehrt of Northumbria, who abdicated in 765. I have seen working spells as old, and older—in Rome, and Athens, and China—but who in miserable, divided, warring eighth century England could perform a ritual so strong, so binding?

It was while studying my equipment, dumbfounded at this discovery, that one of the workers ran up to me, out of breath. "Professor Borthwick," he said, "best coome quick. We've found a gel."

Indeed they had. They had dug a trench about two feet deep in what we termed the Ironmongery, a location toward the center of the fort where we had expected to find a forge, a common feature of fortresses from the period. The rusted remnants of several tools or weapons had already been found there, and the diggers had abandoned spades for trowels and brooms, lest some artifact be damaged by digging. And well that they had, for I shudder to think what a spade might have done to her fair flesh.

About her was loam, evidence of rotted wood; de Laurency, a curious look of epiphany on his face, crouched over her, tenderly brushing away loose dirt with his bare fingers. He had uncovered a hand and a part of an arm.

Her femininity was obvious through the narrowness of the hand. Her fingernails were long, inches in length; God knows when they had last been trimmed.

I cannot count the number of times I have carefully whisked the dirt from a skeleton, uncovering evidence of past violence or disease, looking for artifacts or skeletal damage to learn something of the corpse's fate. *But this was no corpse.* It was a living body, clad in flesh—cool to the touch, but with a slow, slow pulse—buried in the cold earth and yet somehow holding on to life.

Gently, we uncovered her; her hair and nails were preserved along with her body, but her hair was matted and filthy, her poor flesh besmirched with a millennium's dirt.

De Laurency worked by me; the diggers stood back, the other students stood aside to give us room. He said, low enough that I think only I heard him:

> *"How long hast thou rested in England's clay?*
> *How long since the sun on thy tresses played?*
> *How long since thy tender lips were kiss'd?*
> *What power hast brought thee to this?"*

I glanced at him, askance; there are times when I greatly appreciate von Stroheim's brutal practicality. Romanticism is all very well in poetry, but this is science. And *that*, I believe, was doggerel.

We had uncovered her head and shoulder when von Stroheim appeared, returning from an errand.

"Mein Gott," he muttered when he saw her, and turned to me with excitement. "Well, Alistair. Another puzzle, eh? What shall we make of this?"

It took a good two hours to dig her cautiously from the

earth. And then we put her in a litter and carried her down to the encampment.

Clarice was fascinated, and with her little hands helped us to bathe and barber the girl. Though her hair was golden, it was far too matted and filthy to leave; we were forced to cut it off. For the nonce, we covered her with a simple canvas sheet; we had no women's clothing with us.

She appeared to be about sixteen; blond-haired and, when an eyelid was held back, blue-eyed. She was a scant five feet tall—probably large for the period—and just under a hundred pounds. She was well-formed, and her skin fine, though faint scarring gave evidence of a bout with smallpox. She breathed shallowly—a breath every five minutes or so; her pulse ran an impossibly slow beat every thirty seconds. Apparently, she had received enough oxygen, filtered through the soil, to survive. Since her discovery, she has never made water, nor passed stool; never eaten nor drunk. Yet her fingernails and hair slowly grow.

Clarice looked up at me with shining eyes. "It's Sleeping Meg," she said.

Out of such things are discoveries fashioned: a peculiar magical fluctuation, an unexpected finding in the dirt, the words of children.

An intelligent child, Clarice, my sweetheart; eight going on twenty, her mother's dark curls and laughing eyes.

She took me to the house of her playmate, Sybil Shaw, a local girl whose widowed mother eked out a living taking in cleaning and letting out rooms. Mrs. Shaw was a stout, tired-looking woman in her forties, hands reddened with her washing, wispy curls of blond turning gray escaping her cap. She greeted us warmly at the door and offered tea; behind her, I could see irons warming before the fire, petticoats laid out for goffering.

"If you would be so kind, Mrs. Shaw," I told her, a cup

of tea balanced on a knee, "I would very much appreciate it if you could tell me the story of Sleeping Meg."

"Och aye," she said, a little mystified. "Sleeping Meg? 'Tis but a children's tale, ye ken, a story of these parts. What mought a scholar like you to do with tha'?"

And so, patiently, I explained what we had found at Castle Coelwin, and Clarice's words.

Mrs. Shaw snorted. "I misdoubt it has owt to do wi' the tale," she said, "but that's as may be."

I shall set out the story here in plainer language, for Mrs. Shaw (good heart though she has) possesses a thick North Country accent—and a meandering style—that would simply obscure it.

It seems that in the days when Arthur and Guinevere were still much in love, the Queen gave birth to a daughter whom they named Margaret. She was the darling of Arthur's knights, and as a child was dandled on the knees of the likes of Gawain and Lancelot. And at sixteen she was betrothed to the King of Scotland, whose armies had several times ravaged towns along England's northern border, and with whom by this marriage Arthur hoped to cement the peace.

But Morgain heard of this, and saw in it a danger to her son, Mordred, Arthur's bastard; a legitimate daughter, wed to the Scottish monarch, would have a better claim to Arthur's throne. With whispers and magic, she turned the King of Scotland against the proposal.

When Arthur and the Scottish King met in Berwick to seal the marriage, the Scot demanded all of Northumberland as a dowry. To this Arthur could not agree; and the King of Scotland took this as confirming Morgain's words against Arthur. Enraged, he enlisted the sorceress's aid to wreak his revenge; and she cast a mighty spell on Margaret, that she should sleep and never waken till betrothed to a Scottish prince, the betrothal sealed with a kiss.

In horror, Arthur went to Merlin, who could not directly

unweave so mighty a spell; but he altered its terms, so that but a kiss by her own true love would awaken Margaret.

They built her a bed in Camelot, and covered her floor with flowers; many a knight essayed her awakening, but though many loved her, they loved her as a child and not a woman. And dark times soon befell Arthur and his knights; and what became of Margaret none could say, though perhaps she sleeps somewhere still, awaiting her true love's lips.

"What," said von Stroheim, feeding a stick to the campfire under the starry October sky, "are we to make of this old wive's tale?"

"I've asked about, and it's not just Mrs. Shaw's; it seems to be common in the region."

"It's merely a variant on Sleeping Beauty," von Stroheim said. "My own mother told me that story when I was a child."

"I'm sure she did," I told him. "As did mine. But there is often a nugget of truth in legends, as von Schliemann showed at Troy, what? Perhaps rather Sleeping Beauty is a variation on Sleeping Meg. A happier ending, at any rate; surely I would alter the tale in such fashion, if I were to rewrite it."

"Yes, very well," he muttered impatiently. "But Arthur? Centuries off, and problematic in any event, as you well know."

"It's common for stories to become conflated with others," I pointed out. "Suppose the true story goes something like this: Eadberht offered his daughter to one of the Pictish kings to seal a truce. For whatever reason, the deal broke down and a spell was cast. She fell into a slumber, from which she never recovered."

Von Stroheim scowled. "Ach, incredible," he said. "Eleven centuries and no one falls in love with her?" He looked toward the tent where she now lay, properly dressed in my wife's own clothes, guarded by de Laurency. "I'm half in love with her myself."

I grinned at him. "Well, kiss her, then," I told him.

He looked at me startled. "Why not you?"

I raised an eyebrow. "I, sir, am a happily married man."

He snorted. Von Stroheim is a cynic on the subject of marriage. "Very well. And why not?"

We entered the tent. The girl slept on a pallet of straw; de Laurency sat by her, gazing at her fair face by the light of a kerosene lamp. He looked up as we entered.

Von Stroheim went directly to the pallet, knelt, and kissed her: first on the forehead, then on the lips.

De Laurency sprang to his feet, a flush on his pale cheeks. "What the devil are you doing?" he demanded of von Stroheim.

Von Stroheim raised a bushy brow and stood to face the student. "That's 'What the devil are you doing, *Professor*,' " he said.

De Laurency flushed. "Do you often attempt to kiss women to whom you have not been introduced?" he demanded.

The two were silent for a moment, standing in the flickering yellow light under the low canvas roof. It is an image that has stayed with me; the young, sickly Romantic attempting to defend the honor of the girl; the older, bearlike man of science astounded that his simple experiment should rouse such antipathy.

"Be serious," he said at last, and ducked to leave the tent.

De Laurency sat, fists still clenched. "He had best leave her be," he said.

"Simmer down, boy," I told him. "It was an experiment, nothing more. If the story has any truth, it is a kiss that will awaken her."

"Not a kiss from the likes of him," said de Laurency fiercely.

Outside the tent von Stroheim was gazing at Orion, hands in his pockets against the chill. "It is all nonsense, anyway," he said. "You have erected an enormous structure of conjecture on an amazingly small investment of fact."

"Yes, Herr Doktor Professor," I said, a little sardonically, amused at this change in mood. "It is time we telegraphed the Royal Thaumaturgical Society."

Janet sighed when she heard the news from London, sitting on the chaise in the parlor with me, her arm about my waist and her thigh against mine; the children were asleep, coal burned in the fireplace, we sipped hot cider before retiring. "How long?" she said.

"No more than a week," I said. "Sir James has promised to investigate directly we arrive, but I wish to be present for at least the preliminary examination. I do want to return as soon as I may; it is important that we find out as much as we can at the dig, before cold weather sets in."

She laid her head on my shoulder. "And is that the only reason you want to return quickly?" Her lips were on my neck.

"No, dearest," I whispered in her ear. "Neither the only nor the most important."

She kissed me, and I tasted the cider on her tongue.

The trip to London—de Laurency insisted on joining me—was, as usual, quite dull. But Sir James Maxwell made us quite welcome at the Thaumaturgical; after a cursory examination of Meg in his laboratory, he joined us in the society's lounge.

I was not insensible of the honor. While I have a modest scholarly reputation, Sir James outshines me by several orders of magnitude; it was he, after all, who through his discovery of the field equations, put thaumaturgy on a firm mathematical and scientific footing.

Ensconced in leather armchairs, we ordered Armagnac and relaxed.

"Precisely what do you hope from me?" Sir James inquired.

"Two things, I think," I said after a pause for consideration. "First, a spell clearly binds her; it would be useful to learn as much of it as we can, to cast light on the state of magical knowledge during the period. Second, it would be marvelous if we could awaken the girl; wouldn't it be grand if we could talk to and question someone who had actually lived a thousand years ago?"

De Laurency rather darkened at this, and muttered something into his brandy. I glanced at him. "Speak up, Robert," I said.

"She is a freeborn Briton," he said, rather defiantly. "If she should waken, you would have no right to keep her, study her, like some kind of trained ape."

"'Briton' in the period would mean 'Celt,'" I pointed out. "She is Anglo-Saxon."

"Pedantry," he said.

"Perhaps. But I take your point; she would be a free woman. However, I suspect that learning to live in the modern age would be difficult, and that she would be grateful for our assistance. Surely we can expect cooperation in return?"

De Laurency coughed, a little apologetically. "I'm sorry, Professor," he said. "I'm sure you mean her no harm. But we must remember that she is a person, and not an . . . an artifact."

Sir James nodded sagely. "You are quite correct, sir," he said, "and we shall take the utmost caution."

Sir James promised to begin his studies on the morrow, and we parted.

I had taken rooms at the Chemists, my own club and not far from the Thaumaturgical. The next morning—a fine, brisk autumn day, the wind whipping London's skies clean of its normally noxious fumes—I walked back toward the RTS. And as I did, I heard the omnipresent cries of the street hawkers:

"*Globe, Wand, Standard, Times!* Getcher mornin' papers 'ere, gents. Sleepin' Beauty found in North Country. Read hall about it."

"Blast," I muttered, handing the boy a few pence for a *Wand*—one of the yellower of Fleet Street's publications. The article, and the illustration that accompanied it, was rather more fallacy than fact; but it contained the ineluctable truth that our discovery was now at the Royal Thaumaturgical Society.

I fully comprehend the utility of publicity when the need to solicit funds for research arises; but I feared, at this juncture, that public awareness of Meg could only serve to interfere with our investigation.

My fears proved immediately well-founded. While I checked my coat at the Thaumaturgical, a man in a rather loud herringbone suit spied me and approached.

"Dr. Borthwick?"

"I am he," I responded, wondering how he knew me; I caught the eye of the porter at the front desk, who looked down slightly shamefacedly. A little bribery, I supposed.

"I'm Fanshaw, of Fanshaw and Little, promoters," he said, handing me a card. It bore a picture of a Ferris wheel and an address in the East End. "Wonder if we might chat about this Sleeping Beauty girl you've got."

"I fail to see—"

"Well, sir, you see, I read the papers. Can't always believe what they say, but this is a wondrous age, ain't it? Magic and science, the Empire growing, strange things from barbarous lands. *That's* me business."

"Your business appears to be sideshow promotion," I said.

"Dead right, sir. Educational business, educational; bringing the wonders of seven continents and every age to the attention of the British public. *That's* me business. Though the gentry may view us askance, we serve a useful function, you know, introducing the common people to the wonders of the world. The *Wand* says she'll be awoken by true love's kiss, is that right? Can't believe what you read in the *Wand*, of course, but you could make such a spell, could be done, I understand."

Wondering how to get rid of the fellow, I said, "A variety

of theories have been propounded to explain the young woman's state, and this is indeed among them. But until further research is performed—"

"Oh, research, yes, of course," he said. "Research costs money, indeed it does; a shame, that exploration of the wonders of the universe don't come cheap. And *that's* me business."

"Beg pardon?"

"Making money. For all concerned, all concerned; business ain't worth much unless all walk away from the table happy, eh? Now, sez I to meself, be nice to wake up the girl, eh, find out what life was like back in those days, eh? Sez I, bet Dr. Borthwick would be keen on that."

"It would be desirable to be sure, but until we better understand the magic that has so long sustained her—"

"Well now, look here. A kiss to awaken her, eh? But has to be her own true love. Where d'ye find her own true love?"

"Even should the theory prove meritorious, I'm at a loss—"

"Precisely! Impossible to say. So then, kiss her a lot, eh? Many folk. True love bound to burgeon in some young man's breast eventually, eh?"

I blinked at the man. "Precisely what are you proposing?"

"Consider the possibilities. 'Will you be the one to wake up Sleepin' Beauty? Are you her prince?' A shilling a peck, I imagine; bit of a sum, for a sideshow, but this is high-class stuff, Sir James Maxwell investigated, a princess of the ancient world, eh? Bit of pelf for me, bit of pelf for you, bit of pelf for research, eh? And maybe one of the marks wakes up the bint."

I restrained the urge to smite him on his protuberant and rather rugose nose. "Get out of here," I told him, raising my voice, "or I shall have you forcibly ejected."

"Right ho," he said cheerfully. "Jimmy Fanshaw don't stay where he's not wanted. Further research required, and all, maybe the proposition's a little premature. But you've got me card; if you lose it, just remember, Fanshaw and Little, easy to find us, we're big in the business. Once you've finished looking her over, what're you going to do with her, eh? Research costs money, we could make a pretty penny, you and me. And *that's* me business."

Two porters, looking rather worried, were approaching across the marble floor; Fanshaw saw my eyes on them and turned.

"Oh yes, yes," he said, "just going, keep calm, lads," and he strode off toward the big brass doors.

I was glad de Laurency wasn't with me; I didn't fancy a fistfight in the lobby of the RTS.

And what a ludicrous notion! That the poor girl's "own true love," whatever such a thing might mean, might be found in a horde of carney marks nicked at a shilling a head! I'd sooner use her as a hat stand. It would be more dignified.

Some days later I stood with Sir James in his laboratory, at the stroke of noon when white magic is best performed; it was a clear day, despite the lateness of the year and the smokes of London, sunlight spilling through the large French doors and across the pentacle inlaid in the wooden floor. A brazier wafted the scent of patchouli through the air.

Within the pentacle pale Meg lay atop a silver-metaled table, clad in a shift of virgin linen, her arms crossed over her breast; the lines of the pentacle shone blue with force. Sir James's baritone raised in invocation to the seraphim, the Virgin, and (I thought oddly, but perhaps appropriately under the circumstances) the great Boadicea.

The brazier produced a little smoke, enough to show the beams of light shining from the windows—as well as a line of energy stretching northward from Meg's body, across the space demarcated by the pentacle, disappearing through the wall of the laboratory.

Slowly, Sir James touched that line with a wand of ash, then brought the wand toward a manameter, a device of glass and mercury.

The wand touched the manameter. Mercury boiled suddenly over its top, and its glass shattered. The pentacle snapped cold, its blue glow disappearing.

Sir James looked a little shaken. "Well over a kilodee," he said to me. "That answers one of your questions, at any rate."

"It does?" I said.

"*Someone* had a good grasp of magical principles in the eighth century," he said. "As good as a competent Roman mage, at any rate. That is a good, strong spell."

"Could you shield her from that line of power?" I asked.

He nodded warily. "Aye," he said, "but would that waken or kill her? She is more than a thousand years old; magic must sustain as well as suspend her."

As I bent to swab up the mercury with a rag, there was a knock at the door. It was one of the society's porters, a little agitated, bearing a salver with a card. "A . . . a gentlemen has asked to speak with you, Sir James," he said.

Sir James took the card, raised a brow, and handed it to me. It said:

H.R.H.
THE PRINCE OF WALES

Edward, Prince of Wales, is a large man. Large in many ways: large in girth, large in stature, and large in appetites. We bowed, of course.

"Maxwell!" the Prince bellowed. "You look well, man. Haven't seen you at the theater lately."

"Mmm, no, Your Highness. Press of work, you know."

"Ah well, work. Smokes, fumes, and explosions in the lab, eh? Good smelly fun, for a chap like you, I assume. I may smoke in here, may I not?"—this while brandishing a cigar.

"Of course, Your Highness."

"Well sit down, dammit," he said, clipping off the end of the cigar and running a lit lucifer down its length. "Can't smoke at Windsor, you know, Mater won't have it. Can't at any of her residences. Reduced to wandering about the gardens in the most beastly weather just for a smoke. Caught Count von Hatzfeldt, the German ambassador, in his pajamas with his head up the chimney once, can you imagine? Just wanted a cigarette, caused the most dreadful ruckus. I hear you've made quite a discovery, Dr. Borthwick."

I cleared my throat. "An interesting one, certainly, Your Highness," I said.

"Oh, call me Wales, all my friends do," he said, waving the smoke away from his neatly trimmed beard. "Beautiful girl, I understand. Shan't wake till kissed by a Scottish prince."

Sir James cleared his throat. "This is an hypothesis," he said. "We have verified that the binding spell is Scottish in origin, but the rest is speculation based on local legend."

His Royal Highness snorted in amusement. "Trust scientists and wizards for excessive qualification," he said. " 'Hypothesis . . . speculation.' Well, you deal with hypotheses by testing them, what?"

Sir James and I exchanged glances.

"What do you propose, Your Highness?" I inquired.

"Wales, Wales," he said, waving his cigar before his cummerbund. "Ah, case in point; my most important title, to be sure, Prince of Wales. But you know, I've got scads of them—Earl of this and Commander of that. I'm a Rajah, too, did you know? Several of them. In any event, I am also Thane of Fife, as well as Earl of Dumfries and Galloway. Since the Act of Union, I'm the closest thing you'll find to a Scottish prince. And I can't say I object to kissing a pretty girl."

Sir James chuckled. "I've never known you to," he said. "You propose to assist us with our inquiries, I suppose?"

The Prince of Wales gave us a bristly smile.

As we climbed the stairs toward the laboratories, I wondered what the Princess Alexandra would think; but Edward's wife, I suppose, must have inured herself to his infidelities by now, of which this was far from the most egregious.

He bent over her drawn form, her lips almost blue with

the slowness of her circulation, her cheeks lacking the blush of life but somehow still alive, her shorn hair now reshaped into a more attractive coiffure than we had first given her, there in the Cheviot Hills. He bent his stout waist, planted one massive hand to the side of her head and, with surprising tenderness, kissed her through his beard.

She never stirred.

He looked down at her for a long moment, with three fingers of one hand inserted in the watch pocket of his vest. "Poor darling," he said. Then after a moment he turned back to us. "Not much fun if they don't kiss back, eh, lads?"

When I told de Laurency we were to leave Meg with Sir James and return to Alcroft, we had a bit of a tiff. He didn't want to leave her; I believe he felt he could protect her better than the RTS—which, to my certain knowledge, has stronger magical wards than anything in Great Britain with the possible exception of the Grand Fleet's headquarters at Scapa Flow. Eventually, he stomped off into an increasingly bitter night, not reconciled to the decision yet knowing it was mine to make.

He met me the following morning at Paddington Station, reeking of Irish whiskey; I imagine he was out with his radical friends, a passel of socialist trash. Cambridge men mostly, thank God, though we get our share at Oxford. Ten minutes out of the station, he opened the window to vomit down the side of the train, admitting quite a quantity of ash and cinders into the car. Filthy things, trains. He slept for a time thereafter.

Still hours out of Berwick, he awakened, and I told him of the visit by the Prince of Wales. He was appalled. "You let that vile lecher kiss her?" he demanded.

"You *are* referring to your future monarch, you realize."

He snorted. "Lillie Langtry," he said. "Lady Brooke. Mrs. George Keppel. And those are merely the ones that are public knowledge. The man is a scoundrel."

"And was it not you who, scant weeks ago, was lecturing me on the morality of free love?"

He subsided slightly. "That's different," he said. "He married the Princess Alexandra, did he not? Does he owe her nothing?"

"I hadn't heard that she objected to his, um, extracurricular activities," I pointed out.

"Tcha," went de Laurency. "Would you? In her position?"

"See here," I said, "there was no harm done. And how could I have stopped the man in any event? He *is* the Prince of Wales."

"Yes he is," said de Laurency, "and God help England."

As the train sped northward, I contemplated de Laurency's words while he sat quietly on the opposite bench, reading poetry. Byron, of course.

Did I owe Janet, my own dear wife, nothing? On the contrary, I owed her a great deal. But not because a minister said words over us. I am a good C of E man, and believe in the sanctity of the sacrament of marriage; but what I owe her I owe her because she is *my* own true love.

True love. A silly concept, in a way; the stuff of penny novels and Italian opera. God's love, the love of a parent for a child: more tangible and, in a way, more comprehensible. There is love between man and woman: could I deny it? Yet the proximate cause of my love for Janet, and hers for me, was no great fluxion in the celestial sphere, no fated union of souls, no great internal singing when first our glances met. The proximate cause—not the ultimate, you understand, nor the only, but the proximate—was a silly conversation we had one evening at a Christmas party at her father's house. The details are otiose, and we disagreed; but she is one of the very few women I have ever met in whom intelligence, grace, and beauty are united.

She was waiting at Alcroft station.

It was an eternity before the children were at last in bed.

And hours later, studying her sleeping profile by the

half-moon's light, her black hair curling in rings across the pillow, her sweet bosom rising and falling beneath the sheets, I realized that however beautiful she might be, I would surely have never fallen in love with her if we had never had that silly conversation about Bentham, Gladstone, and the Suez Canal. How could I have loved her, never knowing her? And how could I have known her, merely looking?

We stayed in Alcroft a scant few weeks; the weather was turning cold. I spent our remaining time performing such magics as lie within my skill, to try to understand what had transpired here; helping the diggers at their work, laying out plans for future excavation. We found precious little of any value: a few bronze implements, a few Frankish coins, a nicely preserved drinking horn, and various shards.

De Laurency was less a help than a hindrance. He never seemed to be about the dig, and soon lost any interest in keeping his journal notes up to date. I often spied him atop the Cheviot, a small dark figure at such a distance, striking a pose and staring into space. I suspect when he wasn't mooning about the moor, he was imbibing too much of the local ale.

God send me sturdy, even-tempered students!

Soon enough the first frost came, and we decamped to Oxford.

"I've brought Meg back to you," said Sir James, standing in my office and warming his hands before the coal grate. De Laurency moodily fiddled with the fire irons.

"So your cable said you would," I said. "I'm honored that you made the trip yourself."

He sighed, and sat in the armchair to the side of my desk. De Laurency remained standing, staring into the blue flames. "Well," said Sir James, "I felt it incumbent to report in person, though of course I shall be writing up my findings for the Transactions."

"I appreciate that, sir. And what, if I may, have you discovered?"

Sir James cleared his throat. "Precious little, I fear," he said. "The symbology, alas, is foreign."

I blinked. "I don't—"

"Magic is symbolic manipulation, yes?"

"Quite so."

"By noting the effects of a spell cast by another, you can frequently deduce much about the symbolic elements used therein, and possibly re-create the spell yourself—perhaps not in very detail, to be sure, but close enough."

"I have done so many times as an exercise."

"And you have studied Roman magic?"

"Yes, and Mesopotamian."

"And does not the symbology differ from our own?"

I blinked as I came to understand what he was getting at. "Certainly," I said. "They had whole different systems of worship, of color association, of folk tradition; therefore, the symbolic elements used differ greatly from our own. Untangling a Greco-Roman spell is not particularly difficult, since so much has come down to us in both languages, but of the Mesopotamian we have scant understanding."

Sir James nodded. "And this spell was cast by a wild Pictish mage of the eighth century A.D., possibly a Christian but still greatly influenced by pagan traditions. If I were a scholar of the Medieval Celts, I might conceivably be able to untangle the spell better, but as it is, I can really only report on its effects. Which is of dubious utility, as its effects are evident: she sleeps."

De Laurency broke in. "*Why* does she sleep?"

Sir James looked mildly at him. "She is ensorcelled, of course."

De Laurency snorted. "That much is obvious. Can you say nothing of the manner of her ensorcellment, nor how she may be released? Is Professor Borthwick's 'Sleeping Beauty' theory proven or disproven?"

Sir James sighed. "The spell clearly contains a release, a means of ending. I believe, but cannot prove, that the release is tied to love, in some fashion; a strong emotion, love, and it somehow flavors the spell. What further qualifications attend the release, and whether it must be effected by a kiss, I cannot say. As for Dr. Borthwick's theory, it is consistent with the facts as we know them; but it is far from definitively demonstrated."

De Laurency scowled and made a small noise expressive of impatience.

Sir James frowned and said, "Young man, as a scientist, you must learn to be comfortable with a degree of ambiguity. As a system of epistemology, science relies on theories tested and not yet disproven; but even the solidest theory is grounded on quicksand by comparison to the only two things that we can truly know, in the strong philosophical sense of 'to know.' "

"And those are?"

"I know that I exist, because I experience my existence," replied Sir James. "And I know that the Creator exists, through faith. And some would argue with the latter as an adequate proof."

"Is there no hope for her?" I said.

Sir James turned to me. "Oh certainly," he said. "There is always hope. Perhaps her true love will find her. And perhaps as the state of magical knowledge advances, some future wizard, cleverer than I, will untangle the Gordian knot of her spell and release her from slumber."

For some days I left poor Meg sitting in my guest armchair, her head cushioned by a pillow, as I pondered what to do with her. De Laurency was right; she was a free woman, and any experimentation more intrusive than Sir James's gentle exploration was inappropriate. Yet she seemed to need our care not at all; she required no greater sustenance, it seemed, than the very air.

One snowy December afternoon I returned from high table in the company of von Stroheim, with too much capon and a bit of port under my belt. Somewhat to my surprise, we discovered a small, elderly, dark-complexioned gentleman sitting at my desk chair, gloved hands on walking stick, gazing at her visage. He was outlandishly garbed: green velvet pants, paisley vest, silver-buckled shoon. He wore rings on both ring fingers, over the outside of his moleskin gloves.

"Good afternoon, my Lord Beaconsfield," I said, von Stroheim glancing at me in startlement; he had not recognized Disraeli, but I had, of course. I am, to be sure, a lifelong Tory. "To what do I owe the honor?"

He glanced up at me. "Dr. Borthwick, I presume? And can this be Professor von Stroheim? Please forgive an old man's intrusion. I read of your young charge and had wished to see her. I trust I may be forgiven."

"I believe England may forgive you anything, sir," I said. Von Stroheim grinned a sardonic grin at me from behind Beaconsfield's back; he has often accused me of shameless flattery.

Disraeli chuckled. "Well, it seems the public loves me now that I am retired," he said, "but it has not always been so. Nonetheless, I take the compliment in the spirit in which it is offered. Is this fairy tale true?"

"Wholly bosh," said von Stroheim. "The maunderings of old wives and the wistful fancies of middle-aged men."

"My conjecture has not been falsified, Helmut," I said. "You must forgive us, my lord; the disagreements of scientists must sometimes seem like the quarrels of old couples."

"I rather hope the story is true," said the Earl of Beaconsfield. "I came . . . well, it's a peculiar thing. I'm working on a novel, you know; I haven't had time for fifteen years, but now I do. And, as in all novels—well, most—love plays a role. But the devil of it is that I know so little of love; I came to it so late, and in so untidy a fashion. I had thought somehow I might gain an insight from the young lady's plight."

"That is the problem with novels," von Stroheim said. "They revel in pretty lies."

"Late and untidy, my lord?" I said.

"As a young man," said Beaconsfield, "I was too enraptured with my own prospects to pay much heed to 'pretty lies,' if it please you, Professor. 'Woman was to him but a toy, man but a machine,' if I may quote my own *oeuvre*. I married not for love, but for money; Mrs. Lewis was fifteen years my senior, rich and well-connected, when I asked her hand. I did so neither from passion nor affection, but out of cold political calculation, for my modest inheritance had been squandered, my novels did not suffice to keep me in the style to which I had become accustomed, and I desperately needed funds to continue my political career."

"You, my lord? Act from cold, political calculation?" said von Stroheim—a trifle sardonically.

The Earl chuckled. "It is so. Yet I came to love her; she soon let me gently know that she understood my motivations, but loved me nonetheless. And as time passed, a true affection ripened between us. The proudest and happiest day of my life was not when the Queen granted me the title of Beaconsfield, nor when I acquired the Khedive's shares in the Suez Canal, nor yet when I browbeat old Derby into sponsoring the Reform Act; it was in sixty-four, when I obtained for my darling the title of Viscountess."

"Some men give jewelry," von Stroheim said.

Disraeli laughed out loud. "A Prime Minister can do better than that," he said. He sobered, and reached out a gloved hand to trace the line of her jaw. "I found love so unexpectedly; surely this poor creature is as deserving as I?"

"Ach, it is incredible," said von Stroheim. "Eleven centuries! The world is full of idiots. Surely one falls in love with her. Has de Laurency kissed her yet?"

"I haven't the vaguest idea," I said.

"Is it that easy?" Beaconsfield said. "*True* love, as the story goes?"

"*True* love," said von Stroheim incredulously. "*Vas ist?*"

"Yet it exists," said I.

Von Stroheim looked me up and down. "Well," he said at length, "you and Janet almost make me believe it is so."

"You too, my lord," I said, "came to love only after acquaintance."

Disraeli shrugged.

"Is there no hope for her, then?" I asked.

The Earl stood up abruptly. "Perhaps none," he said. "Some stories are tragedies, you know. A fact that presses against me, as the end of my own tale draws near."

He died last year, did you know? But he left us one last novel.

Was it that very night? I think not; the next, perhaps. Certainly within a few days.

I was working late by gaslight; after putting the children to bed, I had found myself wakeful and, begging Janet's pardon, had returned to Balliol to continue my fruitless attempt to decipher the Linear B. I found the shutter to my office window unlatched; sleet and cold wind dashed through it. Cursing, I latched it shut and, fingers shaking with the cold, lit a fire in the grate.

As I crouched before the fender, hands held out to the burgeoning flame, I heard a tenor keening; the drone of words, as faint as an insect buzz. I cocked my head, wondering what on earth this could be, then realized the sound came from up the flue.

I went to the window, threw open the shutters, and peered up at the roof.

My office is on the top floor of the hall; its window is a dormer. About it, and upward, slope slate shingles, slick that night with the freezing rain. And there, atop the curved Spanish tiles that run the length of the roof's peak, clutching the chimney, stood de Laurency, sleet pelting his woolen greatcoat, a scarf about his neck, his lanky hair plastered against his skull.

Into the sleet he said, in a curiously conversational tone of voice:

"Farewell! if ever fondest prayer
For other's weal availed on high,
Mine will not all be lost in air,
But waft thy name beyond the sky.
'Twere vain to speak, to weep, to sigh:

Oh! more than tears of blood can tell,
When wrung from guilt's expiring eye,
Are in that word—Farewell!—Farewell!"

I was tempted to shout, yet I feared to dislodge him from his unsteady perch. I forced my voice to a conversational tone. "What the devil is that?" I demanded.

He blinked down the slick roof at me. "Byron," he said.

I snorted. "No doubt. And what the devil are you doing up there?"

De Laurency gave me a quick smile; a smile that departed as quickly as it had come. "In a moment," he said, "I propose to step onto these tiles and slip to my death on the cobbles below."

I was tempted to tell him to try to hit head first, as he might otherwise simply be crippled.

"And why," I asked, "should you want to do that?"

He closed his eyes, and with real pain in his voice said, "I am unworthy! Truly I love her, and yet I am not her true love!"

"Ah! Kissed her at last, did we?"

He blinked down at me, with some hostility.

"About bloody time," I said. "Mooning about like a silly git. All right, you've had your smoochie, didn't work, carry on, eh? Come on in and I'll fix you a brandy."

"Is it you," he said bitterly, "your age, or *the* age? The age of machines and mechanical magic, all passion and glory a barely remembered palimpsest? Or you, a dried-up old didactic prune with no remembrance of what it is to love and be loved in the glory of the springtime moon? Or were you always a pedant?"

I looked up at him at a loss for a time. Finally, I said, "Oh, I was a pedant always; an insufferable youth, I fear, and barely more tolerable in middle age. And yes, this is a practical age. But I, I know more of love than three of you, de Laurency; for I have three to love, who love me dearly in return."

De Laurency looked at me incredulously. "You?" he said. "You have three lovers?"

"Oh yes," I said. "My darling Janet, my sweet Clarice, and littlest Amelia."

"Oh," he said with dismissal. "Your children."

"My children, yes," I said. "And will you know what that is like if you dash your fool brains out on the cobbles below?"

He straightened up, scowling. "Know this," he said. "I love Meg truly; I have worshiped her since first I saw her, gloried in the scent of her golden hair, longed to see the light of her eyes. I have felt her slow, shallow breath; in dreams have I seen her life amid the court of Northumbria, the gallant knights who served her, the adoration of her royal father." Here I could not restrain a snort; you'd think a prospective archaeologist would better understand the misery of such a primitive and barbaric life. "And I feel we have communed, one spirit to another! And so I gathered my courage, my every hope, and with my lips I gently kissed her! And still she did not stir!"

"Yes, well, so did von Stroheim and the Prince—"

"They did not love her!"

"And you do? You puppy! You pismire! You love yourself rather more than you love her! What vanity, striding about the moor and reciting Byron! I'll wager you spent more time contemplating what a Romantic figure you cut, against the heather, with your windblown hair, than considering the beauties of nature or the nature of beauty! Love! What do mean by that? *Agape* or *eros*? Do you know the difference? Do you care?"

He stared at me, thunderstruck. "Of course I know! Do you think me ignorant? And *agape*, of course; I would hardly dare to desire her, to—"

He sobbed, and swayed, barely holding onto the chimney.

It occurred to me that the lad badly needed a rogering by some down-to-earth, buxom lass. But I dared not suggest such a course.

Love, indeed.

"Come in, Robert," I said at last. "The night is cold, the lady sleeps, and I have brandy waiting."

And to my surprise, he did.

* * *

And, oh dear, what was I to do with her? The finest minds of magic could not help her. If ever she had had her own true love, he was centuries dead, and to love without knowing is an impossibility. She would sleep, sleep on, and sleep forever, if I had my guess.

Hire her out for a shilling a peck? Pshaw.

Leave her be on my guest armchair? Well, you know. I rather need the space.

De Laurency said once that she was a person, not an artifact. True, in its fashion; but she might as well be an artifact, you know. A fine specimen of Medieval English maidenhood, 765 A.D. (est.), Kingdom of Northumbria. You could tie a tag to her toe and stick her in a case.

And why not?

The great and good of England had shown up to gawk at her; and if they, why not the masses? Edify the people of England, preserve the specimen for future study. That is the function of a great museum.

After I packed de Laurency off home, I looked down at the poor dear, and kissed her.

On the forehead, not the lips; I am a happily married man. And though I love her, in a fashion, I have already my own true love.

And the next day I sent a telegraph to the British Museum.

Poor darling Meg; I hope she is happy here, 'tween Athene and Megatherium; surely happier, at any rate, than buried in Alcroft's clay.

The Walking Sticks

Gene Wolfe

Gene Wolfe lives in Barrington, Illinois, with his wife Rosemary. He is widely considered the most accomplished writer in the fantasy and science fiction genres, and his four-volume Book of the New Sun *is an acknowledged masterpiece. Although his novels are most often science fiction, his richly textured far-future worlds often feel like fantasy. His most recent book is* Return to the Whorl, *the third volume of The Book of the Short Sun trilogy, which some of his most attentive readers feel is his best book yet. He has published many fantasy, science fiction, and horror stories over the last thirty years and more, and has been given the World Fantasy Award for Life Achievement. Collections of his short fiction include* The Island of Dr. Death and Other Stories, Storeys from the Old Hotel, Endangered Species, *and* Strange Travelers.

Wolfe published several fine fantasy stories this year. Writer Robert Borski recently published an essay on the thesis that Wolfe often puts a wolf into his fiction, thus inviting the reader to a game of "find the wolf." In "The Walking Sticks," the wolf is not hard to find. This story appeared in Hauntings, *edited by Peter Crowther, a small press limited edition anthology. It is a darkly humorous contemporary sequel to Robert Louis Stevenson's classic novella,* The Strange Case of Dr. Jekyll and Mr. Hyde.

Jo saw something in the back yard day-before-yesterday, and that should have warned me right there. Got me started on this and everything. I should have gone to the big church over on Forest Drive and talked to somebody, yelled for the police and put this out on the net—done everything I am going to do now. Only it did not. It was a man with a funny kind of derby hat on and a big long black overcoat she said, and she went to the door and said, "What are you doing in our back yard?" And he sort of turned out to be smoke and the smoke blew away.

That is what her note said, only I did not believe her because it was practically dark, the sun only just up, and what does it mean when a woman says she saw a man in a black overcoat at night? So much has been happening, and I thought it was nerves.

All right, I am going to go back and tell all of it from the very beginning. Then I will put this on the net and maybe print it out, too, so I can give a copy to the cops and the priests or whatever they have over there.

Mavis and I got divorced six years ago. Guys always talk about what big friends they are with their ex. I never did believe any of that, and that sure was not how it was with us. As soon as it was final I went my way and she went hers. Mine was staying on the job and finding a new place to live, and hers was selling the house and taking off in our Buick for Nantucket or Belize or whatever it was she had read about in some magazine that month. Jo and I got married not too long after that and bought this place in Bear Hill Cove.

All right here I better say something I do not want to have to say. A letter came to Mavis from England, and the people that had bought our old house from her carried it over and stuck it in our box. I ought to have opened it and read it and written to the man in Edinburgh. His name was Gordon Houston-Scudder. I should have said we did not know where Mavis was and not to send anything, but I did not even open it. I thought sooner or later Mavis would turn up and I would give it to her. Now I wonder if she was not behind the whole thing.

Around the end of September a pretty big crate came from England, and there was a good-sized cabinet in it. Jo and I got it out and cleaned up the mess. The key was in the lock, I remember that. And then inside the cabinet there was another mess of wood shavings that got all over the carpet.

Under that was the canes, twenty-two of them. Some were long and some were shorter. There were all kinds of handle shapes; and a dozen different kinds of wood. The handle of one was silver and shaped like a dog's head. It was tarnished pretty bad, but Jo polished it up and showed me hallmarks on it. She said she thought it might be pretty valuable.

About then I remembered the letter for Mavis and got it out of my desk in here and opened it. Mr. Houston-Scudder was a solicitor, he said, and his letter was from what looked like lawyers, Campbell, Macilroy, and somebody else. He said the estate of some doctor from the 1800s had been settled and the canes were supposed to go to a woman named Martha Jenkins or something, but she was dead now and as far as they could see Mavis was her only relative so they were sending them to her.

I thought that was all right. We would just keep them for

her and if she ever came back I would give them to her, and the cabinet, too. Those kids that got killed? I had nothing to do with that. *Nothing*. So help me God.

Anyway, that was that. We put the cabinet in a corner of the dining room, and I locked it and I think I put the key in my pocket. Only the cane with the German Shepherd head was not in there because Jo wanted to keep it out to look at. It was in the kitchen then, I think, leaning against the side of the refrigerator.

Here I do not know which way to go. If I just tell about the walking and the knocking, you probably will not get it. Maybe I should say that the key is lost before I get into all that. I think I must have left it in my pocket, and Jo put my jeans in the wash. For just a cabinet it was a pretty big key, iron. I have tried to pick the lock with a wire, but I could not get it open. I could break the doors, but what good would that do?

The thing is that I do not deserve to go to prison, and I am afraid that is what is bound to happen. But I did not do anything really wrong. In fact nothing I did was wrong at all, except that maybe I should have told somebody sooner. Well, I am telling it now.

It started that night, even though we did not know it. Jo woke me up and said she heard somebody in the house. I listened for a while and it was *tap-tap-tap, rattle-rattle.* I told her it sounded like a squirrel in the attic, which it did. But to shut her up I had to get up and get my gun and a flashlight and have a look around. Everything was just like we had left them when we went to bed. The front door and back door were both locked, and all the windows were closed. There was not any more noise either.

Then when I had turned around to go back to bed, there was a bang and clatter, like something had fallen over. I looked all around with my light and could not see anything, but when I was going back to bed, passing the cabinet, I stepped on it. It was the one with the silver handle. That was the part I stepped on, and it hurt.

So I said some things (that part was probably a mistake) and leaned it back against the cabinet like Jo had probably had it, and went back to bed. Naturally she wanted to know, "What was that?"

And I said, "It was your goddamn cane. I must have knocked it over." Only I knew I had not. Then I asked why she had not told me there were little jewels like rubies or something for the eyes, and she said because there were not any, and we argued about that for a while because I had seen them, and went to sleep. Now I am going to have another beer and go to bed myself. I have locked the pieces in the trunk of my car, and it is not doing that stuff any more anyway.

Here is what I should have written last week. The thing was that I had told it to go to hell, when I stepped on it, I mean. I think that was a mistake and I ought not ever to have done it, but a sharp place had cut my foot a little bit and I was mad. Only I know it walked that first night before I said anything. That was what Jo and I heard, I am pretty sure.

A couple of nights after that Jo heard it again, and next morning it was leaned up against the front door, which was not where we had left it at all.

So that night I put it in the bedroom with us and shut the door, which was a big mistake. About midnight it knocked to be let out, loud enough to wake up both of us. We got up and turned on the lights, and it was exactly where I had left it, and there were dents in the door. I said they had probably been there before and we had not noticed, but I knew it was not true. I took the cane out and leaned it up against the cabinet in the dining room again and went back to bed.

That was the first bad night I had, because it woke me up but it did not wake up Jo. I lay there for hours listening to it tapping on the bare floors and thumping on the carpets. It seemed like it was going through the whole house, room after room, and after a while it seemed like the house it was going through must have been a lot bigger than ours.

I was lying in front of the front door in the morning.

Jo said I had to throw it away, and we had a big fight about it because I wanted to take off the silver dog's head first and saw the wooden part in two, but Jo just wanted me to throw away the whole thing.

Finally I just put it in the garbage, because it was a Saturday and I did not have to go to work. Then when Jo went shopping I got it out and wiped it off and hid it down in the basement. When Jo got back the garbage had been picked up and she thought it was gone.

I know you must think I am a damned fool to do that, but I was wondering about it. In the first place, I was not really so sure any more that I had heard what I thought I had. There were the dents in the bedroom door, but I got to where I was not really sure they had not been there already. Besides, what if I had left it in the garbage and the garbage collectors had taken it away, and I heard the same thing again? Squirrels or something. I would have felt like the biggest damned fool in the world.

Anyway, that is what I did. And that night I did not even try to go to sleep. I just lay in bed listening for it, and when it knocked loud on the basement door to be let out, I got up and put on some clothes and went to the basement door. It was really pounding by then. It seemed like it shook the whole house, and I was surprised Jo did not wake up.

When I put my hand on the knob of the basement door it felt hot. I never have been able to explain that, but it did. I stood there for half a minute or so with my hand on the knob while it pounded louder and louder, wondering what was going to come out when I opened the door, and whether I really should. I was trying to get my nerve up, I guess, and maybe I thought pretty soon Jo would come and there would be two of us. Finally I turned the knob and opened the door.

And what came out was the cane. Just that cane, all by itself, with a sort of cold draft from the basement. As soon as it came out it went up and broke the light over the basement door, but I had gotten a pretty good look at it first.

After that I followed it through the house to the front door, and when it tapped on that to be let out, I opened the door and let it go. After that I closed the door and locked it, and went back to bed.

When I went out in the morning to get the paper, I was expecting to find that cane out there, probably lying in front of the front door. I looked all around for it, in the bushes and everything, and it was gone, and the harder I looked for it and did not find it the better I felt. I was really happy. But now I am going to bed. I should be able to wrap this up tomorrow night.

A cop came today asking questions. I told him I did not know anything about the dead girls except what I had seen on TV. He asked about Jo, and I had to tell him she had left me, which I think is the truth even if her car is still here, and all her stuff. After that he went next door. I saw him, and I think probably he was asking them about me.

Anyway, the next night I followed the cane again, only that time I followed it outside. I had heard it, I thought in the house. I had gotten up and gotten dressed very quietly so as not to wake up Jo and looked all around for it. Finally I heard it down in the basement again, walking and walking, tap-tap-tapping on the concrete floor down there, and I opened the door like before and let it out, and then I ran ahead of it and opened the front door.

And when it went outside, I followed it. I guess I kept about half a block back. Maybe a little bit less. There is no way that I can say how far it was. It did not seem to be very much walking, but pretty soon we were in a neighborhood I had not ever seen before, where all the houses were taller and a lot closer together, and the pavement was not even any more. I got scared then and went back, and when I got inside I locked the door like I had before.

Only something had made Jo wake up, and I told her about how the cane had come back and gotten into the basement somehow, and how I had been following it. She said, "Next time let me throw it out."

So I said, "Well, I hope there never will be any next time. But if you can find it, you can throw it out." After that we went back into bed, and I did not hear anything else that night. In the morning I got up pretty early the way I always do on workdays and got dressed, and Jo fixed my breakfast. Then I went to work the way I always do, figuring Jo would take off for her own job in about an hour. That was the last time I saw her.

When I got home that night and she did not come, I thought she was probably just working late. So I made supper for myself, a can of stew I think it was and rye bread, and drank a couple beers and watched TV. There was nothing on TV that night, or if there was I do not remember what. It got to be practically midnight and still no Jo, so I phoned the police. They said she had to be gone twenty-four hours and to call back if she did not came home, but I never did. That was the only time I called you.

While I was getting undressed somebody knocked on the door. I opened it and all the power went out. The light turned off, and the TV picture shrunk to nothing very fast, so I never did see the dog's head cane come in and by that time I had cut it up anyhow, only I could hear it. I stood as still as I could until I could not hear it any more. Maybe it went down into the basement again, I do not know. I do not know whether the basement door was open or closed, either. It just sort of went away toward the back.

Well, I went in the bedroom and shut the door and moved the bureau to block it, and just about then the lights came back on and I saw there was a note on my pillow. I have still got it, and here it is.

Johnny,

There was someone in the back yard. I saw him as plainly as I have ever seen anything, a big man with a black mustache and a derby hat such as one sees in old photographs. He wore a thick wool overcoat, black or of some dark check, with a wide shawl col-

lar, it seemed, and what may have been a scarf or muffler or another collar of black or dark brown fur.

I watched him for some time, wishing all the while that you were here with me, and asked him more than once what it was he wanted, threatening to call the police. He never replied; I know that you will laugh at me for this, Johnny, but his was the most threatening silence I have ever encountered. It was.

When the sun rose above the Jeffersons', he was *gone. No. You would have* said *that he was gone, that with the first beams he was transformed into something like a mist, which the morning breeze swiftly swept aside. But, he was still there. He* is *still there. I feel his presence.*

I am not going to work today, having already called in sick. But, I am writing this for you to cleanse my spirit of it, and in case I should decide to leave you.

I will *leave, if you will not destroy every last trace of Mavis's stick. I know you did not discard it as you promised me you would last night, and* will *not discard it. I left my poor Georgie for you for much less. I hope you realize this.*

I will go, and once I have I will be out of your life forever.

Very, very seriously,
JoAnne, with all my love

Now I think it is about over. I really do. Either over, or starting something different. Okay, here is the bad part, right up front. The bottom line.

Last night I thought I heard something moving around and I thought oh God, it's back. But then I thought it could not be back because of all the things I did. (I ought to tell about all that, and I will too before I turn in tonight.)

Anyway, I got up to see what it was, and it was all the other canes in the big oak cabinet in the dining room rattling around and knocking to be let out.

So it is not only the one with the silver top, it is all the rest too. But if that one is still doing it, why would the others want to step up? So I think what it really means is I have won. Here is what I plan to do. I am going to call up Union Van Lines and tell them I have got a certain item of furniture I want taken out and stored. I will get them to move the whole cabinet for me. (Naturally it will still be locked, because I have lost the key like I said.) They will put it in a warehouse someplace for me. I think New Jersey, and I can tell them I am planning to move there eventually but I do not know when yet. Every month or whatever they will send me a storage bill for fifty bucks or so, and I will pay that bill, you bet, for the rest of my life. It will be worth every nickel to know that the cabinet is still locked up in that warehouse. I will call them tomorrow.

All right, here is the rest.

There was a night (if you read the paper or even watch the news on TV you know what night it was) when I followed the cane with the silver top outside again. After about four blocks it went to the same place it had before, where the big high houses were up against each other so close you could see they could not have windows on the sides. Where the streets were dirty, like I said, and sometimes you saw people passed out on the cold dirty old pavement. That pavement was just round rocks, really, but the streetlights were so dim (like those friendship lights the gas company used to push) that you could not hardly tell it except with your feet.

We went a long way there, a lot further than the first time.

When we started out, I was trying to keep about half a block behind like before, because I thought somebody would grab that cane sure, and maybe ask if it belonged to me if I was too close. But when we got in among those old houses that leaned over the street like I have told about, I had to move in a lot closer because of the fog and bad light. It was cold and I was scared. I do not mind saying that, because it is the truth. But I had told myself that I was going to follow the cane that night until it came back to the house, no matter what. I did, too.

I kept thinking somebody would notice a cane walking all by itself pretty soon, but it was real late, very few people out at all, and nobody did.

Then there was this girl. She had blond hair and a long skirt, and a coat too big for her it looked like that she was holding tight around her, and hurrying along. I kept waiting for it to register with her that the cane was walking all by itself. Finally when it got real close to her it registered with me that was not how she saw it. Somebody was holding that cane and walking along with it, and even if I could not see him she could.

Just about then he grabbed her, and I saw that. I do not mean I saw him, I did not, but I saw that she had been grabbed and heard her yell. And then the cane was beating her, up and down and up and down, and her yelling and her blood flying like water when a car drives through it fast. It sounded horrible, the yelling, and the *thud-thud-thud* beating, too. I ran and the yelling stopped, but the beating kept right on until I grabbed it.

It felt good. I never hated to write anything this much in my life but it did. That girl was lying down on the dirty pavement stones bleeding terrible, and it was horrible, but it felt good. It felt like I was stronger than I have ever been in my life.

People started yelling and I ran, but before I got very far the houses looked right again, and the streetlights were bright. I was getting out of breath, so I started walking, just walking fast instead of running. I tried to hold the cane so nobody would see it, and when I looked down at it, it was looking up at me. Sure, the handle was bent because of beating on the girl. Or something. But it was looking up at me, a German shepherd or something with pointed ears. The red things were back in its eyes even if Jo had not ever seen them, and it seemed like I could see more teeth.

Then in the morning it was all over the news. I had the

clock radio set to wake me up at five to go to work, and that was all they were talking about this girl that had been a baby sitter over in the Haddington Hill subdivision (it is flatter even than here) and she was on her way back home when somebody beat her to death.

That night they showed the place on TV so you could see the bloodstains on the sidewalk, and it was not right at all, but when they showed her picture from the yearbook, it was her. She had been a sophomore at Consolidated High. I thought I would walk over there and have a look, and when I went out the door that cane with the silver dog on it was in my hand. It stopped me and made it hard for me not to go at the same time.

But I stopped, and that is when I did it. First thing I thought of was I would take off the silver head and put it in my safety deposit at the bank where it could not do anything. But when I twisted it trying to get it off, it unscrewed. I had not even known it was screwed on. There was a silver band under the part that came off that said some name with a J only too worn to read and M.D., all in fancy handwriting. It could have been Jones or Johnson or anything like that, but he had been a doctor.

Then inside that silver band the cane looked hollow. I turned it upside down and this little glass tube came sliding out. It was about half full of something that was kind of like mercury only more like a white powder, some kind of heavy stuff that slid around very easy in the tube and was heavy. I took it way back to the back corner of the back yard where I had noticed a snake hole the last time I cut the grass and poured it in. Jo wanted to know what I was doing there. (She had seen me out the kitchen window while she was washing dishes.) I said nothing, just poking around.

But the funny thing was, when I got back inside the cane was just a cane. There was nothing special about it anymore. I sawed the wood part in two down in my shop like I had planned to, but it was nothing. It was exactly like sawing a broom handle. The next day I took the silver dog head down to the bank on my way home from work, but it did not matter any more and I knew it.

So I thought that everything was fixed until Jo saw that man and went away without taking her clothes or car or anything. Then just before I started writing this I saw him myself, and there was a woman with him, and I think it was Jo. That was what started me doing this. So this is all of it and maybe I will put it on the net like I said, and maybe I will not. I went to sleep on it.

Another cop came a couple of hours ago, and after he went out back I found these papers, which I had stuck in a drawer. (It is December now.) He was friendly, but he did not fool me. He said the New Jersey cops got a court order and broke into the cabinet for them. I said, "What were you looking for?"

And he said, "Jo's body."

So I said, "Well, what did they find inside?"

And he said, "Nothing."

"Nothing?" I could not believe it.

"That's what they say, sir."

Then I told him there had been a collection of valuable canes in there, and they did not belong to me, they belonged to Mavis. He hummed and hawed around, and finally he winked at me and said, "Well those Jersey cops have some real nice canes now, I guess."

I am not ever going to go near New Jersey, and I hope that those other canes do not decide to come back here, or anyway not many of them.

So then I told him about the trespassers and asked him to take a look around my back yard. He went to do it, and he has not come back yet. That makes me feel good and really strong, but probably I will have to call somebody tomorrow because his police car is still parked in front of the house.

Hey, Hey, Something, Something

Jan Lars Jensen

Jan Lars Jensen grew up in Canada, in Yarrow, British Columbia. His first novel, Shiva 3000, *was published (by Harcourt in North America and Macmillan in the U.K.) to glowing reviews. It is set in a future that has brought into literal existence the deities and demons of Hindu mythology but has the comprehension of the technology that produced them. His stories have appeared beginning in the early 1990s in* F & SF, Interzone, On Spec, Prairie Fire, *and elsewhere. "The Secret History of the Ornithopter," an alternate history supposing early success with flapping-wing flying machines, was nominated for a Hugo award in 2000. He lives in Halifax, Nova Scotia, with his wife Michelle, and is finishing his second novel, a re-working of the story of David and Goliath.*

"Hey, Hey, Something, Something" originally appeared in Realms of Fantasy. *It harks back to the innovative fantasy fiction of the 1940s and 1950s, the kind of story that Fritz Leiber published in* Unknown Worlds, *and Shirley Jackson used to publish in* F & SF, *the origins of today's urban fantasy. According to Jensen, it explores two favorite topics of the author: methods of forgetting, and the persistence of cultural artifacts that are no longer fully comprehended by the society that sustains them. Ray Bradbury used to write stories like this.*

"Jack." The principal of the school stood at my doorway and the kids turned to look at him. "Knock knock, Jack. I want a word with you. In the hallway."

I left the chalkboard, and when I reached Olson he took me sharply by the elbow, his habit with both staff and students when he wished to convey something serious. "It's Agnes. She's in her classroom and you need to talk to her. I'll watch yours."

I nodded stupidly and walked down the halls, down the stairs. The refrain from "A Happy Wanderer" warbled from a music class, and I could smell janitorial supplies and grass cuttings the kids had tracked in from outside. Sometimes it was difficult to know how to appear before students, times like this, as I turned the corner and saw my wife's pupils standing in the hall, looking troubled. Their discomfort increased at the sight of me and I badly wanted to say something friendly. When I got to the door, a girl announced, "It was Tim who did it, Mr. Errington. He sassed her." The boy named Tim looked teary-eyed and nervous. "I didn't know she would cry!" he blurted.

"It's not your fault," I said truthfully, and placed my hand on his head. "Why doesn't everyone go to the library for a while?"

They shuffled away and I proceeded into the room where Agnes sat alone, her elbows on the desktop and both hands covering her face. They were pale but red at the knuckles.

"Agnes," I said. "Hi."

"Jack," she said. "What's the matter with me?"

She didn't lower her hands and I supposed she didn't want to show her face. I stood behind her and rubbed her shoulders. Vivid sunset paintings hung on the wall and notebooks from an interrupted lesson lay on the desks. Through the window, I saw the merry-go-round and slide gleaming in the afternoon sunshine. As we remained like this, the first of the buses pulled into view, turning down the driveway, the sound of a big diesel engine reminding me that school was almost over for the day and those kids in the library would soon be picked up and delivered to their homes, where they would tell their parents what had happened in class, and the parents would know that the teacher had had a breakdown.

Agnes must take a stress leave. The realization made me feel guilty—proof that I wasn't suffering as badly as she—but I could feel her sobbing through my hands, and I knew the leave of absence was necessary.

The buzzer sounded. Buses came and went. Our janitor stepped into the room pushing his wheeled trash barrel before him and I asked if he could give us a few minutes. Agnes went through the motions of putting on her jacket and slinging her purse over one shoulder, and while I had her moving, I coaxed her out of the room.

That night, I lay awake. Although she had required the aid of a tranquilizer, I was glad Agnes could sleep.

She had been pregnant for six months, until two Mondays earlier, on an unscheduled, drop-in visit to the clinic, her obstetrician had placed a stethoscope to her belly and heard no heartbeat. Our baby no longer lived, and the shock struck us all like a cannonball. He had to be removed from Agnes, of course, and if that procedure did not undermine our souls, the funeral that followed did. We gave him a name, thinking we could not bury an anonymous child. We attached a word to that boy who had been a wild idea less than a year ago, and I wondered if that wasn't a mistake, if maybe we should have withheld his name so perhaps we wouldn't find ourselves in this state now; maybe we would have buried a vague concept instead of having buried a son.

In my dreams I had seen him, I had seen him alive and on his feet, and the unexpectedness of it woke me.

Or was it a sound?

A rhythm tapped on the street. With minimal disturbance I removed myself from bed and went to the window. Through branches of an alder, I could make out motion, someone hopping on the far sidewalk. Quietly I opened the window and stepped onto the roof, positioning myself so I had a view of him, and he seemed summoned from my imagination, a boy, playing hopscotch. I shook myself. It was past 1 AM, and as I focused I saw this was no boy but an adult, playing, alone.

He stopped.

He turned and scanned the area, and when he spotted me on the roof he raised an arm in greeting.

I returned to our room and closed the blinds. I paced, and wondered if I should just get back under the covers. But after this vision, I wouldn't be able to sleep. Agnes did not stir as I pulled on a pair of jeans and a T-shirt.

Outside, the weather seemed suspended, the air neither warm nor cold. Few lights were on, and I glanced at our house before proceeding to the street. The stranger had returned to his game. He wore trousers and his jacket lay folded on the steps with a tie on top. He picked up a stone and said, "It's difficult to resist, isn't it? The sound of another child playing."

"I haven't been a child for . . . years."

"I wonder if anyone has explored that idea. The sound of play as a lure to other children."

The notion seemed to hold him for a moment before he walked to the end of his chalk drawing.

"Do you know where there's another hopscotch pattern like this? On the pavement of the Roman forum. It's old." He studied it, appreciatively. "Can't you sleep?" he asked.

"Something woke me up. A dream. Or you."

"Sleep disturbances are an indicator of stress. Exercise is one way to be rid of it."

I sat on the steps. "Is that why you're out here?"

"You mean: Why is a grown man playing outside, well after midnight? I'm a professor of folklore at Darby College. My specialty is childhood games, and I believe to truly understand them you must experience them directly."

His face was round and something about it, when he smiled, made me think of the Moon appearing from behind clouds. His eyes were almond shaped and he had long, thin fingers, and when I asked my next question he brought his hands together in a single clap: "What's there to know about kids' games?"

"So much!" he said. "Consider 'Ring Around the Rosy.' You may have heard that it came out of the plague years; 'a ring of rosies' refers to symptoms of plague—sores around the mouth and breath that smells like flowers. 'We all fall down' is what happens in the end: Death. But what motivated children to make up this rhyme? Why walk in a circle while reciting it? Does it have any relationship to druidic rituals for warding off maladies? Interesting questions, but even more startling is how this rhyme came to us: through children, passed orally, from generation to generation. That seems a very unreliable medium, yet here we are, falling down with an idea from a different century, a different continent."

"These games are entwined with our history."

"And one is entwined tighter than most," he said, and pointed at me. "I call it 'Hey Hey Something Something.'"

"That one I don't remember."

"No adult can remember it. But you may have played it."

I frowned.

"Children's games are stepping-stones to more mature ways of thought," he said. "That's their appeal. Kids sense the beginnings of a new paradigm in themselves, but lack the skill to articulate it, or incorporate it into their behavior right away. Games serve as bridges. They nurture more complex ideas about self and groups and social interaction. 'Hey Hey Something Something' has formed—evolved, if you will—around a very specific, transitory phase in mental development. In fact the game is so tuned to this phase that it cannot be understood once higher levels of thinking have been reached. The older you get, the less capable you are of knowing it."

"We forget it."

"No. We become incapable of knowing it."

"How can we be incapable of knowing something?"

"It defies our ideas in such a fundamental way that we are unable to store it in our mind."

"But we could watch kids playing this game. Or they could describe it to us."

"As a concept, though, it will not stick."

"What if we read a description?"

He shook his head. This idea spooked me a little even while I tried to dismiss it as an academic's whimsy. "If it's unknowable to adults," I said, "how can you be sure it's there in the first place?"

"I infer its existence, like a physicist infers the existence of phantom particles. The name of the game is 'Hey Hey Something Something.' The last two words elude me and are perhaps unavailable, as well. I believe the game involves hiding, but not seeking. Players are temporarily elevated in status over others. Partial observations occur in documents from England, Europe, even the Ottoman empire."

"Maybe you've found fragments of other games."

"No—it is a single entity, a concept that has evolved alongside our notions of society. Something that has accompanied our progress, shadowed it; an idea that sustains itself through our psychological need for it."

Lights came on in the upper window of a nearby apartment.

"I better get home," I said.

"I'm Malcolm Welfing. What's your name?"

"Jack Errington."

"Jack!" he said. "A teacher, right?"

I must have looked surprised.

"Your manner of speaking," he explained. "Your house. I have good intuition."

"I imagine that helps, searching for a secret game."

His smile was long. "Indeed it does."

Back in our bedroom, I checked the window and saw the street was empty.

Did kids even play games anymore? Games that didn't involve graphics and a joystick? The answer was yes, and it came to me when I stood monitoring the playground, sometimes thinking of "Hey Hey Something Something." I watched them in big groups, the younger ones especially, socializing, their interaction sometimes blurring into play, the play sometimes stabilizing into rules and leaders. The buzzer ended the break and I followed the swarm toward the building, and had almost stepped inside when I did one last check of the grounds.

Our monkey bars are old—sturdy and old, a structure of iron rising in pentagons from the ground to create an overall cage of potential exercise, seven feet high at its apex, where the girl ignoring the bell hung by her knees. I gestured to indicate she should come along. "Recess is finished," I called, but she made no sign of having heard. I walked across the lawn.

"What's the matter?"

I leaned over, trying to see her face right-side up. I didn't recognize her, but I didn't know every kid.

"Can't you get down? Are you scared?"

She said nothing.

"Don't you want to go to class?"

I entered the cage of bars. She was breathing normally and nothing in her expression suggested distress. She looked like a third-grader.

"You don't want to upset Ms. Molag, do you, being tardy?"

I felt the sunlight on my neck, the playground drained of sound.

"If you don't come down, I'll have to force you." I circled her. "Wouldn't it be easier if you did it yourself?"

Nothing.

"Fine."

I held her midsection and attempted to unhook her from her perch. She didn't struggle but tightened her hold on the bar so it was impossible to remove her without risk of injury.

"If you don't come down right now I'll get Principal Olson out here." I dreaded involving him in another circumstance beyond my control, but having said it, I was obliged to follow through. He came out and loosened his tie and scolded the girl before also declaring that we would remove her by force. "Or maybe we should just leave you until your legs give out!"

She remained hanging.

Olson cursed under his breath before directing me to hold her by the chest. I did so and watched him climb the monkey bars in his dress shoes until he was overhead looking hot and perturbed, his tie hanging down. The girl stiffened, and Olson struggled to grip one of her ankles. "I've had enough foolishness for one day, young lady." She was sun-heated and rigid in my arms. A car rolled into the lot and slowed so the passengers could watch our struggle. Olson held one foot in his hands and clenched his jaw as he worked to pull her leg up and over. "Call your parents . . . enough foolishness . . ."

He was florid with exertion. The girl kept her arms at her sides. I stared at the pattern of paisleys on the principal's tie, and a bead of sweat rolled off his face and landed on the top of my head.

It was a long afternoon.

After Olson and I had finally gotten her off the monkey bars and pulled her inside, we spent more frustrating time trying to determine her identity. The principal stared and stared at her, and I could tell he was mad at himself for not being able to remember her name. "Becky?" he said. "Is it Becky?" We were reduced to bringing her from room to room, asking teachers if she was one of theirs, and after we eliminated the most likely classes, another possibility struck me.

"Do you even go to this school?"

She didn't answer, but after phoning around, Olson determined she was missing from the Dutch Reformed Christian School several blocks away.

"They sent someone over in a green station wagon to pick her up," he told me later. "They weren't even grateful. Didn't even thank me."

"Did you find out her name?"

"Pieternella!" he said. He shook his head in disbelief.

Returning home, I was anxious to tell Agnes about this incident, but I couldn't see her downstairs and she didn't answer my call. I went upstairs, and found her in the room we had prepared for the baby. The wallpaper was of fairytale pigs and wolves. A mobile hung over the empty crib. Agnes sat on a child's stool in the corner.

"You OK?" I asked.

"Perfectly fine."

She didn't ask me about my day so I launched into a summary on my own, saving for last the girl who had hung from the monkey bars. Agnes nodded but didn't look at me. She had been on stress leave for one week, and I got the feeling she had too much time to think and stew; she nodded at everything I said, nothing was unexpected or worthy of comment. After I had stopped and endured a lengthy silence, I said, "Maybe you need a project. Maybe you should redecorate this room."

She snapped, "Maybe you need a project!"

I retreated a step, and felt as if I was swallowing a stone. We both needed something, and soon. But what?

Agnes should get pregnant again. That, I thought, was the best remedy for her and us, but if I wasn't already reluctant to put this idea forward, I became absolutely wary after seeing her toss her maternity clothes into a big garbage bag.

"Are you throwing those out?" I asked.

"Guess I could donate them to the Salvation Army," she replied.

The deeper question—was she giving up on the idea of pregnancy totally—went unasked, unanswered. What was wrong?

At school I took on monitoring duties from my colleagues, and I tried to think what exactly had done this to her, as playground happenings passed back and forth before me like the polished gold watch of a mesmerist. Waves of children rushed from one end of the yard to the other, with no organizing principle other than "boys chase girls." The merry-go-round spun like a dynamo, a boy spinning it faster and faster while squealing passengers clung to the rails, and eventually a game did crystallize, it emerged from the rumble-tumble of lunch as I heard a participant speak the words:

"Mother may I?"

A group of kids stood facing "mother," the sister of one of my students. Justin, take two baby steps. "Mother may I?" he asked dutifully. Mother gave instructions; she had absolute authority, I remembered, dictating who walked and what way, expecting to be asked permission. More kids broke from what they were doing and turned to her, frozen until the little ritual was observed. How big was a baby step? How did you know what a banana step was? We had known in my day, when we stood across a different lawn facing a different mother, listening to her directions and speaking the courtesy, a lesson in humility, playground education passed down through generations of children.

Betty, take one choo choo step. "Mother may I?"

I remembered kids from the neighborhood standing around me, as we looked to mother for instruction. The merry-go-round was a blur. I remembered childhood, putting a buttercup under a friend's chin. Do you like butter?

The glow off the petals told you so. I remembered faces of childhood friends whom I hadn't thought of in years. What were they doing now? Who knew? In the domain of memories they remained forever children, not aged by a single day. I remembered standing on somebody's lawn, playing a similar game. I remembered the far-off sound of adult voices. On the playground now the kids crouched where they stood; the girl was no longer mother but still held control. I remembered twilight, and staying out longer than I was supposed to, and sour cherries, and band-aids. I looked at my finger, which had a cut from a piece of glass. I looked up; other kids crouched on the ground, their backs turned to me, hiding though they remained visible in the Sun. Hey. I couldn't see any faces, and they all seemed so far away, but the voices were familiar, the words, the rules. Hey! I held up my finger and saw a band-aid around it. When I looked again, the leader was pointing at me. Words were repeated, and I felt my legs twitch, I wanted to do what it was that you did whenever someone called out the name of the game, not "Mother May I?" anymore, but another one I knew, I thought I knew, I knew something about how it went, didn't I? I could remember. Almost. I shaded my eyes trying to see the other kids for clues, but they were so far away, and turned from me, they hid in the open, their faces hidden so it was impossible to see who had spoken the words. What was I supposed to do? I held my finger before me and the band-aid was gone, the flesh healed.

What was I supposed to . . . ?

I shook my head and rubbed my eyes.

I stood on the grass, alone. The merry-go-round was motionless and crows jabbed at a dropped sandwich. The kids had gone inside. The buzzer must have sounded.

I spun until the edifice of the school loomed over me, and I made my way to it, hoping it might lend me clarity.

Agnes was crying. Sobbing. A foreign soap opera she'd taped during the day was playing. I hated how these tawdry programs tapped into her emotions, and meant to say so.

"Agnes."

She looked at me.

"It's not worth . . ."

"What?"

"You don't. It's not."

"Go ahead and say it!"

I paddled my hands in the air but . . .

"At lunch hour," I said. "I think I . . ."

"I don't know what you're talking about."

"It's just."

I stood, frustrated. My entire afternoon had been like this, the kids giving me funny looks as I struggled to complete sentences.

Agnes rewound the video to the point where I had interrupted.

I drank a glass of water, then tried reading a novel but had to review the same page several times before any meaning sank in, until finally I tossed the book aside and put on a jacket. Exercise seemed a sure way to unmuddle my head. A brisk walk in the chill October evening would do me good, and when I got outside the first gust of wind was like resuscitation from a divine source. The autumnal sound of leaves skirting along the curb was another welcome stimulation.

On my stroll, I passed a park where adults held hands in a ring and tramped round and round. It seemed so peculiar that I got a closer look, and heard their voices, Ring around the rosy, pocketful of posies . . . One of them was the professor, Malcolm Welfing. They all fell down, without laughter.

"Jack!" said Malcolm. "Glad you could join us."

"I'm just working off some energy."

"You don't want to play games with us?"

"Why would I? What are you doing out here?"

He looked at me. "Research. Like I told you."

"Right. Sorry. I forgot about that."

"Is everything OK, Jack?"

"Got a lot on my mind right now," I said simply.

"Of course, of course. Like what?"

I rolled my eyes skyward.

"I don't mean to pry," he said.

But it wasn't his question that had made me hesitate.

"Has something happened at school, Jack?"

"I blanked out for a while. Watching the kids today."

"That's peculiar. What were the kids doing?"

I shrugged. "Usual lunchtime playground stuff."

"Oh?" Malcolm exchanged looks with the others. "Any sign of 'Hey Hey Something Something'?"

"Of what?"

He smiled, but didn't repeat his question. "A few years ago we interviewed someone," he said, "a camp counselor from Spokane, Washington, who was having memory problems, like you. He was in charge of keeping kids busy, teaching them how to make a fire without matches, use a compass, that kind of thing. But he was also in a position to learn from the kids, always looking for new ways to entertain them. We tried to establish what games he might have encountered, but when questioned along those lines he became less articulate, less able to concentrate—dreamy."

"And?"

Malcolm stared at me. "That's it. I just thought the story might interest you."

I pulled the zipper of my jacket up to my chin. Malcolm rejoined hands with his group, possibly to keep warm. "I need to keep moving," I said. "How late do you people go on like this?"

"Until our mothers call us home!" one of them quipped.

When I imagine it now I see myself walking away as their wheel started turning again, even though they were not reciting the rhyme, staring at one another with smiles on their faces.

The Bible reports that Roman soldiers teased Jesus while He was in their custody. They blindfolded him and struck him from behind, saying, "Prophecy unto us, thou Christ, who is he that smote thee?" This was a child's game, cruel and old, one that may have been ancient even when those centurions smacked the Messiah; a picture in an Egyptian tomb depicts the same game being played, around 2000 BC. In England it persists still, although known for the past three or four centuries as "Hot Cockles." I became an amateur student of games and how they linger throughout the ages, how they move from culture to culture. I was sent a package of materials that started me on this path, but it came later, after what happened at school, the first confrontation.

A young teacher burst into the staff room and announced that someone was parked on the street, watching the kids.

"Should I call the police?" she asked Olson.

"We better find out what's going on, first."

I joined him, emerging to brilliant sunshine. We quickly spotted the suspicious vehicle, an old Volkswagen van parked near the driveway, and as we walked over the driver lowered something he'd been aiming at the kids, which I thought might be a gun until I saw it laying on the passenger seat: a camcorder. The driver gripped the steering wheel and stared straight ahead until Olson banged his fist on the vehicle.

"What's your business, loitering here?" he demanded.

"No concern of yours."

"I happen to be principal of this school and I'm making you my concern."

The driver gave me a significant look.

"I've taken your license plate number," Olson went on. "And I'll be phoning the police, believe it."

"I'm not doing anything illegal."

"Well, whatever the hell you're doing, I suggest you do it elsewhere."

The man looked like he was going to speak but instead turned the ignition and put the van into gear.

"Give me your name," Olson said. "I want your name, buster!"

He said, "I won't be returning," and with a squeal of tires, departed.

The van we never saw again, but other cars came and parked during the breaks over the next few days, anonymous strangers staring at the children, holding cameras or simply jotting notes. "What the hell is going on here?" Olson asked me. "What do they want?"

"I'm not positive, but I think they're interested in how children play."

"Is that so?"

"I met one of them, a few weeks ago. He mentioned a project that might explain this."

"You tell your friend we don't want people hanging around our school. Kapish?"

I hardly know him, I almost said.

I certainly wasn't sure where to find him.

In the evenings I would go for walks, alone, of course, and I hoped to run into him. There was no listing for Malcolm Welfing in the phone book, so I couldn't determine where he lived. Finally it dawned on me that I could try Darby College. I phoned and asked the receptionist to put me through to Malcolm Welfing, and she said she wasn't aware of anybody by that name. The Anthropology, Sociology, Philosophy, even the English department, I tried them all but nobody had heard of him. At school I made use of our Internet access and plugged his name in a search engine which returned a hundred or so hits but didn't help clarify the matter. That same week, Olson called me into his office to show me a letter he'd received from my "friend" Professor Malcolm Welfing, on Darby College stationery, stating that he and his grad students were researching child behavior, and that teachers shouldn't be alarmed if they saw people hanging around near the grounds during recess and lunch hour.

"Do profs use college stationery?" I said.

"Why do you ask?"

"I think the guy might be a fraud. Not a professor of anything."

"I'm definitely reporting this to the police."

So over the next few days a cruiser would occasionally show up, and once or twice, another vehicle sped off. For a while that seemed to scare them away—whoever they were. For a while, I forgot about them.

Nights, I would lay on our bed, and make gestures of intimacy toward Agnes, but she rejected these by rolling over or standing to put herself out of reach. Once she rambled on about restarting an old habit, smoking. I watched her dig through our cupboards until she found a heavy ashtray shaped like a swan; she handled it like an artifact fallen from the sky, then abruptly put it on the kitchen floor and left it there. While she slept, I swung out of bed to stand at the window and look at pools of light cast by street lamps, waiting for profound illumination, or the appearance of a mysterious stranger.

But this was not where they would come.

Soon I wore a long coat doing my monitoring duty at school, and the kids bundled up, too. Days grew colder, but not too cold for energetic play. They moved around the playground like marbles on the deck of a boat, and I lost track of them as individuals and saw them as motes in a pattern of flux. Rules to describe their behavior teased my mind. I heard voices, but it was like listening to a television as you drift toward sleep.

Playing. A game. Hey. They were playing a game.

Children hid in the open. They called without showing their faces. A child in the center was elevated over the others. Hey. She pointed at kids and called out names. The phrase resurfaced. Hey. Hey—and that second, mumbled, word, scrambled, maybe slipped from a nonsense language of no meaning to adults. Thoughts swirled in my head as kids hid in plain view, turning their backs to the one being pointed at. Others dropped off the slow-spinning merry-go-round. Rules spread out and engaged children within hearing distance. They dropped where they stood with arms over heads. I remembered the face of a boy I hadn't thought of in 10 years. I felt a familiar twitch, but I couldn't quite . . . I couldn't quite put a word to it . . . I didn't know what to say, and . . .

Malcolm. The "professor."

He appeared in the front window of a house across the street. Slowly he pulled off a pair of headphones. The game continued to unfold. He left the window and came out the front door. I should cross the lawn, I thought, confront him before he came onto school property. But I remained fixed, as static an observer as a video camera left running on a tripod.

Malcolm walked onto the playground and entered the game. He joined, like any number of joiners, he crouched down, hiding in the open, keeping his mouth from being seen. The kids didn't seem to care.

I heard my name.

Jack . . .

It came to me across a great chasm. "*Jack!*" The voice had an electronic, echoing quality and I turned to see Olson standing by the window of his office, mike in hand. He was speaking over the P.A. system, and the words started to filter into my head. "There's a trespasser, Jack! Can't you see him?! Do something, don't just stand there!" I broke from where I stood, and as I walked I lost consciousness of the game—or perhaps it was like trying to see a cloud by moving into it, too insubstantial to be viewed at close range—or maybe it actually broke up as the kids saw me coming. They started to rise from their crouched positions, but Malcolm remained curled.

"What's the matter with you?" I asked when I got to him. "Who are you?"

He lifted his head to look at me. "An admirer," he said. "Only an admirer."

"Of what?"

"The game."

"What game?"

"See," he said, "already you're forgetting."

"I don't know what you're talking about, Malcolm."

"We're fans," he went on. "We follow it across states, across provinces."

"Why? Are you on the run?"

"We're just people who have things to forget. Understand? I told you it's impossible to remember the game, but that's not everything; if you think about something while playing, you tend to forget that, too. I don't know the reason; something about how the brain arranges memories. We've got things we would rather not remember, so we follow it, and keep our worst memories close at hand. We're fans of the game, Jack, and what it can do for an ordinary person."

I was terribly confused, but I said, "How much can one person want to forget?"

"That's the thing of it. Once you've begun, you keep finding more memories you'd rather not keep."

"You lied about being a professor," I said.

"I used to be a professor. That's how we got started."

"Where are you from?"

A smile spread across his face. "I don't remember."

Behind me, Olson's voice boomed: "ARREST HIM, JACK. MAKE A CITIZEN'S ARREST."

Malcolm said, "Are you going to detain me, Jack?"

I looked to the school, the edifice, with the children watching, curious.

"You better start running," I said, "while I'm still unsure."

The document in my hands had been delivered in a package with no return address. Even before I opened it, I suspected that it came from Malcolm's group. Inside was a collection of information about a game, one that lurks within our culture, perpetuated by generations of children but unknown in the world of adults. I had to go over the material many times. In the top margin of the article I was reading, somebody had scribbled, "apocryphal information."

Nepenthe—The term derives from the Greek *nepenthes* and refers to a potion supposedly used by the ancients to induce forgetfulness of pain or sorrow. Is it possible that Greek scholars, in their philosophical investigations, discovered a means of forgetting memories? If so, it should not surprise us that it got transmuted into the idea of a potion, a better plot element for stories and legend. Perhaps, like our game, their *nepenthe* was too difficult to express without a symbol. . . .

I hadn't seen Malcolm since that day on the playground.

Maybe he was still in Darby, he and his friends, laying low until the alarm at our school subsided. But the stamp on my package had been canceled in Idaho. Olson had been livid when I let Malcolm go without a struggle, and the district had agreed to hire private security to guard the property. I'm sure Malcolm was accustomed to such situations, chasing something as nebulous as a game that couldn't be remembered, and lingering around children to experience it. It would be hard not to seem a crackpot, or worse.

But for a pair of teachers, it was not as difficult.

I folded the article, put it in my pocket.

Agnes stood beside me as we monitored the children. Sure, there was a guard now, but they couldn't do without a teacher, too, to hand out discipline as usual. We sat on the steps and ate lunches we had packed that morning. It was cold in the mornings now, the lawns frosted, the air nippy. We poured soup from a thermos and passed the cup, more to warm our hands than for nourishment.

"What is it we're supposed to watch for?" she said.

"At the outset something will seem vaguely familiar, or you'll even recognize a game from childhood. But the activities change and you feel that you might know the rules, even if you can't articulate them. You hear one word repeated—hey—and another, which doesn't seem part of the English language as it is commonly known. What exactly the kids will be doing I can't say, but the game involves hiding in the open, and players subordinating themselves to others."

She took a sip of the soup. "And you want me to . . . what?"

I reflected a moment before speaking. "I don't know what exactly haunts you, if it was what the doctor said to you in that examination room, or the operation that followed, or maybe the funeral. No! Don't tell me. Don't even think about it. At least not unless the game starts."

"And then?"

She had heard my explanation of the secret game, and the deeper secret, its side effect. She had listened without voicing doubt or skepticism, and this made me realize something about my wife and Malcolm and the others: that it was one thing to live with a chain of disappointments, terrible regrets, big mistakes. It was quite another to live with the possibility of erasing them from your mind.

"Think of what you need to forget, and let the game wash over you. Afterward, I imagine we'll be slightly different people."

She hung an arm over my shoulders, and I was glad for the gesture, the first she had made toward me in many days, and the best insulation I could have asked for as we stared at grounds that became increasingly hard and white and hostile to childish doings. It would not be as long a winter as the one that had first threatened, and if it was harsh, we could take comfort in the fact there was a way to tear it from our book of memories, later.

The Saltimbanques

Terry Dowling

Terry Dowling lives in Hunters Hill, New South Wales, Australia, and is one of the best prose stylists in Australian science fiction and fantasy. His short fiction is widely published in Australia and has appeared in F & SF *and* Interzone. *Although he has never written a novel, his SF stories have been collected in eight volumes in Australia since 1990, most famously in the Tom Rynosseros series, and his influences are most saliently the stories of J. G. Ballard, Ray Bradbury, and Jack Vance. Most recently, he was presented with the special Convenor's Award for Excellence at the 1999 Aurealis Awards for Antique Futures: The Best of Terry Dowling. Web sites for Terry Dowling and many other Australian authors can be found at www.eidolon.net.*

This story, Dowling says, "grew out of the wonderfully mysterious name in the title and the desire to show what a special place the Australian Outback is. There is such a powerful sense of magic and possibility, and what better way to show this than through the eyes of a teenager discovering just how large, wonderful and bittersweet the world can be." "The Saltimbanques," a coming-of-age story, appeared both in Eidolon: The Journal of Australian Science Fiction and Fantasy, *and in* Blackwater Days, *Dowling's collection of linked stories set around the Blackwater Psychiatric Hospital at Everton near Sydney. In the manner of classic Bradbury, teenagers run afoul of a disreputable carnival that takes its name from a Picasso painting.*

For Danny Truswell, his world changed forever that day in 1962 exactly one week before he turned fourteen; a hot dusty day in Reardon, one of those blistering Australian summer days just after Christmas when the air shimmers into haze in every direction and the trees hang and it seems no one is out on the streets.

He followed his usual summer holiday routine, got his chores done early, then planned ways to lie low till about 4 pm when the sun was far enough down the sky for life to ease back towards normal.

'Normal' was hardly the right term with Danny's Dad taking a rig across the top of Australia and not due back for six days, and his Mum away in Dubbo visiting a sick sister. Danny was having his meals with Kenny's folks and sleeping over.

'Lying low' was hardly the right term either, for Danny and Kenny (and sometimes Annie), like most other kids, rarely managed to do the sensible thing. It was summer holidays, after all. And Danny liked to think they had something of an advantage over the others. They had the chart.

When you saw Reardon from the air with its dozen streets and eighty or so houses (population 434), its two pubs, two churches, community hall, school and library, the co-op up by the railhead near the railway station, the sheds and silos, the clumps of trees following a creek pretty well dry for a half of any year, it looked like so many clustered flecks of grey and silver set in a large, mottled red tile, with a splotchy line of dullest green winding across it (the creek with its eucalypts) and a thinner silver hairline dividing the top third (the railway line).

That was the view framed on the office wall of Hendist's Stock and Station Agents. An even larger version, two yards on a side, hung over the saloon bar of the Stockman Hotel, the red sweeping out as if Reardon was a colony on the planet Mars.

But a third such aerial shot, left over from the same 1956 International Geophysical Year shoot, tattered, faded and almost forgotten, was pinned to the wall of a deserted shed at the back of the Woke property, and that's where Kenny Woke, Danny Truswell and 'Sometimes' Annie Hendist had their clubhouse and planned which properties to visit, which parts of the creek to try. It gave them an overview, a sense of the town as finite and just *a* place on the land, not *the* place. Horizontal vistas somehow locked you in too much, were too real, too irresistible to allow that other kind of perspective.

The Reardon Rangers, as they called themselves, were lucky. There'd been six of them in the group originally, but Cathy's folks had moved the family down to Dubbo, and Billy Mack and Keith Spicer, just a year before, had gotten too grown up, they reckoned, for that sort of clubhouse stuff.

Annie Hendist though, curiously, had stayed around. She was already fourteen, a long-legged brunette, disturbingly female, and while her mind often seemed on other things, she'd surprise the boys by dropping in and tagging along just as it used to be. Sometimes it's be for cricket or soccer with other kids, sometimes on one of their Ranger expeditions.

That was how it came to be three not two on that momentous Thursday. The boys were so glad to see her again (awkward as well; they were at *that* age) when she appeared in the doorway in her shorts, striped t-shirt and old sandshoes. She looked so grown-up and knowing that they made it her turn, let her point to a destination on their aerial 'chart'.

Barrack Creek. Dusty and dry until five weeks after the rains in the north when, with all the impact of a miracle, it flooded just like that. But mostly dry and dead, just seeming cool because of the river gums and occasional scrappy willows, because there was shade that wasn't made by blazing, overheated iron and canvas and old boards.

She pointed to a spot close to where the creek, the train tracks and the dirt highway almost came together, creek and road curving in and curving away again, the tracks dividing them.

"How about there?" she said in that calculatedly artless way that had Danny and Kenny swapping looks.

"Roger that," Kenny said, as he so often did, a misuse of old World War II lingo.

Danny grabbed his Dad's army surplus canteen. "Fine with me."

If it had just been the two of them, Danny and Kenny would've been laughing and joking, pushing and shoving, saying goofy things, making a big deal of it. With Annie along they kept it simple, sensing that there was something fragile, special and fleeting in Annie being there. You couldn't talk it, could barely even grasp what it was, but they all knew, which had made Mr Jarvie's words at school for the past two years so much more thrilling and embarrassing.

"Here's Kenny and Danny. Now where is Annie?" Mr Jarvie would say. And when Dan retorted (fairly he'd thought) that Annie was only with them sometimes, that naturally became part of the refrain. "Here's Kenny and Danny and Sometimes Annie," Jarvie would say when they came in, which had the other kids sniggering and singsonging it too. Kids can be cruel, but how often their cues came from adults enjoying a different kind of humour.

Sometimes Annie it was from then on. In fact Kenny

even said "Roger that!" the very first day, because he figured everyone had to have a nickname.

They were a good mile from town when they realised they probably should've picked somewhere closer. The heat was relentless. The land shimmered in every direction; the railway tracks blazed up at the sun as if just freshly poured and still molten; the highway stretched off into the burring of haze, a crusty deserted ribbon. The trees along Barrack Creek danced as if they might vanish at any moment.

When they finally did reach the bank, they found the scant shade barely helped. Leaning against the trunks of the larger river gums, they looked out at the flat stretch of creek-bed, rippling with heat, set with the shifting, black and grey shapes of old tree trunks left by past flash-flooding, set to the mindless sawing of insects, then began moving along to where the trees were thickest.

That's when they saw that someone had set up camp right near the creek. Three drab buses were parked under the thickest stand of river gums, all with roof-racks packed high with bundles and boxes lashed down every which way. No cars were visible, just three old buses, one with its dusty windows catching bits of sun, the second with the windows of the back half painted over, the third all riveted metal with no windows at all that they could tell, just the front windscreen glinting dully.

"Who's that, y'reckon?" Kenny asked, and got no answer. It was so quiet that his words seemed way too loud. Danny and Annie didn't want to speak.

They moved closer, edging along the opposite side to the visitors, slipping from tree to tree.

No one was about. The buses had to be like ovens inside, especially the third one, but Danny couldn't see anyone lying underneath them or leaning against tree trunks. The occupants were in town or off somewhere else, visiting one of the properties maybe. *Inside* only if they were crazy.

There wasn't a lot of mystery in Reardon, so sometimes you made it up. You told other kids stories about the bunyip that lived in Barrack Creek (you knew someone who knew someone who'd actually *seen* it); or the 'bore woman' who appeared around the clanking windmills and poisoned the water and sometimes stole children to drown in one of the artesian dams; or the *min-min* lights you saw flickering over the railway tracks after midnight, sometimes dancing along the creek. But this was the real thing, a real mystery, nothing like the box Mr Jarvie had put on his desk and asked them to write about, what it might contain. Here were three genuine 'mystery boxes', made only more mysterious by the faded letters Danny could make out on the sides of at least two of the vehicles.

"There are words," he said.

Kenny agreed. "Roger that."

Annie turned on him. "Enough of the 'Roger that', will you, Kenny?"

Kenny blinked at her. "Roger. Right. But there *are* words. Can you read 'em?"

None of them could. The buses were angled wrong and too dusty. They discussed moving closer, trying to make out what the words said, but even sneaking out to hide behind one of the bigger logs left by past floodwater still meant crossing the creek-bed in plain view, and, though they didn't say it, none of them wanted to do that right then.

It was just so quiet, so eerie, with insects sawing away in the scraps of grass, the tides of heat rolling along the creek and those dark windows glinting.

If only there was movement, someone visible, maybe a dog about. But it was all heat shimmer and unexpected strangeness.

"Know what?" Kenny said. "We oughta come back later an' spy on 'em. What d'you say? Come back after tea?"

Dan and Annie agreed to it, then all gladly turned and headed back towards the shimmering spill of dirty quicksilver that was Reardon.

It took no effort for Kenny to get his Mum to serve them all an early tea. Monday's leftovers made it easy. The three of them were back at the clubhouse soon after six, killing time till it got darker by testing their flashlights and locating the little caravan of buses on the chart.

"Right here, I reckon," Danny said.

Kenny leant in close. "Roger that. Er, sorry, Annie."

"It's okay, Ken," Annie said, leaning in to see as well, which had Dan suddenly, totally aware of her, of her dark hair and how much her skin smelled of heat and summer. He could've gone crazy on it right then, but just kept pointing at the map, trying to ignore her arm pressing on his, most of all the alarming stirring in his loins, suddenly there, determined not to goof off like Kenny did whenever Annie came too close. He wanted her to like him. He liked her being close.

Then, when the air had cooled by twenty degrees and the sky was a rich, deepening blue, with stars pushing through and a scrap of a moon showing, they set off again, striking out pretty well in a straight line to where they figured the camp ought to be.

This time there were people. The kids smelled the smoke from a cookfire and heard voices well before they could make out the welcoming flicker of the fire itself and see the cheery, calmer points of hurricane lanterns. There were tents set up now too, two of them, large and square, and four people at least, then five, laughing and joking just like people anywhere. Six, Dan counted when someone else stepped from one of the buses: four men, two women.

Without discussing it, Annie moved down onto the creek. The boys followed, moved out to halfway where she was hiding behind an old log and hunkered down next to her.

In a whisper, Annie spelt out the words on the side of the bus nearest the fire. "S-A-L-T-I-M-B-A-N—now what's that? Oh yeah—Q-U-E-S. There's a 'The'. The Saltimbanques, it seems like."

"The Salt in Banks?" Danny said, even as Kenny spoke too.

"Salting Banks? What's that?"

"The name of our carnival," a man's voice answered, right near them.

Kenny yipped in fright. Danny's heart caught in his throat. Someone was there on the creek-bed close by.

"It's French," the voice continued. "I'm Berty Green. Why don't you come over an' say hello?"

The fire, the lanterns, the fact that there were two women—more importantly that Berty, whoever he was, had started walking on ahead—made it seem okay. They were just carny folk camping along the road, tired from driving in the heat.

"Let's go," Kenny said.

Dan and Annie exchanged a half-seen glittering glance, and the three of them followed Berty up into the camp.

Framed above and around by flickering tree-forms in the firelight, warmly lit by yellow lamplight and walled in by the sides of one bus and one of the tents, to Dan it was like walking onto the stage of the Community Hall back in town to do a play, or peering through the eye-hole of a diorama at some painting by that guy Mr Jarvie liked, Breughal. Updated, sure. Australianized, yes, but just odd and interesting people caught in the middle of being easy among themselves. Yet not altogether *his* people.

And there was Berty, fully visible now and quite a sight himself, a short dusty-looking man with a sharp face, his chin and forehead pulling back from his nose like some cartoon figure who'd stood too long in a scorching westerly.

But there was hardly time to take it all in properly because Berty Green was introducing them.

"Some kids from town dropped by to pay their respects. Don't reckon I caught your names, kids."

"Danny."

"Kenny."

"Annie."

Berty gave a deep bow, then gestured at his companions. "Right you are. And here we have Jeffrey, Gwen, Walter, Haunted Jack, May and Robert."

There were nods, smiles, salutes, quick looks at the boys,

longer looks at Annie from all of them, not just the men. Danny couldn't be sure who was who, but it didn't seem important just then.

"Take a seat! Take a seat!" Berty cried. "Gwen, pour our guests some tea, will you? Later we'll take you in to see Mr Hasso."

"Mr who?" Kenny asked.

Berty grinned. "Mr Hasso. Our ringmaster, our maitre'd. The boss. He's been shut away all day doin' his calculations."

"All day?" Danny said. "Not in the bus without windows?"

"Oh, not in there," Berty answered. "That's our dark-wagon. We only go in there on special occasions. His office is in the back o' that one." He pointed to the bus with the closed-off back half. The painted-over panes glowed with dim yellow light.

"All day?" Kenny echoed. "He would've fried to a crisp in there today."

Berty laughed. "You'n me maybe. Not our Mr Hasso. He's a bit of a lizard that way. Likes it warm."

Gwen handed them tin cups of steaming billy tea, sweetened with condensed milk, stirred with a eucalypt twig.

"What are Saltimbanques?" Annie asked, blowing and sipping.

"That depends," Berty replied. "Going traditional now, we're showfolk, mountebanks, jugglers, acrobats, harlequins, ballerinas and buffoons."

"Clowns?" Kenny asked, missing some of the words.

"Inevitably, Kenny," Berty said. "Ask any juggler who drops his balls."

"Or any ballerina past the point of doing pointe," one of the others said, laughing. Walter, Danny thought it was.

"We're all just clowns if the figures aren't right," Gwen said, sitting by the fire again. "How's the tea?"

"Great."

"Beaut."

"Terrific, thank you."

Berty got up. "How 'bout you set your cups down awhile and we'll pay a call on Mr Hasso?"

Danny was glad to, if only to get away from the indulgent gaze of the others around the fire. He didn't much like adults having jokes at his expense. Mr Jarvie was bad enough.

Berty led them between the tents towards the middle bus. There was only the dull yellow glow from the back section, but Berty switched on a front cabin light as they climbed in, illuminating bench seats, a fixed table, some fitted cupboards. A door in the wall halfway down its length had a plaque with the name *Bernard Hasso* on it.

"There. Let's see if he's taking visitors." And Berty winked at them as if they knew a lot more about Bernard Hasso's ways than they let on.

He knocked lightly at the door. "Mr Hasso? We've some young visitors from town come callin'."

There was no reply that Danny could hear, but Berty smiled at them and turned the handle, opening the door on an office that took up the whole back half of the bus.

There were bookshelves and charts along the walls, all aglow in the light of two paraffin lamps, and a big desk at the far end littered with papers, maps, list of calculations. Bernard Hasso sat grinning at them with a pen in his hand, a large blacksmith of a man in a grimy sweat-stained shirt and dark pants. Where Berty Green had sharp features, Bernard Hasso had craggy ones, his eyes set deep under heavy black brows and above a full black moustache. It was as if a gypsy and lion-tamer had been blended with one of those dark mysterious Egyptians from either version of *The Mummy*—the 1932 original or the recent 1959 remake Hank Burgess had shown with it as a midnight double at the Lyceum in town only a month back (surely one of the weirdest choices for a double-feature ever). The smile was amiable enough, but his eyes glittered approvingly at Annie in a way Danny didn't like—the same way the others had looked at her, all except Berty. Hanging on the plywood wall behind the man's chair was a framed picture: a painting of circus figures caught while performing or rehearsing.

"So, kids. What's the verdict? What d'you think of us so far?"

"We haven't seen much yet, Mr Hasso," Kenny said, eager as a puppy. Bernard Hasso nodded and set down his pen. "Not much to see yet, I'm afraid. We don't play many towns during the summer."

"Don't see any animals," Kenny rattled on, clearly on automatic.

"Oh, animals come and go. We don't go in for animal acts too much. Not too much."

And Berty Green sniggered.

"You're Saltimbanques," Annie said, as if identifying a rare breed.

"Why yes, Miss—er?"

"Annie. This is Kenny and Danny."

"Miss Annie, yes." He gave glancing nods at the boys, turned his deep-set, black eyes on her again. "That's exactly what we are. Not your usual troupe of wandering players certainly. Saltimbanques every one!" He indicated the framed print on the wall behind him. "Picasso, 1905. *Family of Saltimbanques*. From his pink or rose period. The name is from the Italian *saltimbanco*, coined in 1646 from *saltare*, to leap, *in*, on, *banco*, bench. Leap-on-benches, yessir. Mountebanks, yes, charlatans and quack-salvers—another marvellous word, from the Dutch *kwakzalver*. Ignorant pretenders. Quacks. That's us."

"Do you do magic?" Kenny asked.

Berty Green sniggered again and sat on a bench seat near the door.

"Why yes, Master Kenny. Sometimes we do." Bernard Hasso patted the papers on his desk. "When the planets are right and the wind blows a certain way. Sometimes it just flows out of the land. Real magic, yessir. A fickle thing though sometimes, just like the favours of pretty young ladies."

"You sure made yourselves disappear today," Annie said, with more pluck, Dan thought, than this Mr Hasso expected. There was something going on that Dan didn't entirely understand.

Bernard Hasso frowned, even as his eyes widened and

his big smile came back. "Ah, Berty, hear that? Our young friends called earlier. We were remiss."

"Couldn't see anyone," Dan said, feeling annoyed yet curious. Something *was* going on. Adult stuff, but not like with Mr Jarvie.

The ringmaster nodded. "Off getting supplies probably."

"Sometimes there's a bunyip here in Barrack Creek," Kenny said, determined not to be left out.

"That so, Master Kenny? What sort?"

"I dunno. You got bunyips?"

"Sometimes. Bunyips are easy." Bernard Hasso's dark eyes twinkled and glittered under his heavy brows, and Kenny looked puzzled, as if not sure if the man were making fun of him or not.

"We should be going, Mr Hasso," Annie said, and it struck Dan that she needed to be the one to say it, that he had just been sort of drifting there in this stuffy, closed part of the bus while some other level of exchange had been going on. He wished he could've re-run everything they'd said, but it was too late now.

"Yeah, we should," he heard himself say, just to be out of there.

Dan wasn't really sure why he had to go back that night. A lot of it had to do with Annie, with how Mr Hasso and the troupe had looked at her, with wanting to both keep her safe and impress her. It was just something he had to do.

He didn't stay at Kenny's long. He told Mrs Woke that there were some chores he'd forgotten to get done like he'd promised but that he'd be back later, that Kenny should expect him in their front verandah sleepout as usual. At 10:12 pm he was pedalling out of town on his bike, riding without a light, using what moonlight there was, heading to where the creek and the highway bowed together, the silver tracks cutting between.

Dan figured he didn't have to tell anyone he'd done it,

maybe Annie later on. He hurried along under a vast field of stars, watching meteors streaking down, now and then looking back at Reardon where it made its neat huddle of yellow light in the greater darkness.

Reaching the closest point to the creek, he left his bike just off the road and moved carefully across to where he figured the buses were. The camp was quiet, with a lantern burning and the fire low. The two tents were dark amid the long hulks of the buses. The only other light came from the back of the second bus where Mr Hasso was probably still working on his mysterious calculations.

The odd thing was that no one slept in the open as you'd expect on such a mild night, arranged about the fire like you did when you camped out. Maybe they were in the third bus, the closed-up one Berty had called the 'dark-wagon', sleeping or practising tricks away from prying eyes.

Dan had intended just to look them over again from the safety of darkness, to maybe eavesdrop on conversations and gather more information about the group, but mainly just to get a better feel for the whole thing, to make up for being so out of it in Mr Hasso's office.

It was seeing the dim yellow glow from the second bus that made him cross the creek-bed and go among the darkened shapes. He'd say he'd lost a ring or something if anyone caught him, say he'd come back looking for it, though that would mean he'd have to be using the torch he had in his back pocket, the last thing he wanted to do.

He made it to the second bus, stood beneath the yellow panes, heard the muffled murmur of voices within. But the windows were closed and Danny couldn't make out words. It was infuriating.

Then the office door opened and Bernard Hasso and Berty Green emerged into the front of the bus.

"I want it brought up first thing," Mr Hasso was saying. "Take Walter and Jack. We've got a little over eighteen hours. Mr Atterling's party will be here at 7 o'clock."

"Right," Berty said (Dan almost expected him to say 'Roger that!').

"And I've reconsidered. Tomorrow you will take the mantacycle into town, drum up some local business. We might as well be seen to be earning our way in case folks get to talking."

"Right you are, Mr Hasso. Good night."

"Good night, Berty."

Bernard Hasso went back into his office and closed the door. Berty clambered out of the second bus and headed for the darkwagon.

Danny stood as motionless as possible, vividly aware of his heart pounding, of the torch stuck in his back pocket, of a stone in his left shoe, of how perspiration had to be making his forehead shine in the moonlight through the trees. But Berty passed obliviously by, climbed into the closed-in bus and shut the door behind him. Only then did Danny cross the intervening space and stand beside that third dark vehicle with its faded legend: *The Saltimbanques*, snaking in the darkness—an incantation to the night and all its silence.

It was *too* quiet. There were insect sounds, the usual clicks and chirrups, but absolute silence from the bus, no footsteps, no voices. But it didn't *feel* like the silence of seven sleeping people, rather more like the silence of people standing, waiting inside till he had gone away so they could resume what they'd been doing before. He imagined them there, eyes wide but catching no light whatsoever, the sighted but unseeing eyes of the living trapped in caves, buried in tombs, caught in air pockets in the holds of sunken ships.

Danny moved away as silently as he could, crept back across the creek, taking care to avoid any logs, reached his bike and hurried back to town, finally joining Kenny in their sleepout.

"You sure took your time," Kenny said drowsily as Danny climbed into bed.

"You know what it's like, Kenny. Sometimes you just get caught up."

"Roger that," Kenny said, and slipped off into sleep again.

Danny lay staring at the night, watching the stars move

round the sky. When he slept at last, he dreamt he was being chased by a terrible creature called a mantacycle with Berty Green perched on its back. Bernard Hasso sat to one side working on his calculations.

Danny had meant to wake early to go spy on the camp and see what it was Berty and the others had to bring up for Mr Hasso first thing, but when Kenny roused him at 8.06 he knew it would be too late for that.

But Annie called by the clubhouse at 9 o'clock and Dan made sure the three of them were at the northwestern end of town, maybe two hundred yards out, when Berty Green came pedalling in from the direction of the creek.

The mantacycle was quite a sight, a tall four-wheeled contraption at least six feet high and six feet square at the base and tapering in, as rusty and weird-looking as an old torture machine, with arms and overhangs and a dozen flags snaking out from as many flagpoles set into the tube-metal frame, all long, faded pennons: blue, orange, red and purple, curling out behind. The whole thing was like the skeleton of a pyramid hauled up from the bottom of the ocean, and Berty was as extraordinary a sight, bent over the pedals on a small saddle seat, elbows out, legs pumping furiously in the early heat, his long, tattered dust-coat flaring behind him. He was wearing a wide-brimmed hat set with corks on strings—no, not corks—set with dancing, swinging, bleached-white things: bird skulls, Danny saw when the mantacycle got closer.

Seeing what they were, Danny realised the little man's name was probably Birdy Green, not Berty. Somehow it just tipped everything further over into strange.

"Mornin' to you, kids!" he called when he recognized them, breathing hard and letting the tall vehicle roll to a stop, its four pumped-up tires making their gritty tearing sound on the hot road surface. "You were a big hit with Mr Hasso last night, I have to tell ya. He figured, what the hell, let's put on a show anyway! Seven o'clock tonight. Five bob admission. Go tell your friends!"

"Roger that!" Kenny cried as Berty—Birdy!—set to pedalling again, and ran off to follow the machine into town, as if there was anything else happening in Reardon this Friday night that might stop folks being available.

In a strange way, standing there in the road with the dust settling around them was the first time Dan had ever felt truly alone with Annie. They watched Birdy ride off with Kenny scrambling back and forth like some native runner in a Jungle Jim movie and the silence just grew up around them, the sense of being together.

"I went back there last night, Annie," he said, expecting her to act annoyed and disappointed.

"So did I," she said.

You could have knocked Danny over. "You what? When? What did you see?" So much for protecting her.

"I went real late. Around midnight, I guess. That Mr Hasso was so creepy, Dan. I just wanted to see the place again."

"See anything?"

"Nope. When did you go?"

Danny told her, describing what he'd heard and felt, growing more and more uneasy at the thought of Annie crouching there in the dark watching the buses and the tents. "What do we do?" he said finally.

Annie shrugged. "I'm just really glad you're here, Dan."

"Me too," Danny said. "That you're here, I mean." And they started walking back towards town.

Birdy Green and his 'Frying' Machine, as townsfolk cheerfully called it (it was 10 am and already 93°), were a definite hit. Locals bought him beers, shouted him an early lunch, offered to give him a tow back. By the time he was pedalling out of town at 11.48, he had had two dozen kids straggling along behind like he was some latter-day Pied Piper doing a practice run. Kenny was one of them.

The kids straggled back ten minutes later, dusty and exhausted, and the day settled into its most terrible phase, the heat lending everything its dreamlike shimmer for what Hank Burgess called the 'wait-out'.

"Whatcha doin' after wait-out?" Hank would say from behind the bar at the Stockman Hotel, asking any number of patrons staring up at the big aerial shot of the town as if expecting some trace of Birdy's carnival to suddenly appear like stigmata or a face on a shroud.

"Dunno," most said as usual, though more and more added, "Might give the circus a look-see" and "Yeah, might give the circus a go."

Pete Byles would invariably correct whoever said it. "Ain't a circus, you blokes."

"Must be," someone would invariably answer. "Seen one clown already."

And round it would go, all through the blazing afternoon.

Annie's mum ran the pub's kitchen, so Danny heard part of it when the three Rangers dropped by so Annie could get permission to go see the show. You always remembered to check in when money was involved.

Now that they had a legitimate reason to visit the carnival (and since Kenny was seeing himself as something of a self-appointed sidekick to Birdy Green), the three Rangers went out to the campsite around 6 pm, this time riding their bikes along the highway and leaving them by the road near where it bowed in to meet the railway line.

They were rather surprised to see two tents set up on the flat hard ground this side of the creek, both warmly lit, one quite large and unusually long, the other smaller and square and placed a few feet away from the bigger one like an afterthought.

No one was about so they looked into the large one first, saw twenty hurricane lamps set on as many supports, warm and welcoming, and lots of benches set up down the far end. All it was really was a large empty space. There was no bunting or posters, no attempt at decoration at all. When they peered into the smaller tent, they saw nothing but one of the bigger, darker logs from the creek. It seemed to swallow the light from the eight lanterns hanging on the uprights. Maybe that's what Birdy had had to carry up.

"Hey, they've got a chain on it!" Kenny said, and laughed. "Maybe they're worried someone'll steal it."

Kenny was right. Around one gnarled length of snapped-off root was an iron ring, with a short chain leading to a spike driven into the hard ground.

"Maybe they're going to turn it into an elephant!" Dan said, more to ease his nerves, he realised, than because he thought it was funny.

Kenny laughed though. "Roger that! Sorry, Annie. Say, why don't we go find Birdy?"

It wasn't a bad idea, Dan thought, given the little man's good humour towards them earlier in the day, and it gave them a reason to cross the creek-bed and go among the buses again, which Danny found was what he wanted to do.

But when they reached the camp, Birdy was nowhere to be seen, which made Danny think of the closed darkwagon and the silence there. The only sign of life was Mr Hasso sitting on the doorsill of the second bus puffing on a pipe.

"Right on time," he said, knocking the pipe against the lowest step to empty it, then getting up. "Come on in awhile. It's almost showtime."

Dan had reservations about going into Mr Hasso's office again, but at the same time wanted to test himself after what had happened the previous night. He followed Annie and Kenny and was soon standing before the ringmaster's big desk, littered as before with charts and pages of figures.

But now there was a different picture on the plywood wall behind where Bernard Hasso was once again seated. Smaller than the Picasso, almost a foot on a side, it showed a washed-out grey landscape under a lowering sky, with shapes like polished river pebbles scattered about, dull and metallic-looking, some set on their ends, some more geometric than others, those in the foreground rising up in columns like those limestone shapes you read about, stalagmites. Among the clustering and spill of grey and white forms were a few touches of colour, here a drab yellow stone, there an ochre one, there a pale red trapezoidal shape, but there was only one distinctive focus in the whole moody scene, a rectangular patch of red on the left side, like a window or door or even a mirror in a worn, rolled, leaden frame.

Dan was about to mention it when Mr Hasso clapped his big hands together and grinned at them, his eyes flashing under dark brows.

"Now you see us at our best!" he said. "This is our emergent phase."

Their what? Danny didn't understand what that could mean.

"And the tents over there?" Annie asked. "All part of your calculations?"

"Exactly so, Annie. Position is crucial. Always crucial. What do they say? Time, place and identity: that's what it's all about. You kids won't know it but the layout of Reardon configures to the sacred geometry of the Vesica—quite by accident, mind you, purest chance, sweetest serendipity. A circle, a square, a triangle, a rhombus, a hexagram and polygons all tipped in together."

"Is that good?" Kenny asked.

"Oh surely it is, Kenny. Very much so. And just there where the road bends in to the creek with the tracks between, we have a most wonderful confirmation of Bruno Taut's *Stadtkrone*, can you believe it? If only I could convey even a fraction of what it means to us, the theosophical blend of ley-line traditions and geomantic corridors with the *axis urbis* of imperial Rome. The cityline. Cities built along lines of force. The ancient scemb lines. No wonder all these crackpot doctrines sprang up, spring up and will forever do so. How else to interpret the truth? But I do forget myself, going on like this. Kenny, Birdy says you were a great help today. How would you like to assist him with his final preparations now?"

"That'd be great! We didn't see him round though."

"Oh, you'll find him, I'm sure. Off you go. You'll see your friends again when the show starts."

"Hey, Roger that!" Kenny cried as he left the office. "See ya!"

Danny heard him clamber out of the bus, heard a dwindling, somehow disturbing, "Hey, Birdy! Hey, Birdy, wait up!"

Now Mr Hasso's smile changed, or rather changed at the eyes, which glittered full of unreadable emotion.

"You changed the picture," Danny said, partly to relieve the tension, the dreadful awkwardness he felt, partly out of determination to stay with it this time no matter what happened.

"I did. We always do. Yves Tanguy, 1954. *The Saltimbanques*. What do you think of it, Danny?"

"It's strange. I prefer the other one."

"The Picasso. You do? Tell me what you see in this one."

Danny studied the strangely lit plain, the clustered eroded shapes and spires in the foreground, the scattered ones farther out, the dramatic patch of red in its frame.

"It's like things waiting for other things to arrive."

"And when they do?" Mr Hasso's voice was rich, his words lulling, soothing. Danny concentrated on the shapes, partly wishing Annie would chip in, partly wanting to impress her and hide the fact that he was truly and deeply afraid.

"I don't know. They change. They grow."

"I see. And the patch of red?"

Danny knew he'd be asked that. "Energy. Force. Or something has scratched through the surface. Made a door maybe. Something showing through under the grey. Peeking through."

"Mr Jarvie never knew what a smart student he had, did he, Dan? Now tell me: did you find your ring?"

"My what?"

"Last night when you came back to pay us a visit. Did you find your ring?"

Danny felt the clutch of panic, pulled back from the picture, from Mr Hasso's incredible voice and eyes and saw that Annie wasn't standing next to him.

"Where's Annie?" he cried. "What have you done with Annie?"

"You didn't hear her? She said she had to—you know—use our convenience."

Danny didn't believe him for a moment. "And where's that?"

Bernard Hasso gestured casually. "Back over there a ways. She'll only be a minute."

"Mr Hasso, what's going on?"

"What do you feel is happening, Danny Truswell?"

"I didn't tell you my last name!"

"Birdy picked it up in town." An answer for everything.

Did not, Danny wanted to shout right into his face, tried to recollect what else he had to remember, something Mr Hasso had just now said. He was forgetting again. Forgetting to notice things. Like Annie going off, leaving the office. She couldn't have. Wouldn't have. Then how . . . ?

"I asked what you feel is happening, Dan," Mr Hasso said, snaring him again with that way he had, killing thoughts by imposing others.

"Something's pushing through," Danny answered.

"Almost right. Almost got it. Now forget the red bit."

How could he? Danny stared at the picture, just couldn't help it.

"Something's getting nearer."

"Now that's really got it!" Bernard Hasso said, seeming genuinely pleased. "Slouching towards Reardon to be born. Something very pure. A network of energy, Dan. Moving across the land, travelling in lines. Lines of force. Spotlights of magic. Some of us know how to plot 'em, track 'em, use 'em. We travel the grid. Sometimes we follow, sometimes we wait for them to catch us up. It's what gives history its buzz and fizz, Danny, me pure boy! Shamans and wizards! Smart old codgers figurin' out the conjunctions. Merlin having a good day. Sacerdotes and mages, seers, sibyls and sorcerers all waiting for auspicious windows of opportunity, knowing how to play the game. Oh, it's an art, I tell ya!"

Dan tried to imagine lines of force, thought of moving spotlights of magic, and something else.

I didn't tell him my last name.

"It's supernatural then!" he managed to say.

"No, it's not! That's precisely *not* what it is. Once your so-called supernatural manifests itself then it's *natural*, don't you see? *Part* of nature. This isn't nonsense about mummies responding to ancient curses. This is things happening as they always happen whether we notice them or not. It's like forgetting to notice gravity because it's always there, or what the Moon's tidal pull does to your body, or negative ions from thunderstorms. This isn't quackery, Dan. Not this! We travel the grid, flexing muscles most of us never get to try, meeting lots of different people, looking for those who think the same way we do, keeping an eye out for apprentices, too, though we're very picky there. Taking turns in trying to pass it on."

Dan was hearing yet not hearing, snared by the smooth round stones, the shadowy sky, the clustering shapes.

"Now Mr Atterling is a politician, see, and this show's really being put on for him. He's one of those secret-handshake Freemason mystic types too, you see, Danny, but he doesn't know how to use it. So it'll do us all good to keep him careful and in his place, in awe of the way it is. Make 'im think it's us. Pay to get bits of it. But for us, for me, it has to be pure, Danny, you do understand that? It's important you do."

Danny understood stones and sky and a shadowy distance, disturbing weights, curves and edges, a comforting patch of red. Though he did hear, part of him did.

"Whatever happens, Dan," Mr Hasso was saying, kindly enough it seemed, "it's all for a good cause. Now you run along and find your friends."

Danny stumbled from the office, blinking, shaking his head, trying to fathom what it had all been, nearly fell out of the bus.

Spotlights of magic. Moving. Getting closer.

The carnival following them.

These Saltimbanques.

The spotlights.

The lanterns. Dan noticed the lamps hanging in the

trees, hanging from the buses, lighting the tents across the way, noticed how the words on the long bus sides seemed brighter, richer, firmer. So magical.

The Saltimbanques.

Performing in spotlights. Moving about. What *had* Mr Hasso said?

Kenny was there then, grinning, excited, seeming too young all of a sudden, just too too young.

"Danny, hi!"

"You seen Annie, Ken?"

Kenny shrugged and grinned. "I think I saw her over at the big tent. Lots of people are arrivin'. You're getting sweet on her, Dan!"

"Hey, she's a Ranger too! Just want to know where she is."

Kenny's grin became a leer. "Whatever you say. But ain't that closed-up bus weird?"

"Sure is. Why, do you reckon?"

Again Kenny shrugged. "Dunno. Just don't like goin' near it. It's real quiet. Spooky."

Like someone's waiting in there, Danny thought. Listening. "You keep clear of it, Kenny, okay?"

"Don't have to tell me. See you at the show."

"See you."

By the time Danny reached the big tent, there were well over two hundred people either crowded on the makeshift benches at the far end or standing along the sides, talking and laughing, poking good-natured fun at the modest set-up. Dan hurried to join them, unable to see Annie in the crowd but sure she'd be there waiting for the show to get underway. After what Kenny had said, he was sort of glad she didn't come over to join him, though another part of him wished she would.

He'd just squeezed in between two kids he knew on one of the front benches when he noticed the four serious-looking men in crumpled dark suits seated further along the row: no doubt Mr Atterling and his party. They were definitely from out of town and were clearly impatient; one of the men kept looking at his watch and muttering to his companions.

When Bernard Hasso entered the tent, it was without a fanfare of any kind. He just strode in looking appropriately splendid in black tails and top-hat, carrying a glossy ebony cane with a silver ferrule at one end and a faceted crystal knob at the other. It glittered and shone in the lamplight.

The chatter subsided immediately. People were grinning. This was more like it.

There ought to be a spotlight, Danny thought, seeing the ringmaster standing before them all. *He looks good but he should be standing in a spotlight.*

"Ladies and gentlemen, boys and girls," Bernard Hasso said in his rich and wonderful voice. "Welcome, one and all! We are The Saltimbanques. Nature's clowns and mountebanks. We have travelled the highways and byways of Australia to be here tonight, to offer an entertainment to the good folk of Reardon. The time is right for magic and merriment once again!"

And he held his arms wide, the crystal knob of his cane twinkling with lamplight. There was no fanfare, but there was a sense of one as the performers ran into the tent: Walter, Haunted Jack and Gwen to the left, Robert, May and Jeffrey to the right, all wearing loose, brightly-coloured bodysuits, stitched all over with shapes and signs like Danny drew with his compass set at school, arcs intersected by straight lines.

All but Mr Hasso himself ran down the length of the tent to shake hands with members of the audience, then, after pinching cheeks and tweaking noses and pulling coloured kerchiefs from the pockets of some of the children, they all rushed back to form up around Bernard Hasso near the entrance.

"Here it comes!" the ringmaster cried, and began twirling his cane, making a Catherine Wheel of flashing light as his troupe began making a human pyramid to one side, Haunted Jack supporting the other six as they climbed aloft to compose themselves in a very impressive display.

Something was wrong about it though, Danny realised. He had done a bit of balancing at school, and this looked like it should topple over any second. But there was Haunted Jack holding them all, and now raising his left leg, supporting the whole thing, *and* going up on his toes.

And—was Dan really seeing it?—now raising his right leg, so the whole pattern of human forms was just hanging in the air, all strobed by the dazzling twirl of Mr Hasso's cane.

It couldn't be.

Everyone was leaning forward trying to be sure of what they were seeing.

That's when Danny noticed how close and warm it was, and that the air smelled of woodsmoke and resin and something else. He kept blinking and sniffing to make sure of what was going on.

These hardly appeared to be the same people as the night before. They all seemed taller, stronger, not so much younger as more, well . . . in control, focused, powerful. They radiated confidence and energy.

And just how had the hovering pyramid been dismantled? For now Haunted Jack balanced Walter and an improbably nimble and alluring Gwen more skillfully than he'd seemed capable of, sitting around the campfire that first night. Robert was juggling twenty balls with casual recklessness, an almost disdainful smirk on his face. May and Jeffrey strode about on stilts, seemed to fall, would catch one another, then go teetering and tottering towards those standing along the sides at that end of the tent before steadying themselves and staggering back the other way. Now Birdy made his appearance, running about in his long coat and bird-skull hat and flinging buckets of confetti over the laughing onlookers.

At first glance, apart from the opening pyramid, the acts weren't anything special, though if you did look close, you started to notice things, how every now and then May and

Jeffrey would lean too far over on their stilts yet not fall, or how one of Robert's hands would lift to wave at someone in the crowd or mop his brow without disturbing the steady flow of the balls. Even when Birdy substituted warm perfumed water for the confetti, the audience responded with delight.

There was a drunkenness, a euphoria surrounding everything. The air became heavier, smokier, dimmer. The lanterns had haloes. The resin smell was stronger than ever. People were still blinking and squinting to be sure of what was going on, but no one complained, no little kids cried, no one got up to leave. It was as if they were in the presence of magic and knew it, and all wanted part of it.

And the players came ever closer as the evening progressed, moving from the far end of the tent towards the benches.

Spotlights of magic.

Danny found himself remembering bits of what Mr Hasso had said. Something about moving points of energy.

The performers were getting nearer. Soon they'd be clambering over the benches.

No, Danny realised. The show would end first. The smaller tent was next-door—*in a straight line to this one!*

What was it Mr Hasso had said about ley-lines and the *urbis axis?* Cities built in lines?

More to the point, why would he have told him?

There was no time to consider it further, for once again Mr Hasso had his arms raised, and his voice was rumbling in the silence.

"Our final treat, ladies and gentlemen, boys and girls, is in the tent next door. Yes, the Barrack Creek Bunyip itself! But it's one at a time, I'm afraid, bunyips being nocturnal and shy creatures when a crowd's around."

Muttering and exchanging uncertain smiles, the townsfolk filed out of the long tent and formed a queue outside the smaller one. Just as Mr Hasso had stipulated, one person was allowed in at a time, to emerge a short while later blinking, with looks of puzzlement on their faces as if not quite sure what they'd seen.

"Keep it short, folks!" Robert kept saying from his place by the entrance. "There's lots of people so keep it short!"

"What did you see? What did you see?" younger kids were calling, eager for their turns, but it was clear that those who'd been inside didn't know what to say and just went off looking bewildered and smiling sheepishly to join relatives and friends.

Danny held back, hoping to see Annie, to share as much of the experience together as Robert made possible.

"You there! Danny!" Robert called. "You wanna see the bunyip or not? You'll need to be quick. Show's over in a few minutes."

Danny pushed into the tent, smelled resin almost immediately, saw the lamps had haloes, saw the log over by the tent's far wall. Someone had moved it; the chain was stretched at full length. That was all.

"Too bad, kiddo," Robert said, right behind him. "Too late, I reckon. Maybe next time."

Danny was glad to be out of there, was relieved to see Kenny right in front of him, a few feet away; noticed too, over near the large tent, Mr Hasso shaking hands with the men in Mr Atterling's party. They no longer looked bored or impatient but were smiling and nodding as they started walking back towards their car.

"Did you see it, Danny?" Kenny asked. "The bunyip, did ya?"

"I missed it. What did you see?"

Kenny frowned and got a silly grin on his face. "I dunno. Hard to describe it really. But it was real neat."

That's when Mr Hasso came over. "Right then, Dan. Thought Kenny might like to help Birdy and the others strike the tents while you and me walk a bit and continue our discussion from before."

And before Kenny could express his pleasure at being a carny roustabout, Danny got in with it first. "Roger that!"

Kenny stared at him in amazement, unable to believe what he'd heard.

Mr Hasso slapped Dan on the shoulder. "That's the way! Never know when you can use twice the pure!"

Danny looked straight at Kenny. "Roger that, too, Mr Hasso!"

And they walked off, leaving Kenny Woke staring after them in confusion and disbelief.

Moments later, Mr Hasso and Danny had left the others and were moving along the creek-bed. Almost all the townsfolk had gone, walking or driving back to town. A few headlights could still be seen heading off to distant properties, and if anyone noticed three bikes left by the highway they would've paid no mind. It was summer holidays, barely 10 pm, and with the days so hot, kids stayed up till all hours.

All Danny could hear apart from their footsteps and the occasional insect sound were members of the troupe calling to one another as they brought down the tents. The voices faded with distance.

"Twice the pure, Dan," Bernard Hasso said, guiding him with a hand on his shoulder. "That's the way. Still workin' on that part of it—why that kind of sacrifice is the best way to go, why sacrifice is necessary at all really. Like to think it's like the Indians killing a buffalo, you know, making an offering to the Buffalo Spirit. Then there's the alchemical angle, reconciling the opposites, and the geomantic tradition. There's just so much to know. But, hey, so long as it works, I say. What d'you reckon, Dan? Ah, but here we are."

Another tent stood in the middle of the creek, square and dark in the thin moonlight.

"In you go, boy," Mr Hasso said. "Don't keep her waiting." And he lit the single hurricane lamp hanging on its wire hook, illuminating the only two things inside.

One of them was Annie Hendist, sitting in the middle of the dirt floor, bound hand and foot, a hankie tied in her mouth. The other was a large black tree-trunk, hooked and broken, shaped by some past flooding, just lying there. The tent had been set up around it.

In line with the other tents, Danny knew.

He hurried across to Annie, pulled the hankie from between her teeth and started freeing her while Mr Hasso took the lantern outside with him and began lacing the tent flaps together behind him. "Won't keep you long," he said, then the lamp was extinguished, plunging them into darkness, and Dan heard footsteps moving away.

"Oh, Dan!" Annie said, grabbing his arm, standing close. "I've been so scared!"

"What happened?" Dan was vividly aware of her.

"I—I'm not sure. One moment I was in the bus with you and Mr Hasso. Then they'd brought me here. I was so terrified, Dan. They just left me here. I didn't know what they'd do."

"It's okay, Annie. You're safe now. It's okay now." So aware of her.

She continued gripping his arm. He could feel her breath on his cheek. "Do you know what's goin' on, Dan?" she asked.

He didn't. He did. He tried to think back, almost had it. It was gone, then bits slipped back again.

"It's something about spotlights of energy. Moving in lines. They follow them." He was surprised to hear himself saying it. "Go from place to place, keeping up. They use it, Annie."

"For what?"

"Everything. Their performance. They were so different, so—changed. And that long tent, remember? Everyone was down one end. Their performance got closer and closer. Then it moved to the bunyip tent."

"The what tent?"

"The smaller tent. The one with the log chained down." And Danny went silent a moment. "Like this one."

Annie's eyes twinkled in the dimness. "This one isn't chained."

"I know."

They peered off to where the hooked, torn silhouette of the old log showed against the moonlit east side of the tent.

"How long we got?" Annie asked him.

"I lose track of time whenever I'm with Hasso. An hour

or two. I don't know how long it takes. Let's try to get out of here."

The sturdy canvas walls had been spiked through brass eyelets on the ground outside; the lacing on the flaps was knotted outside as well. The central and corner uprights were simply too thick and too well planted to break or dislodge, and repeated running against the tent's sides seemed to have no effect at all.

They were standing by the entrance, trying to work the lacing rope so the knot was nearer, when they heard it.

Barely heard it, for it was the softest wrenching, the slightest sound of twisting.

They stared at each other, then at the shape.

And saw one of the snapped-off roots at the top move, twist.

The log was alive.

They could hear it creaking as it lifted slightly, testing the life it had, then heard a scrape, and another. There were a few pounding heartbeats of silence, then a third scrape, this time louder, harsher as it gouged the ground where it lay, made with the determination of something *discovering* itself alive, filled with the desperate chance to live again as something so new.

Annie grabbed Danny by both arms this time.

"You believing all this, Dan?" she said. Such an odd question now.

"Of course."

"He wants us 'cause we're pure, Danny. That's what he told me. You know what that means?"

"Yeah. Sure. Course I do."

"And are you?"

"What? Me? Yes. Of course. You?" He would never have dreamed of asking it. That sort of directness was four, six, ten years in his future at least.

"You know it. Quickly. Take off your shorts!"

Perhaps it was what they did then, perhaps it was Kenny arriving in time, perhaps the enlivening energy simply moved on, but Kenny Woke *was* suddenly there, stirred from his hero-worship of Birdy Green by Danny using *his* signature line like that—a sailor's SOS, a flyer's Mayday, a carny's Hey Rube!—fumbling at the tent rope, undoing the flaps, never noticing how Danny and Annie checked their clothing as they left the tent.

It all remained so dreamlike and uncertain, what happened in those few days, what Mr Jarvie later described as "smoke and mirrors" when school started back, just "so much hypnosis and hallucination."

The heat and the sameness of the days soon wore it down all the more. Blokes at the bar of the Stockman Hotel stopped peering into the aerial shot of Reardon, began looking at their beers again as they talked, and when Danny reminded people (even Kenny) about the carnival that had played out near Barrack Creek, they said, "Oh yeah", as if it had happened years ago not weeks, but sure, of course they remembered it. But what else could you expect in a land where the heat doomed normal folk to the limbo of wait-out, blurred grain trucks and silos into dragons, burred every lonely windmill into Don Quixote tilting at himself?

And just like that, Annie went off to stay with her aunt in Mildura for a while, which was no big deal, she'd done it often enough before, but she didn't say goodbye and it just pushed the whole thing further across into unreality and lack of proper consequence.

Then Mr Hasso's letter came.

Dear Daniel,

We pay our price too. Forfeit things like families. Something to do with the energy, May says, probably where the notion of changelings comes from down through the ages. But no Dannys, Kennys or Annies for The Saltimbanques unless we borrow, find apprentices however we can. Where else do you think we come from? It's the other thing we do. You didn't disappoint us, Dan. The magic passed through you. The child will always be drawn to magic.

For that, our heartfelt thanks.

Bernard Hasso
PS: The 'bunyip' was just to motivate, you understand. Excuse the theatrics.

For a moment Danny actually thought the 'child' reference was to him, but the postscript stole that in an instant. There was only one thought then, a question, desperate, bittersweet and somehow extending his whole life out into something infinitely, ultimately beyond Reardon.

Had she known all along?

In the space it took to read the few dozen words, Danny learned two crucial things, vital to learn at any age but so powerful to have at fourteen: that you always had to grant unlimited possibility, and that happy endings were as fleeting as you let them be. If not protected, they vanished out of lives like the bunyips along Barrack Creek.

Debt of Bones

Terry Goodkind

Terry Goodkind is the most phenomenally successful of all the new fantasy writers of the 1990s, an international bestseller. His official Web site is www.prophets-inc.com, and it is clear from the information there that he is driven to excel in whatever he turns his attention to doing. Suffering from dyslexia, which in high school "brought him constant ridicule and humility from his teachers," he dropped out of college and worked as a carpenter, a violin maker, a hypnotherapist, a wildlife artist, and a restorer of rare artifacts, before turning his thoughts to writing—while constructing his own home on an island off the coast of Maine in the 1980s. After years of planning, he began to write his first novel, Wizard's First Rule, *in 1993, and his writing career was launched with its publication in 1994. The sequels to date include* Stone of Tears, Blood of the Fold, Temple of the Winds, Soul of the Fire, *and* Faith of the Fallen.

He is now one of the most popular fantasy writers in the world, and gaining a larger audience with each book. Most notable in his fiction is his attention to atmosphere and fast-paced storytelling. The atmosphere is generated in part by the exceptional emotional intensity of his characters, that in turn creates continual suspense, driving the reader and the story onward.

"Debt of Bones" is Goodkind's first and only work of short fantasy fiction to date. It was published exclusively in

the showcase anthology, Legends *(1998), edited by Robert Silverberg, which did not permit reprints until this year, and is therefore only now reprinted for the first time. This tale is set in an age earlier than his first novel, and illuminates the world of his famous series. But it is primarily a tale of action and adventure, and of good and evil, in a world of magic and wonders.*

"*What do you* got in the sack, dearie?"

Abby was watching a distant flock of whistling swans, graceful white specks against the dark soaring walls of the Keep, as they made their interminable journey past ramparts, bastions, towers, and bridges lit by the low sun. The sinister specter of the Keep had seemed to be staring back the whole of the day as Abby had waited. She turned to the hunched old woman in front of her.

"I'm sorry, did you ask me something?"

"I asked what you got in your sack." As the woman peered up, she licked the tip of her tongue through the slot where a tooth was missing. "Something precious?"

Abby clutched the burlap sack to herself as she shrank a little from the grinning woman. "Just some of my things, that's all."

An officer, trailed by a troop of assistants, aides, and guards, marched out from under the massive portcullis that loomed nearby. Abby and the rest of the supplicants waiting at the head of the stone bridge moved tighter to the side, even though the soldiers had ample room to pass. The officer, his grim gaze unseeing as he swept by, didn't return the salute as the bridge guards clapped fists to the armor over their hearts.

All day soldiers from different lands, as well as the Home Guard from the vast city of Aydindril below, had been coming and going from the Keep. Some had looked travel-sore. Some wore uniforms still filthy with dirt, soot, and blood from recent battles. Abby had even seen two officers from her homeland of Pendisan Reach. They had looked to her to be little more than boys, but boys with the thin veneer of youth shedding too soon, like a snake casting off its skin before its time, leaving the emerging maturity scarred.

Abby had also seen such an array of important people as she could scarcely believe: sorceresses, councilors, and even a Confessor had come up from the Confessor's Palace down in the city. On her way up to the Keep, there was rarely a turn in the winding road that hadn't offered Abby a view of the sprawling splendor in white stone that was the Confessor's Palace. The alliance of the Midlands, headed by the Mother Confessor herself, held council in the palace, and there, too, lived the Confessors.

In her whole life, Abby had seen a Confessor only once before. The woman had come to see Abby's mother and Abby, not ten years at the time, had been unable to keep from staring at the Confessor's long hair. Other than her mother, no woman in Abby's small town of Coney Crossing was sufficiently important to have hair long enough to touch the shoulders. Abby's own fine, dark brown hair covered her ears but no more.

Coming through the city on the way to the Keep, it had been hard for her not to gape at noblewomen with hair to their shoulders and even a little beyond. But the Confessor going up to the Keep, dressed in the simple, satiny black dress of a Confessor, had hair that reached halfway down her back.

She wished she could have had a better look at the rare sight of such long luxuriant hair and the woman important enough to possess it, but Abby had gone to a knee with the rest of the company at the bridge, and like the rest of them feared to raise her bowed head to look up lest she meet the gaze of the other. It was said that to meet the gaze of a Confessor could cost you your mind if you were lucky, and your soul if you weren't. Even though Abby's mother had said that it was untrue, that only the deliberate touch of such a woman could effect such a thing, Abby feared, this day of all days, to test the stories.

The old woman in front of her, clothed in layered skirts topped with one dyed with henna, and mantled with a dark draping shawl, watched the soldiers pass and then leaned closer. "Do better to bring a bone, dearie. I hear that there be those in the city who will sell a bone such as you need—for the right price. Wizards don't take no salt pork for a need. They got salt pork." She glanced past Abby to the others to see them occupied with their own interests. "Better to sell your things and hope you have enough to buy a bone. Wizards don't want what some country girl brung 'em. Favors from wizards don't come easy." She glanced to the backs of the soldiers as they reached the far side of the bridge. "Not even for those doing their bidding, it would seem."

"I just want to talk to them. That's all."

"Salt pork won't get you a talk, neither, as I hear tell." She eyed Abby's hand trying to cover the smooth round shape beneath the burlap. "Or a jug you made. That what it is, dearie?" Her brown eyes, set in a wrinkled leathery mask, turned up, peering with sudden, humorless intent. "A jug?"

"Yes," Abby said. "A jug I made."

The woman smiled her skepticism and fingered a lick of short gray hair back under her wool head wrap. Her gnarled fingers closed around the smocking on the forearm of Abby's crimson dress, pulling the arm up a bit to have a look.

"Maybe you could get the price of a proper bone for your bracelet."

Abby glanced down at the bracelet made of two wires twisted together in interlocking circles. "My mother gave me this. It has no value but to me."

A slow smile came to the woman's weather-cracked lips. "The spirits believe that there is no stronger power than a mother's want to protect her child."

Abby gently pulled her arm away. "The spirits know the truth of that."

Uncomfortable under the scrutiny of the suddenly talkative woman, Abby searched for a safe place to settle her gaze. It made her dizzy to look down into the yawning chasm beneath the bridge, and she was weary of watching the Wizard's Keep, so she pretended that her attention had been caught as an excuse to turn back toward the collection of people, mostly men, waiting with her at the head of the bridge. She busied herself with nibbling on the last crust of bread from the loaf she had bought down in the market before coming up to the Keep.

Abby felt awkward talking to strangers. In her whole life she had never seen so many people, much less people she didn't know. She knew every person in Coney Crossing. The city made her apprehensive, but not as apprehensive as the Keep towering on the mountain above it, and that not as much as her reason for being there.

She just wanted to go home. But there would be no home, at least nothing to go home to, if she didn't do this.

All eyes turned up at the rattle of hooves coming out under the portcullis. Huge horses, all dusky brown or black and bigger than any Abby had ever seen, came thundering toward them. Men bedecked with polished breastplates, chain mail, and leather, and most carrying lances or poles topped with long flags of high office and rank, urged their mounts onward. They raised dust and gravel as they gathered speed crossing the bridge, in a wild rush of color and sparkles of light from metal flashing past. Sandarian lancers, from the descriptions Abby had heard. She had trouble imagining the enemy with the nerve to go up against men such as these.

Her stomach roiled. She realized she had no need to imagine, and no reason to put her hope in brave men such as those lancers. Her only hope was the wizard, and that hope was slipping away as she stood waiting. There was nothing for it but to wait.

Abby turned back to the Keep just in time to see a statuesque woman in simple robes stride out through the opening in the massive stone wall. Her fair skin stood out all the more against straight dark hair parted in the middle and readily reaching her shoulders. Some of the men had been whispering about the sight of the Sandarian officers, but at the sight of the woman, everyone fell to silence. The four soldiers at the head of the stone bridge made way for the woman as she approached the supplicants.

"Sorceress," the old woman whispered to Abby.

Abby hardly needed the old woman's counsel to know it was a sorceress. Abby recognized the simple flaxen robes, decorated at the neck with yellow and red beads sewn in the ancient symbols of the profession. Some of her earliest memories were of being held in her mother's arms and touching beads like those she saw now.

The sorceress bowed her head to the people and then offered a smile. "Please forgive us for keeping you waiting out here the whole of the day. It is not from lack of respect or something we customarily do, but with the war on our hands such precautions are regrettably unavoidable. We hope none took offense at the delay."

The crowd mumbled that they didn't. Abby doubted there was one among them bold enough to claim otherwise.

"How goes the war?" a man behind asked.

The sorceress's even gaze turned to him. "With the blessings of the good spirits, it will end soon."

"May the spirits will that D'Hara is crushed," beseeched the man.

Without response, the sorceress appraised the faces watching her, waiting to see if anyone else would speak or ask a question. None did.

"Please, come with me, then. The council meeting has ended, and a couple of the wizards will take the time to see you all."

As the sorceress turned back to the Keep and started out, three men strode up along the supplicants and put themselves at the head of the line, right in front of the old woman. The woman snatched a velvet sleeve.

"Who do you think you are," she snapped, "taking a

place before me, when I've been here the whole of the day?"

The oldest of the three, dressed in rich robes of dark purple with contrasting red sewn inside the length of the slits up the sleeves, looked to be a noble with his two advisors, or perhaps guards. He turned a glare on the woman. "You don't mind, do you?"

It didn't sound to Abby at all like a question.

The old woman took her hand back and fell mute.

The man, the ends of his gray hair coiled on his shoulders, glanced at Abby. His hooded eyes gleamed with challenge. She swallowed and remained silent. She didn't have any objection, either, at least none she was willing to voice. For all she knew, the noble was important enough to see to it that she was denied an audience. She couldn't afford to take that chance now that she was this close.

Abby was distracted by a tingling sensation from the bracelet. Blindly, her fingers glided over the wrist of the hand holding the sack. The wire bracelet felt warm. It hadn't done that since her mother had died. In the presence of so much magic as was at a place such as this, it didn't really surprise her. The crowd moved out to follow the sorceress.

"Mean, they are," the woman whispered over her shoulder. "Mean as a winter night, and just as cold."

"Those men?" Abby whispered back.

"No." The woman tilted her head. "Sorceresses. Wizards, too. That's who. All those born with the gift of magic. You better have something important in that sack, or the wizards might turn you to dust for no other reason than that they'd enjoy it."

Abby pulled her sack tight in her arms. The meanest thing her mother had done in the whole of her life was to die before she could see her granddaughter.

Abby swallowed back the urge to cry and prayed to the dear spirits that the old woman was wrong about wizards, and that they were as understanding as sorceresses. She prayed fervently that this wizard would help her. She prayed for forgiveness, too—that the good spirits would understand.

Abby worked at holding a calm countenance even though her insides were in turmoil. She pressed a fist to her stomach. She prayed for strength. Even in this, she prayed for strength.

The sorceress, the three men, the old woman, Abby, and then the rest of the supplicants passed under the huge iron portcullis and onto the Keep grounds. Inside the massive outer wall Abby was surprised to discover the air warm. Outside it had been a chill autumn day, but inside the air was spring-fresh and pleasant.

The road up the mountain, the stone bridge over the chasm, and then the opening under the portcullis appeared to be the only way into the Keep, unless you were a bird. Soaring walls of dark stone with high windows surrounded the gravel courtyard inside. There were a number of doors around the courtyard, and ahead a roadway tunneled deeper into the Keep.

Despite the warmth of the air, Abby was chilled to the bone by the place. She wasn't sure that the old woman wasn't right about wizards. Life in Coney Crossing was far removed from matters of wizards.

Abby had never seen a wizard before, nor did she know anyone who had, except for her mother, and her mother had never spoken of them except to caution that where wizards were concerned, you couldn't trust even what you saw with your own eyes.

The sorceress led them up four granite steps worn smooth over the ages by countless footsteps, through a doorway set back under a lintel of pink-flecked black granite, and into the Keep proper. The sorceress lifted an arm into the darkness, sweeping it to the side. Lamps along the wall sprang to flame.

It had been simple magic—not a very impressive display of the gift—but several of the people behind fell to worried whispering as they passed on through the wide hall. It occurred to Abby that if this little bit of conjuring would frighten them, then they had no business going to see wizards.

They wended their way across the sunken floor of an imposing anteroom the likes of which Abby could never even have imagined. Red marble columns all around supported arches below balconies. In the center of the room a fountain sprayed water high overhead. The water fell back to cascade down through a succession of ever larger scalloped bowls. Officers, sorceresses, and a variety of others sat about on white marble benches or huddled in small groups, all engaged in seemingly earnest conversation masked by the sound of the water.

In a much smaller room beyond, the sorceress gestured for them to be seated at a line of carved oak benches along one wall. Abby was bone-weary and relieved to sit at last.

Light from windows above the benches lit three tapestries hanging on the high far wall. The three together covered nearly the entire wall and made up one scene of a grand procession through a city. Abby had never seen anything like it, but with the way her dreads careered through her thoughts, she could summon little pleasure in seeing even such a majestic tableau.

In the center of the cream-colored marble floor, inset in brass lines, was a circle with a square inside it, its corners touching the circle. Inside the square sat another circle just large enough to touch the insides of the square. The center circle held an eight-pointed star. Lines radiated out from the points of the star, piercing all the way through both circles, every other line bisecting a corner of the square.

The design, called a Grace, was often drawn by those with the gift. The outer circle represented the beginnings of the infinity of the spirit world out beyond. The square represented the boundary separating the spirit world—the underworld, the world of the dead—from the inner circle, which represented the limits of the world of life. In the center of it all was the star, representing the Light—the Creator.

It was a depiction of the continuum of the gift: from the Creator, through life, and at death crossing the boundary to eternity with the spirits in the Keeper's realm of the underworld. But it represented a hope, too—a hope to remain in the Creator's Light from birth, through life, and beyond, in the underworld.

It was said that only the spirits of those who did great wickedness in life would be denied the Creator's Light in the underworld. Abby knew she would be condemned to an eternity with the Keeper of darkness in the underworld. She had no choice.

The sorceress folded her hands. "An aide will come to get you each in turn. A wizard will see each of you. The war burns hot; please keep your petition brief." She gazed down the line of people. "It is out of a sincere obligation to those we serve that the wizards see supplicants, but please try to understand that individual desires are often detrimental to the greater good. By pausing to help one, then many are denied help. Thus, denial of a request is not a denial of your need, but acceptance of greater need. In times of peace it is rare for wizards to grant the narrow wants of supplicants. At a time like this, a time of a great war, it is almost unheard of. Please understand that it has not to do with what we would wish, but is a matter of necessity."

She watched the line of supplicants, but saw none willing to abandon their purpose. Abby certainly would not.

"Very well then. We have two wizards able to take supplicants at this time. We will bring you each to one of them."

The sorceress turned to leave. Abby rose to her feet.

"Please, mistress, a word if I may?"

The sorceress settled an unsettling gaze on Abby. "Speak."

Abby stepped forward. "I must see the First Wizard himself. Wizard Zorander."

One eyebrow arched. "The First Wizard is a very busy man."

Abby reached into her sack and pulled out the neck band from her mother's robes. She stepped into the center of the Grace and kissed the red and yellow beads on the neck band.

"I am Abigail, born of Helsa. On the Grace and my mother's soul, I must see Wizard Zorander. Please. It is no trivial journey I have made. Lives are at stake."

The sorceress watched the beaded band being returned

to the sack. "Abigail, born of Helsa." Her gaze rose to meet Abby's. "I will take your words to the First Wizard."

"Mistress." Abby turned to see the old woman on her feet. "I would be well pleased to see the First Wizard, too."

The three men rose up. The oldest, the one apparently in charge of the three, gave the sorceress a look so barren of timidity that it bordered on contempt. His long gray hair fell forward over his velvet robes as he glanced down the line of seated people, seeming to dare them to stand. When none did, he returned his attention to the sorceress.

"I will see Wizard Zorander."

The sorceress appraised those on their feet and then looked down the line of supplicants on the bench. "The First Wizard has earned a name: the wind of death. He is feared no less by many of us than by our enemies. Anyone else who would bait fate?"

None of those on the bench had the courage to gaze into her fierce stare. To the last they all silently shook their heads. "Please wait," she said to those seated. "Someone will shortly be out to take you to a wizard." She looked once more to the five people standing. "Are you all very, very sure of this?"

Abby nodded. The old woman nodded. The noble glared.

"Very well then. Come with me."

The noble and his two men stepped in front of Abby. The old woman seemed content to take a station at the end of the line. They were led deeper into the Keep, through narrow halls and wide corridors, some dark and austere and some of astounding grandeur. Everywhere there were soldiers of the Home Guard, their breastplates or chain mail covered with red tunics banded around their edges in black. All were heavily armed with swords or battle-axes, all had knives, and many additionally carried pikes tipped with winged and barbed steel.

At the top of a broad white marble stairway the stone railings spiraled at the ends to open wide onto a room of warm oak paneling. Several of the raised panels held lamps with polished silver reflectors. Atop a three-legged table sat a double-bowl cut-glass lamp with twin chimneys, their flames adding to the mellow light from the reflector lamps. A thick carpet of ornate blue patterns covered nearly the entire wood floor.

To each side of a double door stood one of the meticulously dressed Home Guard. Both men were equally huge. They looked to be men more than able to handle any trouble that might come up the stairs.

The sorceress nodded toward a dozen thickly tufted leather chairs set in four groups. Abby waited until the others had seated themselves in two of the groupings and then sat by herself in another. She placed the sack in her lap and rested her hands over its contents.

The sorceress stiffened her back. "I will tell the First Wizard that he has supplicants who wish to see him."

A guard opened one of the double doors for her. As she was swallowed into the great room beyond, Abby was able to snatch a quick glimpse. She could see that it was well lighted by glassed skylights. There were other doors in the gray stone of the walls. Before the door closed, Abby was also able to see a number of people, men and women both, all rushing hither and yon.

Abby sat turned away from the old woman and the three men as with one hand she idly stroked the sack in her lap. She had little fear that the men would talk to her, but she didn't want to talk to the woman; it was a distraction. She passed the time going over in her mind what she planned to say to Wizard Zorander.

At least she tried to go over it in her mind. Mostly, all she could think about was what the sorceress had said, that the First Wizard was called the wind of death, not only by the D'Harans, but also by his own people of the Midlands. Abby knew it was no tale to scare off supplicants from a busy man. Abby herself had heard people whisper of their great wizard, "The wind of death." Those whispered words were uttered in dread.

The lands of D'Hara had sound reason to fear this man as their enemy; he had destroyed countless of their troops, from what Abby had heard. Of course, if they hadn't invaded the Midlands, bent on conquest, they would not have felt the hot wind of death.

Had they not invaded, Abby wouldn't be sitting there in the Wizard's Keep—she would be at home, and everyone she loved would be safe.

Abby marked again the odd tingling sensation from the bracelet. She ran her fingers over it, testing its unusual warmth. This close to a person of such power it didn't surprise her that the bracelet was warming. Her mother had told her to wear it always, and that someday it would be of value. Abby didn't know how, and her mother had died without ever explaining.

Sorceresses were known for the way they kept secrets, even from their own daughters. Perhaps if Abby had been born gifted . . .

She sneaked a peek over her shoulder at the others. The old woman was leaning back in her chair, staring at the doors. The noble's attendants sat with their hands folded as they casually eyed the room.

The noble was doing the oddest thing. He had a lock of sandy-colored hair wound around a finger. He stroked his thumb over the lock of hair as he glared at the doors.

Abby wanted the wizard to hurry up and see her, but time stubbornly dragged by. In a way, she wished he would refuse. No, she told herself, that was unacceptable. No matter her fear, no matter her revulsion, she must do this. Abruptly, the door opened. The sorceress strode out toward Abby.

The noble surged to his feet. "I will see him first." His voice was cold threat. "That is not a request."

"It is our right to see him first," Abby said without forethought. When the sorceress folded her hands, Abby decided she had best go on. "I've waited since dawn. This woman was the only one waiting before me. These men came at the last of the day."

Abby started when the old woman's gnarled fingers gripped her forearm. "Why don't we let these men go first, dearie? It matters not who arrived first, but who has the most important business."

Abby wanted to scream that her business was important, but she realized that the old woman might be saving her from serious trouble in accomplishing her business. Reluctantly, she gave the sorceress a nod. As the sorceress led the three men through the door, Abby could feel the old woman's eyes on her back. Abby hugged the sack against the burning anxiety in her abdomen and told herself that it wouldn't be long, and then she would see him.

As they waited, the old woman remained silent, and Abby was glad for that. Occasionally, she glanced at the door, imploring the good spirits to help her. But she realized it was futile; the good spirits wouldn't be disposed to help her in this.

A roar came from the room beyond the doors. It was like the sound of an arrow zipping through the air, or a long switch whipping, but much louder, intensifying rapidly. It ended with a shrill crack accompanied by a flash of light coming under the doors and around their edges. The doors shuddered on their hinges.

Sudden silence rang in Abby's ears. She found herself gripping the arms of the chair.

Both doors opened. The noble's two attendants marched out, followed by the sorceress. The three stopped in the waiting room. Abby sucked a breath.

One of the two men was cradling the noble's head in the crook of an arm. The wan features of the face were frozen in a mute scream. Thick strings of blood dripped onto the carpet.

"Show them out," the sorceress hissed through gritted teeth to one of the two guards at the door.

The guard dipped his pike toward the stairs, ordering them ahead, and then followed the two men down. Crimson drops splattered onto the white marble of the steps as they descended. Abby sat in stiff, wide-eyed shock.

The sorceress wheeled back to Abby and the old woman.

The woman rose to her feet. "I believe that I would rather not bother the First Wizard today. I will return another day, if need be."

She hunched lower toward Abby. "I am called Mariska." Her brow drew down. "May the good spirits grant that you succeed."

She shuffled to the stairs, rested a hand on the marble railing, and started down. The sorceress snapped her fingers and gestured. The remaining guard rushed to accompany the woman, as the sorceress turned back to Abby.

"The First Wizard will see you now."

Abby gulped air, trying to get her breath as she lurched to her feet.

"What happened? Why did the First Wizard do that?"

"The man was sent on behalf of another to ask a question of the First Wizard. The First Wizard gave his answer."

Abby clutched her sack to herself for dear life as she gaped at the blood on the floor. "Might that be the answer to my question, if I ask it?"

"I don't know the question you would ask." For the first time, the sorceress's expression softened just a bit. "Would you like me to see you out? You could see another wizard or, perhaps, after you've given more thought to your petition, return another day, if you still wish it."

Abby fought back tears of desperation. There was no choice. She shook her head. "I must see him."

The sorceress let out a deep breath. "Very well." She put a hand under Abby's arm as if to keep her on her feet. "The First Wizard will see you now."

Abby hugged the contents of her sack as she was led into the chamber where waited the wind of death. Torches in iron sconces were not yet burning. The late-afternoon light from the glassed roof windows was still strong enough to illuminate the room. It smelled of pitch, lamp oil, roasted meat, wet stone, and stale sweat.

Inside, confusion and commotion reigned. There were people everywhere, and they all seemed to be talking at once. Stout tables set about the room in no discernible pattern were covered with books, scrolls, maps, chalk, unlit oil lamps, burning candles, partially eaten meals, sealing wax, pens, and a clutter of every sort of odd object, from balls of knotted string to half-spilled sacks of sand. People stood about the tables, engaged in conversations or arguments, as others tapped passages in books, pored over scrolls, or moved little painted weights about on maps. Others rolled slices of roasted meat plucked from platters and nibbled as they watched or offered opinions between swallows.

The sorceress, still holding Abby under her arm, leaned closer as they proceeded. "You will have the First Wizard's divided attention. There will be other people talking to him at the same time. Don't be distracted. He will be listening to you as he also listens to or talks to others. Just ignore the others who are speaking and ask what you have come to ask. He will hear you."

Abby was dumbfounded. "While he's talking to other people?"

"Yes." Abby felt the hand squeeze her arm ever so slightly. "Try to be calm, and not to judge by what has come before you."

The killing. That was what she meant. That a man had come to speak to the First Wizard, and he had been killed for it. She was simply supposed to put that from her thoughts? When she glanced down, she saw that she was walking through a trail of blood. She didn't see the headless body anywhere.

Her bracelet tingled and she looked down at it. The hand under her arm halted her. When Abby looked up, she saw a confusing knot of people before her. Some rushed in from the sides as others rushed away. Some flailed their arms as they spoke with great conviction. So many were talking that Abby could scarcely understand a word of it. At the same time, others were leaning in, nearly whispering. She felt as if she were confronting a human beehive.

Abby's attention was snagged by a form in white to the side. The instant she saw the long fall of hair and the violet eyes looking right at her, Abby went rigid. A small cry escaped her throat as she fell to her knees and bowed over until her back protested. She trembled and shuddered, fearing the worst.

In the instant before she dropped to her knees, she had seen that the elegant, satiny white dress was cut square at the neck, the same as the black dresses had been. The long flag of hair was unmistakable. Abby had never seen the woman before, but without doubt knew who she was. There could be no mistaking this woman. Only one of them wore the white dress.

It was the Mother Confessor herself.

She heard muttering above her, but feared to listen, lest it was death being summoned.

"Rise, my child," came a clear voice.

Abby recognized it as the formal response of the Mother Confessor to one of her people. It took a moment for Abby to realize that it represented no threat, but simple acknowledgment. She stared at a smear of blood on the floor as she debated what to do next. Her mother had never instructed her as to how to conduct herself should she ever meet the Mother Confessor. As far as she knew, no one from Coney Crossing had ever seen the Mother Confessor, much less met her. Then again, none of them had ever seen a wizard, either.

Overhead, the sorceress whispered a growl. "Rise."

Abby scrambled to her feet, but kept her eyes to the floor, even though the smear of blood was making her sick. She could smell it, like a fresh butchering of one of their animals. From the long trail, it looked as if the body had been dragged away to one of the doors in the back of the room.

The sorceress spoke calmly into the chaos. "Wizard Zorander, this is Abigail, born of Helsa. She wishes a word with you. Abigail, this is First Wizard Zeddicus Zu'l Zorander."

Abby dared to cautiously lift her gaze. Hazel eyes gazed back.

To each side before her were knots of people: big, forbidding officers—some of them looked as if they might be generals; several old men in robes, some simple and some ornate; several middle-aged men, some in robes and some in livery; three women—sorceresses all; a variety of other men and women; and the Mother Confessor.

The man at the center of the turmoil, the man with the hazel eyes, was not what Abby had been expecting. She had expected some grizzled, gruff old man. This man was young—perhaps as young as she. Lean but sinewy, he wore the simplest of robes, hardly better made than Abby's burlap sack—the mark of his high office.

Abby had not anticipated this sort of man in such an office as that of First Wizard. She remembered what her mother had told her—not to trust what your eyes told you where wizards were concerned.

All about, people spoke to him, argued at him, a few even shouted, but the wizard was silent as he looked into her eyes. His face was pleasing enough to look upon, gentle in appearance, even though his wavy brown hair looked ungovernable, but his eyes . . . Abby had never seen the likes of those eyes. They seemed to see all, to know all, to understand all. At the same time they were bloodshot and weary looking, as if sleep eluded him. They had, too, the slightest glaze of distress. Even so, he was calm at the center of the storm. For that moment that his attention was on her, it was as if no one else were in the room.

The lock of hair Abby had seen around the noble's finger was now held wrapped around the First Wizard's finger. He brushed it to his lips before lowering his arm.

"I am told you are the daughter of a sorceress." His voice was placid water flowing through the tumult raging all about. "Are you gifted, child?"

"No, sir . . ."

Even as she answered, he was turning to another who had just finished speaking. "I told you, if you do, we chance losing them. Send word that I want him to cut south."

The tall officer to whom the wizard spoke threw his hands up. "But he said they've reliable scouting information that the D'Harans went east on him."

"That's not the point," the wizard said. "I want that pass to the south sealed. That's where their main force went; they have gifted among them. They are the ones we must kill."

The tall officer was saluting with a fist to his heart as the wizard turned to an old sorceress. "Yes, that's right, three invocations before attempting the transposition. I found the reference last night."

The old sorceress departed to be replaced by a man jabbering in a foreign tongue as he opened a scroll and held it up for the wizard to see. The wizard squinted toward it, reading a moment before waving the man away, while giving orders in the same foreign language.

The wizard turned to Abby. "You're a skip?"

Abby felt her face heat and her ears burn. "Yes, Wizard Zorander."

"Nothing to be ashamed of, child," he said while the Mother Confessor herself was whispering confidentially in his ear.

But it *was* something to be ashamed of. The gift hadn't passed on to her from her mother—it had skipped her.

The people of Coney Crossing had depended on Abby's mother. She helped with those who were ill or hurt. She advised people on matters of community and those of family. For some she arranged marriages. For some she meted out discipline. For some she bestowed favors available only through magic. She was a sorceress; she protected the people of Coney Crossing.

She was revered openly. By some, she was feared and loathed privately.

She was revered for the good she did for the people of Coney Crossing. By some, she had been feared and loathed because she had the gift—because she wielded magic. Others wanted nothing so much as to live their lives without any magic about.

Abby had no magic and couldn't help with illness or injury or shapeless fears. She dearly wished she could, but she couldn't. When Abby had asked her mother why she would abide all the thankless resentment, her mother told her that helping was its own reward and you should not expect gratitude for it. She said that if you went through life expecting gratitude for the help you provided, you might end up leading a miserable life.

When her mother was alive, Abby had been shunned in subtle ways; after her mother died, the shunning became more overt. It had been expected by the people of Coney Crossing that she would serve as her mother had served. People didn't understand about the gift, how it often wasn't passed on to an offspring; instead they thought Abby selfish.

The wizard was explaining something to a sorceress about the casting of a spell. When he finished, his gaze swept past Abby on its way to someone else. She needed his help, now.

"What is it you wanted to ask me, Abigail?"

Abby's fingers tightened on the sack. "It's about my home of Coney Crossing." She paused while the wizard pointed in a book being held out to him. He rolled his hand at her, gesturing for her to go on as a man was explaining an intricacy to do with inverting a duplex spell. "There's terrible trouble there," Abby said. "D'Haran troops came through the Crossing . . ."

The First Wizard turned to an older man with a long white beard. By his simple robes, Abby guessed him to be a wizard, too.

"I'm telling you, Thomas, it can be done," Wizard Zorander insisted. "I'm not saying I agree with the council, I'm just telling you what I found and their unanimous decision that it be done. I'm not claiming to understand the details of just how it works, but I've studied it; it can be done. As I told the council, I can activate it. I have yet to decide if I agree with them that I should."

The man, Thomas, wiped a hand across his face. "You mean what I heard is true, then? That you really do think it's possible? Are you out of your mind, Zorander?"

"I found it in a book in the First Wizard's private enclave. A book from before the war with the Old World. I've seen it with my own eyes. I've cast a whole series of verification webs to test it." He turned his attention to Abby. "Yes, that would be Anargo's legion. Coney Crossing is in Pendisan Reach."

"That's right," Abby said. "And so then this D'Haran army swept through there and—"

"Pendisan Reach refused to join with the rest of the Midlands under central command to resist the invasion from D'Hara. Standing by their sovereignty, they chose to fight the enemy in their own way. They have to live with the consequences of their actions."

The old man was tugging on his beard. "Still, do you know if it's real? All proven out? I mean, that book would have to be thousands of years old. It might have been conjecture. Verification webs don't always confirm the entire structure of such a thing."

"I know that as well as you, Thomas, but I'm telling you, it's real," Wizard Zorander said. His voice lowered to a whisper. "The spirits preserve us, it's genuine."

Abby's heart was pounding. She wanted to tell him her story, but she couldn't seem to get a word in. He had to help her. It was the only way.

An army officer rushed in from one of the back doors. He pushed his way into the crowd around the First Wizard.

"Wizard Zorander! I've just gotten word! When we unleashed the horns you sent, they worked! Urdland's force turned tail!"

Several voices fell silent. Others didn't.

"At least three thousand years old," the First Wizard said to the man with the beard. He put a hand on the newly arrived officer's shoulder and leaned close. "Tell General Brainard to hold short at the Kern River. Don't burn the bridges, but hold them. Tell him to split his men. Leave half to keep Urdland's force from changing their mind; hopefully they won't be able to replace their field wizard. Have Brainard take the rest of his men north to help cut Anargo's escape route; that's where our concern lies, but we may still need the bridges to go after Urdland."

One of the other officers, an older man looking possibly to be a general himself, went red in the face. "Halt at the river? When the horns have done their job, and we have them on the run? But why? We can take them down before they have a chance to regroup and join up with another force to come back at us!"

Hazel eyes turned toward the man. "And do you know what waits over the border? How many men will die if Panis Rahl has something waiting that the horns can't turn away? How many innocent lives has it already cost us? How many of our men will die to bleed them on their own land—land we don't know as they do?"

"And how many of our people will die if we don't eliminate their ability to come back at us another day! We must pursue them. Panis Rahl will never rest. He'll be working to conjure up something else to gut us all in our sleep. We must hunt them down and kill every last one!"

"I'm working on that," the First Wizard said cryptically.

The old man twisted his beard and made a sarcastic face. "Yes, he thinks he can unleash the underworld itself on them."

Several officers, two of the sorceresses, and a couple of the men in robes paused to stare in open disbelief.

The sorceress who had brought Abby to the audience leaned close. "You wanted to talk to the First Wizard. Talk. If you have lost your nerve, then I will see you out."

Abby wet her lips. She didn't know how she could talk into the middle of such a roundabout conversation, but she knew she must, so she just started back in.

"Sir, I don't know anything about what my homeland of Pendisan Reach has done. I know little of the king. I don't know anything about the council, or the war, or any of it. I'm from a small place, and I only know that the people there are in grave trouble. Our defenders were overrun by the enemy. There is an army of Midlands men who drive toward the D'Harans."

She felt foolish talking to a man who was carrying on a half dozen conversations all at once. Mostly, though, she felt anger and frustration. Those people were going to die if she couldn't convince him to help.

"How many D'Harans?" the wizard asked.

Abby opened her mouth, but an officer spoke in her place. "We're not sure how many are left in Anargo's legion. They may be wounded, but they're an enraged wounded bull. Now they're in sight of their homeland.

They can only come back at us, or escape us. We've got Sanderson sweeping down from the north and Mardale cutting up from the southwest. Anargo made a mistake going into the Crossing; in there he must fight us or run for home. We have to finish them. This may be our only chance."

The First Wizard drew a finger and thumb down his smooth jaw. "Still, we aren't sure of their numbers. The scouts were dependable, but they never returned. We can only assume they're dead. And why would Anargo do such a thing?"

"Well," the officer said, "it's the shortest escape route back to D'Hara."

The First Wizard turned to a sorceress to answer a question she had just finished. "I can't see how we can afford it. Tell them I said no. I'll not cast that kind of web for them and I'll not give them the means to it for no more offered than a 'maybe.'"

The sorceress nodded before rushing off.

Abby knew that a web was the spell cast by a sorceress. Apparently the spell cast by a wizard was called the same.

"Well, if such a thing is possible," the bearded man was saying, "then I'd like to see your exegesis of the text. A three-thousand-year-old book is a lot of risk. We've no clue as to how the wizards of that time could do most of what they did."

The First Wizard, for the first time, cast a hot glare toward the man. "Thomas, do you want to see exactly what I'm talking about? The spell-form?"

Some of the people had fallen silent at the tone in his voice. The First Wizard threw open his arms, urging everyone back out of his way. The Mother Confessor stayed close behind his left shoulder. The sorceress beside Abby pulled her back a step.

The First Wizard motioned. A man snatched a small sack off the table and handed it to him. Abby noticed that some of the sand on the tables wasn't simply spilled, but had been used to draw symbols. Abby's mother had occasionally drawn spells with sand, but mostly used a variety of other things, from ground bone to dried herbs. Abby's mother used sand for practice; spells, real spells, had to be drawn in proper order and without error.

The First Wizard squatted down and took a handful of sand from the sack. He drew on the floor by letting the sand dribble from the side of his fist.

Wizard Zorander's hand moved with practiced precision. His arm swept around, drawing a circle. He returned for a handful of sand and drew an inner circle. It appeared he was drawing a Grace.

Abby's mother had always drawn the square second; everything in order inward and then the rays back out. Wizard Zorander drew the eight-pointed star inside the smaller circle. He drew the lines radiating outward, through both circles, but left one absent.

He had yet to draw the square, representing the boundary between worlds. He was the First Wizard, so Abby guessed that it wasn't improper to do it in a different order than a sorceress in a little place like Coney Crossing did. But several of the men Abby took as wizards, and the two sorceresses behind him, were turning grave glances to one another.

Wizard Zorander laid down the lines of sand for two sides of the square. He scooped up more sand from the sack and began the last two sides.

Instead of a straight line, he drew an arc that dipped well into the edge of the inner circle—the one representing the world of life. The arc, instead of ending at the outer circle, crossed it. He drew the last side, likewise arced, so that it too crossed into the inner circle. He brought the line to meet the other where the ray from the Light was missing. Unlike the other three points of the square, this last point ended outside the larger circle—in the world of the dead.

People gasped. A hush fell over the room for a moment before worried whispers spread among those gifted.

Wizard Zorander rose. "Satisfied, Thomas?"

Thomas's face had gone as white as his beard. "The Creator preserve us." His eyes turned to Wizard Zorander. "The council doesn't truly understand this. It would be madness to unleash it."

Wizard Zorander ignored him and turned toward Abby. "How many D'Harans did you see?"

"Three years past, the locust swarms came. The hills of the Crossing were brown with them. I think I saw more D'Harans than I saw locusts."

Wizard Zorander grunted his discontent. He looked down at the Grace he had drawn. "Panis Rahl won't give up. How long, Thomas? How long until he finds something new to conjure and sends Anargo back on us?" His gaze swept among the people around him. "How many years have we thought we would be annihilated by the invading horde from D'Hara? How many of our people have been killed by Rahl's magic? How many thousands have died of the fevers he sent? How many thousands have blistered and bled to death from the touch of the shadow people he conjured? How many villages, towns, and cities has he wiped from existence?"

When no one spoke, Wizard Zorander went on.

"It has taken us years to come back from the brink. The war has finally turned; the enemy is running. We now have three choices. The first choice is to let him run for home and hope he never comes back to again visit us with his brutality. I think it would only be a matter of time until he tried again. That leaves two realistic options. We can either pursue him into his lair and kill him for good at the cost of tens, perhaps hundreds of thousands of our men—or I can end it."

Those gifted among the crowd cast uneasy glances to the Grace drawn on the floor.

"We still have other magic," another wizard said. "We can use it to the same effect without unleashing such a cataclysm."

"Wizard Zorander is right," another said, "and so is the council. The enemy has earned this fate. We must set it upon them."

The room fell again to arguing. As it did, Wizard Zorander looked into Abby's eyes. It was a clear instruction to finish her supplication.

"My people—the people in Coney Crossing—have been

taken by the D'Harans. There are others, too, who they've captured. They have a sorceress holding the captives with a spell. Please, Wizard Zorander, you must help me.

"When I was hiding, I heard the sorceress talking to their officers. The D'Harans plan to use the captives as shields. They will use the captives to blunt the deadly magic you send against them, or to blunt the spears and arrows the Midlands army sends against them. If they decide to turn and attack, they plan to drive the captives ahead. They called it 'dulling the enemies' weapons on their own women and children.' "

No one looked at her. They were all once again engaged in their mass talking and arguing. It was as if the lives of all those people were beneath their consideration.

Tears stung at Abby's eyes. "Either way all those innocent people will die. Please, Wizard Zorander, we must have your help. Otherwise they'll all die."

He looked her way briefly. "There is nothing we can do for them."

Abby panted, trying to hold back the tears. "My father was captured, along with others of my kin. My husband is among the captives. My daughter is among them. She is not yet five. If you send magic, they will be killed. If you attack, they will be killed. You must rescue them, or hold the attack."

He looked genuinely saddened. "I'm sorry. I can't help them. May the good spirits watch over them and take their souls to the Light." He began turning away.

"No!" Abby screamed. Some of the people fell silent. Others only glanced her way as they went on. "My child! You can't!" She thrust a hand into the sack. "I've a bone—"

"Doesn't everyone," he grumbled, cutting her off. "I can't help you."

"But you must!"

"We would have to abandon our cause. We must take the D'Haran force down—one way or another. Innocent though those people are, they are in the way. I can't allow the D'Harans to succeed in such a scheme or it would encourage its widespread use, and then even more innocents would die. The enemy must be shown that it will not deter us from our course."

"NO!" Abby wailed. "She's only a child! You're condemning my baby to death! There are other children! What kind of monster are you?"

No one but the wizard was even listening to her any more as they all went on with their talking.

The First Wizard's voice cut through the din and fell on her ears as clearly as the knell of death. "I am a man who must make choices such as this one. I must deny your petition."

Abby screamed with the agony of failure. She wasn't even to be allowed to show him.

"But it's a debt!" she cried. "A solemn debt!"

"And it cannot be paid now."

Abby screamed hysterically. The sorceress began pulling her away. Abby broke from the woman and ran out of the room. She staggered down the stone steps, unable to see through the tears.

At the bottom of the steps she buckled to the floor in helpless sobbing. He wouldn't help her. He wouldn't help a helpless child. Her daughter was going to die.

Abby, convulsing in sobs, felt a hand on her shoulder. Gentle arms pulled her closer. Tender fingers brushed back her hair as she wept into a woman's lap. Another person's hand touched her back and she felt the warm comfort of magic seeping into her.

"He's killing my daughter," she cried. "I hate him."

"It's all right, Abigail," the voice above said. "It's all right to weep for such a pain as this."

Abby wiped at her eyes, but couldn't stop the tears. The sorceress was there, beside her, at the bottom of the steps.

Abby looked up at the woman in whose arms she lay. It was the Mother Confessor herself. She could do her worst, for all Abby cared. What did it matter, what did any of it matter, now?

"He's a monster," she sobbed. "He is truly named. He is

the ill wind of death. This time it's my baby he's killing, not the enemy."

"I understand why you feel that way, Abigail," the Mother Confessor said, "but it is not true."

"How can you say that! My daughter has not yet had a chance to live, and he will kill her! My husband will die. My father, too, but he has had a chance to live a life. My baby hasn't!"

She fell to hysterical wailing again, and the Mother Confessor once again drew her into comforting arms. Comfort was not what Abby wanted.

"You have just the one child?" the sorceress asked.

Abby nodded as she sucked a breath. "I had another, a boy, but he died at birth. The midwife said I will have no more. My little Jana is all I will ever have." The wild agony of it ripped through her. "And he will kill her. Just as he killed that man before me. Wizard Zorander is a monster. May the good spirits strike him dead!"

With a poignant expression, the sorceress smoothed Abby's hair back from her forehead "You don't understand. You see only a part of it. You don't mean what you say."

But she did. "If you had—"

"Delora understands," the Mother Confessor said, gesturing toward the sorceress. "She has a daughter of ten years, and a son, too."

Abby peered up at the sorceress. She gave Abby a sympathetic smile and a nod to confirm the truth of it.

"I, too, have a daughter," the Mother Confessor said. "She is twelve. Delora and I both understand your pain. So does the First Wizard."

Abby's fists tightened. "He couldn't! He's hardly more than a boy himself, and he wants to kill my baby. He is the wind of death and that's all he cares about—killing people!"

The Mother Confessor patted the stone step beside her. "Abigail, sit up here beside me. Let me tell you about the man in there."

Still weeping, Abby pushed herself up and slid onto the step. The Mother Confessor was older by maybe twelve or fourteen years, and pleasant-looking, with those violet eyes. Her mass of long hair reached her waist. She had a warm smile. It had never occurred to Abby to think of a Confessor as a woman, but that was what she saw now. She didn't fear this woman as she had before; nothing she did could be worse than what already had been done.

"I sometimes minded Zeddicus when he was but a toddler and I was still coming into womanhood." The Mother Confessor gazed off with a wistful smile. "I swatted his bottom when he misbehaved, and later twisted his ear to make him sit at a lesson. He was mischief on two legs, driven not by guile but by curiosity. He grew into a fine man.

"For a long time, when the war with D'Hara started, Wizard Zorander wouldn't help us. He didn't want to fight, to hurt people. But in the end, when Panis Rahl, the leader of D'Hara, started using magic to slaughter our people, Zedd knew that the only hope to save more lives in the end was to fight.

"Zeddicus Zu'l Zorander may look young to you, as he did to many of us, but he is a special wizard, born of a wizard and a sorceress. Zedd was a prodigy. Even those other wizards in there, some of them his teachers, don't always understand how he is able to unravel some of the enigmas in the books or how he uses his gift to bring so much power to bear, but we do understand that he has heart. He uses his heart, as well as his head. He was named First Wizard for all these things and more."

"Yes," Abby said, "he is very talented at being the wind of death."

The Mother Confessor smiled a small smile. She tapped her chest. "Among ourselves, those of us who really know him call him the trickster. The trickster is the name he has truly earned. We named him the wind of death for others to hear, so as to strike terror into the hearts of the enemy. Some people on our side take that name to heart. Perhaps, since your mother was gifted, you can understand how people sometimes unreasonably fear those with magic?"

"And sometimes," Abby argued, "those with magic really are monsters who care nothing for the life they destroy."

The Mother Confessor appraised Abby's eyes a moment, and then held up a cautionary finger. "In confidence, I am going to tell you about Zeddicus Zu'l Zorander. If you ever repeat this story, I will never forgive you for betraying my confidence."

"I won't, but I don't see—"

"Just listen."

After Abby remained silent the Mother Confessor began. "Zedd married Erilyn. She was a wonderful woman. We all loved her very much, but not as much as did he. They had a daughter."

Abby's curiosity got the best of her. "How old is she?"

"About the age of your daughter," Delora said.

Abby swallowed. "I see."

"When Zedd became First Wizard, things were grim. Panis Rahl had conjured the shadow people."

"I'm from Coney Crossing. I've never heard of such a thing."

"Well, the war had been bad enough, but then Panis Rahl taught his wizards to conjure shadow people." The Mother Confessor sighed at the anguish of retelling the story. "They are so called because they are like shadows in the air. They have no precise shape or form. They are not living, but created out of magic. Weapons have no more effect on them than they would have on smoke.

"You can't hide from the shadow people. They drift toward you across fields, or through the woods. They find you.

"When they touch someone, the person's whole body blisters and swells until their flesh splits open. They die in screaming agony. Not even the gift can heal one touched by a shadow person.

"As the enemy attacked, their wizards would send the shadow people out ahead. In the beginning whole battalions of our brave young soldiers were found killed to a man. We saw no hope. It was our darkest hour."

"And Wizard Zorander was able to stop them?" Abby asked.

The Mother Confessor nodded. "He studied the problem and then conjured battle horns. Their magic swept the shadow people away like smoke in the wind. The magic coming from the horns also traced its way back through the spell, to seek out the one who cast it, and kill them. The horns aren't foolproof, though, and Zedd must constantly alter their magic to keep up with the way the enemy changes their conjuring.

"Panis Rahl summoned other magic, too: fevers and sickness, wasting illnesses, fogs that caused blindness—all sorts of horrors. Zedd worked day and night, and managed to counter them all. While Panis Rahl's magic was being checked, our troops were once again able to fight on even terms. Because of Wizard Zorander, the tide of battle turned."

"Well, that much of it is good, but—"

The Mother Confessor again lifted her finger, commanding silence. Abby held her tongue as the woman lowered her hand and went on.

"Panis Rahl was enraged at what Zedd had done. He tried and failed to kill him, so he instead sent a quad to kill Erilyn."

"A quad? What's a quad?"

"A quad," the sorceress answered, "is a unit of four special assassins sent with the protection of a spell from the one who sent them: Panis Rahl. It is their assignment not only to kill the victim, but to make it unimaginably torturous and brutal."

Abby swallowed. "And did they . . . murder his wife?"

The Mother Confessor leaned closer. "Worse. They left her, her legs and arms all broken, to be found still alive."

"Alive?" Abby whispered. "Why would they leave her alive, if it was their mission to kill her?"

"So that Zedd would find her all broken and bleeding and in inconceivable agony. She was able only to whisper his name in love." The Mother Confessor leaned even closer. Abby could feel the breath of the woman's whispered words against her own face. "When he used his gift to try to heal her, it activated the worm spell."

Abby had to force herself to blink. "Worm spell . . . ?"

"No wizard would have been able to detect it." The Mother Confessor clawed her fingers and, in front of Abby's stomach, spread her hands outward, in a tearing gesture. "The spell ripped her insides apart. Because he had used his loving touch of magic, she died in screaming pain as he knelt helpless beside her."

Wincing, Abby touched her own stomach, almost feeling the wound. "That's terrible."

The Mother Confessor's violet eyes held an iron look. "The quad also took their daughter. Their daughter, who had seen everything those men had done to her mother."

Abby felt tears burning her eyes again. "They did that to his daughter, too?"

"No," the Mother Confessor said. "They hold her captive."

"Then she still lives? There is still hope?"

The Mother Confessor's satiny white dress rustled softly as she leaned back against the white marble balustrade and nested her hands in her lap. "Zedd went after the quad. He found them, but his daughter had been given to others, and they passed her on to yet others, and so on, so they had no idea who had her, or where she might be."

Abby looked to the sorceress and back to the Mother Confessor. "What did Wizard Zorander do to the quad?"

"No less than I myself would have done." The Mother Confessor stared back through a mask of cold rage. "He made them regret ever being born. For a very long time he made them regret it."

Abby shrank back. "I see."

As the Mother Confessor drew a calming breath, the sorceress took up the story. "As we speak, Wizard Zorander uses a spell that none of us understands; it holds Panis Rahl at his palace in D'Hara. It helps blunt the magic Rahl is able to conjure against us, and enables our men to drive his troops back whence they came.

"But Panis Rahl is consumed with wrath for the man who has thwarted his conquest of the Midlands. Hardly a week passes that an attempt is not made on Wizard Zorander's life. Rahl sends dangerous and vile people of all sort. Even the Mord-Sith."

Abby's breath caught. That was a word she had heard. "What are Mord-Sith?"

The sorceress smoothed back her glossy black hair as she glared with a venomous expression. "Mord-Sith are women who, along with their red leather uniform, wear a single long braid as the mark of their profession. They are trained in the torture and killing of those with the gift. If a gifted person tries to use their magic against a Mord-Sith, she is able to capture their magic and use it against them. There is no escaping a Mord-Sith."

"But surely, a person as strong in the gift as Wizard Zorander—"

"Even he would be lost if he tried to use magic against a Mord-Sith," the Mother Confessor said. "A Mord-Sith can be defeated with common weapons—but not with magic. Only the magic of a Confessor works against them. I have killed two.

"In part because of the brutal nature of the training of Mord-Sith, they have been outlawed for as long as anyone knows, but in D'Hara the ghastly tradition of taking young women to be indoctrinated as Mord-Sith continues to this day. D'Hara is a distant and secretive land. We don't know much about it, except what we have learned through unfortunate experience.

"Mord-Sith have captured several of our wizards and sorceresses. Once captured, they cannot kill themselves, nor can they escape. Before they die, they give over everything they know. Panis Rahl knows of our plans.

"We, in turn, have managed to get our hands on several high-ranking D'Harans, and through the touch of Confessors we know the extent of how we have been compromised. Time works against us."

Abby wiped the palms of her hands on her thighs. "And that man who was killed just before I went in to see the First Wizard, he couldn't have been an assassin; the two with him were allowed to leave."

"No, he was not an assassin." The Mother Confessor folded her hands. "I believe Panis Rahl knows of the spell Wizard Zorander discovered, that it has the potential to obliterate all of D'Hara. Panis Rahl is desperate to rid himself of Wizard Zorander."

The Mother Confessor's violet eyes seemed to glisten with a keen intellect. Abby looked away and picked at a stray thread on her sack. "But I don't see what this has to do with denying me help to save my daughter. He has a daughter. Wouldn't he do anything to get her back? Wouldn't he do whatever he must to have his daughter back and safe?"

The Mother Confessor's head lowered and she stroked her fingers over her brow, as if trying to rub at a grievous ache. "The man who came before you was a messenger. His message had been passed through many hands so that it could not be traced back to its source."

Abby felt cold goose bumps running up her arms. "What was the message?"

"The lock of hair he brought was from Zedd's daughter. Panis Rahl offered the life of Zedd's daughter if Zedd would surrender himself to Panis Rahl to be executed."

Abby clutched her sack. "But wouldn't a father who loved his daughter do even this to save her life?"

"At what cost?" the Mother Confessor whispered. "At the cost of the lives of all those who will die without his help?

"He couldn't do such a selfish thing, even to save the life of one he loves more than any other. Before he denied your daughter help, he had just refused the offer, thus sentencing his own innocent daughter to death."

Abby felt her hopes again tumbling into blackness. The thought of Jana's terror, of her being hurt, made Abby dizzy and sick. Tears began running down her cheeks again.

"But I'm not asking him to sacrifice everyone else to save her."

The sorceress gently touched Abby's shoulder. "He believes that sparing those people harm would mean letting the D'Harans escape to kill more people in the end."

Abby snatched desperately for a solution. "But I have a bone."

The sorceress sighed. "Abigail, half the people who come to see a wizard bring a bone. Hucksters convince supplicants that they are true bones. Desperate people, just like you, buy them."

"Most of them come seeking a wizard to somehow give them a life free of magic," the Mother Confessor said. "Most people fear magic, but I'm afraid that with the way it's been used by D'Hara, they now want nothing so much as to never again see magic. An ironic reason to buy a bone, and doubly ironic that they buy sham bones, thinking they have magic, in order to petition to be free of magic."

Abby blinked. "But I bought no bone. This is a debt true. On my mother's deathbed she told me of it. She said it was Wizard Zorander himself bound in it."

The sorceress squinted her skepticism. "Abigail, true debts of this nature are exceedingly rare. Perhaps it was a bone she had and you only thought . . ."

Abby held her sack open for the sorceress to see. The sorceress glanced in and fell silent. The Mother Confessor looked in the sack for herself.

"I know what my mother told me," Abby insisted. "She also told me that if there was any doubt, he had but to test it; then he would know it true, for the debt was passed down to him from his father."

The sorceress stroked the beads at her throat. "He could test it. If it is true, he would know. Still, solemn debt though it may be, that doesn't mean that the debt must be paid now."

Abby leaned boldly toward the sorceress. "My mother said it is a debt true, and that it had to be paid. Please, Delora, you know the nature of such things. I was so confused when I met with him, with all those people shouting. I foolishly failed to press my case by asking that he test it." She turned and clutched the Mother Confessor's arm. "Please, help me? Tell him what I have and ask that he test it?"

The Mother Confessor considered behind a blank expression. At last she spoke. "This involves a debt bound in magic. Such a thing must be considered seriously. I will speak to Wizard Zorander on your behalf and request that you be given a private audience."

Abby squeezed her eyes shut as tears sprang anew. "Thank you." She put her face in both hands and began to weep with relief at the flame of hope rekindled.

The Mother Confessor gripped Abby's shoulders. "I said I will try. He may deny my request."

The sorceress snorted a humorless laugh. "Not likely. I will twist his ear, too. But Abigail, that does not mean that we can convince him to help you—bone or no bone."

Abby wiped her cheek. "I understand. Thank you both. Thank you both for understanding."

With a thumb, the sorceress wiped a tear from Abby's chin. "It is said that the daughter of a sorceress is a daughter to all sorceresses."

The Mother Confessor stood and smoothed her white dress. "Delora, perhaps you could take Abigail to a rooming house for women travelers. She should get some rest. Do you have money, child?"

"Yes, Mother Confessor."

"Good. Delora will take you to a room for the night. Return to the Keep just before sunrise. We will meet you and let you know if we were able to convince Zedd to test your bone."

"I will pray to the good spirits that Wizard Zorander will see me and help my daughter," Abby felt sudden shame at her own words. "And I will pray, too, for his daughter."

The Mother Confessor cupped Abby's cheek. "Pray for all of us, child. Pray that Wizard Zorander unleashes the magic against D'Hara, before it is too late for all the children of the Midlands—old and young alike."

On their walk down to the city, Delora kept the conversation from Abby's worries and hopes, and what magic might contribute to either. In some ways, talking with the sorceress was reminiscent of talking with her mother. Sorceresses evaded talk of magic with one not gifted, daughter or not. Abby got the feeling that it was as uncomfortable for them as it had been for Abby when Jana asked how a mother came to have a child in her tummy.

Even though it was late, the streets were teeming with people. Worried gossip of the war floated to Abby's ears from every direction. At one corner a knot of women murmured tearfully of menfolk gone for months with no word of their fate.

Delora took Abby down a market street and had her buy a small loaf of bread with meats and olives baked right inside. Abby wasn't really hungry. The sorceress made her promise that she would eat. Not wanting to do anything to cause disfavor, Abby promised.

The rooming house was up a side street among tightly packed buildings. The racket of the market carried up the narrow street and flittered around buildings and through tiny courtyards with the ease of a chickadee through a dense wood. Abby wondered how people could stand to live so close together and with nothing to see but other houses and people. She wondered, too, how she was going to be able to sleep with all the strange sounds and noise, but then, sleep had rarely come since she had left home, despite the dead-quiet nights in the countryside.

The sorceress bid Abby a good night, putting her in the hands of a sullen-looking woman of few words who led her to a room at the end of a long hall and left her to her night's rest, after collecting a silver coin. Abby sat on the edge of the bed and, by the light of a single lamp sitting on a shelf by the bed, eyed the small room as she nibbled at the loaf of bread. The meat inside was tough and stringy, but had an agreeable flavor, spiced with salt and garlic.

Without a window, the room wasn't as noisy as Abby had feared it might be. The door had no bolt, but the woman who kept the house had said in a mumble for her not to fret, that no men were allowed in the establishment. Abby set the bread aside and, at a basin atop a simple stand two strides across the room, washed her face. She was surprised at how dirty it left the water.

She twisted the lever stem on the lamp, lowering the wick as far as it would go without snuffing the flame; she didn't like sleeping in the dark in a strange place. Lying in bed, staring up at the water-stained ceiling, she prayed earnestly to the good spirits, despite knowing that they would ignore a request such as she made. She closed her eyes and prayed for Wizard Zorander's daughter, too. Her prayers were fragmented by intruding fears that felt as if they clawed her insides raw.

She didn't know how long she had lain in the bed, wishing for sleep to take her, wishing for morning to come, when the door slowly squeaked open. A shadow climbed the far wall.

Abby froze, eyes wide, breath held tight, as she watched a crouched figure move toward the bed. It wasn't the woman of the house. She would be taller. Abby's fingers tightened on the scratchy blanket, thinking that maybe she could throw it over the intruder and then run for the door.

"Don't be alarmed, dearie. I've just come to see if you had success up at the Keep."

Abby gulped air and she sat up in the bed. "Mariska?" It was the old woman who had waited with her in the keep all day. "You frightened the wits out of me!"

The small flame from the lamp reflected in a sharp shimmer in the woman's eye as she surveyed Abby's face. "Worse things to fear than your own safety."

"What do you mean?"

Mariska smiled. It was not a reassuring smile. "Did you get what you wanted?"

"I saw the First Wizard, if that's what you mean."

"And what did he say, dearie?"

Abby swung her feet down off the bed. "That's my business."

The sly smile widened. "Oh, no, dearie, it's our business."

"What do you mean by that?"

"Answer the question. You've not much time left. Your family has not much time left."

Abby shot to her feet. "How do you—"

The old woman seized Abby's wrist and twisted until Abby was forced to sit. "What say the First Wizard?"

"He said he couldn't help me. Please, that hurts. Let me go."

"Oh, dearie, that's too bad, it is. Too bad for your little Jana."

"How . . . how do you know about her? I never—"

"So, Wizard Zorander denied your petition. Such sad news." She clicked her tongue. "Poor, unfortunate, little Jana. You were warned. You knew the price of failure."

She released Abby's wrist and turned away. Abby's mind raced in hot panic as the woman shuffled toward the door.

"No! Please! I'm to see him again, tomorrow. At sunrise."

Mariska peered back over her shoulder. "Why? Why would he agree to see you again, after he has denied you? Lying will buy your daughter no more time. It will buy her nothing."

"It's true. I swear it on my mother's soul. I talked to the sorceress, the one who took us in. I talked to her and the Mother Confessor, after Wizard Zorander denied my petition. They agreed to convince him to give me a private audience."

Her brow bunched. "Why would they do this?"

Abby pointed to her sack sitting on the end of the bed. "I showed them what I brought."

With one gnarled finger, Mariska lifted open the sack. She looked for a moment and then glided closer to Abby.

"You have yet to show this to Wizard Zorander?"

"That's right. They will get me an audience with him. I'm sure of it. Tomorrow, he will see me."

From her bulky waistband, Mariska drew a knife. She waved it slowly back and forth before Abby's face. "We grow weary of waiting for you."

Abby licked her lips. "But I—"

"In the morning I leave for Coney Crossing. I leave to see your frightened little Jana." Her hand slid behind Abby's neck. Fingers like oak roots gripped Abby's hair, holding her head fast. "If you bring him right behind me, she will go free, as you were promised."

Abby couldn't nod. "I will. I swear. I'll convince him. He is bound by a debt."

Mariska put the point of the knife so close to Abby's eye that it brushed her eyelashes. Abby feared to blink.

"Arrive late, and I will stab my knife in little Jana's eye.

Stab it through. I will leave her the other so that she can watch as I cut out her father's heart, just so that she will know how much it will hurt when I do her. Do you understand, dearie?"

Abby could only whine that she did, as tears streamed down her cheeks.

"There's a good girl," Mariska whispered from so close that Abby was forced to breathe the spicy stink of the woman's sausage dinner. "If we even suspect any tricks, they will all die."

"No tricks. I'll hurry. I'll bring him."

Mariska kissed Abby's forehead. "You're a good mother." She released Abby's hair. "Jana loves you. She cries for you day and night."

After Mariska closed the door, Abby curled into a trembling ball in the bed and wept against her knuckles.

Delora leaned closer as they marched across the broad rampart. "Are you sure you're all right, Abigail?"

Wind snatched at her hair, flicking it across her face. Brushing it from her eyes, Abby looked out at the sprawl of the city below beginning to coalesce out of the gloom. She had been saying a silent prayer to her mother's spirit.

"Yes. I just had a bad night. I couldn't sleep."

The Mother Confessor's shoulder pressed against Abby's from the other side. "We understand. At least he agreed to see you. Take heart in that. He's a good man, he really is."

"Thank you," Abby whispered in shame. "Thank you both for helping me."

The people waiting along the rampart—wizards, sorceresses, officers, and others—all momentarily fell silent and bowed toward the Mother Confessor as the three women passed. Among several people she recognized from the day before, Abby saw the wizard Thomas, grumbling to himself and looking hugely impatient and vexed as he shuffled through a handful of papers covered in what Abby recognized as magical symbols.

At the end of the rampart they came to the stone face of a round turret. A steep roof overhead protruded down low above a round-topped door. The sorceress rapped on the door and opened it without waiting for a reply. She caught the twitch of Abby's brow.

"He rarely hears the knock," she explained in a hushed tone.

The stone room was small, but had a cozy feel to it. A round window to the right overlooked the city below, and another on the opposite side looked up on the soaring walls of the Keep, the distant highest ones glowing pink in the first faint rays of dawn. An elaborate iron candelabrum held a small army of candles that provided a warm glow to the room.

Wizard Zorander, his unruly wavy brown hair hanging down around his face as he leaned on his hands, was absorbed in studying a book lying open on the table. The three women came to a halt.

"Wizard Zorander," the sorceress announced, "we bring Abigail, born of Helsa."

"Bags, woman," the wizard grouched without looking up, "I heard your knock, as I always do."

"Don't you curse at me, Zeddicus Zu'l Zorander," Delora grumbled back.

He ignored the sorceress, rubbing his smooth chin as he considered the book before him. "Welcome, Abigail."

Abby's fingers fumbled at the sack. But then she remembered herself and curtsied. "Thank you for seeing me, Wizard Zorander. It is of vital importance that I have your help. As I've already told you, the lives of innocent children are at stake."

Wizard Zorander finally peered up. After appraising her a long moment he straightened. "Where does the line lie?"

Abby glanced to the sorceress on one side of her and then the Mother Confessor on the other side. Neither looked back.

"Excuse me, Wizard Zorander? The line?"

The wizard's brow drew down. "You imply a higher

value to a life because of a young age. The line, my dear child, across which the value of life becomes petty. Where is the line?"

"But a child—"

He held up a cautionary finger. "Do not think to play on my emotions by plying me with the value of the life of a child, as if a higher value can be placed on life because of age. When is life worth less? Where is the line? At what age? Who decides?

"All life is dear. Dead is dead, no matter the age. Don't think to produce a suspension of my reason with a callous, calculated twisting of emotion, like some slippery officeholder stirring the passions of a mindless mob."

Abby was struck speechless by such an admonition. The wizard turned his attention to the Mother Confessor.

"Speaking of bureaucrats, what did the council have to say for themselves?"

The Mother Confessor clasped her hands and sighed. "I told them your words. Simply put, they didn't care. They want it done."

He grunted his discontent. "Do they, now?" His hazel eyes turned to Abby. "Seems the council doesn't care about the lives of even children, when the children are D'Haran." He wiped a hand across his tired-looking eyes. "I can't say I don't comprehend their reasoning, or that I disagree with them, but dear spirits, they are not the ones to do it. It is not by their hand. It will be by mine."

"I understand, Zedd," the Mother Confessor murmured.

Once again he seemed to notice Abby standing before him. He considered her as if pondering some profound notion. It made her fidget. He held out his hand and waggled his fingers. "Let me see it, then."

Abby stepped closer to the table as she reached in her sack.

"If you cannot be persuaded to help innocent people, then maybe this will mean something more to you."

She drew her mother's skull from the sack and placed it in the wizard's upturned palm. "It is a debt of bones. I declare it due."

One eyebrow lifted. "It is customary to bring only a tiny fragment of bone, child."

Abby felt her face flush. "I didn't know," she stammered. "I wanted to be sure there was enough to test . . . to be sure you would believe me."

He smoothed a gentle hand over the top of the skull. "A piece smaller than a grain of sand is enough." He watched Abby's eyes. "Didn't your mother tell you?"

Abby shook her head. "She said only that it was a debt passed to you from your father. She said the debt must be paid if it was called due."

"Indeed it must," he whispered.

Even as he spoke, his hand was gliding back and forth over the skull. The bone was dull and stained by the dirt from which Abby had pulled it, not at all the pristine white she had fancied it would be. It had horrified her to have to uncover her mother's bones, but the alternative horrified her more.

Beneath the wizard's fingers, the bone of the skull began to glow with soft amber light. Abby's breathing nearly stilled when the air hummed, as if the spirits themselves whispered to the wizard. The sorceress fussed with the beads at her neck. The Mother Confessor chewed her lower lip. Abby prayed.

Wizard Zorander set the skull on the table and turned his back on them. The amber glow faded away.

When he said nothing, Abby spoke into the thick silence. "Well? Are you satisfied? Did your test prove it a debt true?"

"Oh yes," he said quietly without turning toward them. "It is a debt of bones true, bound by the magic invoked until the debt is paid."

Abby's fingers worried at the frayed edge of her sack. "I told you. My mother wouldn't have lied to me. She told me that if not paid while she was alive, it became a debt of bones upon her death."

The wizard slowly rounded to face her. "And did she tell you anything of the engendering of the debt?"

"No." Abby cast a furtive, sidelong glance at Delora before going on. "Sorceresses hold secrets close, and reveal only that which serves their purposes."

With a slight, fleeting smile, he grunted his concurrence.

"She said only that it was your father and she who were bound in it, and that until paid it would continue to pass on to the descendants of each."

"Your mother spoke the truth. But that does not mean that it must be paid now."

"It is a solemn debt of bones." Abby's frustration and fear erupted with venom. "I declare it due! You will yield to the obligation!"

Both the sorceress and the Mother Confessor gazed off at the walls, uneasy at a woman, an ungifted woman, raising her voice to the First Wizard himself. Abby suddenly wondered if she might be struck dead for such insolence. But if he didn't help her, it wouldn't matter.

The Mother Confessor diverted the possible results of Abby's outburst with a question. "Zedd, did your reading tell you of the nature of the engendering of the debt?"

"Indeed it did," he said. "My father, too, told me of a debt. My test has proven to me that this is the one of which he spoke, and that the woman standing before me carries the other half of the link."

"So, what was the engendering?" the sorceress asked.

He turned his palms up. "It seems to have slipped my mind. I'm sorry; I find myself to be more forgetful than usual of late."

Delora sniffed. "And you dare to call sorceresses taciturn?"

Wizard Zorander silently considered her a moment and then turned a squint on the Mother Confessor. "The council wants it done, do they?" He smiled a sly smile. "Then it shall be done."

The Mother Confessor cocked her head. "Zedd . . . are you sure about this?"

"About what?" Abby asked. "Are you going to honor the debt or not?"

The wizard shrugged. "You have declared the debt due."

He plucked a small book from the table and slipped it into a pocket in his robe. "Who am I to argue?"

"Dear spirits," the Mother Confessor whispered to herself. "Zedd, just because the council—"

"I am just a wizard," he said, cutting her off, "serving the wants and wishes of the people."

"But if you travel to this place you would be exposing yourself to needless danger."

"I must be near the border—or it will claim parts of the Midlands, too. Coney Crossing is as good a place as any other to ignite the conflagration."

Beside herself with relief, Abby was hardly hearing anything else he said. "Thank you, Wizard Zorander. Thank you."

He strode around the table and gripped her shoulder with sticklike fingers of surprising strength.

"We are bound, you and I, in a debt of bones. Our life paths have intersected." His smile looked at once sad and sincere. His powerful fingers closed around her wrist, around her bracelet, and he put her mother's skull in her hands. "Please, Abby, call me Zedd."

Near tears, she nodded. "Thank you, Zedd."

Outside, in the early light, they were accosted by the waiting crowd. Wizard Thomas, waving his papers, shoved his way through.

"Zorander! I've been studying these elements you've provided. I have to talk to you."

"Talk, then," the First Wizard said as he marched by. The crowd followed in his wake.

"This is madness."

"I never said it wasn't."

Wizard Thomas shook the papers as if for proof. "You can't do this, Zorander!"

"The council has decided that it is to be done. The war must be ended while we have the upper hand and before Panis Rahl comes up with something we won't be able to counter."

"No, I mean I've studied this thing, and you won't be

able to do it. We don't understand the power those wizards wielded. I've looked over the elements you've shown me. Even trying to invoke such a thing will create intense heat."

Zedd halted and put his face close to Thomas. He lifted his eyebrows in mock surprise. "Really, Thomas? Do you think? Igniting a light spell that will rip the fabric of the world of life might cause an instability in the elements of the web field?"

Thomas charged after as Zedd stormed off. "Zorander! You won't be able to control it! If you were able to invoke it—and I'm not saying I believe you can—you would breach the Grace. The invocation uses heat. The breach feeds it. You won't be able to control the cascade. No one can do such a thing!"

"I can do it," the First Wizard muttered.

Thomas shook the fists of papers in a fury. "Zorander, your arrogance will be the end of us all! Once parted, the veil will be rent and all life will be consumed. I demand to see the book in which you found this spell. I demand to see it myself. The whole thing, not just parts of it!"

The First Wizard paused and lifted a finger. "Thomas, if you were meant to see the book, then you would be First Wizard and have access to the First Wizard's private enclave. But you are not, and you don't."

Thomas's face glowed scarlet above his white bread. "This is a foolhardy act of desperation!"

Wizard Zorander flicked the finger. The papers flew from the old wizard's hand and swirled up into a whirlwind, there to ignite, flaring into ashes that lifted away on the wind.

"Sometimes, Thomas, all that is left to you is an act of desperation. I am First Wizard, and I will do as I must. That is the end of it. I will hear no more." He turned and snatched the sleeve of an officer. "Alert the lancers. Gather all the cavalry available. We ride for Pendisan Reach at once."

The man thumped a quick salute to his chest before dashing off. Another officer, older and looking to be of much higher rank, cleared his throat.

"Wizard Zorander, may I know of your plan?"

"It is Anargo," the First Wizard said, "who is the right hand of Panis Rahl, and in conjunction with Rahl conjures death to stalk us. Quite simply put, I intend to send death back at them."

"By leading the lancers into Pendisan Reach?"

"Yes. Anargo holds at Coney Crossing. We have General Brainard driving north toward Pendisan Reach, General Sanderson sweeping south to join with him, and Mardale charging up from the southwest. We will go in there with the lancers and whoever of the rest of them is able to join with us."

"Anargo is no fool. We don't know how many other wizards and gifted he has with him, but we know what they're capable of. They've bled us time and time again. At last we have dealt them a blow." The officer chose his words carefully. "Why do you think they wait? Why wouldn't they simply slip back into D'Hara?"

Zedd rested a hand on the crenellated wall and gazed out on the dawn, out on the city below.

"Anargo relishes the game. He performs it with high drama; he wants us to think them wounded. Pendisan Reach is the only terrain in all those mountains that an army can get through with any speed. Coney Crossing provides a wide field for battle, but not wide enough to let us maneuver easily, or flank them. He is trying to bait us in."

The officer didn't seem surprised. "But why?"

Zedd looked back over his shoulder at the officer. "Obviously, he believes that in such terrain he can defeat us. I believe otherwise. He knows that we can't allow the menace to remain there, and he knows our plans. He thinks to draw me in, kill me, and end the threat I alone hold over them."

"So . . ." the officer reasoned aloud, "you are saying that for Anargo, it is worth the risk."

"If Anargo is right, he could win it all at Coney Crossing. When he has finished me, he will turn his gifted loose, slaughter the bulk of our forces all in one place, and then, virtually unopposed, cut out the heart of the Midlands:"—

Zedd swept his arm out, indicating the city below the Wizard's Keep—"Aydindril."

"Anargo plans that before the snow flies, he will have killed me, annihilated our joint forces, have the people of the Midlands in chains, and be able to hand the whip to Panis Rahl."

The officer stared, dumbfounded. "And you plan to do as Anargo is hoping and go in there to face him?"

Zedd shrugged. "What choice have I?"

"And do you at least know how Anargo plans to kill you, so that we might take precautions? Take countermeasures?"

"I'm afraid not." Vexed, he waved his hand, dismissing the matter. He turned to Abby. "The lancers have swift horses. We will ride hard. We will be to your home soon—we will be there in time—and then we'll see to our business."

Abby only nodded. She couldn't put into words the relief of her petition granted, nor could she express the shame she felt to have her prayer answered. But most of all, she couldn't utter a word of her horror at what she was doing, for she knew the D'Harans' plan.

Flies swarmed around dried scraps of viscera, all that was left of Abby's prized bearded pigs. Apparently, even the breeding stock, which Abby's parents had given her as a wedding gift, had been slaughtered and taken.

Abby's parents, too, had chosen Abby's husband. Abby had never met him before: he came from the town of Lynford, where her mother and father bought the pigs. Abby had been beside herself with anxiety over who her parents would choose for her husband. She had hoped for a man who would be of good cheer—a man to bring a smile to the difficulties of life.

When she first saw Philip, she thought he must be the most serious man in all the world. His young face looked to her as if it had never once smiled. That first night after meeting him, she had cried herself to sleep over thoughts of sharing her life with so solemn a man. She thought her life caught up on the sharp tines of grim fate.

Abby came to find that Philip was a hardworking man who looked out at life through a great grin. That first day she had seen him, she only later learned, he had been putting on his most sober face so that his new family would not think him a slacker unworthy of their daughter. In a short time, Abby had come to know that Philip was a man upon whom she could depend. By the time Jana had been born, she had come to love him.

Now Philip, and so many others, depended upon her.

Abby brushed her hands clean after putting her mother's bones to rest once more. The fences Jana had watched Philip so often mend, she saw, were all broken down. Coming back around the house, she noticed that barn doors were missing. Anything an animal or human could eat was gone. Abby could not recall having ever seen her home looking so barren.

It didn't matter, she told herself. It didn't matter, if only Jana would be returned to her. Fences could be mended. Pigs could be replaced, somehow, someday. Jana could never be replaced.

"Abby," Zedd asked as he peered around at the ruins of her home, "how is it that you weren't taken, when your husband and daughter and everyone else were?"

Abby stepped through the broken doorway, thinking that her home had never looked so small. Before she had gone to Aydindril, to the Wizard's Keep, her home had seemed as big as anything she could imagine. Here, Philip had laughed and filled the simple room with his comfort and conversation. With charcoal he had drawn animals on the stone hearth for Jana.

Abby pointed. "Under that door is the root cellar. That's where I was when I heard the things I told you about."

Zedd ran the toe of his boot across the knothole used as a fingerhold to lift the hatch. "They were taking your husband, and your daughter, and you stayed down there? While your daughter was screaming for you, you didn't run up to help her?"

Abby summoned her voice. "I knew that if I came up, they would have me, too. I knew that the only chance my family had was if I waited and then went for help. My mother always told me that even a sorceress was no more than a fool if she acted one. She always told me to think things through, first."

"Wise advice." Zedd set down a ladle that had been bent and holed. He rested a gentle hand on her shoulder. "It would have been hard to leave your daughter crying for you, and do the wise thing."

Abby could only manage a whisper. "You speak the spirits' own truth." She pointed through the window on the side wall. "That way—across the Coney River—lies town. They took Jana and Philip with them as they went on to take all the people from town. They had others, too, that they had already captured. The army set up camp in the hills beyond."

Zedd stood at the window, gazing out at the distant hills. "Soon, I hope, this war will be ended. Dear spirits, let it end."

Remembering the Mother Confessor's admonition not to repeat the story she told, Abby never asked about the wizard's daughter or murdered wife. When on their swift journey back to Coney Crossing she spoke of her love for Jana, it must have broken his heart to think of his own daughter in the brutal hands of the enemy, knowing that he had left her to death lest many more die.

Zedd pushed open the bedroom door. "And back here?" he asked as he put his head into the room beyond.

Abby looked up from her thoughts. "The bedroom. In the rear is a door back to the garden and the barn."

Though he never once mentioned his dead wife or missing daughter, Abby's knowledge of them ate away at her as a swelling spring river ate at a hole in the ice.

Zedd stepped back in from the bedroom as Delora came silently slipping in through the front doorway. "As Abigail said, the town across the river has been sacked," the sorceress reported. "From the looks of it, the people were all taken."

Zedd brushed back his wavy hair. "How close is the river?"

Abby gestured out the window. Night was falling. "Just there. A walk of five minutes."

In the valley, on its way to join the Kern, the Coney River slowed and spread wide, so that it became shallow enough to cross easily. There was no bridge; the road simply led to the river's edge and took up again on the other side. Though the river was near to a quarter mile across in most of the valley, it was in no place much more than knee-deep. Only in the spring melt was it occasionally treacherous to cross. The town of Coney Crossing was two miles beyond, up on the rise of hills, safe from spring floods, as was the knoll where Abby's farmyard stood.

Zedd took Delora by the elbow. "Ride back and tell everyone to hold station. If anything goes wrong . . . well, if anything goes wrong, then they must attack. Anargo's legion must be stopped, even if they have to go into D'Hara after them."

Delora did not look pleased. "Before we left, the Mother Confessor made me promise that I would be sure that you were not left alone. She told me to see to it that gifted were always near if you needed them."

Abby, too, had heard the Mother Confessor issue the orders. Looking back at the Keep as they had crossed the stone bridge, Abby had seen the Mother Confessor up on a high rampart, watching them leave. The Mother Confessor had helped when Abby had feared all was lost. She wondered what would become of the woman.

Then she remembered that she didn't have to wonder. She knew.

The wizard ignored what the sorceress had said. "As soon as I help Abby, I'll send her back, too. I don't want anyone near when I unleash the spell."

Delora gripped his collar and pulled him close. She looked as if she might be about to give him a heated scolding. Instead she drew him into an embrace.

"Please, Zedd," she whispered, "don't leave us without you as First Wizard."

Zedd smoothed back her dark hair. "And abandon you all to Thomas?" He smirked. "Never."

The dust from Delora's horse drifted away into the gathering darkness as Zedd and Abby descended the slope toward the river. Abby led him along the path through the tall grasses and rushes, explaining that the path would offer them better concealment than the road. Abby was thankful that he didn't argue for the road.

Her eyes darted from the deep shadows on one side to the shadows on the other as they were swallowed into the brush. Her pulse raced. She flinched whenever a twig snapped underfoot.

It happened as she feared it would, as she knew it would.

A figure enfolded in a long hooded cloak darted out of nowhere, knocking Abby aside. She saw the flash of a blade as Zedd flipped the attacker into the brush. He squatted, putting a hand back on Abby's shoulder as she lay in the grass panting.

"Stay down," he whispered urgently.

Light gathered at his fingers. He was conjuring magic. That was what they wanted him to do.

Tears welled, burning her eyes. She snatched his sleeve. "Zedd, don't use magic." She could hardly speak past the tightening pain in her chest. "Don't—"

The figure sprang again from the gloom of the bushes. Zedd threw up a hand. The night lit with a flash of hot light that struck the cloaked figure.

Rather than the assailant going down, it was Zedd who cried out and crumpled to the ground. Whatever he had thought to do to the attacker, it had been turned back on him, and he was in the grip of the most terrible anguish, preventing him from rising, or speaking. That was why they had wanted him to conjure magic: so they could capture him.

The figure standing over the wizard glowered at Abby. "Your part here is finished. Go."

Abby scuttled into the grass. The woman pushed the hood back, and cast off her cloak. In the near darkness, Abby could see the woman's long braid and red leather uniform. It was one of the women Abby had been told about, the women used to capture those with magic: the Mord Sith.

The Mord-Sith watched with satisfaction as the wizard at her feet writhed in choking pain. "Well, well. Looks like the First Wizard himself has just made a very big mistake."

The belts and straps of her red leather uniform creaked as she leaned down toward him, grinning at his agony. "I have been given the whole night to make you regret ever having lifted a finger to resist us. In the morning I'm to allow you to watch as our forces annihilate your people. Afterward, I am to take you to Lord Rahl himself, the man who ordered the death of your wife, so you can beg him to order me to kill you, too." She kicked him. "So you can beg Lord Rahl for your death, as you watch your daughter die before your eyes."

Zedd could only scream in horror and pain.

On her hands and knees, Abby crabbed her way farther back into the weeds and rushes. She wiped at her eyes, trying to see. She was horrified to witness what was being done to the man who had agreed to help her for no more reason than a debt to her mother. By contrast, these people had coerced her service by holding hostage the life of her child.

As she backed away, Abby saw the knife the Mord-Sith had dropped when Zedd had thrown her into the weeds. The knife was a pretext, used to provoke him to act; it was magic that was the true weapon. The Mord-Sith had used his own magic against him—used it to cripple and capture him, and now used it to hurt him.

It was the price demanded. Abby had complied. She had had no choice.

But what toll was she imposing on others?

How could she save her daughter's life at the cost of so many others? Would Jana grow up to be a slave to people who would do this? With a mother who would allow it? Jana would grow up to learn to bow to Panis Rahl and his minions, to submit to evil, or worse, grow up to become a willing part in the scourge, never tasting liberty or knowing the value of honor.

With dreadful finality, everything seemed to fall to ruin in Abby's mind.

She snatched up the knife. Zedd was wailing in pain as the Mord-Sith bent, doing some foul thing to him. Before she had time to lose her resolve, Abby was moving toward the woman's back.

Abby had butchered animals. She told herself that this was no different. These were not people, but animals. She lifted the knife.

A hand clamped over her mouth. Another seized her wrist.

Abby moaned against the hand, against her failure to stop this madness when she had had the chance. A mouth close to her ear urged her to hush.

Struggling against the figure in hooded cloak that held her, Abby turned her head as much as she could, and in the last of the daylight saw violet eyes looking back. For a moment she couldn't make sense of it, couldn't make sense of how the woman could be there when Abby had seen her remain behind. But it truly was her.

Abby stilled. The Mother Confessor released her and, with a quick hand signal, urged her back. Abby didn't question; she scurried back into the rushes as the Mother Confessor reached out toward the woman in red leather. The Mord-Sith was bent over, intent on her grisly business with the screaming wizard.

In the distance, bugs chirped and clicked. Frogs called with insistent croaks. Not far away the river sloshed and burbled as it always did—a familiar, comforting sound of home.

And then there came a sudden, violent concussion to the air. Thunder without sound. It drove the wind from Abby's lungs. The wallop nearly knocked her senseless, making every joint in her body burn in sharp pain.

There was no flash of light—just that pure and flawless jolt to the air. The world seemed to stop in its terrible splendor.

Grass flattened as if in a wind radiating out in a ring from the Mord-Sith and the Mother Confessor. Abby's senses returned as the pain in her joints thankfully melted away.

Abby had never seen it done before, and had never expected to see it in the whole of her life, but she knew without doubt that she had just witnessed a Confessor unleashing her power. From what Abby's mother had told her, it was the destruction of a person's mind so complete that it left only numb devotion to the Confessor. She had but to ask and they would confess any truth, no matter the crime they had previously attempted to conceal or deny.

"Mistress," the Mord-Sith moaned in piteous lamentation.

Abby, first staggered by the shock of the soundless thunder of the Mother Confessor's power, and now stunned by the abject anguish of the woman crumpled on the ground, felt a hand grip her arm. It was the wizard.

With the back of his other hand he wiped blood from his mouth. He labored to get his breath. "Leave her to it."

"Zedd . . . I . . . I'm so sorry. I tried to tell you not to use magic, but I didn't call loud enough for you to hear."

He managed to smile through obvious pain. "I heard you."

"But why then did you use your gift?"

"I thought that in the end, you would not be the kind of person to do such a terrible thing, and that you would show your true heart." He pulled her away from the cries. "We used you. We wanted them to think they had succeeded."

"You knew what I was going to do? You knew I was to bring you to them so that they could capture you?"

"I had a good idea. From the first there seemed more to you than you presented. You are not very talented at being a spy and a traitor. Since we arrived here you've been watching the shadows and jumping at the chirp of every bug."

The Mother Confessor rushed up. "Zedd, are you all right?"

He put a hand on her shoulder. "I'll be fine." His eyes still held the glaze of terror. "Thank you for not being late. For a moment, I feared . . ."

"I know." The Mother Confessor offered a quick smile. "Let us hope your trick was worth it. You have until dawn.

She said they expect her to torture you all night before bringing you to them in the morning. Their scouts alerted Anargo to our troops' arrival."

Back in the rushes the Mord-Sith was screaming as though she were being flayed alive.

Shivers ran through Abby's shoulders. "They'll hear her and know what's happened."

"Even if they could hear at this distance, they will think it is Zedd, being tortured by her." The Mother Confessor took the knife from Abby's hand. "I am glad that you rewarded my faith and in the end chose not to join with them."

Abby wiped her palms on her skirts, shamed by all she had done, by what she had intended to do. She was beginning to shake. "Are you going to kill her?"

The Mother Confessor, despite looking bone-weary after having touched the Mord-Sith, still had iron resolve in her eyes. "A Mord-Sith is different from anyone else. She does not recover from the touch of a Confessor. She would suffer in profound agony until she died, sometime before morning." She glanced back toward the cries. "She has told us what we need to know, and Zedd must have his power back. It is the merciful thing to do."

"It also buys me time to do what I must do." Zedd's fingers turned Abby's face toward him, away from the shrieks. "And time to get Jana back. You will have until morning."

"I will have until morning? What do you mean?"

"I'll explain. But we must hurry if you are to have enough time. Now, take off your clothes."

Abby was running out of time.

She moved through the D'Haran camp, holding herself stiff and tall, trying not to look frantic, even though that was how she felt. All night long she had been doing as the wizard had instructed: acting haughty. To anyone who noticed her, she directed disdain. To anyone who looked her way, thinking to speak to her, she growled.

Not that many, though, so much as dared to catch the

attention of what appeared to be a red-leather-clad Mord-Sith. Zedd had told her, too, to keep the Mord-Sith's weapon in her fist. It looked like nothing more than a small red leather rod. How it worked, Abby had no idea—the wizard had said only that it involved magic, and she wouldn't be able to call it to her aid—but it did have an effect on those who saw it in her hand: it made them melt back into the darkness, away from the light of the campfires, away from Abby.

Those who were awake, anyway. Although most people in the camp were sleeping, there was no shortage of alert guards. Zedd had cut the long braid from the Mord-Sith who had attacked him, and tied it into Abby's hair. In the dark, the mismatch of color wasn't obvious. When the guards looked at Abby they saw a Mord-Sith, and quickly turned their attention elsewhere.

By the apprehension on people's faces when they saw her coming, Abby knew she must look fearsome. They didn't know how her heart pounded. She was thankful for the mantle of night so that the D'Harans couldn't see her knees trembling. She had seen only two real Mord-Sith, both sleeping, and she had kept far away from them, as Zedd had warned her. Real Mord-Sith were not likely to be fooled so easily.

Zedd had given her until dawn. Time was running out. He had told her that if she wasn't back in time, she would die.

Abby was thankful she knew the lay of the land, or long since she would have become lost among the confusion of tents, campfires, wagons, horses, and mules. Everywhere pikes and lances were stacked upright in circles with their points leaning together. Men—farriers, fletchers, blacksmiths, and craftsmen of all sorts—worked through the night.

The air was thick with woodsmoke and rang with the sound of metal being shaped and sharpened and wood being worked for everything from bows to wagons. Abby didn't know how people could sleep through the noise, but sleep they did.

Shortly the immense camp would wake to a new day—a day of battle, a day the soldiers went to work doing what they did best. They were getting a good night's sleep so they would be rested for the killing of the Midlands army. From what she had heard, D'Haran soldiers were very good at their job.

Abby had searched relentlessly, but she had been unable to find her father, her husband, or her daughter. She had no intention of giving up. She had resigned herself to the knowledge that if she didn't find them, she would die with them.

She had found captives tied together and staked to trees, or the ground, to keep them from running. Many more were chained. Some she recognized, but many more she didn't. Most were kept in groups and under guard.

Abby never once saw a guard asleep at his post. When they looked her way, she acted as if she were looking for someone, and she wasn't going to go easy on them when she found them. Zedd had told her that her safety, and the safety of her family, depended on her playing the part convincingly. Abby thought about these people hurting her daughter, and it wasn't hard to act angry.

But she was running out of time. She couldn't find them, and she knew that Zedd would not wait. Too much was at stake; she understood that, now. She was coming to appreciate that the wizard and the Mother Confessor were trying to stop a war; that they were people resolved to the dreadful task of weighing the lives of a few against the lives of many.

Abby lifted another tent flap, and saw soldiers sleeping. She squatted and looked at the faces of prisoners tied to wagons. They stared back with hollow expressions. She bent to gaze at the faces of children pressed together in nightmares. She couldn't find Jana. The huge camp sprawled across the hilly countryside; there were a thousand places she could be.

As she marched along a crooked line of tents, she scratched at her wrist. Only when she went farther did she notice that it was the bracelet warming that made her wrist itch. It warmed yet more as she proceeded, but then the warmth began fading. Her brow twitched. Out of curiosity, she turned and went back the way she had come.

Where a pathway between tents turned off, her bracelet tingled again with warmth. Abby paused a moment, looking off into the darkness. The sky was just beginning to color with light. She took the path between the tents, following until the bracelet cooled, then backtracked to where it warmed again and took a new direction where it warmed yet more.

Abby's mother had given her the bracelet, telling her to wear it always, and that someday it would be of value. Abby wondered if somehow the bracelet had magic that would help her find her daughter. With dawn nearing, this seemed the only chance she had left. She hurried onward, wending where the warmth from the bracelet directed.

The bracelet led her to an expanse of snoring soldiers. There were no prisoners in sight. Guards patrolled the men in bedrolls and blankets. There was one tent set among the big men—for an officer, she guessed.

Not knowing what else to do, Abby strode among the sleeping men. Near the tent, the bracelet sent tingling heat up her arm.

Abby saw that sentries hung around the small tent like flies around meat. The canvas sides glowed softly, probably from a candle inside. Off to the side, she noticed a sleeping form different from the men. As she got closer, she saw that it was a woman; Mariska.

The old woman breathed with a little raspy whistle as she slept. Abby stood paralyzed. Guards looked up at her.

Needing to do something before they asked any questions, Abby scowled at them and marched toward the tent. She tried not to make any noise; the guards might think she was a Mord-Sith, but Mariska would not long be fooled. A glare from Abby turned the guards' eyes to the dark countryside.

Her heart pounding nearly out of control, Abby gripped the tent flap. She knew Jana would be inside. She told herself that she must not cry out when she saw her daughter. She reminded herself that she must put a hand over Jana's mouth before she could cry out with joy, lest they be caught before they had a chance to escape.

The bracelet was so hot it felt as if it would blister her skin. Abby ducked into the low tent.

A trembling little girl huddled in a tattered wool cloak sat in blankets on the ground. She stared up with big eyes that blinked with the terror of what might come next. Abby felt a stab of anguish. It was not Jana.

They stared at each other. The child's face was lit clearly by the candle set to the side, as Abby's must be. In those big gray eyes that looked to have beheld unimaginable terrors, the little girl seemed to reach a judgment.

Her arms stretched up in supplication.

Instinctively, Abby fell to her knees and scooped up the little girl, hugging her small trembling body. The girl's spindly arms came out from the tattered cloak and wrapped around Abby's neck, holding on for dear life.

"Help me? Please?" the child whimpered in Abby's ear.

Before she had picked her up she had seen the face in the candlelight. There was no doubt in Abby's mind. It was Zedd's daughter.

"I've come to help you," Abby comforted. "Zedd sent me."

The child moaned expectantly.

Abby held the girl out at arm's length. "I'll take you to your father, but you mustn't let these people know I'm rescuing you. Can you play along with me? Can you pretend that you're my prisoner, so that I can get you away?"

Near tears, the girl nodded. She had the same wavy hair as Zedd, and the same eyes, although they were an arresting gray, not hazel.

"Good," Abby whispered, cupping a chilly cheek, almost lost in those gray eyes. "Trust me, then, and I will get you away."

"I trust you," came the small voice.

Abby snatched up a rope lying nearby and looped it

around the girl's neck. "I'll try not to hurt you, but I must make them think you are my prisoner."

The girl cast a worried look at the rope, as if she knew the rope well, and then nodded that she would go along.

Abby stood, once outside the tent, and by the rope pulled the child out after her. The guards looked her way. Abby started out.

One of them scowled as he stepped close. "What's going on?"

Abby stomped to a halt and lifted the red leather rod, pointing it at the guard's nose. "She has been summoned. And who are you to question? Get out of my way or I'll have you gutted and cleaned for my breakfast!"

The man paled and hurriedly stepped aside. Before he had time to reconsider, Abby charged off, the girl in tow at the end of the rope, dragging her heels, making it look real.

No one followed. Abby wanted to run, but she couldn't. She wanted to carry the girl, but she couldn't. It had to look as if a Mord-Sith were taking a prisoner away.

Rather than take the shortest route back to Zedd, Abby followed the hills upriver to a place where the trees offered concealment almost to the water's edge. Zedd had told her where to cross, and warned her not to return by a different way; he had set traps of magic to prevent the D'Harans from charging down from the hills to stop whatever it was he was going to do.

Closer to the river she saw, downstream a ways, a bank of fog hanging close to the ground. Zedd had emphatically warned her not to go near any fog. She suspected that it was a poison cloud of some sort that he had conjured.

The sound of the water told her she was close to the river. The pink sky provided enough light to finally see it when she reached the edge of the trees. Although she could see the massive camp on the hills in the distance behind her, she saw no one following.

Abby took the rope from the child's neck. The girl watched her with those big round eyes. Abby lifted her and held her tight.

"Hold on, and keep quiet."

Pressing the girl's head to her shoulder, Abby ran for the river.

There was light, but it was not the dawn. They had crossed the frigid water and made the other side when she first noticed it. Even as she ran along the river's bank, before she could see the source of the light, Abby knew that magic was being called there that was unlike any magic she had ever seen before. A sound, low and thin, whined up the river toward her. A smell, as if the air itself had been burned, hung along the riverbank.

The little girl clung to Abby, tears running down her face, afraid to speak—afraid, it seemed, to hope that she had at last been rescued, as if asking a question might somehow make it all vanish like a dream, upon waking. Abby felt tears coursing down her own cheeks.

When she rounded a bend in the river, she spotted the wizard. He stood in the center of the river, on a rock that Abby had never before seen. The rock was just large enough to clear the surface of the water by a few inches, making it almost appear as if the wizard stood on the surface of the water.

Before him as he faced toward distant D'Hara, shapes, dark and wavering, floated in the air. They curled around, as if confiding in him, conversing, warning, tempting him with floating arms and reaching fingers that wreathed like smoke.

Animate light twisted up around the wizard. Colors both dark and wondrous glimmered about him, cavorting with the shadowy forms undulating through the air. It was at once the most enchanting and the most frightening thing Abby had ever seen. No magic her mother conjured had ever seemed . . . aware.

But the most frightening thing by far was what hovered in the air before the wizard. It appeared to be a molten sphere, so hot it glowed from within, its surface a crackling of fluid dross. An arm of water from the river magically turned skyward in a fountain spray and poured down over the rotating silvery mass.

The water hissed and steamed as it hit the sphere, leaving behind clouds of white vapor to drift away in the gentle dawn wind. The molten form blackened at the touch of the water cascading over it, and yet the intense inner heat melted the glassy surface again as fast as the water cooled it, making the whole thing bubble and boil in midair, a pulsing sinister menace.

Transfixed, Abby let the child slip to the silty ground.

The little girl's arms stretched out. "Papa."

He was too far away to hear her, but he heard.

Zedd turned, at once larger than life in the midst of magic Abby could see but not begin to fathom, yet at the same time small with the frailty of human need. Tears filled his eyes as he gazed at his daughter standing beside Abby. This man who seemed to be consulting with spirits looked as if for the first time he were seeing a true apparition.

Zedd leaped off the rock and charged through the water. When he reached her and took her up in the safety of his arms, she began to wail at last with the contained terror released.

"There, there, dear one," Zedd comforted. "Papa is here now."

"Oh, Papa," she cried against his neck, "they hurt Mama. They were wicked. They hurt her so . . ."

He hushed her tenderly. "I know, dear one. I know."

For the first time, Abby saw the sorceress and the Mother Confessor standing off to the side, watching. They, too, shed tears at what they were seeing. Though Abby was glad for the wizard and his daughter, the sight only intensified the pain in her chest at what she had lost. She was choked with tears.

"There, there, dear one," Zedd was cooing. "You're safe, now. Papa won't let anything happen to you. You're safe now."

Zedd turned to Abby. By the time he had smiled his tearful appreciation, the child was asleep.

"A little spell," he explained when Abby's brow twitched with surprise. "She needs to rest. I need to finish what I am doing."

He put his daughter in Abby's arms. "Abby, would you take her up to your house where she can sleep until I'm finished here? Please, put her in bed and cover her up to keep her warm. She will sleep for now."

Thinking about her own daughter in the hands of the brutes across the river, Abby could only nod before turning to the task. She was happy for Zedd, and even felt pride at having rescued his little girl, but as she ran for her home, she was near to dying with grief over her failure to recover her own family.

Abby settled the dead weight of the sleeping child into her bed. She drew the curtain across the small window in her bedroom and, unable to resist, smoothed back silky hair and pressed a kiss to the soft brow before leaving the girl to her blessed rest.

With the child safe at last and asleep, Abby raced back down the knoll to the river. She thought to ask Zedd to give her just a little more time so she could return to look for her own daughter. Fear for Jana had her heart pounding wildly. He owed her a debt, and had not yet seen it through.

Wringing her hands, Abby came to a panting halt at the water's edge. She watched the wizard up on his rock in the river, light and shadow coursing up around him. She had been around magic enough to have the sense to fear approaching him. She could hear his chanted words; though they were words she had never heard before, she recognized the idiosyncratic cadence of words spoken in a spell, words calling together frightful forces.

On the ground beside her was the strange Grace she had seen him draw before, the one that breached the worlds of life and death. The Grace was drawn with a sparkling, pure white sand that stood out in stark relief against the dark silt. Abby shuddered even to look upon it, much less contemplate its meaning. Around the Grace, carefully drawn with the same sparkling white sand, were geometric forms of magical invocations.

Abby lowered her fists, about to call out to the wizard, when Delora leaned close. Abby flinched in surprise.

"Not now, Abigail," the sorceress murmured. "Don't disturb him in the middle of this part."

Reluctantly, Abby heeded the sorceress's words. The Mother Confessor was there, too. Abby chewed her bottom lip as she watched the wizard throw up his arms. Sparkles of colored light curled up along twisting shafts of shadows. "But I must. I haven't been able to find my family. He must help me. He must save them. It's a debt of bones that must be satisfied."

The other two women shared a look. "Abby," the Mother Confessor said, "he gave you a chance, gave you time. He tried. He did his best, but he has everyone else to think of, now."

The Mother Confessor took up Abby's hand, and the sorceress put an arm around Abby's shoulders as she stood weeping on the riverbank. It wasn't supposed to end this way, not after all she had been through, not after all she had done. Despair crushed her.

The wizard, his arms raised, called forth more light, more shadows, more magic. The river roiled around him. The hissing thing in the air grew as it slowly slumped closer to the water. Shafts of light shot from the hot, rotating bloom of power.

The sun was rising over the hills behind the D'Harans. This part of the river wasn't as wide as elsewhere, and Abby could see the activity in the trees beyond. Men moved about, but the fog hanging on the far bank kept them wary, kept them in the trees.

Also across the river, at the edge of the tree-covered hills, another wizard had appeared to conjure magic. He too stood atop a rock as his arms launched sparkling light up into the air. Abby thought that the strong morning sun might outshine the conjured illuminations, but it didn't.

Abby could stand it no longer. "Zedd!" she called out across the river. "Zedd! Please, you promised! I found your daughter! What about mine? Please don't do this until she is safe!"

Zedd turned and looked at her as if from a great distance, as if from another world. Arms of dark forms caressed him. Fingers of dark smoke dragged along his jaw, urging his attention back to them, but he gazed instead at Abby.

"I'm so sorry." Despite the distance, Abby could clearly hear his whispered words. "I gave you time to try to find them. I can spare no more, or countless other mothers will weep for their children—mothers still living, and mothers in the spirit world."

Abby cried out in an anguished wail as he turned back to the ensorcellment. The two women tried to comfort her, but Abby was not to be comforted in her grief.

Thunder rolled through the hills. A clacking clamor from the spell around Zedd rose to echo up and down the valley. Shafts of intense light shot upward. It was a disorienting sight, light shining up into sunlight.

Across the river, the counter to Zedd's magic seemed to spring forth. Arms of light twisted like smoke, lowering to tangle with the light radiating up around Zedd. The fog along the riverbank diffused suddenly.

In answer, Zedd spread his arms wide. The glowing tumbling furnace of molten light thundered. The water sluicing over it roared as it boiled and steamed. The air wailed as if in protest.

Behind the wizard, across the river, the D'Haran soldiers were pouring out of the trees, driving their prisoners before them. People cried out in terror. They quailed at the wizard's magic, only to be driven onward by the spears and swords at their backs.

Abby saw several who refused to move fall to the blades. At the mortal cries, the rest rushed onward, like sheep before wolves.

If whatever Zedd was doing failed, the army of the Midlands would then charge into this valley to confront the enemy. The prisoners would be caught in the middle.

A figure worked its way up along the opposite bank, dragging a child behind. Abby's flesh flashed icy cold with sudden frigid sweat. It was Mariska. Abby shot a quick glance back over her shoulder. It was impossible. She squinted across the river.

"Nooo!" Zedd called out.

It was Zedd's little girl that Mariska had by the hair.

Somehow, Mariska had followed and found the child sleeping in Abby's home. With no one there to watch over her as she slept, Mariska had stolen the child back.

Mariska held the child out before herself, for Zedd to see. "Cease and surrender, Zorander, or she dies!"

Abby tore away from the arms holding her and charged into the water. She struggled to run against the current, to reach the wizard. Part way there, he turned to stare into her eyes.

Abby froze. "I'm sorry." Her own voice sounded to her like a plea before death. "I thought she was safe."

Zedd nodded in resignation. It was out of his hands. He turned back to the enemy. His arms lifted to his sides. His fingers spread, as if commanding all to stop—magic and men alike.

"Let the prisoners go!" Zedd called across the water to the enemy wizard. "Let them go, Anargo, and I'll give you all your lives!"

Anargo's laugh rang out over the water.

"Surrender," Mariska hissed, "or she dies."

The old woman pulled the knife she kept in the wrap around her waist. She pressed the blade to the child's throat. The girl was screaming in terror, her arms reaching to her father, her little fingers clawing the air.

Abby struggled ahead into the water. She called out, begging Mariska to let Zedd's daughter go free. The woman paid no more heed to Abby than to Zedd.

"Last chance!" Mariska called.

"You heard her," Anargo growled out across the water. "Surrender now or she will die."

"You know I can't put myself above my people!" Zedd called back. "This is between us, Anargo! Let them all go!"

Anargo's laugh echoed up and down the river. "You are a fool, Zorander! You had your chance!" His expression twisted to rage. "Kill her!" he screamed to Mariska.

Fists at his side, Zedd shrieked. The sound seemed to split the morning with its fury.

Mariska lifted the squealing child by her hair. Abby gasped in disbelief as the woman sliced the little girl's throat.

The child flailed. Blood spurted across Mariska's gnarly fingers as she viciously sawed the blade back and forth. She gave a final, mighty yank of the knife. The blood-soaked body dropped in a limp heap. Abby felt vomit welling up in the back of her throat. The silty dirt of the riverbank turned a wet red.

Mariska held the severed head high with a howl of victory. Strings of flesh and blood swung beneath it. The mouth hung in a slack, silent cry.

Abby threw her arms around Zedd's legs. "Dear spirits, I'm sorry! Oh, Zedd, forgive me!"

She wailed in anguish, unable to gather her senses at witnessing a sight so grisly.

"And now, child," Zedd asked in a hoarse voice from above, "what would you have me do? Would you have me let them win, to save your daughter from what they have done to mine? Tell me, child, what should I do?"

Abby couldn't beg for the life of her family at a cost of such people rampaging unchecked across the land. Her sickened heart wouldn't allow it. How could she sacrifice the lives and peace of everyone else just so her loved ones would live?

She would be no better than Mariska, killing innocent children.

"Kill them all!" Abby screamed up at the wizard. She threw her arm out, pointing at Mariska and the hateful wizard Anargo. "Kill the bastards! Kill them all!"

Zedd's arms flung upward. The morning cracked with a peal of thunder. As if he had loosed it, the molten mass before him plunged into the water. The ground shook with a jolt. A huge geyser of water exploded forth. The air itself quaked. All around the most dreadful rumbling whipped the water into froth.

Abby, squatted down with the water to her waist, felt

numb not only from the cold, but also from the cold knowledge that she'd been forsaken by the good spirits she had always thought would watch over her. Zedd turned and snatched her arm, dragging her up on the rock with him.

It was another world.

The shapes around them called to her, too. They reached out, bridging the distance between life and death. Searing pain, frightful joy, profound peace spread through her at their touch. Light moved up through her body, filling her like air filled her lungs, and exploded in showers of sparks in her mind's eye. The thick howl of the magic was deafening.

Green light ripped through the water. Across the river, Anargo had been thrown to the ground. The rock atop which he had stood had shattered into needle-like shards. The soldiers called out in fright as the air all about danced with swirling smoke and sparks of light.

"Run!" Mariska screamed. "While you have the chance! Run for your lives!" Already she was racing toward the hills. "Leave the prisoners to die! Save yourselves! Run!"

The mood across the river suddenly galvanized with a single determination. The D'Harans dropped their weapons. They cast aside the ropes and chains holding the prisoners. They kicked up dirt as they turned and ran. In a single instant, the whole of an army that had a moment before stood grimly facing them were all, as if of a single fright, running for their lives.

From the corner of her eye, Abby saw the Mother Confessor and the sorceress struggling to run into the water. Although the water was hardly above their knees, it bogged them down in their rush nearly as much as would mud.

Abby watched it all as if in a dream. She floated in the light surrounding her. Pain and rapture were one within her. Light and dark, sound and silence, joy and sorrow, all were one, everything and nothing together in a caldron of raging magic.

Across the river, the D'Haran army had vanished into

the woods. Dust rose above the trees, marking their horses, wagons, and footfalls racing away, while at the riverbank the Mother Confessor and the sorceress were shoving people into the water, screaming at them, though Abby didn't hear the words, so absorbed was she by the strange harmonious trills twisting her thoughts into visions of dancing color overlaying what her eyes were trying to tell her.

She thought briefly that surely she was dying. She thought briefly that it didn't matter. And then her mind was swimming again in the cold color and hot light, the drumming music of magic and worlds meshing. The wizard's embrace made her feel as if she were being held in her mother's arms again. Maybe she was.

Abby was aware of the people reaching the Midlands side of the river and running ahead of the Mother Confessor and sorceress. They vanished into the rushes and then Abby saw them far away, beyond the tall grass, running uphill, away from the sublime sorcery erupting from the river.

The world thundered around her. A subterranean thump brought sharp pain deep in her chest. A whine, like steel being shredded, tore through the morning air. All around the water danced and quaked.

Hot steam felt as if it would scald Abby's legs. The air went white with it. The noise hurt her ears so much that she squeezed her eyes shut. She saw the same thing with her eyes closed as she saw with them open—shadowy shapes swirling through the green air. Everything was going crazy in her mind, making no sense. Green fury tore at her body and soul.

Abby felt pain, as if something inside her tore asunder. She gasped and opened her eyes. A horrific wall of green fire was receding away from them, toward the far side of the river. Founts of water lashed upward, like a thunderstorm in reverse. Lightning laced together above the surface of the river.

As the conflagration reached the far bank, the ground beneath it rent apart. Shafts of violet light shot up from the ripping wounds in the earth, like the blood of another realm.

Worse, though, than any of it were the howls. Howls of the dead, Abby was sure. It felt as if her own soul moaned in sympathy with the agony of cries filling the air. From the receding green wall of glimmering fire, the shapes twisted and turned, calling, begging, trying to escape the world of the dead.

She understood now that that was what the wall of green fire was—death, come to life.

The wizard had breached the boundary between worlds.

Abby had no idea how much time passed; in the grip of the strange light in which she swam there seemed to be no time, any more than there was anything solid. There was nothing familiar about any of the sensations upon which to hang understanding.

It seemed to Abby that the wall of green fire had halted its advance in the trees on the far hillside. The trees over which it had passed, and those she could see embraced by the shimmering curtain, had been blackened and shriveled by the profound touch of death itself. Even the grass over which the grim presence had passed looked to have been baked black and crisp by a high summer sun.

As Abby watched the wall, it dulled. As she stared, it seemed to waver in and out of her vision, sometimes a glimmering green gloss, like molten glass, and sometimes no more than a pale hint, like a fog just now passed from the air.

To each side, it was spreading, a wall of death raging across the world of life.

Abby realized she heard the river again, the comfortable, common, sloshing, lapping, burbling sounds that she lived her life hearing but most of the time didn't notice.

Zedd hopped down from the rock. He took her hand and helped her down. Abby gripped his hand tightly to brace against the dizzying sensations swimming through her head.

Zedd snapped his fingers, and the rock upon which they

had just stood leaped into the air, causing her to gasp in fright. In an instant so brief that she doubted she had seen it, Zedd caught the rock. It had become a small stone, smaller than an egg. He winked at her as he slipped it into a pocket. She thought the wink the oddest thing she could imagine, odder even than the boulder now a stone in his pocket.

On the bank, the Mother Confessor and the sorceress waited. They took her arms, helping her out of the water.

The sorceress looked grim. "Zedd, why isn't it moving?"

It sounded to Abby more like an accusation than a question. Either way, Zedd ignored it.

"Zedd," Abby mumbled, "I'm so sorry. It's my fault. I shouldn't have left her alone. I should have stayed. I'm so sorry."

The wizard, hardly hearing her words, was looking off to the wall of death on the other side of the river. He brought his clawed fingers up past his chest, calling something forth from within himself.

With a sudden thump to the air, fire erupted between his hands. He held it out as he would hold an offering. Abby threw an arm up in front of her face at the heat.

Zedd lifted the roiling ball of liquid fire. It grew between his hands, tumbling and turning, roaring and hissing with rage.

The three women backed away. Abby had heard of such fire. She had once heard her mother name it in a hushed tone: wizard's fire. Even then, not seeing or knowing its like, those whispered words forming a picture in Abby's mind as her mother recounted it, had sent a chill through Abby. Wizard's fire was the bane of life, called forth to scourge an enemy. This could be nothing else.

"For killing my love, my Erilyn, the mother of our daughter, and all the other innocent loved ones of innocent people," Zedd whispered, "I send you, Panis Rahl, the gift of death."

The wizard opened his arms outward. The liquid blue and yellow fire, bidden by its master, tumbled forward, gathering speed, roaring away toward D'Hara. As it crossed the river, it grew like angry lightning blooming forth, wailing with wrathful fury, reflecting in glimmering points from the water in thousands of bright sparkles.

The wizard's fire shot across the growing wall of green, just catching the upper edge. At the contact, green flame flared forth, some of it tearing away, caught up behind the wizard's fire, trailing after like smoke behind flame. The deadly mix howled toward the horizon. Everyone stood transfixed, watching, until all trace of it had vanished in the distance.

When Zedd, pale and drawn, turned back to them, Abby clutched his robes. "Zedd, I'm so sorry. I shouldn't—"

He put his fingers to her lips to silence her. "There is someone waiting for you."

He tilted his head. She turned. Back by the rushes, Philip stood holding Jana's hand. Abby gasped with a jolt of giddy joy. Philip grinned his familiar grin. At his other side, her father smiled and nodded his approval to her.

Arms reaching, Abby ran to them. Jana's face wrinkled. She backed against Philip. Abby fell to her knees before her.

"It's Mama," Philip said to Jana. "She just has herself some new clothes."

Abby realized Jana was frightened by the red leather outfit she was wearing. Abby grinned through her tears.

"Mama!" Jana cried at seeing the smile.

Abby threw her arms around her daughter. She laughed and hugged Jana so hard the child squeaked in protest. Abby felt Philip's hand on her shoulder in loving greeting. Abby stood and threw an arm around him, tears choking her voice. Her father put a comforting hand to her back while she squeezed Jana's hand.

Zedd, Delora, and the Mother Confessor gathered them and herded them up the hill toward the people waiting at the top. Soldiers, mostly officers, some that Abby recognized, a few other people from Aydindril, and the wizard Thomas waited with the freed prisoners. Among the people liberated were those of Coney Crossing; people who held Abby, the daughter of a sorceress, in no favor. But they were her people, the people from her home, the people she had wanted saved.

Zedd rested a hand on Abby's shoulder. Abby was shocked to see that his wavy brown hair was now partly snow white. She knew without a looking glass that hers had undergone the same transformation in the place beyond the world of life, where, for a time, they had been.

"This is Abigail, born of Helsa," the wizard called out to the people gathered. "She is the one who went to Aydindril to seek my help. Though she does not have magic, it is because of her that you people are all free. She cared enough to beg for your lives."

Abby, with Philip's arm around her waist and Jana's hand in hers, looked from the wizard to the sorceress, and then to the Mother Confessor. The Mother Confessor smiled. Abby thought it a cold-hearted thing to do in view of the fact that Zedd's daughter had been murdered before their eyes not long before. She whispered as much.

The Mother Confessor's smile widened. "Don't you remember?" she asked as she leaned close. "Don't you remember what I told you we call him?"

Abby, confused by everything that had happened, couldn't imagine what the Mother Confessor was talking about. When she admitted she didn't, the Mother Confessor and the sorceress shepherded her onward, past the grave where Abby had reburied her mother's skull upon her return, and into the house.

With a hand, the Mother Confessor eased back the door to Abby's bedroom. There, on the bed where Abby had placed her, was Zedd's daughter, still sleeping. Abby stared in disbelief.

"The trickster," the Mother Confessor said. "I told you that was our name for him."

"And not a very flattering one," Zedd grumbled as he stepped up behind them.

"But . . . how?" Abby pressed her fingers to her temples. "I don't understand."

Zedd gestured. Abby saw, for the first time, the body lying just beyond the door out the back. It was Mariska.

"When you showed me the room when we first came here," Zedd told her, "I laid a few traps for those intent on harm. That woman was killed by those traps because she came here intent on taking my daughter from where she slept."

"You mean it was all an illusion?" Abby was dumbfounded. "Why would you do such a cruel thing? How could you?"

"I am the object of vengeance," the wizard explained. "I didn't want my daughter to pay the price her mother has already paid. Since my spell killed the woman as she tried to harm my daughter, I was able to use a vision of her to accomplish the deception. The enemy knew the woman, and that she acted for Anargo. I used what they expected to see to convince them and to frighten them into running and leaving the prisoners.

"I cast the death spell so that everyone would think they saw my daughter being killed. This way, the enemy thinks my daughter dead, and will have no reason to hunt her or ever again try to harm her. I did it to protect her from the unforeseen."

The sorceress scowled at him. "If it were any but you, Zeddicus, and for any reason but the reason you had, I'd see you brought up on charges for casting such a web as a death spell." She broke into a grin. "Well done, First Wizard."

Outside, the officers all wanted to know what was happening.

"No battle today," Zedd told them. "I've just ended the war."

They cheered with genuine joy. Had Zedd not been the First Wizard, Abby suspected they would have hoisted him on their shoulders. It seemed that there was no one more glad for peace than those whose job it was to fight for it.

Wizard Thomas, looking more humble than Abby had ever seen him, cleared his throat. "Zorander, I . . . I . . . I simply can't believe what my own eyes have seen." His face finally took on its familiar scowl. "But we have people already in near revolt over magic. When news of this spreads, it is only going to make it worse. The demands for relief from magic grow every day and you have fed the fury. With this, we're liable to have revolt on our hands."

"I still want to know why it isn't moving," Delora growled from behind. "I want to know why it's just sitting there, all green and still."

Zedd ignored her and directed his attention to the old wizard. "Thomas, I have a job for you."

He motioned several officers and officials from Aydindril forward, and passed a finger before all their faces, his own turning grim and determined. "I have a job for all of you. The people have reason to fear magic. Today we have seen magic deadly and dangerous. I can understand those fears.

"In appreciation of these fears, I shall grant their wish."

"What!" Thomas scoffed. "You can't end magic, Zorander! Not even you can accomplish such a paradox."

"Not end it," Zedd said. "But give them a place without it. I want you to organize an official delegation large enough to travel all the Midlands with the offer. All those who would quit a world with magic are to move to the lands to the west. There they shall set up new lives free of any magic. I shall insure that magic cannot intrude on their peace."

Thomas threw up his hands. "How can you make such a promise!"

Zedd's arm lifted to point off behind him, to the wall of green fire growing toward the sky. "I shall call up a second wall of death, through which none can pass. On the other side of it shall be a place free of magic. There, people will be able to live their lives without magic.

"I want you all to see that the word is passed through the land. People have until spring to emigrate to the lands west. Thomas, you will warrant that none with magic make the journey. We have books we can use to insure that we purge a place of any with a trace of magic. We can assure that there will be no magic there.

"In the spring, when all who wish have gone to their

new homeland, I will seal them off from magic. In one fell swoop, I will satisfy the large majority of the petitions come to us; they will have lives without magic. May the good spirits watch over them, and may they not come to regret their wish granted."

Thomas pointed heatedly at the thing Zedd had brought into the world. "But what about that? What if people go wandering into it in the dark? They will be walking into death."

"Not only in the dark," Zedd said. "Once it has stabilized, it will be hard to see at all. We will have to set up guards to keep people away. We will have to set aside land near the boundary and have men guard the area to keep people out."

"Men?" Abby asked. "You mean you will have to start a corps of boundary wardens?"

"Yes," Zedd said, his eyebrows lifting, "that's a good name for them. Boundary wardens."

Silence settled over those leaning in to hear the wizard's words. The mood had changed and was now serious with the grim matter at hand. Abby couldn't imagine a place without magic, but she knew how vehemently some wished it.

Thomas finally nodded. "Zedd, this time I think you've gotten it right. Sometimes, we must serve the people by not serving them." The others mumbled their agreement, though, like Abby, they thought it a bleak solution.

Zedd straightened. "Then it is decided."

He turned and announced to the crowd the end of the war, and the division to come in which those who had petitioned for years would finally have their petition granted; for those who wished it, a land outside the Midlands, without magic, would be created.

While everyone was chattering about such a mysterious and exotic thing as a land without magic, or cheering and celebrating the end of the war, Abby whispered to Jana to wait with her father a moment. She kissed her daughter and then took the opportunity to pull Zedd aside.

"Zedd, may I speak with you? I have a question."

Zedd smiled and took her by the elbow, urging Abby into her small home. "I'd like to check on my daughter. Come along."

Abby cast caution to the winds and took the Mother Confessor's hand in one of hers. Delora's in the other, and pulled them in with her. They had a right to hear this, too.

"Zedd," Abby asked once they were away from the crowd in her yard, "may I please know the debt your father owed my mother?"

Zedd lifted an eyebrow. "My father owed your mother no debt."

Abby frowned. "But it was a debt of bones, passed down from your father to you, and from my mother to me."

"Oh, it was a debt all right, but not owed to your mother, but by your mother."

"What?" Abby asked in stunned confusion. "What do you mean?"

Zedd smiled. "When your mother was giving birth to you, she was in trouble. You both were dying in the labor. My father used magic to save her. Helsa begged him to save you, too. In order to keep you in the world of the living and out of the Keeper's grasp, without thought to his own safety, he worked far beyond the endurance anyone would expect of a wizard.

"Your mother was a sorceress, and understood the extent of what was involved in saving your life. In appreciation of what my father had done, she swore a debt to him. When she died, the debt passed to you."

Abby, eyes wide, tried to reconcile the whole thing in her mind. Her mother had never told her the nature of the debt.

"But . . . but you mean that it is I who owe the debt to you? You mean that the debt of bones is my burden?"

Zedd pushed open the door to the room where his daughter slept, smiling as he looked in. "The debt is paid, Abby. The bracelet your mother gave you had magic, linking you to the debt. Thank you for my daughter's life."

Abby glanced to the Mother Confessor. Trickster indeed. "But why would you help me, if it was really not a debt of bones you owed me? If it was really a debt I owed you?"

Zedd shrugged. "We reap a reward merely in the act of helping others. We never know how, or if, that reward will come back to us. Helping is the reward; none other is needed nor better."

Abby watched the beautiful little girl sleeping in the room beyond. "I am thankful to the good spirits that I could help keep such a life in this world. I may not have the gift, but I can foresee that she will go on to be a person of import, not only for you, but for others."

Zedd smiled idly as he watched his daughter sleeping. "I think you may have the gift of prophecy, my dear, for she is already a person who has played a part in bringing a war to an end, and in so doing, saved the lives of countless people."

The sorceress pointed out the window. "I still want to know why that thing isn't moving. It was supposed to pass over D'Hara and purge it of all life, to kill them all for what they have done." Her scowl deepened. "Why is it just sitting there?"

Zedd folded his hands. "It ended the war. That is enough. The wall is a part of the underworld itself, the world of the dead. Their army will not be able to cross it and make war on us for as long as such a boundary stands."

"And how long will that be?"

Zedd shrugged. "Nothing remains forever. For now, there will be peace. The killing is ended."

The sorceress did not look to be satisfied. "But they were trying to kill us all!"

"Well, now they can't. Delora, there are those in D'Hara who are innocent, too. Just because Panis Rahl wished to conquer and subjugate us, that does not mean that all the D'Haran people are evil. Many good people in D'Hara have suffered under harsh rule. How could I kill everyone there, including all the people who have caused no harm, and themselves wish only to live their lives in peace?"

Delora wiped a hand across her face. "Zeddicus, sometimes I don't know about you. Sometimes, you make a lousy wind of death."

The Mother Confessor stood staring out the window, toward D'Hara. Her violet eyes turned back to the wizard.

"There will be those over there who will be your foes for life because of this, Zedd. You have made bitter enemies with this. You have left them alive."

"Enemies," the wizard said, "are the price of honor."

Story Copyrights